WAYNE MA,

D0451805

780-489-4992

Martin Booth, novelist, critic, biographer, children's author, and social historian, died of a brain tumor in 2004. Shortly after diagnosis, he began to write his acclaimed memoir of his childhood in Hong Kong, *Gweilo* (published in America as *Golden Boy*), which he completed shortly before his death. Among his acclaimed novels were *Hiroshima Joe,* based on the life of a real down-and-out Briton who had survived the Nagasaki atomic raid, and *The Industry of Souls,* which was short-listed for the Man Booker Prize.

Also by Martin Booth

FICTION

Hiroshima Joe
The Jade Pavilion
Black Chameleon
Dreaming of Samarkand
The Humble Disciple
The Iron Tree
Toys of Glass
Adrift in the Oceans of Mercy
The Industry of Souls
Islands of Silence

NONFICTION

The Doctor and the Detective: A Biography of Sir Arthur Conan Doyle
Carpet Sahib: A Life of Jim Corbett
The Triads
Rhino Road
The Dragon and the Pearl: A Hong Kong Notebook
Opium: A History
The Dragon Syndicates
A Magick Life: A Biography of Aleister Crowley
Cannabis: A History
Golden Boy: Memories of a Hong Kong Childhood

CHILDREN'S BOOKS

War Dog
Music on the Bamboo Radio
Panther
P.O.W.
Doctor Illuminatus
Soul Stealer
Midnight Saboteur
Coyote Moon

EDITED BOOKS

The Book of Cats (with George Macbeth)

The American

Previously Published as
A Very Private Gentleman

Martin Booth

Picador

A Thomas Dunne Book
St. Martin's Press
New York

A VERY PRIVATE GENTLEMAN. Copyright © 2004 by Martin Booth. All rights reserved. Printed in the United States of America. For information, address Picador, 175 Fifth Avenue, New York, N.Y. 10010.

www.picadorusa.com

Picador® is a U.S. registered trademark and is used by St. Martin's Press under license from Pan Books Limited.

For information on Picador Reading Group Guides, please contact Picador. E-mail: readinggroupguides@picadorusa.com

The Library of Congress has cataloged the first Picador edition as follows:

Booth, Martin.
    A very private gentleman / Martin Booth.—1st Picador ed.
        p. cm.
    ISBN 978-0-312-30909-1
        1. Painters—Fiction. 2. Deception—Fiction. 3. Butterflies in art—Fiction. 4. Italy—Fiction. 5. Large type books. I. Title.

    PR6052.O63V47 2004b
    823'.914—dc22

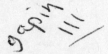

2004057252

Second Picador Edition ISBN 978-0-312-43001-6

Originally published in Great Britain by Century

First published in the United States by St. Martin's Press

First Picador Edition: February 2005

Second Picador Edition: August 2010

10 9 8 7 6 5 4 3 2 1

For Hugh and Karen

People begin to see that something more goes to the composition of a fine murder than two blockheads to kill and be killed . . . a knife . . . a purse . . . a dark lane.

THOMAS DE QUINCEY

The American

HIGH IN THESE MOUNTAINS, THE APENNINES, THE SPINAL CORD of Italy, with its vertebræ of infant stone to which the tendons and the flesh of the old world are attached, there is a small cave high up a precipice. It is very difficult to reach. The narrow path is littered with loose stones and, in the spring when the thaw comes, it is a running stream, an angled gutter two hundred metres long, slicing across the sheer surface of the rock face, collecting melt-water as the scar incised in the bark of a rubber tree channels the sap.

Some years, the local people claim, the water runs crimson with the sacred blood of the saint who lived in the cave as a hermit, dined on lichen or moss, consumed the pine nuts fallen from the firs over-hanging the precipice high above, and drank only the stony water seeping through the roof of his abode.

I have been there. It is not an outing for the faint-hearted or suffer-ers from vertigo. In parts, the path is no wider than a scaffolder's plank and one is obliged to move upwards crab fashion, one's back to the rock, facing down into the valley below, across to a purple haze of mountains jagged like the scales of a dragon's back. This, they say, is a test of one's faith, a trial to be taken on the route to salvation. They say you can see two hundred kilometres on a fine day.

There are scrubby pines growing at intervals along the path, the off-spring of those far overhead. Each is festooned, as if for a religious festi-val, with clots of spiders' webs hanging like the dense gossamer ghosts of Chinese lanterns. They say to touch one is to be burned, to be inculcated with original sin. The poison on the web is reported to restrict respira-tion, choke one to death as readily as if the spider was vulture-sized, its hairy legs locked about your throat. Lizards green as emeralds dart through the litter of dead needles, mountain succulents and wind-bent herbs. The reptiles have black beads for eyes and might be brooches of precious stones were it not for their lithe, impulsive movements.

The cave is about five metres deep and just high enough for an average man to stand. I do not have to bow my head in there. A ledge cut in the rock on one side served as the saint's hard bed of contri-tion. At the cave-mouth, there is usually to be found the remnant of a campfire. Lovers use the place as a rendezvous, a spectacular place to couple, perhaps to ask the saint's blessing be called upon their fornica-tions. At the rear of the cave the devout, or those greedy for heavenly intervention in the petty disasters of their lives, have erected an altar of concrete blocks clumsily smeared with plaster. Upon this crude sacrarium stands a dusty wooden cross and a candlestick made of cheap metal painted gold. Wax has marked the stone table of the altar: no-one bothers to chip it off.

It is red wax. One day, someone will claim it to be the sacred flesh of the saint. Anything is possible where faith is concerned. The sinner searches forever after a sign to prove it is worth his while to recant. I should know: I have been a sinner, and a Catholic, too.

All men want to make their mark, know upon their deathbed the world has changed because of them, as a result of their actions or philosophies. They are arrogant enough to think, when they are dead, others will see their accomplishments and say, 'Look. He made that— the man of vision, the man who got things done.'

Years ago, when I was living in an English village, I was surrounded by people trying in vain, tiny ways to stamp their signatures upon the course of time. Old Colonel Cedric—a major in the Pay Corps when he was discharged, without one day's action in six years of war—paid for the fifth and six bells in a mediocre peal. A local estate agent, well-off from the proceeds of selling the village over and over, planted an avenue of beeches from the lane up to his renovated mansion, a one-time derelict tithe barn; caustic rain, village youths and a main sewer, all in their own way, put paid to the symmetry with which he hoped the fields of history would be bisected and his memory preserved. The local bus driver was the one who topped them all: Brian of the beer gut and greasy hair slicked forward to camouflage a balding pate. Brian was simultaneously a district councillor, Parish Council chairman, churchwarden, vice-chairman of the Village Hall Development Committee and co-president of the Village Association of Change-Ringers. The old Colonel was the other co-president. It stood to reason.

I shall not name the village. It would be unwise. I am not silent from a fear of litigation, you understand. Simply from the concern of wanting to retain my privacy. And my past. Privacy—which some might call secrecy—is of immense value to me.

One could not be private in a village. No matter how one kept to oneself, there were always those who pried, nosed, thrust sticks under my stone, flipped it over to see what lay beneath. These were the people who could not make the tiniest mark on history, could not affect their world—the village, the parish—no matter how they tried. The best they could hope for was to share vicariously in others' petty achievements. Their ambition was to be able to say, 'Him? I knew him when he bought The Glebe,' or 'Her? I was with her when it happened,' or 'I saw the car skid, you know. There's still a hole in the hedge: a nasty corner: someone should do something about it.' Yet they never did and if I were a betting man, prone to taking a gamble, I should wager tyres still squeal on the bend, doors dent of a frosty morning.

In those days, I was a jobbing silversmith, a pots-and-pans man, not a maker of rings and mounter of diamonds. I repaired teapots, soldered salvers, straightened spoons, polished or copied church plate. I did the rounds of the antique shops and the bazaars put on to snare the tourists. It was not a skilled job and I was not a skilled man. I had no training other than a basic tuition in metalwork picked up by chance in the workshops of my boarding school.

Occasionally, I fenced. The villagers had no idea of this nefarious activity, and the local bobby was a dullard bent more on snaring poachers of pheasants and scrumpers of apples than apprehending criminals. Such activity put him in the good books of the Colonel's son, an ardent hunter and shooter who owned orchards under licence to the cider makers, raised the pheasants for his own guns or those of his cronies. The constable's place in local history was thus assured: the Colonel was the repository of local records, being the landowner and, as he thought, the squire. For evermore, the constable would be remembered in anecdotes of petty arrests, for he served his masters well.

It was the fencing which gave me a notion to move away, diversify into other lines of business. The criminality added a certain spice to an otherwise stultifying existence in an utterly boring location. It was not for the money I took to it, I can assure you. I made little profit melting down or re-polishing the minor silver from insignificant country house robberies and the break-ins at provincial antique shops. I did it to fight the mundane. It gave me contacts, too, in the ethereal twilit world of the law-breaker, the milieu I have inhabited ever since.

Yet now I am back on a one-track existence, undiversified, all my eggs in one basket; but they are golden eggs.

I am getting old and have made my marks on history. Vicariously, perhaps. Secretively, certainly. Those who want to snuffle in the parish records of that village will discover who hung those two bells or who perhaps, by now, has put a 'Slow' sign at the icy corner. Few know what my contributions to history have been, and no-one shall, save the reader of these words. And that is good enough.

Father Benedetto drinks brandy. He likes cognac, prefers armagnac, yet is not too fussy. As a priest, he can ill afford to be: his small private income is subject to the vagaries of the stock market. Religious observance and church attendance are declining in Italy, less money falling in the offertory. Only old crones in black shawls smelling of mothballs attend his services, and old men in berets and musty jackets. The urchins in the streets catcall *bagarozzo* after him as he passes in his soutane on his way to Mass.

Today, as is customary for him, he is dressed in his commonplace uniform, the pastoral apparel of a Roman Catholic priest: a black suit of unstylish, outmoded tailoring with a few of his short, white hairs in evidence on his shoulders, a black silk stock and a deep Roman collar wearing at the edge. His priestly uniform has looked faintly shabby and old-fashioned since the moment it left the tailor's bench, the last thread cut like an ecclesiastical umbilical cord tying it to the secular bolt of cloth. His socks and shoes are black, the latter polished by his soutane on his walk home from Mass.

So long as the quality of his brandy is good, the liquor smooth and the glass warmed by the sun, Father Benedetto is satisfied. He likes to sniff his drink before he sips it, like a bee hovering over a bloom, a butterfly pausing on a petal before taking the nectar.

'The only thing good to come of the *francesi*,' he declares. 'Everything else . . .'

He raises one hand dismissively and grimaces. To him, the French are not worth thinking about: they are, he is fond of saying, intellectual vagabonds, usurpers of the True Faith—no good Pope, in his opinion, came of Avignon—and Europe's troublemakers. He thinks it more than fitting that truancy is termed, in English, French leave and the hated *preservativo* called a French letter. French wine is too effete (as are Frenchmen) and French cheese too salty. By this, he implies, they are too given to the indulgence of sexual pleasures. This is not a new trait, recently discovered. Italians, Benedetto claims with the authority of having been there, have known this throughout history. When Rome called France the province of Gaul they were just the same. Heathen rabble. Only their brandy is worthy of attention.

The priest's house is halfway along a twisting alley off the Via dell' Orologio. It is a modest fifteenth-century edifice, reputed to have once been the home of the best of the clockmakers from whom the nearby street derived its name. The front door is of heavy oak blackened with age and studded with iron bolts. Within there is no courtyard but, at the rear, snuggles a walled garden, overlooked by other buildings yet remaining secluded. Being on the side of a hill, the garden catches more of the sun than one might expect. The buildings down the slope being lower, the sun lingers longer on the little patio.

We are sitting on this patio. It is four o'clock in the afternoon. Two-thirds of the garden is in shade. We are in lazy, soporific sunlight. The brandy bottle—today, we have armagnac—is globulous, made of green glass and bears a plain label in black printing on cream paper. It is called, simply, *La Vie*.

I like this man. Certainly, he is holy but I do not hold that against him. He is pious but acceptably so, a raconteur when he wants to be, an erudite conversationalist who is never dogmatic in his arguments or pedantic in the presentation of them. He is about my age, with short grey-white hair and quick, laughing eyes.

It was only a few days after I arrived in the town when we first met. I was wandering about with apparent nonchalance, taking in the sights, it would seem. In fact, I was studying the town, memorising the streets and the escape routes I should use should the necessity arise. He came up to me and addressed me in English: I must have looked more English than I hoped.

'Can I help you?' he offered.

'I am just looking about,' I said.

'You are a tourist?'

'I am newly resident here.'

'Where are your lodgings?'

I avoided this inquisition and obliquely replied, 'Not for long, I suspect. Until my work is done.'

This was the truth.

'If you are to live here,' he declared, 'then you should share a glass of wine with me. As a welcome.'

It was then I visited, for the first time, the quiet house down the alley off the Via dell' Orologio. I am almost certain, in retrospect, he saw me as a soul for potential redemption, a reclamation for Christ, even after but a few words.

Ever since the whole garden was in sunlight, we have been sipping, talking, sipping, eating peaches. We have been talking of history. It is a favoured argument we have. Father Benedetto believes history, by which he means the past, is the single most important influence upon a man's life. This opinion has to be his standpoint. He is a priest who lives in the house of a long-deceased watchmaker. Without history, a priest can have no job, for religion feeds upon the past for its veracity. Besides, he lives in the house of a long-deceased watchmaker.

I disagree. History has no such grand influence. It is merely an occurrence which may or may not affect a man's activities and attitudes. Foremost, I proclaim, the past is an irrelevancy, a jumble of dates and facts and heroes many of whom were impostors, sciolists, *blagueurs,* get-rich-quick merchants or men fortuitously present at the right moment in the timetable of fate. Father Benedetto, of course, cannot accept fate. Fate is a concept invented by men. God controls us all.

'People are trapped in history, and history resides within them like the blood of Christ in the chalice,' he says.

'What is history? Certainly not a trap,' I reply. 'History does not affect me save, perhaps, materially. I wear polyester because of an historical event—the invention of nylon. I drive a car because of the invention of the internal combustion engine. But to say I behave as I do because history is in me and influencing me is wrong.'

'History, Nietzsche states, is the enunciator of new truths. Every fact, every new event exercises an influence upon every age and every new generation of Man.'

'Then Man is an idiot!'

I cut into a peach, the juice running like plasma onto the wooden boards of the table. I prise the stone out and flick it with the knife point into the flower bed. The pebble-like stones of our afternoon feasting litter the ground between the golden-headed marigolds.

Father Benedetto balks at my facetiousness. For him, to insult Mankind is to reproach God in whose image men were forged.

'If man is so imbued with history, then he seems not to have taken much of it to heart,' I continue. 'All that history has taught us is that we are too stupid to learn anything from it. At the end of the day, what is history but the truth of reality twisted into convenient lies by those whom it suits to see a different record made? History is but the tool of man's self-worship.' I suck at the peach. 'You, Father, should be ashamed!'

I grin, so he is assured I do not seek to slight him. He shrugs and reaches for a peach. There are five left in the wooden bowl.

He peels his peach. I eat mine in silence.

'How can you live here in Italy,' he asks as his peach stone hits the wall and drops to the marigolds, 'with history around you, crowding in on you, and treat it with such disdain?'

I look around his private garden. The shutters on the building beyond the peach tree are like eyelids shut demurely in case they should see something embarrassing in the windows of Father Benedetto's house—like the priest in his bathtub.

'History? All around me? There are ruins and ancient buildings, yes. But history? With a capital H? History, I maintain, is a falsehood. Real history is the commonplace, unrecorded. We speak of the history of Rome with the eloquence of grandeur but most Romans did not know of it or want to know it. What did the slave or the shopkeeper know of Cicero, or Virgil, the Sabines or the magics of Sirmio? Nothing. History was for them half-registered fragments about geese saving a city or Caligula eating his unborn child. History was an old man mumbling in his cups. They had no time for history when a clipped coin was worth less by the week, their taxes rose by the month, the price of their flour rocketed and hot weather frayed their tempers.'

'Men like to be remembered . . .' Father Benedetto begins.

'So legend might build them into someone grander,' I interrupt.

'Do you not want to make your mark, my son?'

He calls me that when he wants to annoy me. I am not his son, nor a child of his church. Not any longer.

'Perhaps,' I admit, smiling. 'But whatever I do shall be irrefutable. Not open to misinterpretation.'

His glass is empty and he reaches for the bottle.

'So you live for the future?'

'Yes.' I am emphatic. 'I live for the future.'

'And what is the future but History yet to arrive?'

His eyebrows rise questioningly and he gives my glass a wink.

'No, no more. Thank you. I must be going. It is late and I have some preliminary sketches to complete.'

'Art?' Father Benedetto exclaims. 'That is irrefutable. Your signature on a unique painting.'

'One can put one's signature on more than paper,' I reply. 'One can write in the sky.'

He laughs and I bid him farewell.

'You should come to Mass,' he says, quietly.

'God is history. I have no use for him.' This, I realise, may hurt the priest, so I add, 'If he exists I am sure he has no use for me.'

'There you are wrong. Our Lord has a use for everyone.'

Father Benedetto does not know me, though he thinks he does. If he did know me, he would most certainly readjust his judgment. But then, just maybe—it would be a supreme irony worthy of God—he is correct.

Signor Farfalla! Signore! La posta!'
Signora Prasca calls every morning from the fountain in the courtyard below. It is her ritual. It is a sign of being old, maintaining a routine. My routine, however, is temporary. I do not yet have the luxury afforded those of my age of being able to set my life to a series of conformities.

'Thank you!'

Every weekday, when there is mail for me, is identical. She calls in Italian, I reply in English, she invariably responding, *'Sulla balaustrata! La posta! Sulla balaustrata, signore!'*

When I come down a storey to lean over the edge of the third floor balcony, and peer down into the gloom of the courtyard into which the sun only strikes for an hour and half in the middle of the day in the middle of the year, I can see the letters balancing on the stone pillar at the foot of the banisters. She always stacks them with the largest letter on the bottom of the pile, the smallest on top. As the smallest is usually a postcard or a letter in a small envelope, it is inevitably the brightest, glimmering in the half-light like a coin or a religious medal cast optimistically down a well.

Signor Farfalla, she calls me. So do the others in the neighbourhood. Luigi who owns the bar in the Piazza di S. Teresa. Alfonso in the garage. Clara the pretty one and Dindina the plain one. Galeazzo the bookshop owner. Father Benedetto. They do not know my real name, so they call me Mr. Butterfly. I like it.

To the confusion of Signora Prasca, letters come addressed to me either as Mr. A. Clarke, Mr. A.E. Clarke or Mr. E. Clark. These are all aliases. Some even come addressed to M. Leclerc, others to Mr. Giddings. She does not question this and her gossip causes no conjecture. No suspicion is aroused, for this is Italy and people mind their own business, accustomed to the Byzantine intrigues of men who live alone.

I send most of the mail: if I am away, I post an empty envelope or two to myself, or write out a postcard, disguising my hand, purporting to be from a relative. I have a fictitious favourite niece who addresses me as Uncle and signs herself Pet. I send off prepaid envelopes to life insurance companies, travel agents, time-share operators, trade magazines and other sources which generate junk mail: now I am bombarded with colourful trash informing me I may have won a cheap car, or a holiday in Florida, or a million lire per annum for life. To most people, this unsolicited garbage is a curse. To me it lends an air of perfection to the lie.

Why Mr. Butterfly? It is simple. I paint them. They think this is how I make my money, painting butterflies' portraits.

It is a most efficient cover. The countryside around the town, as yet unadulterated by agro-chemicals, unharmed by the clumsy footsteps of men, abounds with butterflies. Some are the minuscule blues: to study them delights me, to paint their portraits enthrals me. They seldom have a wingspan further across than a penny. Their colours iridesce, fade from tone to tone, from bright summer sky blue to washed dawn blue in just a few millimetres. They have tiny dots upon them, black and white rims, and the trailing edges of their hind wings have near-microscopic tails pricking out like tiny thorns. To paint one of these creatures successfully is a major achievement, a triumph of detail. And I live by detail, by minute particulars. Without such ardent attention to detail, I would be dead.

To further the efficacy of my deceit, I have allayed any possible suspicion by explaining to Signora Prasca that Leclerc is French for Clark (with or without an *e*) and Giddings is the name under which I paint—a pseudonym to scrawl upon my pictures.

To aid this misconception, I once hinted that artists often use a fake name to protect their privacy: they cannot, I explain, be forever hampered by intrusion. It destroys the concentration, decelerates output, and galleries and printers, editors and authors, demand deadlines.

Since then, I am sometimes asked if I am working on a new book.

I shrug and say, 'No, I am building up a stock of pictures. Against a rainy day. A few go to galleries,' I say. They are bought, I suggest, by collectors of miniatures, or entomologists.

One day, I received a letter posted in a South American republic. It bore postage stamps of gaudy tropical butterflies, those flashy stamps so loved by dictators. The colours of the insects were too vivid to be real, too garish to be believable, bright as the rows of self-appointed medals which are part of every generalissimo's costume.

'Ha!' exclaimed Signora Prasca, knowingly. She waved her hand in the air.

I smiled knowingly back at her and winked.

They think I design postage stamps for banana republics. I leave them with this convenient illusion.

For some men, France is the country of love, the women poutingly beautiful with eyes widely innocent with lust, lips which beg to kiss and press. The countryside is mellow—the rolling neolithic hills of the Dordogne, the rugged Pyrenees or the boggy marshes of the Camargue, it matters not where they travel. All are imbued with the aura of warm sun ripening the vine. The men see a vineyard and think only of lying in the sun with a bottle of Bordeaux and a girl who tastes of grapes. For women, French men are hand-kissers, the slight-bow-brigade, the charming conversationalists, the gentle seducers. How unlike the Italians, they say. The Italian women have hairy armpits, smell of garlic and grow quickly fat on pasta: Italian men pinch arse on the buses of Rome and thrust too hard when making love. Such are the cries of xenophobia.

For me, France is a country of provincial banality, a land where patriotism flowers only to hide the bloodied earth of revolution, where history was begun at the Bastille by a horde of peasants running amok with pitchforks, decapitating their betters because they were just that. Before the Revolution, the French insist in their clipped accent, with a Gallic shrug of the shoulders meant to disarm contradiction, there was only poverty and aristocracy. Now . . . the shoulders shrug again and a jutting chin points to the dubious grandeur of France. The truth is they have now a poverty of spirit and an aristocracy of politicians. Italy is different. Italy is romance.

I like it here. The wine is good, the sun hot, the people accept their past and do not crow about it. The women are soft, slow lovers—at least, Clara is; Dindina is more anxious—and the men enjoy a good life. There is no poverty of the soul. Everyone is rich of spirit. The civil servants keep the streets clean, keep the traffic moving, keep the trains running and the water flowing in the taps. The *carabinieri* and the *polizia* fight the criminals, after a fashion, and the *polizia stradale* keeps the speed on the autostrada down. Taxes are collected with only a modicum of thoroughness. In the meantime, the people live, drink wine, earn money, spend money and let the world turn.

Italy is the Land of Laissez-faire, a bucolic anarchy governed by wine and the connivances of various loves—of good food of sex, of liberty, of devil-may-care, of take-it-or-leave-it—above all of a love of life. The national motto of Italy should be *senza formalità* or *non interferenza*.

Let me tell you a tale. The authorities in Rome wanted to catch tax dodgers—not as in England where they seek out the meanest evader of pennies, hounding him until his dues are settled. No, they wanted only the Caesars of the State Swindlers, the Emperors of Eludance. To catch them they set no paltry traps in banks, no covert studies of stocks and shares transactions. They sent a team of men around the marinas and harbours of Italy checking on the registration of every yacht over twenty metres. There was a wonderful Mediterranean logic at work: under twenty metres, and the yacht was a rich man's plaything; over, and it was a super-indulgence of the truly rich. They found one hundred and sixty seven yachts the owners of which were utterly unknown to the authorities—no tax records, no state benefit records, in some cases no birth certificates. Not even in Sicily. Not even in Sardinia.

Did they find these men? Did they pay up the owed billions of illicit lire? Who can tell? It is just a fairy story.

For me, no better place could exist. I could stay here forever, quite possibly, undiscovered like an Etruscan tomb disguised as a culvert on the side of the Via Appia. So long as I don't buy a yacht over twenty metres long and keep it at Capri. No chance of that now. Besides, had I wanted such a toy, I should have bought it long ago.

Today, the courtyard is as ever cool. It is like a vault the roof of which has caved in so the sky might peer down and bear witness to what little dramas are unfolding therein.

Some say a nobleman was murdered by the fountain in the centre, that every year on the anniversary of his assassination, the water flows pink. Others tell me the courtyard was the scene of the murder of a Socialist in the Mussolini years. Whether the water is pink from blood, from the nobleman's reputation (so they say) of always dressing in the pink of fashion or because the Socialist was only moderately leftist, I cannot tell. Perhaps a saint lived here and they have all got it wrong. So much for history.

The flagstones are buff-coloured as if worn from centuries of scrubbing and stoning. The fountain, which dribbles cooly through a necklace of pendant moss and algæ, the drips resonant in the cavern of the yard, is of marble shot through with black veins. It is as if the ageing building has contracted varicose veins in its heart. For the fountain is the heart of the building. Within it stands the figure of a girl bedecked in a toga and holding a clam shell from which the water falls, delivered by a two-and-a-quarter-millimetre diameter pipe made of bronze. This girl is not fashioned of marble but of alabaster. Looking at her, I wonder if it is the water or her skin which cools our building.

Doorways face the fountain, slatted shutters look down upon it, balconies lean over it. On the hottest day, it keeps the building moist and cool, the drip-drip of water never ceasing, flowing through a nick cut in the marble on to the flags, disappearing down an iron grid from beneath which sprouts a frond of aquatic fern.

In winter, with the mountains capped with snow, the alleyways of the town icy underfoot, the fountain tries to freeze. Yet it cannot. No matter how still and cold the air, no matter how long the icicles suspended from the maiden's shell, the water still drips, drips, drips.

No one turns the fountain on. There is no electric pump or similar device. The water seeps from deep in the earth as if the building were erected upon a wound in the soil.

Beyond the fountain is the heavy wooden door leading into the alley, the *vialetto*. It is a narrow passageway through the buildings with two right angled corners in it. Once, it was a garden walk. Or so Signora Prasca claims. She would have it on the authority of her grandmother that the house was surrounded by gardens in the seventeenth century and that the alleyway follows the line of the walk through the arbour. Hence *vialetto* rather than *vicolo* or *passaggio*. I say it is bunkum. The buildings around are contemporary with this one. There were never any gardens in the old quarter, only courtyards where noblemen and Socialists were stabbed in the shadows.

To one side of the fountain is the start of the steep stone steps which run up to the fourth floor where I live, one flight per side of the square court. They are worn in the centre. Signora Prasca walks at the sides, especially if it is raining and the steps are wet A leaky gutter dribbles water on to the second flight. No one fixes it. I shall not. It is not my role to alter petty histories, to repair the guttering and cause the steps to last a hundred years more. That is what most Englishmen would do. I do not want them to think of me as necessarily English. I am concerned with greater affairs.

At each storey there is a landing, a balcony open to the courtyard, the square of sky, but otherwise unseen by anyone save the inhabitants and their respective gods.

The walls are painted the colour of café-au-lait, the finials of the columns of the balconies touched off in white distemper which is peeling. I am told the plaster cracks every winter with the first snow on the mountains, as reliable as the most expensive barometer. All the shutters are of varnished wood—beech, to judge by their colour. An unusual wood for shutters in Italy.

I like the building. I was attracted to it as soon as I heard the fountain trickle and was told of the assassinations. It was appropriate. I had no option but to rent the fourth floor apartment on a long lease, six months' rental paid in advance. I have always believed in fate. There is no such thing as coincidence. My customers will confirm this opinion.

I have no truly close friends: such friends can be dangerous. They know too much, become too involved in one's well-being, take too much of an interest in how one is, where one has been, where one is going. They are like wives but without the suspicion: still, they are curious, and curiosity I can do without. I cannot afford to take the risk. Instead, I have acquaintances. Some are closer than others and I allow them to look over the outer ramparts of my existence, yet none are what are generally termed close friends.

They know me: more exactly, they know of me. A few know in which quarter of the town I live but none have entered my eyrie: entrance to my present abode is reserved only for a very select group of professional visitors.

Several have approached to within a hundred metres and discovered me coming or going: I have greeted them with smiles and bonhomie, suggested it is time to quit work. The sun is high. A bottle of wine, perhaps? We have gone to the bar—the one in the Piazza di S. Teresa, or the other in the Piazza Conca d'Oro, say—and I have talked of *Polyommatus bellargus, P. anteros and P. dorylas* and the delicate blue of their wings, of the latest government scandal from Rome or Milan, of the chamois-like abilities of my little Citroën on the mountain roads. I call the car *il camoscio,* to everyone's humour. Only a foreigner, probably an Englishman and an eccentric, would give his automobile a name.

Duilio is one of my acquaintances. He is, he announces with disarming modesty, a plumber: in truth, he is a wealthy entrepreneur of pipes and ducts. His company builds sewers, underground conduits, water catchment drains and, of late, has branched out into avalanche barriers. He is a merry man with a bacchanalian love of good wines. His wife, Francesca, is a jolly, rotund woman who never ceases to smile. She smiles in her sleep, Duilio claims and he winks obscenely to hint at the cause thereof.

We met when first he came to survey the gutter. As a friend of a friend of Signora Prasca. It was hoped one of his men would see to the job in an off day, for cash. We fell to talking—Duilio speaks some English but better French—and went to the bar. The gutter was not repaired but no one seemed to care. Friendship can be forged over a handyman's task, not broken by it. Then, some weeks later, I was invited to his house to try his wine. It was an honour.

Duilio and Francesca have several homes: one by the sea, one in the mountains, an apartment in Rome for business and, perhaps, the dalliances with which Italian men fill their extramarital hours. Their mountain home is set in vineyards and apricot orchards about fifteen kilometres from the town, higher up the valley. It is just too high for olives, which is a shame: there are few greater luxuries in the world than lazing a long afternoon under the scant shade of an olive grove, the sunlight pricking through the branches and the roots of the trees digging into one's daydreams like fingers into dough.

The house is a three storey modern building built on the site of a Roman cistern, appropriate for a man who constructs drainage systems: Duilio laughs at this irony.

He is, he states, keeping up with the tradition of the land, restoring the irrigation channels in the orchards. He, too, wants to leave his mark on history.

He makes his own wine: it is red, light red, the grapes Montepulciano.

The house has no wine cellar. Instead a cavernous garage suffices, the rear as dark and musty as any cave, and as mysterious. Behind a breeze-block wall, behind shelves of small bore piping and pump spares, massive wrenches and tube-cutting machines, boxes of faucets and valves, is the wine. It is covered in cement dust, plaster and bat-shit. To reach a particular shelf, Duilio has to stand upon the hood of his brand-new Mercedes. Reaching over, he wheezes with the effort. He is not a well man. It is the wine.

'*Violà!*' he declaims, then relies upon his weak command of English in honour of his guest. 'This is a fine wine.' He is as proud as a father of his son, of a daughter wed above her station. 'I make it.'

He slaps the bottle as if it were a whore's buttocks. 'She is good.'

He wipes the neck of the bottle in the cleft of his elbow, the grey dust staining his flesh. From between a box of washers and a crate of tins of machine oil he produces a corkscrew, the bottle opening with a tiny explosion like a high velocity round leaving a silencer. He pours the wine into two glasses on the table and we sit, waiting for it to warm in the sun. Lizards scuttle over the blinding white earth of the driveway, rustle in the dry thistles and grass beneath the swelling apricots.

'*Alla salute!*'

Like a true connoisseur, he sips and washes the wine around his mouth, squeezing a drop between his lips and swallowing slowly.

'She is good,' he declares again. 'You think?'

In Italy, anything worth having appears to be feminine: a good car, a good wine, a good salami, a good book and a good woman.

'Yes,' I agree.

If the wine were a woman, I say, she would be young and sexy. Her kisses would tear your heart out. Her hands would revive the limpest old man into a stud of Herculean proportions. Stallions would stampede with envy. Her eyes would beg for love.

'Like blood,' Duilio says. 'Like Italian blood. Good red.'

I nod at the thought of blood and history. I should be back at my work. I take my leave and reluctantly accept a gift of a bottle of this unlabelled grape-blood. Receiving it places me at a disadvantage. A man who receives wine from an acquaintance risks the development of friendship and, as I say, I want no friendship for it brings with it perils.

P ermit me to give you a word of advice, whoever you are. Do not attempt to find me.

I have hidden in the crowds all my life. Another face, as anonymous as a sparrow, as undistinguishable from the next man as a pebble on a beach. I may be standing next to you at the airport check-in, at the bus-stop, in the supermarket queue. I may be the old man sleeping rough under the railway bridge of any European city. I may be the old buffer propping up the bar in a rural English pub. I may be the pompous old bastard driving an open Roller—a white Corniche, say—down the autobahn with a girl a third of my age at my side, her breasts moulded under her T-shirt and her skirt hitched high up her tanned and endless thighs. I may be the corpse on the mortuary slab, the derelict without a name, without a home, without a single mourner at the maw of a pauper's grave. You cannot know.

Ignore the apparent clues. Italy is a big country and ideal for hiding in.

But Piazza di S. Teresa, you think, where there is a bar owned by one Luigi. Signora Prasca, you think. Duilio the millionaire sewerman and Francesca, you think. Clara and Dindina. A good sleuth could track these down, put one and two together and make four. Search the tax records for a spinster or widow Prasca, the police computers for two whores called Clara and Dindina in the same bordello, the lists of the Italian Sewer Manufacturers' Directory. Look for every Piazza di S. Teresa with a bar in it close to an alleyway with two right angled bends and pretentiously called a *vialetto*.

Forget it. Do not waste your time. I may be old, but I am no fool. If I was, I should not be old, I should be dead.

The names are changed, the places changed, the people changed. There are a thousand Piazzas di S. Teresa, ten thousand alleys which have no names, exist on no maps save those in the heads of the occupants and the local *postino* who knows of it only as a dead end he has to walk down every morning, only to return to the Via Ceresio to continue his round.

You will not find me. I will not permit it and without my consent, you are lost. The British Anti-Terrorist Squad, MI5, the CIA and the FBI, Interpol, Russia's KGB or GRU and Romania's Securitate, even the Bulgarians, those expert trackers of men—they have all looked but never discovered me, although a few have drawn quite close. You have no chance.

The apartment is self-contained. No one can gain access except through the one main door; there are no rear stairs, no buildings overtowering it from which an intruder could be lowered, no fire escape. In case of need, I have an escape but you are not to know of it: such a disclosure would be extremely foolish on my part.

In truth, the apartment has three levels, the building being constructed on the slope of the hill upon which the town is built. Entering through the door from the fourth floor balcony, you would find the short hallway and the main sitting room. It is spacious, fully ten metres by seven. The floor is tiled in once red, now ochre, seventeenth century slabs and, in the center, is a fire grate raised on a twenty-centimetre dais over which hangs a copper hood and chimney. It can be cold here in the winter. Several modern settees surround the fireplace, the sort made from kits purchased in furniture warehouses. The chairs are canvas and wood, like those used by film directors on a movie set. The table, of heavy nineteenth-century oak, has only two chairs. That is one more than is essential.

Along one wall is a row of windows: like the fireplace, they are a modern addition. Opposite them are the bookshelves.

I enjoy books. No room is fit for occupation without a lining of books. They contain the condensed experiences of humanity. To live fully, one has to read widely. I do not intend to face a man-eating lion in the African veldt, fall from an aircraft into the Arabian Sea, soar through outer space or march with the legions of Rome against Gaul or Carthage, yet books can take me to these places, to these predicaments. In a book, Salome can seduce me, I can fall in love with Marie Duplessis, have my own Lady of the Camellias, a private Monroe or exclusive Cleopatra. In a book I can rob a bank, spy on the enemy, kill a man. Kill any number of men. No, not that. One man at a time is enough for me. It always was. And I do not always seek experience second-hand.

Books are a drawback for, when I move on, they must be abandoned, jettisoned like bags of sand from a sinking balloon, ballast from a listing ship fighting the hurricane. Every new place, I have to start again, constructing a library. I am always tempted to have the books returned for storage but that necessitates an address, a fixed point and I cannot afford such an indulgence. Looking at these shelves, however, I consider that they may be more permanent than those in the past.

Music is also an enjoyment of mine, an indulgence, an escape from realities. On the shelves I have a compact disc player. There are fifty or so discs besides it. Mostly classical. I am not a lover of the modern musics. Some jazz. Yet that also is the classical of the genre—the Original Dixieland Jazz Band, King Oliver, Bix Beiderbecke, the Original New Orleans Rhythm Kings, McKenzie and Condon's Chicagoans. Music is also an excellent device for distorting or dampening other sounds.

On the end walls of the room I have paintings. They are not valuable. They were purchased from a market frequented by artists in front of the cathedral on Saturdays. Some are distinctly modernistic, cubes and triangles and worms of paint. Others are inept representations of the countryside around: a church with a poorly executed campanile, a water-mill surrounded by willows, a castle perched on a hilltop. There are many castles balanced on ridges in the province. The paintings are cheerful and merrily primitive in the way children's art is attractive. They add colour and light.

I need light. In a dark world, light is essential.

At the end of the room is a small kitchen with a gas stove, fridge, sink and work surfaces of fake marble. Along a narrow and dark passage from this is a lavatory containing a water closet and, redundant in my abode, a bidet. At the facing end of the room is another door leading to five rising steps and another passageway, the whole side of which is a long window broken only by pillars. Once a balcony, this was glazed by the previous occupant.

Off this passageway are two large bedrooms and an adequately appointed bathroom—a bath, shower, lavatory, linen cupboard with hot water tank and another redundant bidet. The previous inhabitant, Signora Prasca informs me, was a prodigious *amante*. This she states with a smile of fond remembrance as if she, too, had been one of his conquests. When she recalls the inconvenience of his parties, the quickness of his temper and the loud moaning of a young mistress through an open summer's night window and echoing in the courtyard, she speaks of him as *seduttore*. There is no pleasing old women.

The first bedroom is simply furnished with a double bed, a pine chest of drawers, cane-seated chair and wardrobe. I am not a man desirous of luxurious sleep. I sleep lightly. It is part of my business. A room full of satins, cushions and mirrors and scents lulls the mind as effectively as morphine. Besides, I bring no pretty girls up here. The bed may be double but that simply gives me space. In my business, one sometimes needs space, even in slumber. The mattress is firm, for soft foam and springs are another soporific, and the frame does not squeak. There is no—what is the current euphemism?—horizontal jogging done in this bed. A noisy bed-frame is the last sound many a man has heard. I do not intend to join the august company of deceased fools.

The bathroom, tastefully lined with white tiles upon which are printed, at random around the room, colourful depictions of mountain flowers, is between the bedrooms.

The second bedroom I shall leave for now.

At the end of the one-time balcony is another flight of stone steps as well worn as the main staircase. Until the building was sub-divided into apartments twenty years or so ago, whoever entered the front door was sure, unless he was a menial or tradesman, to make the pilgrimage to the top. For up these steps is the crowning glory of Italian architecture, an octagonal loggia.

I have furnished this with a wrought-iron chair and table, painted white. Nothing more. Not so much as a cushion. There is no electric light. A low wooden shelf under the parapet wall, holds an oil lamp.

Signora Prasca expresses occasional dismay that I have no guests to enjoy the loggia and its panoramic view, with whom to share the dawn and the twilight, the balmy summer breezes and the rising of a wintry, coruscating Venus down the valley.

The loggia is mine, more precious than any guest who could tread it. It is my utterly private place, more so than the remainder of my apartment. Up in the loggia, I survey the panorama of the valley and the mountains and I think of Ruskin and Byron, of Shelley and Walpole, of Keats and Beckford.

If I sit in the centre of the space, under the dome of the roof, I cannot be seen from below or from the buildings on either side. I can be seen from the roof or the parapet on the façade of the church up the hill, but it is locked at night and the walls are as impregnable as a penitentiary. There is no tower and it would take a most determined man to scale the building.

The interior of the dome is most curiously painted with a fresco I should guess to be at least three hundred years old. It depicts the horizon of the view, the tops of the mountains and the façade of the church, the outline unaltered by time. Above is painted the sky in royal azure, the stars pricked out in gold. In places, the paint has faded and peeled but, generally, the fresco is still in good condition. I cannot recognise the stars and assume they are either an invention of the artist's imagination or hold some symbolic meaning I have not attempted to fathom. Time is too short to allow for my delving into history. It is enough to assist in the shaping of it in my own little way.

I do not often venture out at the height of the day. This is not a case of being deliberately non-expatriate. Noël Coward's 'Mad Dogs and Englishmen' does not apply to me. I do not claim to be either English or French, German, Swiss, American, Canadian, South African. Nothing, in fact. Signora Prasca (and, indeed, all my acquaintances) assume I am English for I speak the language and receive mail in English. I listen—and they must hear it from time to time—to the BBC World Service on my transistor radio. I am also mildly, harmlessly eccentric for I paint butterflies, very rarely receive visitors, am a very private man. The English do not go out in the height of the day. I could be nothing but English in their eyes. I do not disabuse them of their assumptions.

My preference for remaining indoors, which I do when it suits me, is for a variety of reasons.

Firstly, it is more convenient for me to work during the day. Any noise I make can be camouflaged by the general hum of the town. Any smell which might emanate is lost in the odium of car fumes and cooking food. It is better for me to work by daylight than artificial light. I need to see, very exactly, what I am doing. The advantage of Italy is the number of sunlit hours it affords.

Secondly, the streets are crowded in the day time. Crowds are, I know it only too well, a superlative hiding place—yet not only for myself: there are those who would hide from me in order to watch me, to wonder at me, to try to assess what I am up to.

I do not like crowds unless they are to my advantage. A crowd is to me as a tropical forest is to a leopard. It can be a habitat of great safety or great danger depending on attitude, position, the innate senses. To move in crowds, I have to be ever alert, ever cautious. After a while, a constant state of watchfulness becomes tiring. This is the time of most danger, when the attention is weakened. It is then the hunter bags his leopard.

Thirdly, if someone were to wish to burgle the apartment, he would more likely do it under cover of day.

The inaccessibility of the apartment would make a night intrusion awkward at least, highly dangerous at best. No burglar, not even an idiot of an amateur apprentice, would be prepared to scale roofs of loose pantiles, haul up a seven-metre ladder, swing it over an open space fifteen metres above ground, clamber precariously over it and all for a few baubles, a wristwatch or two and a tv set.

No: any burglar would come by day, disguised as a meter-reader, census-counter, health official, building inspector. It would not be easy for him even then: he would have to gain entry through to the courtyard, bluff his way past the wily Signora Prasca, who has been a concierge since before the war and knows all the tricks, and open my apartment door. It is double deadlocked with two Chubbs, and the timber is over an inch thick. I have lined the inner side of the door with seven gauge steel plate.

The ordinary burglar's time would anyway be wasted. I wear my one wristwatch and, with no desire to vegetate before inane quizzes and Milanese housewives' breasts, I have no television, only the compact disc player and the transistor radio, which are not popular with the Italian Society of Fagins.

The more intelligent burglar, however, is the one I fear. What he would steal from me is not material wealth. It is knowledge, a knowledge which could be fenced more readily than a filched brooch or a Rolex Oyster Perpetual. Not everyone wants a hot watch but the whole world wants information.

Fourthly, I like the apartment in day. The windows let in the breeze, the sun moves inexorably across the floor, disappears, starts in through the opposite windows. The pantiles click in the heat and lizards scuttle along the sills. Martins nest in the eaves to chirp and cheep through the hot day, diving into their mud bowls like acrobats, as if being swung on trajectories of invisible wires. The countryside moves through phases of light: the mists of dawn, the harsh bright early sunlight, the haze of midday and afternoon, the purpling wash to dusk, the first sparks of lights coming on in the mountain villages.

There is a romantic side to me. I do not deny it. With my concern for intricacy, my adoration of exactitudes, my perception of detail and my awareness of nature, I should perhaps have been a poet, one of the unacknowledged legislators of the world. Certainly, I am an unacknowledged legislator, but I have written not a jot of verse since I left school. I have even been acknowledged on several occasions, albeit under a pseudonym.

Finally, when in the apartment, I am in complete control of my destiny. I may be subjected to an earthquake, for this part of Italy is prone to such. I may be poisoned by the daytime car fumes. I may be struck by lightning during the summer storm—there is no finer spot in the world to watch the gods sport than in the loggia—or have a loose piece of aircraft fall on me. That is by the way. No one can avoid such unpredictabilities.

What I am safe from are the predictables, the risks which can be assessed, analysed and accounted for, the vagaries of men.

I walk out in the early morning. The *vialetto* holds the night for half an hour after dawn has broken. At the Via Ceresio I turn left and go to the corner with the Via de' Bardi. Opposite is an old house, the oldest in the town according to Signora Prasca. Just below the roof line is a ten-centimetre crack caused by age, the shaking of distant volcanoes and the vibrations of lorries in the Viale Farnese. In this crack lives a colony of bats, thousands of them. Standing at the junction at dawn, I watch them returning for the day and think of D.H. Lawrence and his *pipistrello*. He was right. Bats do not so much fly as flicker-splash in neurasthenic parabolæ.

In the first light, I sometimes walk down the Via Bregno, cross the

Viale Farnese and enter the Parco della Resistenza dell' 8 Settembre. The pine trees and poplars hiss as the first breezes swell from the valley. Sparrows jig about searching for crumbs left by yesterday's strollers. A few wayward bats take the last of the night's insects. In the bushes rustle small rodents competing for the sparrows' gleanings.

There is no one abroad so early. I could be a ghost wandering the streets, blind to the living. I usually have the park entirely to myself and that is best, is safe. If there should be other persons about, a janitor making his way to work, a pair of lovers entwined about each other after a night of what Signora Prasca would doubtless term *l'amore all'aperto*, a man taking exercise as myself, I can see them, determine their motives for being in the park with me, assert the threat they may pose and react accordingly.

Alternatively, I go out in the evenings. The town is alive then, but not too crowded. There are crowds, but there are also shadows into which to slip, archways and doorways in which to shelter, alleys down which to make good an escape. I can meld with the crowds, disappear into them silently like a ship into fog.

These are but sensible precautions. Outside those in the discreet fraternity of my profession, no one knows I am here or, if they do, not where exactly in the long leg of Italy I make my living. Yet I must be prepared.

I know this town, every street, alley and passageway. I have wandered them, learnt them, studied their curves and bends, their straights and their angles of ascent or descent. I can walk swiftly from the west to the east gate in fifteen minutes, not once deviating more than eight metres off a straight line drawn through the buildings. I doubt I have a fellow citizen who can do likewise.

As regards leaving the town, I can drive out of it at the height of rush-hour, even in the middle of the tourist season, in less than three minutes from where I keep my Citroën. In seven, I can be through the toll-gate, ticket clipped for convenience in the ashtray, and on the autostrada. In fifteen, I can be well into the mountains.

Let me tell you of the view from the loggia. Signora Prasca is correct when she chides me for not enjoying it with others, so I shall share it with you. It is a shame you cannot actually be here with me. I could now allow that, not knowing you. You must understand I may in any case be lying. Not falsifying the truth. Truth is an ineluctable absolute. I am merely readjusting it.

From the loggia, I have a panoramic view over the rooftops of the valley and mountains from the south-south-west round to the east-north-east. I can also see over the roofs of the town to the church and a long row of trees which line the Viale Nizza.

The rooftops are all pantiled, the chimneys squat with sloping pantiled covers like miniature roofs. Television aerials mounted on aluminium poles are the only concession to modernity. Remove these and the view would be like the one painted around the rim of the dome. The rooftops descend in steps as the hill goes towards the cliff which drops to the river and railway line below.

Beyond is the valley, running south-east to north-west for about thirty kilometres. On either flank are mountains rising to one thousand and fifty metres with foothills between the valley plain and the peaks which, despite their height and cragginess, are not overbearing and stand more like friendly sentinels than warders. In winter, the snowline comes down to just a hundred metres from the valley floor. In the distance, down the valley, are other hills rising from the plain. They are, like the mountains, wooded where there is no rock, the slope not too steep and the snow generally temporary. Across the valley are villages. Upon the hills, small communities cling to plateaux. The living is agricultural, harsh but rich with contentment.

In the town there are industries: electronics, service industries, pharmaceuticals—all high-tech and low pollution. The workforce live in anonymous suburbs to the north, sterile communities in cossetted houses surrounded by pine trees scarred by the construction companies' bulldozers, or in blocks of low-rise condominiums. These are the homes of the people who want to shape no history at all.

Fortunately, I cannot see these disimmaculate conceptions, as Father Benedetto refers to them, the barren and effete developments, the pretentious enclaves of the *borghesia Italiana*. What I can see, with my pair of compact pocket Yashica binoculars, are five thousand years of history laid out before me as if it was a tapestry upon a cathedral wall, an altar-cloth to the god of time spread over the world.

On one ridge, jutting from the mountains like a cockerel's spur of rock, is a castle. It is in ruins now, only the curtain walls remaining, surrounding a three hectare site of derelict barracks and stables, storage barns and noblemen's quarters. There is only one entrance, sealed with a heavy iron grid and secured with three titanium steel chains and heavy duty padlocks. The chains bear the signs of ineffectual hacksawing: on the ground lie the remains of several saw blades, shattered by temper or poor usage. Someone, more ingenious than the hacksawers, has attempted to widen the gap between two of the bars with a hydraulic jack. He has been partially, but not completely, successful.

Except to me, it seems, the castle remains as impregnable as in the days of the Crusades. I have found an entrance, my head containing a similar mind to that of the fortress builders, a mind accustomed to the convolutions of intrigue, the diversity of necessity and the ever-present requirement of a bolthole, a rope out of the window or a ladder down the wall.

Not far from the castle stands the ruins of a monastery, the Convento di Vallingegno. It is a ghostly place. As with the castle, the walls stand firm. The buildings within, however, are in better condition. Not all the roofs have caved in. Spirits are said to be active here. Local witches, for there are still a good many in this part of Italy, rifle the tombs of the monks. The monastery was the scene of black magic ceremonies conducted by the area Gestapo hierarchy in 1942. It is said a Gestapo senior officer is buried there. The witches have searched zealously for this prize but as yet to no effect.

Around these ruins are little villages—San Doménico, Lettomanoppello, San Martino, Castiglione, Capo d'Acqua, Fossa. Tiny places, half abandoned by their populations who departed for Australia, America, Venezuela, eluding plague or drought or unemployment or the grinding rural, montane misery of the Twenties and Thirties.

I know all these places. And others, farther afield, over the mountain passes, along tracks only the chamois use, or the shepherds, or the wild boar or the courageously stupid cross-country skiers come the first heavy falls of snow.

The valley is history. The mountains are history. I cannot see it from the loggia, for the line of poplars in the Parco della Resistenza dell' 8 Settembre blocks it, but there is a bridge over the river seventeen kilometres away which is buried by undergrowth, tangles of brambles and old-man's beard. The road no longer uses it, has not for fifty years. A motor bridge bypasses it twenty metres downstream.

Thrusting through the snagging cover, I have stepped on this cobbled arch. I know, for I have read the local history, Otto and Conrad IV, Charles I of Anjou and both Henry III and Edward I of England have crossed it, not to mention Popes—the diplomatist Innocent III, the cunning crusader Gregory X, the mendacious Boniface VIII and the gullible miracle worker Celestino V. All were men of history, men of destiny, men who wanted to leave their marks upon time.

Being a romantic—not a poet, yet still a legislator: do not forget that—I imagine the drum and slip of hooves upon the cobbles, the banners furling from lances, the chink of bridle and clatter of armour, the shifting sound of chain mail and creak of leather. I can see, reflected in the river, the glint of sword-steel and the riot of colour from silks and flags.

History: the castle and the monastery, the villages, the bridge, the roads and the churches and the fields. I like it, this ordinary history of everyday things.

Today, upon the ridge, it is viciously hot. I have struggled up the rocky track for nearly twenty minutes. The hillside is bleak: wild thyme, sage, low brush and thistles to the stems of which cling white and brown striped snails, their shells sealed by hardened mucus against the heat of the sun, displayed like pearls upon the stalks, like globs of sap oozed out and baked by the day.

The rocks are loose and large, as blindingly white as bleached enamel, the track uneven. If the way was less stony, I should have driven a car up here, yet I cannot risk a punctured oil pan or cracked axle. I need reliable mobility.

At the top of the track, which hairpins to and fro up the hill, is a ruined tower and a small church, hardly more than a chapel, once confined within the walls of a small fort, but one of huge importance, for it surveys the southern end of the valley where the land starts to drop off steeply to the plains. From here, the winding route down the narrowing valley can be observed for ten kilometers. The road is little used now: there is a brand new motor road to the east. Yet it was down here the Crusaders passed and the tower and church belonged to the world's first bankers, the Knights Templar.

I arrive at the top and find a convenient boulder upon which to sit beside the tumbled-down tower. The sun is merciless. I pull my water bottle out of my knapsack and guzzle the water. It is lukewarm, tastes tepid and smells of plastic.

I admire those knights. They took control of history. They fought. They changed destiny. They killed. They kept secrets. They were reticent men and, like all men of discretion, they made many enemies because of their diffidence, their engrossing fetish for privacy. As I have done. The tower against which I lean was theirs. From here destiny was controlled.

The grand destiny. Not the little tweaks to the line of time. The grand twists, the snaps in the whip of time which curl and flick and make thunder. Which hurt.

These were not men who built churches by which to be remembered, if not by God then at least by their fellows. These were not men who constructed towers by which the future might admire them. Indeed, few hereabouts in the valley or down the road they paved to the plains know of their work. Their churches are for the most part insignificant and austere, their towers heaps of rubble. They changed not the shape of the landscape but the shape of their own and my existences. Yours, too.

I am of their ilk. In my quiet way, I too play a role on the wide stage of time. I erect no towers, establish no monuments and yet, because of me and my actions, the cast of history is configured. Not the sort of history Father Benedetto refers to, the making and breaking of grand treaties, the forging of alliances, the exalted intermarriages of princes and peoples which only bear slightly upon the rest of humanity, but the kind which alters the air we breathe, the water in which we bathe, the soil upon which we tread our brief spans, which affect the way we think.

It is better to change the manner in which a man perceives the world than it is to change the world he perceives. Think upon this.

Rested, my breath back and my heart thumping less loudly from the exertions of the climb, I set about the reason for my trip out of the town. Reasons: there are two.

The first is quickly accomplished. It takes but a few minutes. With my binoculars, I survey the western hillside to the narrow valley. It is wooded, oaks and chestnuts, mountain ash. There is no discernible pathway up from the valley floor where the nearest village huddles like a group of travellers sheltering from an oncoming storm. Indeed, the houses are travellers, time's travellers and the storm, time's storm. I know the village, not a house newer than a hundred years and two erected in the twelfth century. One is the village bakery, as it has ever been, the other a moped garage and repair-shop.

Knowing the topography of these mountains, I can tell the ridge at the top of the woods hides an alpine meadowland beyond.

One cannot buy maps in Italy, not detailed ones such as the British foolishly sell in every bookstore and stationery shop. Ordnance Survey maps are unobtainable in Italy. Only the authorities keep them, the military or the water companies, the *polizia*, the provincial govern-ments: Italy has had too many wars, too many bandits, too many politicians to risk such information getting out. Maps which show contours, mountain tracks, derelict and uninhabited mountain vil-lages, disused roads are not publicly available. A 1:50,000 map of the region would be of immense value to me: for a 1:25,000 I should willingly pay three quarters of a million lire. Yet I dare not seek it. I am sure the map would be there for the asking, but he who asks is known. Instead, I have to rely upon my experience of the mountains and my knowledge tells me there is an alpine meadow over there, ideal for future requirements.

I make a few notes, decide to drive over the mountain and spy out the land as soon as there is an overcast day. On sunny days, a car win-dow can flash like a heliograph in the mountains. From the loggia, I have seen the reflection of a vehicle twenty-seven kilometres off.

That done, I set to my next task, a portrait of *Papilio machaon*, the common swallowtail.

Anyone who has never seen this creature is much the poorer for the omission of such beauty from their lives. It is, to quote the 1889 edition of Kirby, a large, strong butterfly with broad triangular fore-wings and dentated hind-wings. The wings are sulphur-yellow, fore-wings black at the base, and with black veins. They also have black spots on the costa, and a broad black sub-marginal band dusted with yellow. The hind-wings are broadly black, dusted with blue, before the hind margin, and the eye-spot is red, bordered in front with black and cobalt blue. All the wings have yellow lunules before the hind margins. It expands to three or four inches in width, flying with a gracile speed, the wings beating rapidly. Suffice to say it is exquisite.

There is a warm updraught between the ruined tower and the lit-tle church, blowing from the valley floor, from the barley and lentil fields, from the patch of saffron, from the vineyards and the orchards. It wafts only here and the butterflies use it as a highway to cross the ridge from one part of the valley to the next, rising upon it as raptors ride thermals. I pour my trap upon the earth, a medicine bottle of honey and wine mixed with an eggcupful of my own urine. It soaks into the gravellous soil, leaving a dark, damp stain.

Art is only a matter of observing. The novelist examines life and re-creates it as narrative; the painter scrutinises life and imitates it in colour; the sculptor pores over life and immortalises it in everlasting marble, or so he thinks; the musician listens to life and plays it on his violin; the actor pretends reality. I am no true artist, not one of these breeds. I am merely an observer, one who stands in the world's wings to behold the action occurring. The prompter's chair has always been my place: I whisper the words, the stage directions, and the plot unfolds.

How many books have I seen burned, how many paintings faded and grimed, how many sculptures smashed by weapons, chipped by frost or split by fire? How many millions of notes have I heard drift in the air to peter out like the smoke of an abandoned cigar?

I do not have long to await. By chance, the first arrival is *P. machaon*. The butterfly settles on the damp spot in the earth. It has smelt the trap. One of its eye-spots is missing. A gash has ripped the wing. The tear is the exact V shape of a bird's beak. The butterfly uncoils its proboscis like a watch-spring losing tension. It lowers it to the ground and probes for the dampest area. Then it sucks.

I watch. This beautiful creature is drinking up a part of me. What I waste, it enjoys. I imagine my urine salty, the honey sickly sweet and the wine heady. It is not long before there are half a dozen of *P. machaon* supping at my drug accompanied by other species in which, today, I have no interest. The first swallowtail, with the torn wing, has had enough and stands in the scant shade of a thistle, opening and shutting its wings. It is drunk on my salt and the wine. This will not last long. In twenty minutes, it will be recovered to flit down the hillside in search of flowers, more wholesome yet less wonderful.

I do not understand how men can kill such beauty. There can be no joy, surely, in capturing such a masterpiece of evolution, gassing it

with chloroform or squeezing its thorax until it is dead, setting it on a
cork board until rigor mortis is advanced then pinning it, frozen by
death, in a glass-topped case, hung over with a curtain to keep the
light from fading the colours. To me, this is the height of frivolous
insanity.

Nothing can be gained from killing a butterfly. Killing a man is a
different matter.

The piazza in the village of Mopolino is triangular, eight trees standing in a row shading the western end, their trunks scarred and
gouged by careless parking, their projecting roots stained by dog urine
and fertilised by cigarette butts. They grow from beds of dirty gravel
and are surrounded by kerbstones which afford them no protection.
Kerbstones are not guiding marks but mere inconveniences to Italian
drivers.

At the eastern apex of the piazza is the village post office, a tiny
place no bigger than a small shop which smells of hessian, stale
tobacco, cheap paper and glue. The counter is at least as old as the
postmaster, who I should say is not under sixty-five. The wooden surface is highly polished by wax and the sleeves of jackets, but it is also
cracked, the splits filled with an accumulation of the dust of years.
The postmaster's face is similarly polished and cracked.

The advantage of the piazza is that it contains two bars, one on
either side. This is of great use to me for I can sit in one and cast an
eye over not only the piazza but the other bar, too.

There is little likelihood of a watcher drinking in the same bar as
myself. He would feel he had to move away if I was to enter, or go to
sit at one of the tables outside. This would make him conspicuous. He
would prefer to be across the piazza, observing me from a distance.

I took a long time finding the right post office.

In the town where I reside, the main post office is too big, too
busy, too public. There is always a throng of people milling about it

and the telephone company next door, many of them waiting to make a call from a kiosk, post a letter, send a telegram, meet a friend. They read newspapers, chat to each other or stand and survey the crowds. Some walk up and down impatiently. They are a perfect cover for a clandestine observer.

There is no bar in sight. If there were one there, it would bring its owner many riches, and it surprises me no wily entrepreneur has recognised the potential. It would also present to me a perfect vantage point from which I could inspect the crowds and assess any possible threat. Yet it is inconceivable that I could be entirely safe in such a place of teeming onlookers. What I required as soon as I came to live in this region was a spot I could approach cautiously, like a tiger returning to its kill, aware there may be a hunter in a *machan* in the trees who has been waiting, patiently.

And so, whenever I drive out to Mopolino, I always park my little Citroën 2CV by the end tree in the line, walking to the bar on the left of the piazza. I sit at the same table every time, order the same refreshment—an *espresso* and a glass of iced water. The patron, who is not quite as old as the postmaster, knows me by now and I am accepted as a regular, if taciturn, visitor.

I do not call always on the same day of the week, nor do I call always at the same hour: so rigid a timetable would invite problems.

For a while, I sip my coffee and behold the slow pace of village life unfolding. There is a farmer who arrives in a cart pulled by a tubby pony. The cart is made from the truck-bed of a Fiat pick-up, with wooden shafts from a gig many decades older. They are intricately carved with leaf designs, as much a work of aesthetic art as the rest of the cart is one of ingenuity. The wheels are adapted from those of a heavy lorry and have bald pneumatic Pirelli tyres, half inflated. There is a number of rowdy teenage boys who zoom into the piazza upon mopeds, their engines and voices echoing momentarily off the walls. There is a rich man with a Mercedes-Benz sedan who drives to the post office and leaves his vehicle in the centre of the thoroughfare while he does his business: he cares not a jot that he holds up the daily meat delivery to the butcher's shop. There are also two very pretty young girls who drink coffee at the other bar, their laughter light yet simultaneously serious with the concerns of their youth.

I wait for up to an hour. If there is nothing to alarm me, I go smartly across to the post office.

'*Buon giorno*,' I say.

The postmaster grunts his reply, jutting his chin. It is his way of asking what I want although he is well aware. It is always the same. I buy no stamps and seldom post a letter.

'*Il fermo posta?*' I enquire.

He turns to a rack of pigeonholes behind a sack of mail hanging in a metal frame like an old person's walking aid. I wonder if, when the day's collection has been made, he borrows the framework to see himself home.

From one pigeonhole he draws a bundle of general delivery envelopes held together by an elastic band. Some have been there for weeks, months even. They are the relics of love affairs turned sour, petty crimes abandoned or long since carried out, deals reneged upon and tourists long since passed by on their restless itineraries. They are a sad comment upon the feckless, shifting, unfeeling character of human nature.

Deftly, like a teller counting through a thick wad of banknotes, he flicks through the mail. At the end, he stops and repeats the process until he comes to my letter. There is always only the one. This he extracts with thin, wasted fingers and tosses on to the counter with an incomprehensible grunt. He knows me well by now, no longer asking for identification. I put one hundred lire in change upon the counter by way of payment or gratuity. With his bony fingers, he scoops the coins across the counter and into the palm of his hand.

Leaving the post office, I do not go directly to my little car. I walk around the village first. The streets are so placid, so cool in the shade, the cobbles smooth and hard underfoot, the windows shuttered against the heat of the day. By some of the doorways sleeping dogs lie prone, too bushed by the heat to bother to growl at a stranger; or perhaps they too know me by now. Cats hide suspiciously in the deep shadows under steps or lintels, their alert eyes bright and devious like those of child pickpockets in Naples.

One doorway always has an old woman sitting within it. She makes lace, her gnarled fingers like the roots of the trees in the piazza but still nimble, flicking the bobbins over on the frame with a practised dexterity I admire. She sits in the shade but her hands and lace are in the brilliant sunlight, the skin over her knuckles tanned as leather.

Every time I pass her by I smile. Often I pause to appreciate her handiwork.

Her greeting is, regardless of the time, 'Buona sera, signore,' delivered in a high, squeaky voice like that of a cat mewing.

I wondered at first if she was blind, every hour being evening tinted, but soon realised it is because her eyes see everything in twilight, permanently dazzled by the sun on the white tracery of the lace.

I point at her lace and remark, 'Molto bello, il merletto.'

This remark invariably prompts a wide and toothless smile and the same retort spoken through a porcine snort of comical derision.

'Merletto. Si! I lacci. No!'

This is her reference to my first meeting with her when, in searching for the word, I assumed laccio was lace. It was: a shoe-lace.

Today, as I walk, I open my letter, read it and memorise the contents. I also watch out for someone following me. Before I return to the car, I stand and survey the piazza, pausing to tie my shoelace. During this time, I cast an eye over the vehicles in the piazza. Most I know to be owned by locals. Those I do not recognise I momentarily study, committing their details to mind. This way I can ensure one does not follow me back to the town.

Satisfied I am safe—or at least prepared—I leave. I take several other precautions as well, but you are not to know of these. I cannot afford to give away every detail. It would not be circumspect.

On the way back to the town—a distance of some thirty-five kilometres—I watch to see if I am being tailed and, bit by bit, I shred the
letter into the tiniest confetti and let it blow, a pinch at a time, out of
the window.

The second bedroom in my apartment is a workroom. It is quite
large, almost too large, for I prefer to work in enclosed surroundings. This preference is not good for my health, not with the kind of
work I do, but I have become accustomed to it and so am inured to
small rooms.

In Marseilles, I had to operate from what had once been a wine
cellar. There was no ventilation at all except a grid high in the wall
and a sort of flue rising from one corner. There was no natural light,
which was awful. I strained my eyes for weeks in there, on just one
job. The results were superb, possibly my best ever, but it ruined my
eyesight and scoured my lungs. For months, I suffered from bronchi-
tis and sore throats and was obliged to wear sunglasses, gradually less-
ening the density of the lenses until I could once more face raw
daylight. It was hell. I thought I was finished. But I was not.

In Hong Kong, I rented a two-room flat in Kwun Tong, an indus-
trial area near Kai Tak airport. The pollution was atrocious. It lay
upon the district like the strata of leaves collecting in a pond. At
ground level was offal, waste food, strips of rattan scaffolding ties, Sty-
rofoam fast-food containers, discarded plastic shoes, paper, filth. At
first floor level—in the building in which I rented my temporary
workshop this was ironically termed the mezzanine—up to third or
fourth, the air stank of diesel and petrol fumes. From there on up, the
smell was predominantly carbon tetrachloride delicately impinged
upon, depending on the direction of the stifling breeze, by burning
sugar, sewage, melting plastic, textile dyes and frying fat. The floors
below my own were occupied variously by a dyeing works, a toy
manufacturer, a fish-ball kitchen, a candy-maker, a dental laboratory

making false teeth, a plastic spectacles frame company and a dry cleaning processor. The sewage came from a badly corroded twelve-inch pipe which leaked at the fifth floor level.

I hated the place. The ventilation to my flat, one of a dozen 'residences' on the top floors, the occupants of all of them engaged like myself in some manufacturing process, was adequate but, in removing the noxious gases produced by my processes, it merely imported the others. Down the centre of the street outside ran the underground railway system, supported on concrete piers like the New York subway only far more up-to-date and, astonishingly, spotlessly clean.

The place was indescribably noisy, too: the trains passing at three minute intervals, trucks, cars, machinery, human shouting, car horns, hammering and thumping and grinding and hissing. Every few minutes for most of the day, a jet aircraft roared momentarily.

I was there five weeks. I worked without ceasing. The job was quickly done for I wanted to get out. Delivery had to be made to Manila. After that, I took a long break in Fiji, lying in the shade like a retired pirate, living as a spendthrift on my loot.

In London, I rented a garage built into the archway of a railway viaduct south of the Thames. It was a grotty locality—grotty was an in-word then—yet it served me well. I could work with the door open, by daylight. The other archways were used as lock-up storage units, an auto body shop, a television repair works and a fire extinguisher recharging plant. No one intruded upon the others' businesses. We all drank in the nearby pub at lunchtime, eating Scotch eggs and pickled herring with tough-crusted buns and drinking Bass. There was a camaraderie in that row of archways with its muddy, puddled approach, its grimy brickwork and dusty mortar, its rusting chain-link fencing and the strangely comforting rumble of commuter trains overhead making for Charing Cross or Waterloo.

The others thought I custom-made bicycle frames. I bought a racing cycle to further the deception. When I left, it was a close call. The cops were only hours behind me with their bullhorns and plain-clothes snipers. One of the auto body mechanics was an informer. He tipped them off I was stealing lead: he could smell it when I melted and recast the metal. It was a ridiculous accusation. The man was judging me by his standards, a bad error.

I went back two years later. I found the muddy approach had become a pedestrian precinct with pretty posts made of iron and painted with the crest of the council. The archways had become a trendy restaurant, a photographic studio and a unisex hair salon. I also found the mechanic living in a quiet, tree-lined square off the Old Kent Road. According to the tabloids, he and his young common-law wife committed suicide. A lovers' pact, the articles suggested. I fixed it to look that way.

It was the only time I ever returned. Marseilles, Hong Kong . . . I never went back. Athens, Tucson, Livingstone. Fort Lauderdale, Adelaide, New Jersey, Madrid . . . I never saw them again.

Of all the workshops I have had, however, the second bedroom in this, my Italian refuge, is by far the best. It is airy. Even with the shutters closed on a hot day in high summer, there is a continuous, transient breeze passing through. Enough daylight enters through the door or the shutter slats for me to dispense with the spotlamps unless I am doing the most detailed of work. Any pernicious redolence I might cause from time to time, as a part of this or that stage in one or another process, blows away to be replaced with fresh air. Outside, it is quickly diluted in the sky. The floors being made of stone are strong and absorb a good deal of the sound.

The room contains no furniture as such. In the centre is a large workbench. Beside it stands a bank of metal shelves upon which I keep tools. Against the wall, to the right of the window, is a small lathe of the sort jewellers use. It is mounted upon iron legs which stand upon two blocks of wood between which is sandwiched a layer of solid rubber of the sort used in car engine mountings. Screwed onto the wall beside the lathe is the stereo speaker; across the room is another. I have installed a steel kitchen sink in the room and a cold water tap, connected to the water and outflow pipes in the bathroom next door. I have a stool upon which to sit and a square of carpet beneath it. By the workbench is an electric fan heater. To the left of the door is an architect's drawing board and another stool. That is all.

The lathe was awkward. Signora Prasca understood the workbench. Artists use such tables, she thought. Besides, I made sure she noticed my easel and drawing board arrive at the same time. And the spotlamps. The workbench was therefore disguised as a part of the artist's requirements. But the artistry of miniatures necessitates no lathe. This I kept in pieces in the rented van in which I had driven up from Rome, parked in the Largo Bradano. Bit by bit, over four days, I moved it to the apartment. The bed of the lathe was too heavy for me to lift. I obtained the help of one of Alfonso's mechanics from his garage in the Piazza della Vanga. He believed he was carrying a printing press: after all, artists made prints of their work. He said so himself. Signora Prasca was out shopping in the market at the time.

Should the lathe be making too much noise, I turn on the stereo loudly. The speakers are wired to the compact disc player in the sitting room. If the metal tends to screech in the turning, I play one of three pieces: Bach's Toccata and Fugue in D minor, Mahler's Symphony No. 1 'Titan', the second movement and, most appropriately, for I appreciate twists of irony, Mendelssohn's Symphony No. 4 in A, the 'Italian'. Perhaps, in order to complete the irony, I should add to my little repertoire of covering music the closing five minutes of Tchaikovsky's 1812 Overture (opus 49). The cannon fire would be a suitable accompaniment for the lathe.

Imbert. He was a quiet man, as I recall. Antonio Imbert. You will not have heard of him unless you are a specialist in Central American affairs, or an elderly official in the CIA. Nor will you know of his associates, his comrades-in-deed, his co-conspirators. They were important men in their world, in their history: Diaz was a brigadier-general,

Guerrero a presidential aide, Tejeda and Pastoriza both engineers (I never knew of what). There were also Pimentel and Vasquez and Cedeno. And Imbert.

Of the assassination squad, I met only him and only on the one occasion, for about twenty minutes over a cocktail in a hotel in South Miami Beach. It was a most apt rendezvous. The hotel was a seedy joint once glorious in the days of bootlegging, Tommy-gun-toting gangsters. It was an art deco building, all rounded edges and curving lines like an old-fashioned American limousine, a Dodge say, or a Buick, a Great Gatsby automobile. It was said Al Capone had spent a holiday there, once: Lucky Luciano, too. I ordered, I remember, a manhattan whilst Antonio had a tequila, sipping it with salt and lemon.

It was reported he was the only one to escape the subsequent fusillade of bullets which chase after such men as him, just as angry wasps pursue him who kicks the hive. They were all hive-kickers. Their hive was the Dominican Republic and the wasps were the followers of Generalissimo Rafael Leonidas Trujillo.

He disappeared—Antonio, that is; Trujillo just died. I never knew where he went, though I have an inkling of a suspicion he went first to Panama. As agreed, on July 30, two months to the day after the event, I received a bank draft drawn on the First National City Bank mailed to me in Colon.

It was all so long ago, late February 1981, when we met. Trujillo's assassination was that May.

It was a traditional killing. Al Capone would have been more than satisfied by it. It had all the hallmarks of a gangster-slaying, the same type of planning, the same type of execution. I am not given to flippant absurdity: it is no clumsy pun but a bald statement of irredeemable fact. Such a conception is rare nowadays: the grand assassinations are no more, gone with the eloquent, decadent age of the ocean liner, the flying boat and macabre dowagers in mink overcoats and thick cosmetics. Now it is just the bomb and the blitz, the spraying of bullets, the radio-controlled landmine, the random explosions of uncontrolled violence. There is no artistry left, no pride taken in the job, no assiduity, no coolly-collected, assimilated deliberation. No real nerve.

Trujillo was a man of habit. He visited his very elderly mother every night at San Cristóbal, thirty-two kilometres from Ciudad Trujillo. They, Antonio and his chums, blocked the road with two cars. Another followed on behind. As the Generalissimo's vehicle slowed, the men in the car opened fire. From the roadside, the others let rip with machine-guns. Or so the report went. The Generalissimo fired back with his personal revolver. His chauffeur returned fire with the two submachine guns kept in the car. The chauffeur survived. The assailants were not aiming at the front seat. They were directing their fire exactly at the rear, at the wound down window, at the single spits of flame which were the target's handgun.

Once they had felled their target, it was not enough to see him dead. They came out of the cover, kicking his body, smashing it with the butts of their guns, pulverising his left arm. They dumped his body in the trunk of one of the road block cars and drove off to abandon it, in the darkness, with a last look at the bruised, contorted face of the dictator.

What they did was wrong: not the killing, for death can always be justified. It was the mutilation that was wrong. They should have been satisfied with the end of their enemy. It is not a matter of aesthetics or moralities, of political expediency or humanity. It is simply a waste of time.

The dead feel nothing. For them, it is over. For the killers, there is nothing to gain from the beating of a corpse. I can see no pleasure in such actions, no self-justification, although I accept there must be some. It dehumanises the killers and they abase themselves by such actions. After all, the act of killing cleanly, exactly, quickly is such a human action that to bestialise it is to reduce it to mere carnality.

Yet I suppose I can appreciate their reasoning, the hatred which bubbled within them for Trujillo, for what he had done, to which they were opposed.

At least they left the chauffeur, injured and unconscious. They did not beat him, kill him. He was merely a bystander in history's unfolding tapestry.

That, too, was a mistake. Never leave an involved onlooker. They should become a part of the history they witness. It is their right as much as their lot. To deprive them is to deprive history of another victim.

If you were to tell Europeans it was taboo to urinate against a kapok tree—that by doing so they would release the devil inhabiting the trunk and it would escape, climb up the stream of piss and enter the genitals, rendering them infertile—you would be ridiculed. Taboo is not a word considered with any seriousness in the Old World. It is the stuff of primitive tribes, of head-hunters and face-painters.

Yet, for every supposedly civilised man, death is a taboo. We fear it, abhor it, wonder superstitiously about it. Our religions warn us of it, of the brimstone and flames, of red-tailed demons armed with pitchforks, eager to ensnare us, press us into the pit. As I see it, there is no dybbuk in the kapok tree, nor is there a hell. Death is but a part of a process, inescapable and irrevocable. We live and we die. Once born, these are the only certainties, the only inevitabilities. The only true variable is the timing of the event of death.

It is as pointless to fear death as it is to fear life. We are presented with the facts of both and have to accept them. There is no Faustian avoidance on offer. All we can do is attempt to delay or accelerate the approach of death. Men strive to postpone it. They do this instinctively, for life, it seems, is preferable to death.

I admit that I too seek to put off the coming of the dark. I do not know why. There is nothing I can do about it. It will come, and only the manner of its coming can potentially be controlled.

Tomorrow, it is within my power to kill myself. The bottle of codeine is on the bathroom shelf, waiting. There is a through train to the south from Milano every day bar Sunday which does not stop at the station: it would take but a step forward there to end it all. The mountains too have cliffs as high as the sky, and there is always the gun, the clean quick way to die.

I may have the quotation wrong—my classical languages were never good—but I think it was Simonides who wrote 'Somebody is happy because I, Theodorus, am dead; and someone else will be glad when that somebody dies as well, for we are, everyone of us, in arrears to death.'

Certainly, there will be those who shall celebrate my passing should they get to hear of it, for whom the dictum of Charles IX of France will ring so true: 'Nothing smells so good as the body of a slain enemy.' Just as sure is the fact there will be few mourners at my graveside. Perhaps, if I was to die today, Signora Prasca might weep. Clara and Dindina too. Father Benedetto would mutter a few words, be sorrowful he had not heard my last confession. Indeed, if he values my friendship as I think he does, he might pretend he heard a final, faint breath of contrition or catch the merest flicker of an eyelid in response to the last, great question. There would be no such thing, of course. Any twitch of the flesh would be caused by the nerves fading, the flesh discharging its electricity, the muscles relaxing and starting their genteel corruption into dust.

What name might be spoken in my eulogy or carved upon my tablet in the cemetery, I cannot say. 'A.E. Clarke', perhaps. I should prefer 'il Signor Farfalla'. I have to accept, when death rears up before me, so too will arise the question of my identity. Whatever happens, the headstone will not bear my true name. I shall forever be an administrative error in the affairs of the graveyard.

I am not afraid of death nor of dying. I do not consider it where I am concerned. I just accept that it will arrive, in its own due time. I am of the opinion of Epicurus. Death, purportedly the most terrifying ill, is nothing to me. So long as I am alive, it does not exist for it is not here, has not occurred, is neither tangible nor foreseeable. When it arrives, it is nothing. It merely implies I no longer exist. It is of little concern therefore, for the living have it not and the dead, being no more in existence, similarly know nothing of it. It is no more than a swing-door between being and ceasing to be. It is not an event of living. It is not experienced as a part of life. It is an entity of its own. So long as I live, it is non-existent.

As I care little for death, it follows I care not that I create it for others. I am not an assassin. I have never killed a man by pulling a trigger and taking a pay-off. I wonder if you thought I had. If this is so, then you are wrong.

My job is the gift-wrapping of death. I am the salesman of death, the arbiter who can bring death into existence as easily as a fairground magician conjures a dove from a handkerchief. I do not cause it. I merely arrange for its delivery. I am death's booking-clerk, death's bell-hop. I am the guide on the path towards darkness. I am the one with his hand on the switch.

It is the case I support assassination. It is the best of deaths. Death should be noble, clean, final, exact, specific. Its beauty lies in its finality. It is the last brushstroke to the canvas of life, the final daub of colour which completes the picture, which rounds it to perfection. Life is ugly with uncertainties, its unsureness abhorrent. One can become bankrupt and beggared, lose love and respect, be hated and downcast by life. Death does none of these.

Death should be tidy, as precise as a surgeon's cut. Life is a blunt instrument. Death is a scalpel, sharp as light and used but once then thrown away as dulled.

I cannot bear those who dole out death in ragged slovenliness, the hunters of fox and stag, for example. For those cruel and empty souls, death is not a mastery of beauty, though they claim it is, but a long-drawn-out journey of barbarity into an obscenity, into a degraded death. For them, death is fun. They should wish themselves to die quickly,

avoid the deathbed scene and the agony of cancers, the slow deteriora-
tion of the flesh and the spirit: they would wish to die as if struck by
lightning, one minute fully aware of the sun cutting its rays under broil-
ing storm clouds, the next gone. Yet they want to issue death as slowly as
they can, extort its every twist of fate, its every ounce of anguish.

I am not like them, the obscene men in their hunting uniforms,
the colour of arterial blood. You see, they even fear to call their jackets crimson, vermilion or bloody red. They call them pink.

The dining room in Father Benedetto's house is as sombre as an
advocate's office. No paintings hang in there save a dusty oil in a
chipped, gold lacquer frame, of the Virgin Mary holding the infant
Christ almost at arm's length. It is as if the baby Jesus was not her own
offspring: perhaps he smelled as babies always do, from a soiled diaper
or the cloying stink of soured milk. The walls are panelled in dark
wood stained by centuries of polish, smoke from the baronial fireplace
and previous incumbents' cigarettes and soot from paraffin lamps.
Upon the sideboard stand two such lamps, their funnels of clear glass
protruding from frosted orbs upon which are exquisitely engraved
scenes from the life of Our Lord.

The room is mostly filled by the dining table, a massive edifice of
oak, black as ebony and five inches thick, with six legs carved like the
fluted pillars of a grotesque cathedral. Up these clamber fertile vines
bearing little smirking demons.

The priest's best crockery is antique, fine porcelain and china
edged with maroon and gold, big dinner plates and neat finger bowls
which ring to the flick of a fingernail, solid soup dishes and oval plat-
ters for fish. Each serving dish could hold an entire meal for a peasant
family of four. The vegetable dishes and soup tureen could contain
sufficient to feed a small hamlet in the mountains. In the centre of
each piece is a crest, a coat of arms surrounded by three golden birds,
each with its head thrown back and its beak open in song.

Father Benedetto comes from a well-to-do background. His father was a merchant in Genova, his mother a noted beauty of her time, courted by many and famously flirtatious but cautious: like all the wise women of her day, she guarded her virginity until she could trade it in wedlock to a wealthy man. I have never discovered in what line the priest's father was a merchant. He has hinted at chemicals, which could be a euphemism for armaments, but I have heard rumours he made a fortune after the war by the illegal excavation and exportation of antiquities rifled by peasants from Etruscan tombs. He died before he could fully enjoy his riches, his eight children—Father Benedetto is quick to point out his father was a good Catholic—inheriting what the government allowed them after taxation.

Now, the wealth and opulence of Father Benedetto's youth have faded into a shabby and dusty decay, like the cuffs of his canonicals.

When I first sat at this table, I admired the crockery.

'The crest is that of the family of my father,' he explained 'The birds are Guazzo's.'

'Guazzo's?' I asked.

'His *Compendium Maleficarum*,' he replied as if I should know of it. 'My family were Crusaders. A long time ago, you understand,' he added, should I think this to be a recent calling, a contemporary crusade. 'They fought for death and the remission of their sins. Guazzo wrote in his book of the wonders of the East, of the golden singing birds belonging to the Emperor Leo. My family owned one once, so it is said . . .'

He spoke with a sudden, deep sorrow.

Tonight, we are dining together, just the two of us. Father Benedetto has an old woman who keeps house for him, a crone from the town. She does not live in, and every Wednesday, unless it is a Feast Day in the Catholic calendar, he gives her the afternoon and evening off. It is then he cooks his meal.

Cooking is an art with him. He relishes it, enjoys the intricacies of transforming raw flesh into meat, dough into bread, hard earth nuggets into succulent vegetables. He spends the whole afternoon preparing the meal, humming operatic arias to himself in the high-ceilinged kitchen, hung about with tarnished copper pans and old-fashioned, redundant utensils which look more like instruments of torture than culinary tools.

I always arrive an hour early, talk to him as he busies himself at his play.

'You only do this because it is an evilness you can allow yourself to indulge in,' I tell him. 'This is the nearest you can get to alchemical practices without jeopardising your soul.'

'If only alchemy were possible,' he muses. 'If it were, I should change these copper pots to gold and sell them for the poor.'

'You should not keep some for yourself?'

'No,' he answers emphatically. 'But I should give some to Our Lord for his glorification. A new vestment for the cardinal, a gift to our Holy Father in Rome . . .'

He potters about the stove. It is wood-fired and he stokes the flames with a brass poker. The pans are simmering on the hot-plates.

'Cooking is good. I sublimate my want for sex in here. Instead of stroking a woman, shaping her into an object of desire, I form food into . . .'

'Objects of desire?'

'Quite so!'

He pours another glass of wine and hands it to me. He has his own which he sips as he works between bouts of humming.

After some time, we go to the table. I sit at one side, he the other. He mutters a grace in Latin, speaking the words so quickly they form one long incantation, as if he is in a hurry to begin. This may be the case, for he does not want the main course to spoil.

His soups are always chilled. Tonight, we have carrot and sorrel soup. It is both sweet and tart and whets the palate. We do not talk during this first course. This is customary. As soon as his bowl is empty, he invites me to help myself to more from the tureen. He bustles out to the kitchen, humming once more.

The soup ladle is made of silver and is, I should guess, about three hundred years old. Decades of ardent polishing have all but erased the crest and three birds. The assay marks are invisible. The place cutlery comes from several sets: the forks are silver, the soup spoons silver-plated and the knives Sheffield steel with serrated blades and rounded ivory handles the colour of a corpse's teeth.

'*Ecco!*' he exclaims, returning with a silver dish upon which sit two plump poultry carcasses covered in sauce and steaming into his face.

'What is it?'

'*Fagiano*—wild roast pheasant with oranges. The birds come from Umbria. A friend . . .'

He puts the dish carefully on the table and rushes out to return balancing three bowls upon his arms like an experienced waiter: one contains salsify soaked in garlic butter, another *mange-tout* peas and the third fried button mushrooms with shreds of truffle mixed with them. He pours a white wine into our glasses and serves each of us with a complete bird.

'The sauce is orange juice, rind, garlic, chestnuts, Marsala and *brodo di pollo*. How do you say it in English?' His hands supplicate and he looks up to the lofty ceiling for a translation: God gives him one. 'Chicken broth, of bones.'

I help myself to vegetables and we eat. The meat is sweet yet gamey, the salsify soft and delicious. The wine is dry but bland and the bottle bears no label. He must have purchased it locally, from an acquaintance with a few hectares of vines on the sides of the valley.

'This is sinful,' I declare, indicating the food with my fork. 'Decadent. Hedonistic. We should be living a thousand years ago to eat so.'

He nods but makes no answer.

'At least,' I continue, 'we have the table for it. Laden with a repast fit for a Pope.'

'The Holy Father eats better than this,' Father Benedetto declares, swilling the wine around his mouth. 'And this is the correct table. It is said it was once the property of Aldebert.'

He rightly interprets my silence as ignorance and goes on, laying down his knife and fork.

'Aldebert was an antichrist. French.' He shrugs as if to imply this was an inevitability. 'He was a Frankish bishop who abandoned his see and preached to peasants near Soissons. San Bonifacio—the English one—had much trouble with him. Aldebert practised apostolic poverty, was able to cure the sick and claimed he was born of a virgin. He was born by the caesarean method. At a synod in the year of Our Lord 744, he was excommunicated. Yet he continued to preach and was never arrested.'

'What happened to him?'

'He died,' Father Benedetto says with finality. 'Who knows how?' He picks up his knife and fork again. 'The French have never been good Catholics. Consider this recent schism, this . . .' again he looks up for divine translation but this time without assistance '. . . *buffone* who wants to keep to the old ways. He is French. He causes much trouble for the Holy Father.'

'But do you not adore history, my friend?' I interject. 'Is not such tradition the stuff of life, the blood of the continuity of the church? Did you not say a Latin grace before we ate?'

He sticks his fork into the breast of his pheasant as if it was a French priest of dubious piety and does not reply. He just grins.

After a few more mouthfuls, I ask, 'How can you dine at the table of the Antichrist? And was he not a Frenchman . . .?'

He smiles and excuses himself, 'He was a bishop when he owned the table. Also, he was not antichrist. I think this. He was a man of God. He cured the sick. Even today, there is the charismatic Catholic church. I do not . . .' He lifts his fork, burdened with flesh. 'But it exists. Often Jesuits.'

I cannot tell if he is in favour of the Society or against it.

We finish the meat and I help him clear the plates away. He produces nuts and cognac. We sit again at the table.

'Did you never want to be other than a priest?' I ask.

'No.'

He splits an almond with the pair of silver-plated nutcrackers.

'Not a doctor or teacher or something else you could do within the church?'

'No. And how about you, Signor Farfalla?'

He almost smirks. He must know I receive mail in the name of Clarke, Clark, Leclerc and Giddings. He is certain to have asked Signora Prasca and she, a good and god-fearing woman, will have told him, for he is her priest and she an elderly lady with a devout faith in such men. I do not share this unquestioning trust.

'Have you never wanted to be other than an artist?' he enquires.

'I have not considered it.'

'You should do so. I am sure you have other talents. Other than with the brush and the paper, the aquatints and the pencil. Perhaps you should do something else also. You have the hands of a craftsman, not an artist.'

I do not show my unease. He is treading too close to my path.

'Perhaps you should also make other things. Things of beauty . . . Things to bring you greater wealth than little pictures of insects. This cannot make you a rich man.'

'No, it cannot.'

'Perhaps you are rich already?' he suggests.

'As rich as you are, my friend.'

He laughs lightly.

'I am very rich. I have God in my vaults.'

'Then I am not so affluent as you,' I allow, 'for that is one valuable I do not possess.'

I sip my cognac.

'You could . . .' he begins, but then he stops. He knows better than to try and gain a convert over the pheasant and brandy.

'What do you suggest I do or make?'

'Fine jewellery. You should be a goldsmith. Make plenty of money. With your drawing skill . . . Maybe you should make banknotes.'

He is looking at me shrewdly. I imagine, should the mesh be removed from the wall of the confessional, this is how he would regard the sinners who come to him for release and a penance. Years of experience have given him the knack of looking through dissemblance.

'That would indeed be sinful.' I attempt to make light of his subtle probing. 'Even more so than eating a sensualistic meal at the table of an antichrist.'

I sense he knows something is not right. He knows I have money. He knows I cannot subsist on the portraits of swallowtails. I must be careful.

'I am not a young man. I have my savings. From past work.'

'And what was your work?'

He is quite forthright with his question. There is no subterfuge in the man yet I do not feel I want to trust him. He would surely not betray me but it is still for the best he should not know, have so much as an inkling.

'This and that. I owned a tailor's shop for a while . . .'

I lie. He is fooled, for I have seemingly given in to him.

'I knew this!' He is triumphant at his skilful piece of detection. 'You have the hands of a master needle-craftsman. Perhaps you should do this again. There is much prosperity in designing clothes.'

He smiles broadly and raises his cognac in a mute toast, either to my proficiency as a tailor or his as a detective. I cannot tell which and follow suit.

As I leave, bid him goodnight and walk through the shadows down the alleyway to the Via dell' Orologio, I consider our conversation. I like this priest a good deal but I must keep him at bay. He must not uncover the truth.

There are almost as many saints in Italy as churches dedicated to them. At the birthplace of the Venerated One, at the site of his or her miracles, monastic home or hermit's cave, the place of death or martyrdom, there is a church. Some are grandiose edifices with lofty bell towers, imposing façades and spacious quadrangles of flagstones before them: others are, as religious houses go, hovels of the meanest sort. Yet even the very rudest has at least a piazza.

If you go down the *vialetto*, turn left on the Via Ceresio and then left again at the Via de' Bardi, you will come to the foot of a long flight of marble steps. They are but a metre or two wide at the base but, halfway up the hill, they widen until, at the piazza at the top, they are perhaps fifteen metres wide. The steps are worn smooth with age and the tread of pilgrims. Today, however, only shoppers struggle up or down them, lovers with their arms about each other's waist, tourists with cameras and video camcorders. Sparse wisps of grass grow between the stones and litter blows over them. Of late, and in the early hours, the steps have become the haunt of addicts. Several times recently, I have noted discarded hypodermic needles lying against the side walls.

The marble is of poor quality, chosen for durability rather than colour. It is veined with dark, sooty stains like the forearms of the addicts.

Traffic zips by the top of the steps. The pavement is very wide there and a number of street entertainers and vendors gather at this spot in the tourist season. One is a flautist. He has his stand under an umbrella tied to a no-parking sign upon which a frustrated driver has spray painted a derisive *non sempre*.

The flautist is a tubercular young man, his skin pasty and his eyes hollow. I suspect he is one of the early hours crowd, the heroin fixers and dope smokers, the twentieth-century lost, the modern leper or plague victim. He carries no bell. Instead, he has a chipped and dirty flute.

Despite the condition of his instrument, he makes the most beautiful music. His speciality is the baroque. He has adapted several pieces for the flute and plays these with a detachment both moving and pathetic. He squats beneath his umbrella, a grubby cushion under his haunches, and his fingers run up and down his black flute with a rapid fluidity of which one would not expect him capable. He seems never to run short of breath and only takes a break between tunes in order to sip at a bottle of cheap, coarse wine. He takes his lunch in a nearby bar, if he has had a good morning's custom, eating bread with a few anchovies and drinking Cerasuolo diluted with mineral water.

Sometimes, I can hear him in the evenings, his music drifting over the rooftops to the loggia, competing with the sundown chorus of cicadas. I sit quietly, the lantern glowing from the shelf under the parapet, and think of him as a part of my trade, my profession. I am the bringer of infinity, the harbinger of eternity and he is my minstrel, my Blondel playing up to me in my tower of death.

Another entertainer is a puppeteer. In the daytime, he stands behind a stage draped with candy-striped cloth like a Victorian Punch-and-Judy stall. His daytime puppets move to the pull of strings. They dance and cavort, a red-faced clown executes skilful somersaults without tangling his wires, and recount nursery rhymes or local legends in high, squeaky voices. Local school-children, tourists' offspring and old folk make up the audience. They laugh together, the young and old infantiles, and throw small change or telephone tokens into a tin bowl placed beside the stall. Every so often, the puppeteer's foot appears from beneath the cloth and toes the bowl out of sight. There is a rattle of coins and the bowl, almost empty, reappears. As with every busker the world over, the bowl is never seen totally void of generosity. Money begets more money as if pennies in the basin are an investment and the audience provide the interest.

At night, the puppeteer changes his show. The string puppets are folded into a case, and he dons glove puppets. These are not the ridiculous figures of the daytime performances, the clowns and policemen, the schoolteachers and dragons, old ladies and wizards. These are now monks and soldiers, ladies of fashion and gentlemen of leisure. The stories they tell do not centre upon legend but upon sex. The characters speak no longer in shrill voices but now sound like modern, real men and women. Every tale involves a seduction and at least one puppet has a rampant cock filled, no doubt, by the puppeteer's little finger, which he thrusts up the skirts of one of the ladies in the narrative. For obvious reasons, the puppeteer not being double jointed and his stall being narrow, the puppets fuck standing up.

Local men watch these tales with hilarity. Lovers stand before the stall and giggle, later to disappear into the Parco della Resistenza dell' 8 Settembre to try out the method for themselves. The tourists, usually with their children in tow, watch for a while, not understanding a word of the story and walking off hastily as the screwing begins. French tourists are the only group not to drag their children away when the pornography commences. Honeymooners, I have noticed, watch the longest.

Of the vendors at the steps, my favourite is toothless old Roberto, who always wears a pair of stained black trousers, a grey and filthy waistcoat, a collarless shirt and chain-smokes black tobacco. He also has a thumbnail fully three centimetres long. This is the only clean part of his anatomy. Roberto sells watermelons.

I buy my melons only from him. He is convenient, his barrow being comparatively close to my apartment: the way there is downhill and a melon can weigh over ten kilos. He also cuts open a melon for one to judge the quality of his wares. When a melon is chosen, he tests it for ripeness and solidity, tapping a tattoo upon the skin with his long nail. He listens to the echo. I have yet to buy unripe or over-ripe fruit from him.

The church across the piazza from the pornographic puppeteer, the dying flautist and the sounder of watermelons is dedicated to San Silvestro. Which Silvestro has his memory enshrined in this foundation I do not know. The townsfolk claim it is Silvestro I, the Roman pope who climbed on to the Throne of Christ in 314 and of whom little is known or supposed save that, in trying to establish his notch on history's tree, he claimed the Emperor Constantine donated to him, and his successors in the see of Rome, primacy over all Italy. It was a shrewd move for a man destined to be one of the first saints who was not a martyr. However, it could equally well be Silvestro Gozzolini, a twelfth century lawyer who turned to the priesthood, criticised his bishop for loose living, went into self-imposed solitary confinement, came out to found a monastery near Fabriano and had a dozen monasteries named after him on his death, as a strict interpreter of the rule of Benedict. To this day, the Silvestrines are a Benedictine congregation: Gozzolini was therefore even shrewder than his namesake. Today the monasteries mostly reduced to rubble, there is still a nearby street named after his followers. But, there again, there are many other Silvestros, men who lived and died in tiny villages, divined a well or cured a sick cow and were seen as vessels of the Holy Spirit.

For whomever it exists, the building is impressive. It has a square front, such as is commonly found in these mountains, with a round window above the main door and sets of columns rising against the stonework. Within, the cavern of the church is as cool as the interior of one of Roberto's watermelons.

The floor of the nave is tiled with black and white slabs of marble intended, no doubt, to imitate a fifteenth-century carpet without affording the worshippers the true touch of fabric on shoe or bare sole. So much of religion is an offering of the fake, of the representation rather than the reality.

The ceiling is a vast, ornately carved wooden monstrosity, painted entirely in gold and inset with panels of oil paintings depicting key events in the saint's life. It is as tastelessly florid and ornate as the surround to a prewar cinema screen or the proscenium arch of a music hall. Well-aimed spotlights illuminate this rococo extravaganza and tourists bend their necks and *ohh* and *ahh* at the ghastly sight as if it was a static firework display, or a presentation of the entrance to heaven itself.

The saint's tomb is no more restrained. It stands in a side aisle for all the world like a fairground organ. Fluted pillars, gold flecked black marble and embroidered cloth surround an evacuated glass box in which the corpse can be seen. It is a wizened thing, the face reconstituted in wax but the hands in view and looking like beachcombed driftwood. The chest appears to have collapsed under the robe draped around it. The feet are bedecked in a pair of elaborate slippers of the sort more usually seen dangling from the toes of whores in bordello windows in Amsterdam. So much glory, all for one man who was shrewd enough to see he was not forgotten: so much history encased in one building, in one grotesque funereal monument, in one pair of tart's sandals.

Yet what has the man achieved, whoever he may be? Nothing. A feast day in the calendar (December 31 or November 26, or some other date depending on the identity of the wax face and sunken chest) and a paragraph in a hagiography no one reads. A few fat old women in black dresses and sombre shawls hover like carrion crows about the altar, lighting candles perhaps for an intercession on their behalf, or punishment on a daughter for running off with an actor, a son for marrying beneath him, a husband for enjoying the poking puppets across the piazza.

History is nothing unless you can actively shape it. Few men are afforded such an opportunity. Oppenheimer was lucky. He invented the atom bomb. Christ was lucky. He invented a religion. Mohammed was just as fortunate. He invented another religion. Karl Marx was lucky. He invented an anti-religion.

Note this: everyone who changes history does so by destroying his fellow man. Hiroshima and Nagasaki, the Crusades and the spoliation of millions of primitives in the name of Christ. Pizarro massacred the Incas, missionaries corrupted the Amazon Indians and the blacks of central Africa. During the Taiping Rebellion in China more died than in both World Wars put together: the leader of the Taipings thought he was the new-come Christ. Communism has killed millions in purges, by starvation, in ethnic wars.

To alter history, you have to kill your fellow man. Or cause them to be killed. I am no Hitler, no Stalin, no Churchill, no Johnson or Nixon, no Mao Tse-t'ung. I am no Christ, no Mohammed. Yet I am the hidden one who makes the changes possible, provides the means to the end. I too alter history.

The wine shop is owned by an elderly dwarf who serves behind the counter standing on two wooden boxes nailed one on top of the other. He does nothing but take the order and write it on a slip of onionskin, accept payment or enter the transaction in a ledger for settlement at the end of the month and then bawl out to the dark recesses of his store. From there appears a man almost two metres high who reads the order slip and disappears, returning in due course with the bottles in boxes on a trolley. He does not smile and the dwarf is sarcastic at his every turn: the wooden boxes are chipped, the bottles are rattling, the wine is being shaken, the wheel on the trolley squeaks. I wonder every time I visit the place how long it will be before the tall one, who must spent his life crouching in the cellars, murders the dwarf, who spends his life reaching for the till on a level with his head.

Yesterday, I went to the shop to purchase a dozen bottles of Frascati and an assortment of other wines. I drove there, through the narrow mediaeval streets, frequently sounding the horn and twisting the wheel to avoid jutting doorsteps, stubborn pedestrians and the door-mirrors of illegally parked cars, the Citroën bucking from side to side. Once at the shop, I had not long to wait. There were no other customers and the tall cellarman was behind the dwarf, restocking shelves high up by the ceiling.

I gave my order, the dwarf screamed at his assistant as if he was a hundred metres underground, and the wine, in two boxes, quickly arrived. The assistant pushed the trolley out to my car and loaded the boxes into the trunk. I tipped him two hundred lire. As usual, he did not smile. He has, I suspect, forgotten how; but I could tell from his eyes he was pleased. Not many of the customers tip him.

It was then, as I closed the trunk, twisted the handle and turned towards the driver's door, I sensed him. A shadow-dweller.

I was not unduly alarmed. This may surprise you. The fact is that I was expecting him. I have a visitor coming soon, and my visitors often send a scout ahead to spy out the lie of the land, the look of the man, of me.

Cautiously, for I did not want to spook him, I cast glances about the street. He was four parked cars off, leaning against a Fiat 500 standing in front of a small pharmacy, his right hand on the roof. He was bending over as if speaking to the occupant. Twice he looked up, gazing along the street in both directions. This is a natural reaction with citizens of the town: standing so in a narrow street, one keeps an eye open for cars approaching over the cobbles.

I settled myself in the driving seat, pretending to fumble for my ignition key. All the while I played my little act, I studied him in the driving mirror.

He was in his mid-thirties with short, brown hair and a good tan, was of average height and slim, not muscular, more of an athlete. He wore sunglasses, a pair of stone-washed designer jeans, very neatly pressed with a sharp crease, a light blue shirt open at the neck and expensive buff suede shoes. It was these which gave him away and confirmed my suspicion: no one wears suedes in the summer in Italy.

I watched him for perhaps twenty seconds, taking in every detail, then started the Citroën and drove away. No sooner was I out of my parking space than he was walking after me. This was not difficult for him for I had to drive slowly in the narrow thoroughfare. He could easily have caught me up but chose to keep his distance. At the end of the street the traffic lights changed and the thoroughfare was suddenly busy, vehicular progress invariably slow.

A van came towards me. The driver gesticulated through the windscreen, signalling me to give him room to pass. I edged the Citroën into a doorway and halted. It was quite natural for me to look over my shoulder: I wanted to assure myself there was space for the van to get by. The shadow-dweller had stepped between two parked cars. He was looking my way, in the direction of the van which edged by the rear bumper of my vehicle.

By chance, there was no traffic queued behind the van. I quickly backed out of the doorway and drove smartly down the street. In the door-mirror, I saw the man nip out from between the cars but the van was stuck with its door-mirror snagged on that of a blue Peugeot 309 with Rome registration and a small yellow disc in the rear window, a rental car company logo. The mirror had twisted loose. Already a crowd of onlookers was gathering for the argument. Just as the lights changed again, I turned right and was gone.

Somewhere, someone is always waiting in the shadows, living there, patiently loitering pending the order to act, hidden like a disease biding its time to waste the muscles or poison the blood. This I accept unequivocally, just as the priest does the existence of a sinner in his congregation, the schoolmaster a miscreant in his class, or the general a coward in his army. It is a fact of the life I live, and my task is to keep a keen weather eye open, to avoid a confrontation, to give this vague presence of a man the slip.

Once, in Washington, DC, I had to dodge a shadow-dweller. There is no need for you to know why I was in Washington. Suffice to say it was to case the stage for which I was providing one of the scene-shifters' tools. I was a novice in those days, but fortunately he was not a thorough expert: the really accomplished shadow-dweller is one who could blend into the spines of a cactus standing solitary in the desert.

In the heart of Washington, one of the most beautiful of America's cities—if you ignore the black suburbs where the indispensable working classes who keep the white man's metropolis going live—is the Mall. It is a green park of grass and trees a third of a mile wide and one and three quarters long, traversed by drives and bounded by avenues. At the east end, on its grand, arrogant little hillock, stands the

US Capitol: it is like a wedding cake left on the table while the sweep
cleaned the chimney. At the other end broods Lincoln in his white
marble box, gruff as a judge and sternly gazing out at the corruption
of the nation he vainly sought to unite. Halfway between the two
stands the phallic needle of Washington's Monument. To the north,
set back behind the Ellipse, is the White House around which security
is tight: too many presidents have been premature in their ride across
the Potomac and up the rise to the Arlington National Cemetery.

Tourists are not always what they seem. I have seen at least a dozen,
within fifty yards of the presidential mansion, packing heat, as the
Americans say. Two were women. They mingle and they watch, and
they listen as they eat ice creams or popcorn, suck at Cokes or Pepsis in
the summer heat. These, too, are not the experts but the rank-and-file
workers of my world, the expendables, the cannon-fodder.

It was here that it began, in the National Museum of Natural History. I was wandering the display rooms, cursorily gazing at dinosaur
skeletons, when I sensed a shadow-dweller. I did not see him, yet I
knew he was about. I looked for him, in reflections in the glass cases
and around the groups of school children and tourists. I could not
find him.

This was not a fancy on my part. I was, as I say, a novice, but I was
already attuned to my seventh and eighth senses. The ninth and the
tenth came in later years.

I went to the museum shop area and lingered to make a few purchases. Nothing valuable; a pyrite crystal glued to a magnet, a fos-
silised fish from Arizona, some postcards and an American flag made
of nylon with a tiny label upon it reading 'Made in Taiwan'.

To buy something, even a bagel or a hot dog at a street-side stall,
gives one good cover from which to observe. The tail thinks the target is busy with his money or his conversation with the vendor. For
those with practice, the purchase and observation can be mingled so
any surreptitious glancing about is unnoticed.

He was there. Somewhere. I still could not see him. He might have been the man in the open-neck shirt and Daks with a camera hanging from his shoulder. He might have been the young husband with the plump wife. He might have been the schoolteacher with his class or the old man tagging along behind a group of senior citizens from Oklahoma. He might have been the fattish man wearing his holiday tour company lapel badge upside-down on his navy blue windbreaker: this could have been a signal to a compatriot shadow-dweller. He could have been the party guide. He might even have been the Japanese tourist. I just could not tell.

I left the museum, turned right along Madison Drive, pausing at a van selling hot cookies. I could not discern him in the passers-by or those coming out of the museum, yet his reality was with me still. I bought two cookies in a waxed paper bag, walked past the National Museum of American History and across 14th Street.

There were a lot of people drifting my way along the sidewalks, over the grassy parkland. In the open air, in the wide space of the Mall, I stood a better chance of identifying the shadow-dweller.

I headed for the Washington Monument. Some boys of about ten, released momentarily from the strictures of their school party, were playing on the grass, throwing a softball to each other, catching it in cow-hide mitts. I could hear the thud of leather from some distance.

Nearing the monument, I suddenly stopped and turned. Others were doing likewise, to see the dramatic view down the centre of the Mall, towards the Capitol.

I saw no-one flinch, not even in the distance, not even for an instant. Yet I knew now who he was. He was a man with his wife and child, about thirty or thirty-five, six feet tall, 160 pounds, slimly built. He was dark-haired and wore a fawn jacket and brown trousers, a light blue shirt and a tie which he had loosened. His wife was auburn-haired, quite pretty in a flowery print dress with a leather shoulder-bag. Their child was a girl of about eight, incongruously blonde. She was holding the woman's hand and it was this which gave them away. I could not exactly define what was wrong, what tiny cues told me this was not a family. The little girl's hand just did not fit in the woman's. The child did not walk, somehow, with the familiarity of a daughter with her mother.

I realised as I saw them that they had been in the museum shop. There, in the crush of museum visitors, the unnaturalness of the relationship between the mother and child had not been discernible. Now, in the open, it was obvious. I had to dodge these people.

The man, I reasoned, would be the one to follow me if I headed off at speed. He looked fit and athletic. I should not stand much of a chance over the open grass. The woman and the child would not follow: the former would contact other operatives in the field to head me off. The child would be a minor inconvenience.

I pretended not to notice them and carried on towards the monument. Just on the edge of its shadow, I stopped and sat on the grass to eat my cookies, now lukewarm. The pseudo-family continued towards me. They had not realised I had rumbled them.

Coming quite close to me, the woman reached inside her shoulder-bag for a Kleenex. I was sure I heard the minute click of a shutter snapping, but it did not matter. I was prepared, had my face half-covered by my hands and a large piece of cookie.

The man pointed to the top of the obelisk.

'This, Charlene honey,' he said in what I recognised as just marginally too loud a voice, 'was built by the people of America to honour the great George Washington. He was the first President of our country.'

The little girl craned her head back and peered up, her blonde curls hanging loose.

'My neck hurts,' she complained. 'Why did they have to make it so high?'

After a while, they moved away informing the child all about Washington and his monument. Most of the tourists walked all around the obelisk: they wanted to see the Lincoln Memorial reflected in the oblong pool made for the effect. Yet my little family did not. It was the final confirmation I required.

Casually, I set off the way I had come, against the drift of pedestrians. Most were, I guessed, following a city walk plan which dictated a stroll to see Lincoln after pausing by the Washington needle. My family dutifully followed me. I skirted the White House and Lafayette Square and started up Connecticut Avenue. I was booked into a hotel beyond Dupont Circle and assumed they knew this: they would be thinking I was going there.

I halted at a pedestrian crossing, waiting for the walk sign to light up. They halted some way back and the man pretended to re-tie the little girl's shoe. This was a farce: I had noticed her white sandals were buckled. The mother busied herself with her shoulder-bag. I guessed she had a walkie-talkie in it and was reporting my position.

The light changed. A taxi drew along the street. I hailed it and got quickly in.

'Patterson Street,' I ordered. The taxi swung round in an illegal U and headed off eastward down K Street.

I looked back. The walkie-talkie was out of the shoulder-bag. The man was looking round frantically for another taxi, his right hand inside his jacket. The little girl stood against a scarlet fire hydrant looking perplexed.

At Mount Vernon Square, I changed my instruction to the driver, to his chagrin. He drove down 9th Street, over the Washington Channel and the Potomac to the airport. Within twenty minutes, I was on the next flight out of town. It did not matter to where.

There are always those who live in the shadows. I know them because I am one of them. We are brothers in the freemasonry of secrecy.

Yesterday, my visitor called. I shall not give you a name. It would be foolish, the height of professional indiscretion. Besides, I do not know it myself. I have only Boyd, for that is how the note was signed.

This person was of average height, quite thin but well-formed in a lean way with mousy brown hair which may have been dyed. A firm handshake. I like that: a person who grips you can be trusted within the established parameters of a relationship. A quietly spoken person, of few words, conservatively dressed in a well-cut suit.

We did not meet at the apartment but near the fountain in the Piazza del Duomo. The person was standing, as we arranged, by the cheese stall, wearing dark glasses and reading the day's edition of *Il Messaggero* with the front page folded in half upon itself.

It was the agreed opening signal. I had to make mine. I went to the cheese stall.

'*Un po' di formaggio,*' I ordered.

'*Quale?*' the old woman replied. '*Pecorino, parmigiano?*'

'*Questo,*' I answered, pointing. '*Gorgonzola. E un po' di pecorino.*'

Gorgonzola, then pecorino: this was the formula, another cue in the game of recognition.

All the while, I was being watched. I paid with a five euro note. The page of the newspaper slipped to the ground. I picked it up.

'*Grazie.*'

As the word was spoken, I saw the head tilt to one side. There was a smile. I could see lines form at the corner of the eyes, a young person's eyes.

'*Prego,*' I answered, adding, 'you are most welcome.'

The newspaper was folded, I collected my change and followed some paces behind through the market stalls to the *gelateria*-cum-bar outside of which stood some tables and chairs on the pavement. My contact sat beneath a Martini umbrella. I sat opposite across the metal table which rocked unevenly on the pavement.

'It is hot.'

The sunglasses were removed and put down. The eyes were deeply hazel, but contact lenses can tint an iris and I guessed these were coloured.

The waiter came out, flicked a cloth over the table and emptied the tin ashtray down a draining grate in the gutter.

'*Buon giorno. Desidera?*'

He spoke with a tired voice. It was nearly midday and the sun was hot.

I did not order. This was the final fail-safe, the final check. My visitor said, '*Due spremute di limone. E due gelati alla fragola. Per favore.*'

Again, there was a smile and I saw the skin by the eyes line once more. The waiter nodded. I noticed my visitor's smile was devious, cunning: there was something sharp about it, acutely discerning. It was like the crafty, falsely subservient expression one sees in the eye of an artful dog which has just robbed the butcher's shop.

We did not speak until the drinks and ice creams arrived.

'It is hot. My car has no air conditioning. I asked for one but . . .'

The words trailed off. Thin, artistic fingers like a musician's removed the plastic straw from the drink and sipped at it.

'What car have you?' I asked but received no reply. Instead, the hazel eyes moved quickly across the market crowd, from one passer-by to the other.

'Do you live far off?'

The voice was subdued, more suited to an intimate *tête-à-tête* in a private cubicle in a cosy restaurant than conversation across a rickety street café table.

'No. Five minutes walk at the most.'

'Good! I've had enough in the sun for today.'

We ate our ice creams and drank our drinks. We did not speak again until it was time to leave. The waiter brought the bill.

'Let me,' I offered, reaching for the slip.

'No. My shout.'

Such an English expression, I thought: British, at any rate.

'Are you sure?'

'Quite.'

It was if we were old friends sparring in a comradely fashion over a bill in a London restaurant. Business friends. In part, this is the case, for we are doing business.

'You leave. I'll get my change and come after you.'

We made our way to the *vialetto*. At all times, my visitor kept at least thirty metres back.

'Very nice,' was the comment as I let us in to the cool canyon of the courtyard, the fountain dripping gently in the quiet. 'You've found a very nice spot. I do like fountains. They add such—such peace to a place.'

'I like it,' I replied.

It was at that moment, perhaps, for the first time, I felt a distinct affinity for the little town, the valley and the mountains, sensed their deep pacificity and wondered if, when it was all over, I should stay this time, eke out my leisure years here, not move on to another temporary abode and subterfuge.

We went up the stairs and into my apartment, my visitor sitting in one of the canvas chairs.

'I wonder if I might beg a glass of water? It is so frightfully hot.'

Frightfully: another English phrase.

'I have cold beer. Or wine. Capezzana Bianco. It is semi-sweet.'

'A glass of wine. Please.'

I went into the kitchen and opened the refrigerator. The beer bottles clinked in the door rack. I could hear movement in the chair as the wood frame creaked. I knew what was going on: my room was being surveyed, searched for whatever that sort of person looked for in a strange place, something to offer reassurance, security.

I poured the wine into a tall stemmed glass, a tumbler of beer for myself, then carried the refreshments through on an olive-wood tray. I handed the wine glass over and watched as my guest sipped it.

'Much better.' The smile half-formed. 'We should have arranged for wine in the bar, not lemon juice.'

I sat on another of the chairs, put the tray on the floor and raised my beer.

'Cheers!' I said.

'I do not have long.'

'Quite.' I took a pull of my beer and set the tumbler back down on the tray. 'What exactly are your requirements?'

The eyes moved across to the windows.

'You have a fine view from here.'

I nodded.

'You're not overlooked. That is most important.'

'Yes,' I replied, unnecessarily.

'The range will be about seventy-five metres. Certainly not over ninety. Possibly much closer. I shall have not more than five seconds. Possibly seven, at the most.'

'How many . . .' I paused. One never knows how to phrase it. I have had this discussion so many times over the last three decades and I still do not have it worked out to perfection '. . . targets?'

'Just the one.'

'Anything else?'

'A rapid fire rate. A reasonably large magazine capacity. Preferably 9mm Parabellum.'

The wine glass twisted in those artistic fingers. I watched as the reflection of the windows spun round against the mellow yellow of the wine.

'And it must be light. Fairly small. Compact. Possible to be broken down into its constituent parts.'

'How small? Pocket-size?'

'Bigger would be permissible. A small case. Say a briefcase. Or a lady's vanity case.'

'X-rays? Camouflage—transistor radio, tape cassette, camera? In amongst tins, aerosols, that sort of thing?'

'Not necessary.'

'Noise?'

'It needs to be silenced. To be on the safe side.'

The wine glass chimed as the base touched the stone floor and my visitor stood up to leave.

'Can you do it?'

I nodded again.

'Most certainly.'

'How long?'

'A month. To a trial. Then, say, a week for any final touches.'

'Today is the sixth. I shall need a trial on the thirtieth. Then four days to delivery.'

'I do not deliver, not these days,' I pointed out. I had said as much in my letter.

'To collection, then. How much?'

'One hundred thousand. Thirty now, twenty at the trial, fifty on completion.'

'Dollars?'

'Of course.'

The smile was less cautious now. There was an edge of relief to it, a hint of satisfaction such as one sees on the face of anyone who has what they want.

'I shall need a 'scope. And a case.'

'Of course.' I smiled now. 'I'll also prepare . . .'

I left the rest unsaid. A pen is no use without ink, a plate without food, a book without words or a gun without ammunition.

'Excellent, Mr. . . . Mr. Butterfly.'

The manila envelope fell heavily on to the chair.

'The first payment.'

The bills, judging by the thickness, must have been hundreds.

'Until the end of the month, then.'

I rose to my feet.

'Please don't get up. I can let myself out.'

It is not good to be a man of habit. I hold in contempt those men who rule their lives by timetables, who run their existence with the efficiency of the German national railway network. There can be nothing more despicable than for a man to be able to declaim, without demur, that at 13.15 on Tuesday he will be seated at the eighth table on the right from the door in the *pizzeria* on Via Such-and-Such, a glass of Scansano by his plate and a *pizza ai fungi* before him.

Such a man is puerile, has never been able to escape the security of parental order, the insistent but safe sequence of the school timetable. What for many years was mathematics or geography is now the *pizzeria* or the barber-shop, the office coffee break or the morning sales meeting.

How one can determine one's life seems obscure to me. I could not do this. I escaped from such a routine through fencing stolen knick-knacks and entering into my present life.

When I lived in that English village, hounded by Mrs. Ruffords from across the lane, whom I secretly called the Daily News, for she was an inveterate gossip, an enduring community snooper, the one person who had the longest stick to prise under my stone of solitude, my day was as compartmentalised as that of a schoolmaster. I rose at six, made coffee, emptied the night's accumulation of slag from the coke burner, made toast and watched the milkman deliver the milk. At seven thirty, I entered the workshop and set about the day's tasks, written on a sheet of paper the night before and pinned over the end of the bench. I switched on the radio, the volume low. I heard nothing. It was just a noise to break the tedium.

At noon, exactly, as the time pips bleeped the end of the morning, I downed tools, made a cup of soup and drank it at the table in the pokey sitting room of my cottage, peering out on a tiny, drab garden upon which the seasons seemed to make little impression.

At one o'clock, I returned to the workbench. I did not immediately recommence work. The morning's toil had untidied the surface. I spent half an hour organising my tools. The saws hung from hooks over the bench, the chisels and gouges along the windowsill, the hammers in a rack at the end of the bench: that everything was into the original disorder within thirty minutes, and that I knew where everything was in any case, was immaterial. It was the routine I was serving, not the logicality of work.

At six o'clock, I stopped work, listening to the television news as I prepared my evening meal. Even this was routine. I had steak most nights, or lamb chops for variation. They required only grilling. I forced myself to cook a different vegetable each night, my concession to originality.

Saturday mornings I went to the supermarket. Wednesday afternoons I went to the antique fair and did a round of the dealers, buying and selling, accepting commissions for repair.

Now, I deliberately fight routine. Not only to stave off boredom but also, I admit, as an act of preservation. Not just the preservation of which a man in my line of business has to be constantly conscious, the stranger on the corner, the reader of a newspaper under a street lamp, the man who changes trains at the same station, but the preservation of the mind. I should go crazy if I had to follow the hours with the religious observance of a time-server.

So it is I never go to the bar every Monday, or every lunchtime, and I have several which I patronise. No one can say of me it is Thursday because I am in the Piazza Conca d'Oro, in the Bar Conca d'Oro, at the table by the counter.

Let me tell you of this bar. It is on the corner of the piazza, which is cobbled with those square stones so loved of Italian street pavers, set in patterns, shell patterns in this piazza, quite obviously. There are two islands in the piazza: one contains a fountain, the other three trees. The fountain does not work and has no water in it. Students from the university use it as a bicycle park. Where there should be the music of water there is a tangle of cycle frames, handlebars and pedals. Under the trees, the proprietor of the bar has set tables, monopolising the public space for the sake of his profit-margin and, he claims, the good of the residents. If he had no tables there the space would be filled with parked Fiats and mopeds, all leaking oil and fouling the air with fumes. In fact, few vehicles drive into the *piazza* which is a backwater of the town.

The interior of the bar is indistinguishable from that of any other throughout Italy. British pubs are all, in their own fashion, unique. They may have jukeboxes or one-armed bandits in common but there the similarities end. Bars are not like this: they all have a plastic curtain at the doorway, a shop-window to let in the light, plastic or wooden chairs around shaky tables, a bar and a hissing *cappuccino* maker, racks of fly-blown bottles of obscure liquors and tumblers with chipped rims and sides scratched from many thousands of washings. There is often a dusty radio hidden on a high shelf muttering pop music and on the bar one of those gambling machines into which one puts a coin and receives a coloured wooden bead in the centre of which is a hole drilled through, containing a paper slip with a national flag printed upon it. Get the correct flag and win a plastic digital wristwatch worth next to nothing.

I am known in the Bar Conca d'Oro as an irregular regular. Sometimes I sit at the tables in the piazza, sometimes in the bar. I may have a cup of *cappuccino,* or an *espresso.* If it is cold I order hot chocolate. I may, if it is early in the day, request a *brioche* to break my fast.

The other customers who frequent the place are slaves to timetables, are regular regulars. I know them all by name. I remember names. It is an important part of the preservation process.

They are a jolly crew: Visconti is a photographer with a tiny studio nearby in the Via S. Lucio, Armando is a cobbler, Emilio (whom everyone calls Milo for he has lived in Chicago and was so named over there) operates a watch-repairing stall in the Piazza del Duomo, Giuseppe is a street-sweeper, Gherardo owns a taxi. They are men of little future but huge and happy vision.

When I enter, they all look up. I may be a stranger and worth talking to, or about. They all say, '*Ciao! Come stai? Signor Farfalla.*' It is a chorus.

'*Ciao!*' I reply. '*Bene!*'

My Italian is poor. We converse in a bastard esperanto of our own invention, the language changing as the mood changes, as the *grappa* is drunk or the wine uncorked.

They ask after my butterfly hunting. They have not seen me for a week or two, maybe longer, not since the feast day of San Bernadino di Siena: Gherardo remembers it was that day because it was when the taxi broke its rear shock absorber on the road to his mother's house.

I say the butterfly-hunting is good, the paintings coming along. I say I have an exhibition coming off in a gallery in Munich. The German collectors are starting to take an interest in European wildlife. Milo, I suggest, should start painting the portraits of wild boars, not illegally shooting them in the mountains for salami. He should become green. Europe is turning green, I say.

They laugh. Milo is already green, they say: a 'greenhorn'. It is one of his favourite Americanisms which he throws as an insult to anyone who questions his knowledge. *Un pivello.* Behind his back and without any spite they call him *il nuovo immigrato* although he returned home over twenty years ago and has lost much of his command of both English and American.

Yet this is a diversion. Soon they are discussing the green revolution. They are trying to save the world, these five working-class men in a bar in the middle of Italy, in the middle of the seventeenth century.

There is not a building in the Piazza Conca d'Oro newer than 1650. The iron balconies, the shuttered windows, have seen more of history than any professor. The fountain was reputedly built by a cousin of the Borgias. The cellar of a building opposite is said to have been a Templar lodge in the thirteenth century. Now it is a vaulted wine store rented by the bar owner. Up a little dead-end alley, the Vicolo dei Silvestrini, is a chapel incorporated into the basement of a house: it is said San Silvestro once prayed there. From the balcony over the pork butcher's shop behind the fountain was once hanged a famous brigand, caught *in flagrante delicto* by a nobleman whose wife was bouncing on the brigand's belly in the nobleman's own bed. No one can agree on who the amorous culprit was, nor when he was lynched. It is one of the evening stories the puppeteer enacts.

Together, they come to a unanimous decision. To save the world, all cars must run on water. Visconti claims there exists the process whereby water can be split into its component hydrogen and oxygen, by solar-power electricity. The two gases are mixed in the cylinder head and ignited by a spark of electricity as with a petrol engine spark plug. Hydrogen explodes. Everyone knows that. The hydrogen bomb. His hands create a mushroom of destruction over the table. The explosion drives the piston down. And—he laughs ironically at the simplicity of the chemistry—what happens when you explode hydrogen with oxygen? You get water. No need for fuel top-ups. The exhaust pipe gets the burnt-off water and returns it to the fuel tank. A never-ending engine. All it needs is sunlight to charge the batteries.

Gherardo is most pleased. His taxi will run forever. Giuseppe is doubtful. He sees a fault in the logic. He has much time to think, he says, as he sweeps the streets: street-sweeping is, he suggests, an ideal occupation for a philospher, for one has to think of nothing except how to avoid getting hit from behind by a Roman driver.

'*Cosi!* Problem—what?' Visconti asks in our spurious tongue. His hands shake palm up in the air. His shoulders shrug with defiance.

If the idea is so good, Giuseppe suggests, why has it not yet been introduced? The hole in the ozone is big already. The petrol fumes still choke you in Rome.

Visconti looks from one to the other of us, seeking support for his disgust at Giuseppe's ignorance. We all look glum. It is the way.

If the process were made public now, Visconti declares, the petrol companies would go bankrupt. They bought up the process years ago and are sitting on it to protect their profits.

The others shrug now. This they believe. Italy is a land of big business corruption. The conversation moves on to the fortunes of AC Milano.

I drink the last of my *cappuccino* and leave. They wave farewell. They will see me again, they say. Have good luck hunting butterflies.

———

At the very end of the cul-de-sac formed by the southern half of the Via Lampedusa there is a brothel. It is not a grand place. It has no maroon velvet curtains or plush settees, no red lights, either. Downstairs is a hair salon. Upstairs is a three storey whorehouse.

From time to time, I go: there I am not ashamed of this. It is my way. In my world, one cannot afford the luxury of a wife, or a steady companion. They would be a liability and wives can turn against you. At least lovers seldom do.

There are four full-time whores in the Via Lampedusa.

Maria is the oldest at about forty. She runs the establishment but she does not own it. The owner is an Italian American who lives in Sardinia. Or Sicily. Or Corsica. His actual whereabouts are unknown and subject to rumour. Some say he is in the government, which would not surprise anyone. His cut of the action is paid by direct credit into a bank in Madrid. Maria sends this to him fortnightly. She does not work a great deal, keeping only to three specific clients, men of about her own age who must have been visiting her for years.

Elena is about twenty-eight. She has brazen red hair and the complexion of a Pre-Raphaelite model. She never goes into direct sunlight and only leaves the building to shop or visit the doctor's surgery in the Via Adriano, when the sun is low enough to cast a shadow across at least half of each street. She is the tallest of the whores at about six feet.

Marine and Rachele are both twenty-five. The former is a brunette, the latter a dark blonde. Both turn as many tricks as they can in a day, vying with each other for every occasional customer. It is their intention, for I am convinced they are lesbian lovers, to earn half a million euros and establish a dress-shop in Milan. Both have the dreams which sustain every whore the world over: that, one day, they will be able to sleep one full night uninterrupted in their own bed and be a respectable, if aloof, member of the community. As with their employer, rumours are spread about them: they were models in Milan, sacked from a top agency for scarring another girl's breasts with a nail file; they are the illegitimate daughters of a Vatican cardinal; they were schoolteachers dismissed for seducing teenage boys, or girls, depending on the source. The truth, I suspect, is they are country girls out to make money as best they can in the way they know best.

In addition to the four full-timers, there are a number of part-timers: students at the university or the language school in need of extra funds; girls supporting a heroin habit, and who are screwed only by the most ignorant labourers or stupid tourists; and fresh-faced teenagers from the countryside who come into town of a Saturday afternoon to do a bit of shopping in the boutiques in the Corso, sit around with their friends in the bars and pay for their day out by taking their new clothes off in the presence of the young men of the town.

My two favourites are both students. Clara is twenty-one, Dindina nineteen.

Clara's family lives in Brescia. Her father is an accountant, her mother a bank clerk. She has two brothers, both in school. She is studying English and enjoys our meetings for she has an opportunity to test her language skills out on me. Indeed, her standard has improved beyond all recognition since we first met. She is a pretty girl of five foot six, with auburn hair, dark brown eyes and long, tanned legs. Her back and shoulders are slim, her buttocks small but rounded. Her breasts are nothing to write home about and she often wears no bra. She has about her a veneer of sophistication, for she comes from the North.

An exact opposite is Dindina. She is five foot four, arrogant, as black-haired and black-eyed as a Moor, with firm breasts and a tight, smooth belly. Her legs seem to be longer than the rest of her body: Gherardo says she is one of those girls whose thighs start in their armpits. She is not as pretty as Clara nor as clever. She is studying sociology. She says Clara is a snob from the north. Clara says Dindina is a peasant from the south. Her family owns a small farm and a few hectares of olives between Bari and Matera.

They do not work every night. Like me, they do not obey a schedule.

If one of them is present, I may stay. If not, I drink a beer with Maria and leave. I have no interest in the others.

Sometimes, both are present and then I employ the two of them.

Understand, I am not a young man. I shall not give you my exact age: accept the fires are not yet out but they require a little stoking to get the water hot. Like the damn coke boiler I had in the cottage in England.

When we make a threesome, it can be fun. I book the biggest room in the house, on the top floor overlooking the narrow street. In the room there is a two-metre-wide four-poster bed, a dressing table, a full length mirror and several Windsor chairs. We undress each other slowly. Clara will not let Dindina undress her so I do it. Dindina is not so fussy. Perhaps Clara is a snob: perhaps she is jealous of Dindina's fuller breasts. They both strip me.

'You are getting fatter,' Clara remarks every time.

I deny it.

I am not ashamed of my body. Over the years, by dint of necessity, I have kept myself in good trim. When travelling, I always stay in hotels which offer a sauna and gymnasium for guests. In Miami, I took a room with a gym of its own *en suite*. If there are no facilities, I run. Butterfly-hunting is good exercise in the mountains.

'You eat too much pasta. You should marry and have a woman diet you. Perhaps . . .', I detect a wistfulness, '. . . a young woman to look after you. Perhaps Italy is bad for you. You should move away where there is no pasta and wine is pricey.'

Dindina does not talk. She prefers to get down to business. We lie on the bed, with the window open and the light of the street lamp slicing through the closed shutters. Clara talks first, but Dindina is already busy, stroking my stomach or winding her fingers through the hairs of my chest. She kisses my nipples, sucking and nibbling at them like a mouse at a wafer.

Clara kisses my lips. She kisses very softly, even when at the height of passion. Her tongue does not force itself into my mouth as Dindina's does but inveigles itself in. I hardly notice it until it touches my own.

Dindina gets on top first. She lies along me and transfers her nibbling from my chest to my ear lobes. Clara touches Dindina's buttocks, slipping her fingers down between her thighs and rubbing my legs as well as Dindina's. I think it is strange how Clara will not let Dindina undress her, yet she touches her up and allows her to reciprocate.

I cannot afford to be emotional, not in my way of life. If emotion gets involved then risks start to accumulate. Emotion prompts thought and thought elicits misgivings, doubts and dubieties. I have spent many hours controlling emotion and it pays off now. I do not allow myself to climax with Dindina. She knows this and does not feel cheated. She has her orgasm and slides off me as Clara takes her place.

With Clara, it is different. With Clara, I let myself go.

This, I readily admit, is a self-indulgence, one of my very few.

Afterwards, we lie to gain our breath then cavort some more, with less urgency. At ten o'clock or thereabouts—I will not clock-watch— we dress and I take them out to a *pizzeria* at the end of the Via Roviano. We have to buy two bottles of wine: Clara drinks Chiaretto di Cellatica because is it northern, from her native Lombardy, and Dindina demands Colatamburo because it hails from Bari. I take a glass of each. Dindina eats her *pizza napoletana* as she makes love, business-like, not wasting time on words. She is a girl of action. Clara has *pizza margherita* and talks a lot. In English. She speaks of nothing of importance but then, after sex, one does not want to discuss major issues of the day.

Our dining over, I pay the girls. They are quite open about taking money before we leave the *pizzeria*. As we part, Dindina kisses me as she would her uncle.

'*Buona sera*,' she whispers lightly, close to my ear.

I smile and return her kiss as an uncle might.

Clara kisses me too, but like a lover. She puts her arms around my neck and hugs me, her lips on mine. She tastes of oregano and garlic and sweet red wine. I think of Duillio's bottled blood every time we kiss in the Via Roviano.

Clara always touches upon two subjects in the closing moments of our evening. The first is what she intends to do with her money. It is as if she has to justify her screwing in some material way.

'I am going to buy a book—*An Unofficial Rose* by Iris Murdoch.' Or she might declare, 'I shall buy a new fountain pen. A Par-ker.' She divides some words into the component syllables when the word is unfamiliar or she is not sure of it. Sometimes, she says, almost shame-facedly, 'Now I can pay my rent.'

The second is always an attempt to discover where I live.

'Take me to your home. We can do it some more. With no Dind-ina. For free! Just for love.' Another tack is, 'You should not live alone. You need your bed warm as flesh.' This is an extension of the good-woman/eat-less-pasta ploy.

I always refuse, politely but emphatically. Sometimes she accuses me of having a wife already, a harridan who sleeps with her legs crossed. I deny this and she knows this to be the truth. Though she is no professional whore, she has the instincts. Possibly all women have. I am not one who can tell.

To be on the safe side, though I live to the east, only a few streets from the brothel, I walk north. Clara heads west to her digs near the barracks. I double back only when I know she is gone. Only once has she tried to follow me and giving her the slip was simplicity itself.

I look at my notes: 90 metres. It is a long way for some, but for a bul-let it is a brief instant in which to restructure history. Yet how much of the past has been altered by just such a transient moment. How long did it take the 6.5 mm slug to travel from the top of the Texas School Book Depository to John F. Kennedy's neck? How long the other shot to go through his skull? Infinitesimally short instances during which the world shook, the existence of men was threatened and the temple of politics altered for ever.

Often, as I sit in the loggia with the light coming down like the last rays of life itself, I think of the second man, the one under the trees on the grassy knoll in Dealey Plaza, the ghost of death to Oswald's spirit of assassination. He must have fired. All the reports indicate it. He seems not to have hit the target. Yet perhaps he did, and Oswald was a dupe and a lousy shot. Who knows? Someone does.

The weapon needs to be light, fairly small, easily assembled and broken down. It has to have a long range for what it is to do and a rapid fire rate. Five seconds indicates to me the possibility of a rapidly moving target. And it must be silenced.

I think about the problem for a whole day, perched on the stool before the drawing board, later sitting in the loggia as the sun goes down. It is not an easy task. Not in three weeks.

Eventually, I decide upon a modified Socimi 821. It has a silencer but I shall have to discard it. Another will have to be made. My customer is not a spray-it-and-see hit-and-misser, but a person who, like myself, lives by circumstantialities. Hence the requirement of a telescopic sight.

The Socimi is Italian made, by Società Costruzioni Industriali Milano. It is a new gun, first available in 1983 and based in design upon the Israeli Uzi sub-machine gun, the darling of the hijackers, the artless hit squads, the motorcycle passenger killer. It has the same form of telescoping bolt, the same safety mechanisms and the magazine in the hand grip. The receiver, which is rectangular, the barrel housing and pistol grip are made of light alloy not gunmetal or steel. It can take a laser sight. The barrel is short, not really intended for perfect aiming, not ideal for the distant target. The weapon is only 400 mm long, with the stock folded, and weighs only 2.45 kg. The barrel is six-grooved with a right-hand twist, 200 mm long. The box magazine holds 32 rounds, 9 mm Parabellum. The fire rate is 600 rpm and the muzzle velocity 380 mps. The silencer, however, reduces this significantly, which is a problem I must overcome.

I can see only one way around this obstacle. The barrel has to be lengthened but instead of putting on a silencer which will reduce velocity, I shall fit a sound suppressor such as the Americans use on the Ingram Model 10. This muffles the sound of the discharge but does not seek to silence the report of the round. Muzzle velocity is thus unimpaired. The crack of the bullet can be heard but it is hard to trace the direction of the firing position.

I should like to give my client as near five full seconds of fire power as I am able. This means an extended magazine. Ten rounds a second for five seconds equals a fifty round box magazine. That should be all right: sixty might make it too large, upset the balance of the piece.

The longer barrel will require a good deal of Bach's Toccata and Fugue in D minor. The rest should be fairly easy.

I have, in my time, had to build a complete weapon from scratch. Purchase the metal, forge it and shape it, drill it, sleeve and rifle the barrel, design the mechanism. It was just such a job that had me sweating and stinking in the back of beyond past Kai Tak airport. Not only had I to build the weapon, I also had to disguise it as a briefcase.

It was masterly, though I say so myself. The butt was the handle, the top frame the barrel. The magazine was in the spine and hinged open on what seemed the case hinges. The mechanism was mounted in a false combination lock in the centre of the front. It went through several customs checks. I took it through to Manila myself. The gun was used three times, each time successfully. Each time in a different country. I understand it is now in the FBI museum or somesuch. Of course, that was in the days before rigorous X-ray checks at airports. The hijackers have made my life so very much more difficult.

To this end, I am surprised my client is not bothered with such a risk. Clearly, this weapon is to be used on mainland. Europe or somewhere easily accessible without air travel.

As I sit at my workbench, carefully bending the sheet steel for the extra long magazine, I wonder who the target is. Such thoughts fill those long minutes when the hands are busy but do not need the brain.

The most likely hit is, I think, Arafat or Sharon. If he is the target, my client must be working for a government. I have prepared weapons for freelance agents of the Americans, French, and British before now. I am careful not to operate for government salaried staff.

If Qaddafi is not the contract, it could be any head of state in Europe, even a visiting head of state. The British Prime Minister would be a likely candidate: in many quarters, and not all of them foreign or anti-British by a long way, she is sufficiently hated to be a hit. There would be muted cheering in many streets at such an outcome. The German leader is another possibility. So is his entire cabinet. Andreas Baader may be dead but his ideals live on.

I met Baader just the once. He was introduced to me by a Briton, Iain MacLeod, in Stuttgart in the winter of 1971. He was a quiet man, very good looking in the way of popular revolutionaries. He had thick, bushy eyebrows and a trim moustache. His hair was cut short. He looked like a German Che Guevara. His eyes shone with the fire of conviction one sees in monks and mercenaries, the blaze of ideological certainty, the inner conflagration of the sure knowledge the course one follows is right.

So many of those for whom I work have this burning in their soul. It consumes them. It is their drug, their sex, the very air they breathe. You cannot poison them, or shoot them, or blow them up, or drown them, or toss them off a cliff. Even when their bodies are consigned to the earth, or the ash of their flesh spread on the wind, the forest fire of their belief lives on. The man can die but the ideals cannot. You cannot crush a concept.

I am a good gun-maker. One of the best in the world. Certainly in my world. I do not refer to myself as a gunsmith: it rings too much of artisanery. I am not an artisan. I am an artist. I fashion a weapon with as much care for form and attention to detail as a cabinet-maker does a fine piece of furniture. No painter lavishes more of himself on a picture than I do of myself on a gun.

How I came to develop this facility was purely by chance. I never sought to work in weaponry, did not anticipate armoury as a career. It started as a favour to one of the other petty criminals who lived in the village, that centre of all that is banal in the world. He was one of the few who spoke to me other than to pass the time of day or weather. Perhaps he knew, or innately felt, there was more to me than repairing silver teapots. In my world, one can sense a kindred spirit with an almost instinctive ability.

His name was Fer. He was about sixty. I never discovered the origins of his name: he might have been Fergus, or perhaps Ferguson. He may have been Farquarson, for all I know, born the wrong side of the sheets and condemned to life as a peasant. He resided in a derelict Bedford van in an orchard a mile from the village: the tyres were perished, grass and docks grew against the panels, the radiator and hood were missing as was half the engine. Where the gearbox should have been grew a sturdy ash sapling. By now, the trunk will have split the rusting hulk.

Fer was the neighbourhood poacher: he kept ferrets in the cab of the van and lived in the back with a black lurcher bitch called Molly. In winter, he was a ready source of pheasants, rabbits and, on occasion, hares or venison. In the summer, he supplied pigeons to the Chinese restaurants in the nearby towns. He was also able to provide summer trout and, if the waters ran well, autumn salmon. When the season was inappropriate, he worked as a woodsman, felling or thinning trees and taking the timber as payment, selling it by the sackload in a lay-by on the main road. He had an axe one could shave with; he could work a two-man saw single-handed; he had a countryman's eye for the main chance and a shotgun.

The weapon was a side-by-side twelve-bore. It was not a Purdey or a Churchill, nothing grand, no teak case chased in brass with a filigreed lock and velvet compartments. It was just a working gun. Fer kept it in pristine condition, oiled and cleaned and polished it with devotion. He lavished more attention upon it than he did upon Molly the dog, the ferrets, the van or himself. Yet even loved ones fall sick.

The connector guide plate fractured one autumn evening and he came to me.

The excuse was that the gun was old, spare parts no longer available, but that the weapon was otherwise sound and he could not afford to replace it. The truth was that it was unlicensed and probably of dubious history. Fer could not risk taking it to a gun dealership.

I agreed, under the strictest of secrecy, to repair the fault. The broken part was easily duplicated. He offered me money but I suggested he pay me with a pheasant or two.

In my little workshop, I disassembled the shotgun. I was like a child being given a clockwork motor to dissect. The interlocking of the pieces, the neat order of metal upon metal, the chain reaction of finger muscle to explosive charge fascinated, captivated me. I effected the repair overnight. Fer paid me with fish and game for three months, always visiting after dark and always calling me 'Sir.'

A year later, one of my acquaintances asked the same of me. His gun was similar to Fer's except that the left hand firing pin was the part which had failed and the barrels were sawn short at twelve inches from the breech.

In such workmanship as mine, there are no adult education evening classes in the local secondary school. This is not clay-throwing and pot-making, not tapestry weaving. This is the choreography of cut steel. It is self-taught.

Consider a gun. Most people think of it only as an explosive device. There is a bang, something or someone drops dead. They know there is a bullet which zips through the air. They know there is a cartridge case either of brass, compressed card or plastic, which remains, empty and smoking. They know there is a trigger which does this. Otherwise they see it as do head-hunters in the jungle: the fire-stick which speaks with the voice of the gods, the thunder-pole, the spear-no-one-throws, the lightning-tube. They think the pull on the trigger is all that is required. Pull the trigger and the target is hit. They watch too many television gangster shows, believe all they see on the movies where no policeman or cowboy ever misses, where the bullets fly straight and true, according to the script.

Life and death are not scripted.

A gun is a beautiful thing. The trigger does not just click backwards and the cartridge go bang. It operates a series of levers, springs, catches which move with the precision of a Swiss watch. Each has to be machined to the finest of tolerances, cut and shaped with as much accuracy as is demanded of a neuro-surgeon cutting into a brain. Each has to relate exactly to the next. The smallest of deviations, the merest one hundredth of a millimetre, and the mechanism will not obey the order of the other parts, and it will jam.

Only once has a weapon of mine jammed. It was some time ago, some twenty years ago, in fact. The weapon was a rifle, not based upon another's design but entirely upon my own. I made it in its entirety, even sleeving the barrel and rifling it. I was foolish, arrogant enough to think I could improve upon a design proven through half a century of wars, assassinations, murders, riots and civil unrest.

It was to be used upon one of the few non-political targets for which I have provided the weapon and one of the few I have known about beforehand.

In truth, the target was political in a manner of speaking: it was the motive which was not. The hit was the American multi-millionaire proprietor of several international companies—pharmaceuticals, newspapers and television networks, a chain of international hotels, an airline or two. He was also known as an important philanthropist, donating drug rehabilitation clinics to hard-pressed, under-funded American cities. I shall not give you his name. He is still alive and he has my fault to thank for this, although he does not know it.

I was staying on Long Island at the time and was asked to telephone a number in New Jersey, instructed by an American lawyer, a Manhattan attorney to the Mafia, for whom I had done some occasional work in the past. His letter of introduction was short. I remember it well *Dear Joe*, it began: he always addressed me as Joe—I was Joe

Doe to him. It was best that way. *Give a callow youth a call, will you? He's only eighteen, but he's no mug. Do not judge him until you have heard his whole spiel. I realize you may not like the job, but as a favor to me, will you consider it? The money is guaranteed. I have it on hold for you. Larry.*

His name, of course, was not Lawrence, or Larry, or anything like it. That, too, was best.

A request from Larry was as good as Royal Command from the Queen of England. He had clout I could not refuse. So I rang the boy and listened to him out of courtesy to my lawyer friend and with misgivings about the job.

The boy wanted his father killed. This was not only his intention, it was also the express wish of his mother. The millionaire, I was informed, was as good at philandering as he was at running multi-national corporations. His sexual conquests, which the boy told me his father referred to when amongst his cronies as asset-stripping, were various and many. In the course of his stripping asses, as it were, he had contracted syphilis and had passed this on to his wife.

The motive was understandable but I was still loath to take on such a commission, even for my friend. I did not want to become known merely as a murderer's assistant. Nothing can be gained from that.

The boy, no doubt inheriting some of his father's shrewdness, sensed my reluctance, even over the 'phone.

'You don't want to do it,' he said.

He spoke in a very classy Bostonian accent. I wondered if he was to be a graduate at the Harvard Business School: he had the right voice.

'It is not my usual line of work,' I agreed.

'Larry said you'd take that stance. But there is something more. I'll send it round. You call me back.'

Within the hour, an envelope was delivered by courier. It contained several documents, photostats of US Government memos, all marked secret and all concerning Latin America. There were also three photographs. One showed the hit with a rebel leader known for his genocidal ideologies, another had him with a well-known cocaine baron and the third was a very compromising photograph of the hit humping a very pretty girl on the side of a swimming pool. I rang the number again.

'The clinics are funded by the dope,' the boy bluntly informed me. 'And the girl's the one that gave my mother the . . .'

He fell silent and the line hummed. I looked at the photographs lying on the desk beside the telephone. I thought I could hear him faintly sobbing and felt an immense sorrow for him.

'Do you have someone in mind . . . ?' I began.

'Larry has,' he replied, a catch in his voice.

'I see. And what exactly do you want of me?'

'The piece,' he said.

How strange it was to hear a Boston voice speak like a hoodlum in the cinema.

'I can do that. But I shall need to meet the man who is to do it. I have to know the requirements.'

'Rifle, long barrel, telescopic sight fitting—you don't need to provide that—automatic.'

'A good man only needs one bullet,' I remarked.

'We want the girl rubbed out, too.'

I nodded. It was human nature.

'Very well,' I agreed. 'I shall give Larry a call and tell him I accept. He'll have to contact me for collection and payment. But understand this: I am not doing this because I want to help your or your mother. I do not work for the simple motives of vengeance or petty retribution. It is my opinion that your mother should have been wiser in her choice of husband at the start.'

'I understand,' he said. 'Larry said this would be your attitude.'

'Larry, no doubt,' I went on, 'also said that if you sent me the envelope the contents would clinch the deal.'

'Yes. He did,' he admitted and he hung up.

I made the gun. It was untraceable. No numbers, no patterning, no mass-produced or purchased parts. I tested it. It worked well. I fired twelve shots from it in six seconds, just the required fire rate.

Yet it jammed on the day. I cannot account for this malfunction but I accept, for I am a professional, that it was my sole responsibility.

The hit was not killed. He was winged, a slug in the shoulder and another in the liver. The assassin should have gone for two head shots. The problem was the swimming pool was close and the target rolled into it on the first shot. The second, in his side, was deflected by the water. The third and last struck the concrete pool surround and ricocheted. The girl was killed outright. The assassin, unable to defend himself, was gunned down by bodyguards. He had no back-up weapon and that was foolish.

Larry was upset but I was still paid. He did not believe the gun jamming was my fault. He assumed the hitman had done something to the weapon, dropped it, tried to adjust it. But I know better. I did the job in a rush, my heart was not in it and I took insufficient care. The failure was my fault, unequivocally. I have always regretted it.

Galeazzo's secondhand bookshop smells of dust and dry biscuits. It is a crowded little place. Books stand in piles upon the floor, upon tables. Shelves are lined with books. Extra volumes lie on top of those standing upright. The wooden floorboards creak underfoot. If the beams of the cellar below were not made of thick blocks of mountain chestnut, 40 cms square, the shop would long since have collapsed. The first floor is also piled high with books, the back-stock. Galeazzo lives in a two-storey apartment above that.

He is a man of about my age, grey-haired and stooping as befits a book-dealer. He is a widower, jokes that his wife was crushed to death under a collapsing bookshelf. The truth—Giuseppe informed me: he saw it in a newspaper blowing in the street—is less amusing and just as bizarre. She was visiting relatives in Sulmona when an earth tremor struck. A third floor balcony broke and a motorcycle parked upon it fell on her as she ran to the centre of the street for safety. She was killed instantly. It was a neat, tidy, correct death, as it should be.

Remarkably, the bookshop stock is not restricted to books in Italian. Almost every European language is represented on Galeazzo's shelves and in reasonable quantities. Just as remarkable is the shop itself: the Italians do not pride themselves in owning secondhand goods. Look about the Italian countryside at the buildings falling down, at the ruins of structures which could make solid, even superior homes if they were renovated. Instead, close by you see the concrete frame of a modern shanty going up. If the Italians prefer new houses to old, there is no way they will buy old books.

Yet Galeazzo makes a reasonable living. He sends out quarterly catalogues to professors on his mailing list, receives mail orders which he fulfils by return of post. He even has, he tells me, customers in Britain, Germany, the Netherlands, and the USA. The Americans want only books about the Old Country. Here, of course, they are searching for their Italian roots. The British request books in English on Italy. The professors are on the look-out for folklore, mediaeval religious books and tomes on regional architecture.

With his good command of English, Galeazzo and I get along well. We sit in the Bar Conca d'Oro some days and talk about books. He keeps his eye open for volumes on butterflies and has sold me a number of valuable editions illustrated by artists far superior to myself. Several are nineteenth-century publications with exquisite hand-tinted steel engravings.

'Why do you live in Italy?'

This is a question often upon his lips. I usually make no verbal response but shrug in the Italian manner, and grimace.

'You should live in . . .' Every time, he pauses to consider a new country, one not mentioned previously. '. . . Indonesia. They have many forests, many strange reptiles. Many butterflies. Why do you paint Italian butterflies? Everyone knows Italian butterflies.'

'They do not,' I remonstrate. 'For example, the genus *Charaxes*— *Charaxes jasius.* Hardly known elsewhere in Europe, it has frequently been seen in the past on Mediterranean shores and in Italy, wherever the strawberry tree grows. Even the *Danaidæ* have been discovered in Italy. A hundred years ago, I grant you, but I may find another. The Monarch. The rare *Danaus chrysippus*.'

'Meagre creatures. You should go to Java.' He pronounces it Yarvah, like a Jewish festival. 'There are butterflies as big as birds.'

'I live in Italy,' I confide in him, 'because the wine is cheap, the women beautiful and the rent low. At my age such things are important. I have no pension.'

He pours more wine, Lacrima di Gallipoli. My glass balances unsteadily on an Everyman edition of Darwin's *Voyage of the Beagle* which Galeazzo has read and knows intimately: his glass teeters on an edition of Ciano's diary, also in English. He claims to be named after Count Ciano but I believe this to be romantic piffle. The wine he purchases on his book-buying forays to Apulia. Somewhere on the heel of Italy he knows of a library which he can raid from time to time. I try to suss out this seemingly endless supply of cosmopolitan editions. It gives me the opportunity to steer the conversation away from butterflies of which I have only enough knowledge to fool the casual listener. Put me in a room with even an amateur lepidopterist and he will see through my sham in minutes.

'Where do you get your books from?' I ask for the umpteenth time. 'You never cease to amaze me with your range.'

He smirks secretively and taps his temple with his plastic ballpoint pen. The sound reminds me of Roberto testing a watermelon.

'You would like to know! But does the man who owns the diamond mine tell his friends of its location? Of course not.' He sips his wine. The base of the glass has made a ring upon the dust wrapper of the diary. 'In the south. Far south. In the mountains there. An old lady, old as Methuselah's mother-in-law and just as ugly. She has nothing. A few hectares of peach trees and some olives, just enough to press her own oil. Cloudy stuff her oil, and somehow gritty. She gave me some once: useless for salad, good only for preserving. Her peaches are stripped by caterpillars: if only you studied moths! So she has no harvest but books.'

'How many hectares of books?'

'Don't be foolish! Drink your wine.'

I obey.

'Her books are measured not in hectares but kilometres.'

'So how many has she?'

'No one can tell. I have yet to walk all her shelves.'

A few weeks ago, partly to allay any local gossip and strengthen my artistic credentials, I gave Galeazzo one of my paintings of *P. machaon*. He has, as I guessed he would, had it framed and hangs it prominently over the till where everyone can see it. This serves my purpose well. I am Signor Farfalla.

Signora Prasca has been very worried. She tells me so when I return. I said I would be away for two days and have been gone four. She has been most distressed in case her Signor Farfalla met with an accident on the autostrada, been mugged in Rome whither I told her I was going, been caught in the terrible thunderstorms whilst driving through the mountains. She fusses around me as I let myself into the courtyard and start up the stairs with my wooden box. In her hands she holds the four days' accumulation of mail. It includes a postcard from Pet which I sent three days ago from Firenze.

I calm her fears. Rome was fine, I assure her. The storms did not reach the capital. The autostrada was free of water. Only tourists are mugged. I do not tell her I have been no nearer to Rome than the staircase I am mounting.

Do not attempt to guess where I have been. It is not for you to know and I shall give you no clues. Suffice to say I picked up a Socimi 821, a good quality German telescopic sight with Zeiss optics and an assortment of other bits and pieces for under eight thousand US dollars. The sight was a low-light model, too. Just in case. The profit margin on this job will be good.

The task at hand is not as difficult as I first imagined it might be.

There will be little actual fabrication involved, less Bach. I was extremely lucky in being able to obtain a barrel. You need not know the details. No inventor or craftsman divulges his secrets.

When this job is done, I might sell you the information. If you want to enter the business. When I am gone there will be very few others to carry on the art. I know of only two freelance—how shall I put it?—specialist gun merchants. One of those may well be dead by now. I have not heard of him for several years.

Perhaps he has retired. As I shall, after this final job.

It is a pity, really. I had hoped my final project would be much harder than this is proving to be. Another briefcase rifle, perhaps a dart gun inside a typewriter. Miniaturisation is the name of the game these days: lap-top computers, digital watches, PDAs, heart pacemakers, mobile phones the size of a cigarette pack. Evolution will have to start shortening and thinning our fingers.

An umbrella gun would be a challenge. Of course, it has been done. The Bulgarians used one on a dissident, Georgi Markov, in London in 1978. A 1.52 mm pellet was fired by compressed gas into the target's thigh. The pellet was a masterpiece of micro-engineering long before the super-chip was laser cut from a silicon sliver the thickness of a human hair, or whatever other miracle dimensions are involved. It was spherical and cast from an alloy of platinum and iridium. Two .35 mm holes drilled into it led to a minuscule central reservoir filled with ricin, a poison obtained from the castor oil plant and unconquered by the antidote-makers. Two weeks before, the Bulgarians had used the same weapon unsuccessfully upon another so-called undesirable, one Vladimir Kostov, in Paris. He survived.

The concept of the weapon was brilliant: perfect disguise, astonishing projectile, simplicity itself. Two seconds and it was all done. Two seconds to change the world and end it for the target. The sadness here was that the poison was slow. Markov took three days to die. That is not a beautiful death, that is a fox-hunter death.

The bullet is the better way.

There are some modifications to make to the Socimi. The longer barrel will have to be fitted. This is not too difficult. Merely a matter of milling and lathe-work. The barrel is simply attached with a nut and will allow easy dismantling and re-assembly. I shall have to adjust the connector, only a tiny amount, to make the trigger lighter. My customer, I suspect, has a light finger despite the firm grip.

The stock will need to be reshaped completely. The present one is too short. It is ideal for a spray-gun, but not for an exact weapon with a 'scope on top. I shall build another. I have to thread the muzzle for the sound suppressor, which will take a while. One has to turn the thread-cutter so carefully, so slowly.

The barrel I have obtained is already rifled: six lands. I have not fired it and shall have to bed it down, so to speak. It is a technical business. I do not intend to burden you with the jargon of gun-smithing. Just be assured the job will be done to the highest tolerances, to the most precise specifications, to the best standard to be found anywhere in the world.

I am a craftsman. It is a pity my craftsmanship will be used only the once, like a McDonald's plastic foam hamburger box, but that is the lot of craftsmen these days. We are fast disappearing in a world of the throw-away. Perhaps that is why we experts tend to seek each other out—why I often look for what I need from Alfonso, why I go to him now.

Alfonso's garage is in the Piazza della Vagna. It is a cavernous space beneath a seventeenth-century merchant's house. Where he repairs Alfa Romeos, Fiats and Lancias there were once stored silks from China, cloves from Zanzibar, dried dates from Egypt, gemstones from India and gold from wherever there was gold to be stolen, bartered or murdered for. Now the place reeks of gearbox oil, the shelves lined with tools, boxes of nuts, bolts and spare parts, most of them second-hand and many retrieved from crashes attended with the breakdown truck. The lights are garish neon strips. In the corner, like a household shrine, blinks the computerised tuning machine. The blip on the oscilloscope screen zig-zags as if registering the death-wheeze of a dying engine block. It reminds me of sickness.

Alfonso calls his business a hospital. Ill cars arrive and leave healthy. He does not speak of a damaged Mercedes. For him, the vehicle is 'wounded' in a battle with a Regata. 'Wounded' sounds noble. The Regata on the other hand is merely 'injured'. He holds Fiats in contempt, declaring them to be rust-buckets. A few weeks ago, he told me that he saw a 'dead' Lamborghini on the autostrada south of Florence. Nearby was a 'slightly hurt' articulated Scania lorry. Alfonso is the Christiaan Barnard of the BMW, the Fleming of the Fiat. For him, a socket spanner is a scalpel, a pair of pliers and a monkey wrench delicate instruments of surgery.

'*Ciao*, Alfonso!' I greet him. He looks sideways at me from beneath the hood of a Lancia.

'She is lazy,' he declares and thumps his hand against the inside of the wheel arch. 'This old Roman woman . . .' he nods in the direction of the license plate '. . . can't climb hills no more. Time she had new blood.'

For Alfonso, blood is oil, food is fuel, plasma is hydraulic fluid, a coat of paint is a dress or a smart suit. Filler or undercoat is invariably panties or bra, depending on the positioning of the repair.

I require some pieces of iron. Steel, preferably. Alfonso keeps scrap lying all over the place. Nothing cannot be recycled by him. Once, I heard tell, he welded the burner rings of an old gas stove into the floor of a baby Fiat that had rotted through. The owner knew no different and the car went on burbling about the valley for years until the brakes failed on a bend. They say the car was a write-off but the burner rings did not so much as buckle.

He waves his hand in the general direction of the shelves. His gesture implies take what you want, help yourself, my garage is your garage, what are a few scraps of steel between friends.

Behind an oil pan with a jagged hole in it I discover several off-cuts of steel: then I find three gear wheels with the teeth sheared off. I hold the biggest up.

'*Bene?*' I ask.

'*Si! Si! Va bene!*'

'*Quant'è?*'

He growls at me and grins.

'*Niente!*'

Nothing. We are friends. A gear wheel with no bite is useless to him. What do I want it for, he asks. A doorstop, I reply. He says it is heavy and should make a good one.

I wrap it in a sheet of oily newspaper and take it home. Signora Prasca is on the telephone. I can hear her chattering away like a parrot.

In my apartment, I put the Bach on loud. Then I take it off. I put on my latest purchase, the Tchaikovsky 1812 Overture. As the French artillery repulses the Russians, I smash the wheel into five pieces with a four pound mallet.

I am death's telegram boy, death's kissogram. And that is the beauty of it. In my line of business, everything I do flows uncompromisingly towards one tiny moment, a final destination of perfection. How many artists can claim as much?

The painter finishes his painting and steps back. It is done, the commission met. The picture goes to the framer and from him to the owner. Months later, the artist sees it hanging in his patron's home and he notices a tiny error. A bee on a flower has only one antenna. Perhaps an oak leaf is the wrong shape. The perfection is imperfect.

Take a writer: for months, he strives upon a story, finishes it, sends it to his publisher. It is edited, re-written, copy-edited, set, proof-read, corrected, printed. A year later, it stands in the book-shops. The reviewers have praised it. The readers are buying it. The writer skips through his free copy. The gravel driveway to his hero's Malibu beach-house in Chapter 2 has mysteriously been paved by Chapter 37. The whole is flawed.

Yet for me, this does not occur. Save just that once. There will come a time when my endeavours succeed. The chain of events which starts with the shattering of a steel gear will culminate in two seconds of action. The finger will tighten, the trigger will move, the connector will shift, the sear will rise, the slide will move, the bolt lock go up, the hammer will hit the firing pin, which will strike the cartridge, the explosion will happen and the bullet will travel to the heart or the head and the perfection be complete. Everything happens to a logical, preordained and flawless design.

Such a choreography and I am the dancing master of this ballet towards eternity. I am the accomplisher, the cause, the first step and the last step, the producer and director.

In collaboration with my client, I am the greatest impresario on earth, the Barnum of bullets, the Andrew Lloyd Webber of assassination, the D'Oyly Carte of death. Together, we choose the method and I make it possible. I write the libretto, I write the score. My client chooses the theatre but I dress the stage. I am the spotlights and the backdrop, I am the director. My client is half the cast. You can guess who the other player is in this drama.

My client is my puppet. I am no different from the puppeteer in front of the church of San Silvestro. I entertain. I put on perhaps the biggest show on earth. But my puppet does not have a precocious penis to pop up. It has an adapted Socimi 821 and a clip of 9 mm specials.

What I like so much about this play, this tragi-comedy of fate, is that I have a say in the method, the place, the moment. How many people can state unequivocally when they shall die, where and how? Only the suicide can be certain and he cannot be sure, not one hundred per cent, that someone will not come along and cut him down, or drag him from the water, or pump the pills out of his stomach or switch the gas off and open wide the windows. Let in the life again. How many know, are irrefutably certain, when and in what place another will die, shuffle off the mortal coil? The assassin knows. It is this that makes him God.

The ordinary murderer does not. He is an amateur. He acts on impulse or through panic. He does not think his actions through, does not see the authority he holds by an almost divine right. He blunders and wonders afterwards, as the cuffs lock on his wrists or the bullhorns demand he comes out with his hands up, what it was all about.

The assassin knows.

So do I.

This is the utter, phenomenal miracle of it all.

The newspaper stand close by Milo's pitch in the Piazza del Duomo sometimes offers foreign journals and magazines, in the summer when the tourists are about. Today, there is *Time, Newsweek* and the English *Daily Telegraph,* as well as the *International Herald Tribune* and last Sunday's *New York Times.* The front cover of *Time* portrays a revolutionary of indeterminate nationality wearing the international terrorist uniform of flak jacket and balaclava helmet with a Yasser Arafat scarf bunched at the throat, standing before a pile of burning car tyres and brandishing what is clearly, to my practised eye, a Chinese Type 68 automatic rifle.

I study the picture under the shade of the news-stand awning. It is an interesting rifle. I have not handled one for a number of years. It looks like the Russian Simonov SKS but the barrel is longer and the gas regulator different. The bolt locking is similar to the AK47, the magazine dissimilar. To use AK47 magazines on this rifle one has to file down the bolt stop: I had to do so once. I remember the statistics: a heavy-ish weapon at nearly four kilos loaded, a 15 round magazine—30 if the AK47 version is attached—cyclic rate 750 rounds per minute, muzzle velocity 730 metres per second. Fires a 7.62 mm round, Soviet M43 ball slug, 25 gr charge weight, 122 gr bullet weight. The title over the portrait, which is a half length photograph, reads 'Men of Violence: the enemy in our midst.'

I thumb over the pages. The drift of the article is that we must root out these forces of brutality, these perpetrators of quick death and the transistor radio bomb. There is no place in the world for the priests of gunfire, the missionaries of pain.

I put the magazine down. I have no time for proselytising. Life is too short to spend it reading messages from presidential aids in political bunkers preaching peace from behind the stock of a legal weapon.

Men of violence. There is no such exclusive category. Everyone is a terrorist. Everyone carries a gun in his heart. Most do not fire simply because they have no cause to pursue. For want of a rationale, or courage, we are all assassins.

The propensity men have for causing terror is boundless. The British and, even here in the heart of civilisation, the Italians, hunt foxes and throw live cubs to the hounds for the pleasure of seeing the blood, hearing the pain, sensing the thrills of agony pulse in their own veins; the Swedish hamstring wolves; the Americans disembowel live rattlesnakes. Violence is an inherent characteristic of the species *Homo*. I should know. I am a man.

There is no difference between a Simonov look-alike in the fist of a freedom-fighter, my bastardised Socimi in a young person's brief-case, and an M16 carbine in the hands of a US Marine.

People accept violence. On television, men die by the gun, by the fist of righteousness as if every film producer was a finger on the hand of his God. Death by violence is a commonplace. No-one crowds to see the drunk dead of booze in the gutter, the old man dead of cancer in the terminal ward of the old folks' home. A few relatives mourn, cluck about like grateful hens, thankful the departed was not in pain long. A dignified death: that is what they want for him, want for themselves. Yet look at the rubber-necking drivers at a pile-up on the autostrada, the sightseeing hordes massing at the trackside of a railway crash, flocking to see where the plane came down, where the unfortunates were killed.

And the brutalities of law: people accept violence if it is legitimised by authority, accept it as a way of doling out justice. Certain people, certain classes of people, the niggers and the wops and the kafirs and the chinks and the trash, may be dealt violence rightfully, no matter who governs it, who dispenses it. It has always been like this. It always will be.

I am one of that class, one of those who may be gunned down in the name of peace. I am the bounty. I and my visitor whom I am to meet again in a few days.

Violence is the monopoly of the state, like the post office and the revenue department. We buy violence with our taxes, live under its protection.

Or most do. I do not. I pay no taxes. No-one knows me. I have no long, sleek yachts moored in the best marinas.

I live by the rule of Malcolm X: I am peaceful, I am courteous, I obey the law, I respect all the world. Yet if someone puts his hand on me, I send him to the cemetery.

I should expand this a little for you will otherwise label me a liar. The law I obey is that of natural justice. The peace to which I adhere is that of quietude.

As I sit in the second bedroom, the compact disc quietly playing, let us say, Pachelbel and work on the connectors, fashioning them from the smashed steel gear, I think of assassination and I think of poison, the coward's way of killing, and I think of Italy, the home of poisoning.

It was the Romans who refined the poisoner's prowess and the Church of Rome which perfected it. Livia, the Emperor Augustus' wife, was an expert: she drugged and laid low half her family. In ancient Rome, there was a guild of poisoners, but it was popes and cardinals who were the real experts.

To bring death by the gun is noble. To bring it by poison is not: it is to corrupt. It is borne of a corruption, of the machinations of a malignant and ruthless soul. True assassination is impersonal yet the assassin takes an active part in the process. Poisoning involves hatred and envy and is, therefore, personal but the perpetrator merely applies the drug and runs, does not join in the meting out of death.

I always think it so ironic it was the Vatican which made so much use of toxins and venoms.

The first Pope to be murdered, John VIII, was done away with poison in the year 882: his followers did it but they were apprentices at the game and eventually had to club him to death. In this way, they were not true poisoners for they had an active, if reluctant, hand in the matter.

A decade later, Formosus was poisoned; then, in the worst act of brutality ever committed by a killer, his successor Stephen VII had the body exhumed, excommunicated, mangled and dragged through the streets of Rome before being tipped into the Tiber like a sack of household waste, a bucket of night soil. Draw your own conclusions: poisoners are driven by hatred, assassins by justice and a cause, by the tide of history.

It did not end there. John X was poisoned by his mistress's daughter: similarly disposed of were John XIV, Benedict VI, Clement II and Silvester II. Benedict XI ate figs in sugar, save the sugar was adulterated with powdered glass. Paul II ate dosed watermelons. Alexander VI drank wine laced with white arsenic which was intended for his enemy. How sweet is right! His flesh turned black, his tongue darkened like Satan's and swelled to fill his mouth. Gas frothed from every orifice and, it is said, they had to jump on his belly to compress him into his sarcophagus.

Such disgusting exhibitions those must have been. All committed by hatred and avarice. No true assassin would behave so. Death of this variety displays the nadir of human capability. This is not my business.

In preparation for my excursion into the mountains, I packed myself a picnic: a bottle of Frascati, chilled in the refrigerator and packed with ice inside a polystyrene cool box such as vintners use to mail their wares; a loaf of coarse bread; 50 gms of *pecorino*; 100 gms of *prosciutto*; a small jar of black olives; two oranges and a Thermos of black, sweet coffee. All these are stuffed into a large rucksack with my pocket binoculars, drawing pad and crayons and a magnifying glass. A second rucksack carries the rest of my equipment.

Signora Prasca asked me, as I left, if I was going to paint more butterflies: I replied I was not. This was an expedition to the high mountains to draw the flowers upon which the butterflies feed. A gallery in Luxembourg, I informed her, had requested a series of butterflies on blooms. The insects themselves I knew. The blossoms I did not.

'*Sta' attento!*' were her last words, called as I closed the courtyard door.

I have every intention, my dear Signora Prasca, of taking care in every waking moment. Great care. I have always done so. It is why I am still here.

She envisages me crawling along the rims of precipices, leaning over precariously to focus my glass upon some obscure weed clinging to the rock, or jumping from boulder to boulder, chamois-like, at the foot of what in winter is a glacier of white death, the conception of the avalanches one sometimes hears rumbling in the February night. If this were winter, she would be afraid of my getting lost in the snowfields to be killed and eaten by wolves or the packs of feral dogs which prey upon loose horses and the wandering shepherds' flocks.

The road climbs the escarpment of the valley cutting through steep, narrow gorges and meandering across near vertical hillsides. It passes meagre settlements, the houses stunted by the enormity of the mountains, the churches falling into a slow and senatorial decline for lack of congregations. Up here there are few trees: a few stunted walnuts and, in sheltered spots, copses of oak and sweet chestnut.

After half an hour's continuous ascent, the Citroën—like *il camoscio*, the chamois, its namesake—gains the summit of the pass where the road levels onto the Piano di Campo Staffi. This plateau is a rich place of alfalfa, wheat and barley fields. Buffalo graze here and provide the town's daily fresh supply of *mozzarella*, driven down the mountain road in a fleet of rattling vans and pick-up trucks, some sufficiently antiquated to have seen service in the Mussolini era.

A few kilometres from the pass is the village of Terranera, Black Earth. I decide to stop here, at the bar, and take a coffee. It is not a sunny day, and I am high in the mountains, yet it is still hot and I need the refreshment.

'*Sì?*'

The woman behind the counter is young, perhaps twenty years of age. She has full lips and large breasts. Her eyes are dark, sullen with the boredom of village life. The fleeting thought occurs to me that it will not be long before she joins Maria's ranks at the end of the Via Lampedusa.

'*Un caffè lungo.*'

I do not want the strong stuff. She turns to pour the coffee into a small, thick cup which rattles on the saucer. I spoon sugar into it from a bowl by the till.

'*Fare caldo,*' I say as I pay her.

She nods dismissively.

There is an ice cream counter at the back of the bar. I drain my coffee and look at it. One of the delights of Italy is the ice cream.

'*E un gelato, per favore.*'

She moves lazily to the counter and walks behind it, lifting the Perspex cover.

'*Abbiamo cioccolata, caffè, fragola, limone, pistacchio . . .*'

'*Limone e cioccolata.*'

She scoops the ice cream into a cone and I pay. The tariff is chalked on a child's blackboard suspended from hooks in the ceiling by orange plastic baling string.

Standing in the doorway licking the ice cream, the lemon acidic and the chocolate cloying, I survey the fields through the buildings. The earth is truly black where the plough has turned it. Some people call this the Plain of the Fields of the Inquisition. The black earth is, it is suggested, the result of melted human flesh. Burn a body slowly and it chars then melts like rubber. I have seen it.

On the road once more, I drive for ten minutes then take a track off to the left. I halt the Citroën a hundred metres along it and get out, leaving the driver's door open. Standing by the car, I piss into the bushes. I do not need to relieve myself for the coffee has not run through me yet. I am not so old. I am just checking that no one has seen the car turn off. There is not a soul in sight, not so far as I can see over the black earth and waving brown grass.

The track has not been used by a vehicle for a long while. I halt again, once I am into the trees, and study the blades of grass growing from the hump in the centre of the track: there is no oil, no sludge of a car belly upon it. There are sheep droppings here and there but even they are old. The cow dung is desiccated into patches of insect-masticated dust.

Setting the tripmeter to zero, I drive on, the Citroën bouncing on its soft springs like a toy boat in a rough pond. I do not halt again until I have counted off ten kilometres. For the penultimate three or four, the track has been just an elongated clearing through woodland, dropping some two hundred metres in altitude. The Citroën makes tracks in the grass, which is still green here under the trees, but it will spring back in a few hours and cover my presence.

Eventually, passing a ruined shepherd's hut, turning a corner by a pile of boulders and descending a slope through the last of the woods, I arrive at what I had expected to find, an alpine meadow about a kilometre long and four hundred metres wide at the centre. At the far end is a small lake, the banks overrun with reeds. To the right is a heavily wooded ridge behind which tower steep grey cliffs, perhaps 700 metres high. To the left is another ridge upon which stands the ruined *pagliara* which I had also anticipated.

Paglia: straw. Many of the mountain villages have a *pagliara*, a second settlement still higher up the mountains to which the inhabitants used to migrate for the summer grazing. Today, these places are abandoned, the footpaths overgrown, the buildings roofless, the windows bereft of shutters and the chimneys of smoke. Occasionally, cross-country skiers may come upon these places but they seldom stop.

Locking my knapsacks in the car trunk, I walk across the meadows and make my way up to the ruined hamlet. The sun comes out but this is of no consequence now. No one can see the flash of a windscreen here.

The grass is long, the trees offer deep shade. Everywhere there is a profusion of wild meadow flowers. I have never seen anywhere so beautiful, so utterly uncorrupted: delicate yellows and mauves, brash whites, harsh and brilliant crimsons, exquisite blues. The field is as if an artistic god has spattered it with colour, shaken his dripping brush over the lush emerald of the valley. The ground is firm but there is water here and everything thrives. The air is humming with insects, bees fumble the long-stemmed mountain clover. Small butterflies of species I do not recognise dart up as my feet disturb them.

My ankle boots affording protection against vipers, I start to scramble up towards the houses. I cannot set about my business until I am certain no one comes here. Possibly, there is another, easier way to this valley from the south west and the houses are frequented by lovers seeking a remote, romantic spot.

Quickly, I pass from one ruin to the next. No signs of recent disturbance. No soot marks upon the stones, no campfire circles, no discarded tins and bottles, no condoms hanging in the bushes. From beside the end building, I survey the valley with the binoculars. There are no signs of recent human activity.

Assured I am sharing this place only with the insects, birds and wild boar—for there are trotter prints in a muddy rill leading to the lake—I return to the Citroën and drive down into the valley, swaying over stones hidden in the grass. I turn the car to face the way I have come and park it under the shade of a squat but ample walnut, laden with half-formed nuts, close to where I left the trees. I remove the knapsacks.

It takes approximately one hundred and fifty seconds to assemble the bastardised Socimi. I rest it on the driver's seat and unroll the length of flannel in which I have forty rounds. I press ten into the magazine, slotting it into the base of the hand grip. I snuggle the butt into my shoulder, putting my eye to the rubber cup on the telescopic sight. Carefully, I survey the pond.

My hand is not as steady as it was. I am getting older. My muscles are too used to moving or, if they are immobile, to relaxing. To be still and tensed is no longer a skill over which I have complete mastery.

Being sure I am in the shade of the walnut, I rest the gun on the car roof and aim at a clump of reeds on the far side of the pond. Very gently, I hold my breath and squeeze the trigger as if it was one of Clara's insignificant but supple breasts.

There is a brief put-put-put sound. Through the sight I watch the water churn at four o'clock to the reed clump and perhaps four metres off.

From the knapsack I take a watch-maker's steel-handled screwdriver and adjust the sight. I load another ten rounds into the magazine. Put-put-put! The reeds are clipped, the bullets slapping into the bank behind. I can see the mud spurt tinily. I adjust again and reload. Put-put-put! The reed clump is shot to shit. Feathers drift upon the breeze. There must have been a water-bird's nest there, deserted now for it is late in the summer and the breeding season is over, the chicks on the wing.

Satisfied, I dismantle the Socimi, returning it to the knapsack which I lock in the boot. There are a few modifications to be made yet, a few refinements to be considered. The sound suppressor must be made a little more efficient and the connector filed down further. The trigger still takes a little too much pressure. Yet, overall, I am smugly pleased with myself.

I spread a blanket upon the grass, lay out my picnic, open the Frascati and eat and drink. The meal over, I collect up the spent cartridge cases, put them in my pocket, walk down into the meadow and sketch and colour over two dozen different flowers. Signora Prasca will need to see the evidence of my excursion.

By the lake, I idly toss the used shell casings, one by one, into the lake. As the last hits the surface, a big fish rises to its brassy gleam.

Clara has given me a gift. It is nothing grand, a tie-pin made of base metal coated with fake gold. It is about four centimetres long with a spring-loaded clip on the back bearing little serrated teeth. In the centre of the gold-coloured bar is an enamel coat of arms. It is that of the town and contains features of the Visconti crest within it. The Viscontis, according to a printed slip in the presentation box, poorly printed in English, French, German and Italian, once held the town and most of the surrounding countryside. This makes it an appropriate present for me, although Clara cannot know this: the Viscontis were pastmasters of the arts of assassination, grand viziers of the game of killing. Indeed, for them, it was a way of life. Or death.

The manner of her giving me this memento was, to say the least, surreptitious although whether from shyness or the fear of a taunting from Dindina I cannot tell. She slipped it into the pocket of my jacket either when it lay over the back of the chair in our room in the Via Lampedusa or when we were in the *pizzeria*. I did not find it until after Dindina had left us, giving me her customary public peck on the cheek.

'Look in your pocket,' Clara instructed me.

I felt for the inner pocket of my jacket. This was a natural action for me. I never put anything in the outer for fear of pickpockets. Clara laughed scornfully.

'Not inside. In your pocket.'

I tapped my jacket and felt the box.

'What is this?'

I was genuinely surprised. I would never, under normal circumstances, have left myself so open. It is nothing to slip three ounces of Semtex and one of those minuscule detonators into a coat. I have known two people go to their maker in such a fashion: it is another of the skills accredited to the Bulgarians. Or was it Romanians? Maybe Albanians. All the Balkan-*ians* are alike when it comes down to it, devious bastards with an instinctive deceitfulness borne of centuries of invasion, inbreeding and survival subterfuge.

I took the box out and looked at it. If Clara had not been my mistress and standing close to me, if she had looked ready to bolt, I should have tossed the box as far as I could and thrown myself down on the cobbles. Or, perhaps, I would have thrown the box at her, at her feet. On reflection, that is probably what I would have done. Survival and retribution are not the property of the Balkan peoples alone.

'*Dono. Regalo.* A—a pre-sent. For you.'

She was smiling at me, the light from a street lamp casting pretty shadows across her face and highlighting her cleavage. She was, I could see, also blushing.

'This is not necessary.'

'No. Of course. Not necessary. But it is from me. For you. Why do you not open it?'

I lifted the lid of the box which was hinged with a little spring. The historical explanation fluttered to the ground. My heart missed a beat, my every nerve taut. She bent and picked it up.

The tie-pin shone in the lamplight. I moved it to and fro to make it glisten.

'It is just a small trinket.'

She must have been practising the words for she spoke them perfectly, not dividing the noun into its syllables.

'This is very sweet of you, Clara,' I smiled, 'but you should not spend your money so. You need it.'

'Yes. But also . . .'

I leaned forward and kissed her just as Dindina had kissed me. Clara put her hand on the nape of my neck and twisted her face into mine, her lips pressing against my own. She held me for a long moment, her lips not moving, not opening to let her tongue push into me.

'Thank you very much,' I said as she let me go.

'For what?'

'For this tie-pin and such a firm kiss.'

'These are both because I love you, so much.'

I made no reply. There was nothing I could say. She looked into my eyes for a few seconds and I could tell she was pleading in her soul for me to return her love, to say the emotion was mutual, binding, wonderful. Yet I could not. It would not be fair to her.

She turned, not huffily but a little sadly, and walked away.

'Clara,' I called softly after her.

She stopped and looked over her shoulder. I held the box up.

'I shall treasure this,' I said, and that much was the truth.

She smiled and answered, 'I shall see you again. Soon. Tomorrow?'

'The day after. I must work tomorrow.'

'*Bene!* The next day!' she exclaimed and walked off with a light step.

Clara loves me. This is not a fallacy but a stark truth. She does not love me as Dindina does, for the lust and the experience and the pocket money, but for what I am, or what she thinks I am. And this is where the fallacy begins.

Her love is a complication. I cannot really allow it, cannot risk it. I do not want to bring her misery, nor do I want to deceive myself. Yet I have to admit to myself that I feel for her: if not love, then certainly a fondness. Her cheap tie-pin has increased this sentiment, this dangerous weakness getting into me and worrying me.

I watched her go and made my way home with feelings of anxiety.

Everyone needs a refuge, be it from a spouse or a monotonous job, an objectionable situation or a dangerous enemy. It need not be far off. Indeed, it is often best if it is not. The rabbit, when startled, often stops stock-still before diving for the warren. This can be his error yet it can also save him. A well-placed tussock can be as advantageous as a well-dug tunnel. The hunter expects the rabbit to go subterranean. If he remains on the surface, he may still remain undetected for his continued presence above ground is not anticipated. The Polish have a card game called, I seem to recall, *gapin*. It means one who looks but does not see. The rabbit is a *gapin* player par excellence.

In searching for just such a tussock, I yesterday discovered a church not far from the town in which resides one of the most astounding works of art I have ever been privileged to view.

There is no way under the sky to force me to share the knowledge with you. I may be a rabbit after all and hold a good hand. Perhaps I should do as *Charaxes jasius* does: squat low and close my wings, be a dead leaf, lie low. I should then at least be living up to my name.

The church is no bigger than an eighteenth century English coach-house. It stands next to a barn from which it is detached by a lane scarcely wide enough for my Citroën, definitely too narrow for, say, a *carabinieri* Alfa Romeo. Even in the Citroën, I had to fold in the side-view mirror to squeeze the vehicle through.

I went to the place because the farmhouse beside the church was for sale. A sun-warped board was nailed to the wall, with *Vendesi* written crudely upon it in pink distemper. The paint had run like the blood flowing from the stigmata, drying in the fierce heat of the sun before it could reach the bottom of the board.

Knocking upon the door, I received no reply. The windows were firmly shuttered as if the building had closed its eyes tight against the glaring sun. It was a baking hot day. Grass and weeds grew against the wall. I went round to the back. There was a straw-strewn courtyard of square cobbles and a near-derelict barn. From the smell, cattle were lodged there. A crabby hen scratched in the debris of a broken-open bale of hay from which protruded several three-pronged pitchforks. Upon my approach, the fowl clucked its vehement annoyance at my intrusion and flew clumsily into the rafters.

The back door was ajar. I knocked again. No response. Carefully, I edged the door wider open.

It was not that I was afraid or suspicious. I had told no one where I was going: I might have been in the Piazza del Duomo buying cheese. Yet one never knows when the end might come, when someone else, holding hands with fate or the butt of a Beretta 84, decides the time has come.

Quite often, rising in the dawn hour to dress and commence my work, I let my mind weigh up the odds. Not those of surviving the day, the week, the month: they are too long to estimate. I consider the chances of the method of my death. A bomb is always possible but only if a client decided I need rubbing out, can or would identify him, talk under torture or sodium pentothal: there is a code of honour in my world, but many do not trust it. I rate odds against a bomb at, say, twenty to one. A bullet is much more likely. Generally, three to one. There can be side bets on this one, to increase the profitability of the gamble. Take the rifle or machine-gun bullet. Long odds on a 5.45 mm. My stalking angel, for this is how I think of my assassin, may be a Bulgarian but they prefer umbrellas, as I have indicated. Shorter odds on a 5.56 x 45 mm: that covers the Americans, the Ml6 and the Armalite combat rifle. I would offer you six to one. Evens for the 7.62 mm NATO round. Where hand-guns are concerned, there is no bet. If bullet it is to be, then the 9 mm Parabellum is the most likely one, the enforcer of treaties and the settler of old scores. Odds on my dying of disease, a car accident, unless the vehicle was tampered with, a self-admistered drug overdose are slim. Death by boredom is always a possibility but unquantifiable and so therefore not open for a wager.

The farmhouse was uninhabited, at least by humans. The parlour-cum-kitchen contained a wrought-iron stove, the door welded by rust, a chair with no seat and a rickety table which had plainly been used in recent times as an execution block for the beheading of the scrawny hen's cousins. Two other downstairs rooms were empty of all but dust and fallen plaster. The stairs were rotten. I trod cautiously, close to the wall. Each step creaked ominously, painfully even. At the top were three rooms. One had a bed-frame in it, the springs awry and tangled. In another, a cat had recently kittened. The mother was absent, but the blind offspring mewed piteously as they sensed my foot upon the floor. From the third, was a view of the valley, the Citroën and an old man studying my insurance and licence dockets on the windscreen.

Holding on to the wall, trying not to put my full weight on each complaining step for more than a split second, I went down the stairs and out into the yard. The old man was standing there. He was not antagonistic. He assumed there was nothing a man who drives a seven-month-old Citroën 2CV would wish to steal.

'*Buon giorno*,' I said.

He shook his head and mumbled. For him, perhaps, it was not a good day.

I pointed first to the house and then to myself and said, '*Vendesi!*'

He grimaced, shaking his head again. The sound of a car passing on the road below, grinding uphill in second gear, drew his attention and he ambled off without uttering a word to me. Either he was dumb, or did not like strangers, or distrusted foreigners, or thought anyone who would wish to purchase the building to be insane and therefore beneath either contempt or conversation.

I do not know what drew me to the church. Perhaps the chicken pecking at the ground caught my attention, some communication passing between us at a bestial level of telepathy, recognition of which has been lost to civilised man. More likely, it was a hot day and holiness is cool. Putting my hand on the ancient handle, I went in.

Once upon a time, as I have stated, I was a Catholic. It was a long time ago. I have no use for religion now. The older one gets, either the more pious one becomes or the more cynical. My parents were devout beyond the call of duty. My mother wore her knees raw scrubbing the church floor tiles after a burst water main flooded the place. My father paid to have them waxed and sealed with varnish. This was as an indemnity against further damage by flooding, not to save my mother from future hours of agony. My father, I recall, was much angered when the man from the Ecclesiastical Insurance Society referred to the burst main as an Act of God.

To the age of eight, I was educated in a convent school. There were seven boys in the establishment. The nuns taught us well, indocrinated us to a higher, more invidious standard than that to which our parents or Father McConnell could aspire. The other six kowtowed to the domination of these virgins with wilted souls and milky flesh. I would not. I thought of them as bats with white faces. The Mother Superior, a dumpy Irish woman endowed with the quick temper of piety, looked like a corpse in its shroud, only mobile. Witches in my dreams wore wimples, not pointed hats.

At eight, I was sent to a Catholic preparatory school. Here, the brothers from the nearby community taught us. They were not as spiritually shrivelled as their sisters-in-God. Instead, they had been somehow brutalised by prayer and solitude. They beat us for the most inconsequential misdemeanours. They caned hands, always the left, even on left-handed pupils, bare buttocks and the soft fleshy rear sides of thighs. They boxed ears and cuffed heads. They were obscene.

Yet, through them, I learnt so much of such value to me ever since: Geometry to assess trajectory and range; English; Geography to know the world and its hiding places; History, that I might know it and shape it and take my back-seat place in its cavalcade; Metalwork; Hate.

When I was thirteen, I was sent to a Catholic public school in the shires. I will not tell you which one. You could trace me through it. I was academically competent, particularly at mathematics and the sciences. I have never been much of a linguist. I was never beaten as others were because I kept a low profile, as they say. I did not creep to the masters. I merely kept my head well down behind the barricades.

Public school teaches you how to hide in the crowd. I got on with my studies, played the required sports with enough gusto and house spirit to get by without achieving house colours. I was never the scorer of goals, always the handy lad on the right wing who passed the ball at the appropriate moment to the centre-forward, to the striker. In the school's Combined Cadet Force, I was the best shot, though. They taught me how to assemble a Bren gun when I was fourteen. And they taught me how to pray without thinking. Both skills have served me well.

Catholicism—all the perversions of Christianity—is not a faith of love. It is a faith of fear. Obey, be good, toe the line, and heaven is yours, the first prize in the lottery of eternity. Disobey, react, cut the lifeline, and never-ceasing damnation is the booby prize. The dogma is, love the only god and you shall be safe. Fail in that love and he will not rescue you, not until you crawl and apologise and fawn before the altar. What kind of a religion demands such indignity? As you can tell, age makes me contemptuous.

The little church was not cool inside. It was cold. There were no windows save for a few thin slices of sunlight like archers' slits. It took a while for me to adjust my eyes to the gloom. I left the door open so I could see. Once accustomed to the midday twilight, I was astounded by the sights surrounding me.

Every square inch of the interior was painted. The frescoes started at the flagstones and went up to the roof timbers. Over the simple altar—a table bedecked with a white cloth smutted by mould—the ceiling was domed and entirely decorated in royal blue with gold stars and a pale, limpid moon.

The paintings were pre-Brunelleschi, with no sense of perspective. They were visually two-dimensional yet had the third dimension of magic about them. Upon one wall was a five-metre long depiction of the Last Supper. All the diners had halos, but Christ's was primrose yellow with golden radiates, the others mere circles drawn with a dull red line and coloured in black, light brown or blue. Upon the table was a loaf of bread like a large hot cross bun and some objects looking remarkably like leeks. No other food. They must either have been waiting for the meal to arrive or had finished it and were about to depart. There was some crockery, two jugs of wine, several bowls and a chalice. The only cutlery was a knife like a butcher's cleaver.

All the diners looked alike. Men with beards, men with halos, men with staring eyes and long hair. One was a red-head, with no halo. Of course. At the foot of the table was a dog, lying asleep with its muzzle upon its paws. The meal must have been over, for the dog appeared well-fed and contented.

The same wall carried several portrayals of Knights Templar on piebald mounts with white shields and red crosses: one was Saint George, or his archetype, slaying a dragon of almost oriental appearance. The artist was reasonably competent with figures and horses but the trees looked more like multi-stemmed fungi of the genus *Amanita*. Quite possibly, they were meant to represent these toadstools, the magic mushroom, the soma plant, the bringer of the dreams of the gods.

Across the little nave, Adam and Eve were receiving their just deserts for having it off in Eden. Nearby, the Three Wise Men knelt to the Virgin and Child, the latter reaching out for the gold. How appropriate, I think: ever since, the Catholics have been after the money.

I ignored the other scenes from the lives of Christ and the saintly ones. They made me seethe. So much time and effort spent to decorate this unknown chapel in the middle of the mountains, to record a history much of which is trivial poppycock.

I turned to leave. It was then the horror struck, the horror of history, of religion, of politics, the manipulation of people, the twisting of lives to unquestioning acquiescence, the bowing to the status quo.

The wall in which the door was set was entirely decorated by hell. Open coffins lay with the rotting dead rising from their delicious corruption. Whores, with their bosoms bare and their sex in full, pinkly view, lay on their backs, spread for a phalanx of red demons to enter them. Words spewed from the mouth of one whore in a bubble, as if from a modern cartoon character.

I cannot read stylised Latin script but guess, if it were translated by a modern academic, it would say 'Here comes the Devil syphilis.'

Other Satans, with three-pronged pitchforks just like those in the derelict barn outside, were prodding sinners into a well of fire. Jasmine and scarlet flames licked around their buttocks. A cauldron of sulphur, the devil's own brew, was pouring upon them like syrup. A huge fiend, the master Beelzebub himself, stood close to the ceiling, close to heaven. He was grey black with red eyes like the fog lamps on expensive cars. His feet were a phoenix's, his head was a gryphon's, his hands were those of a man. A naked woman balanced upon his tail, the tip in her cunt. She was screaming with pain. Or pleasure. I could not tell.

I walked quickly out, into the daylight. The door slammed behind me. I looked up and the sun burnt into me.

By stepping from the fantasy of the little church into the reality of the day, I had seemed to pass through hell, yet, as I started the Citroën, the engine ticking over, it occurred to me I had not passed through but entered into it. For what is hell if it is not the modern world, crumbling into dissolution, polluted by sins against the people and the earth mother, twisted by the whims of politicians and soured by the incantations of hypocrites.

I drove away in a hurry. My spine itched as if the devils were tailing me—as if the shadow-dweller was in the vicinity.

On the road, I passed the old man standing beside a blue sedan with a driver's side mirror awry and catching the sun. To my surprise, he waved to me as I went by: perhaps he was pointing at me, telling his friend in the car of the fool of a foreigner who was considering the purchase of the old farmhouse.

Later, in the solitude of my apartment, I remembered Dante.

Lasciate ogni speranza voi ch'entrate.

With considerable thought and care, I have decided to remove the telescopic sight mountings, shifting them slightly forward. The rubber eye-cup was just a little too far back. I could have altered the length of the butt yet that would have put the gun off-balance.

Balance is vitally important. This gun will not be used from a stable platform, a safe position. It will be fired from a rooftop, from a casement window open only a few centimetres, from beneath a bush, on a tree, from the rear of a stationary van, from a precarious place. The shooter must have utter confidence in the weapon so that all concentration can be given to the target and to remaining inconspicuous.

Re-aligning the sight mountings is not difficult but it is finicky. One has to work to minute tolerances.

Long into the evening, I work on the task, every so often weighing the gun, poising it on a ruler over the pencil mark I have determined to be the centre of balance. At last, about eleven o'clock, I am finished. My eyes are sore from the spotlamp over my workbench. My fingers are tired. My head aches monotonously.

I put the gun down, switch off the lights, take a beer from the refrigerator and go up to the loggia.

The town still hums but indistinctly. The old quarter around me is quiet, the peace broken only now and again by the echo of a vehicle in the canyons of the narrow ways or the call of a voice from the Via Ceresio.

I sit at the table and sip the beer. Though it is late, the stones are still warm. The sky is moonless, the stars punctures of light on the satin of the night. The mountains are the veils of black-clad widows peering into an open casket, the villages the glint of funeral candles in their eyes.

If the old widows are peering into a coffin, then I am the corpse. We all are. We are all the dead. We are done with life and it is done with us. The game is over, the long trick finally ended. We are being paid off.

Certainly, I shall soon be paid off. The visitor will return, the Socimi handed over, the job completed.

Then what?

This is my last task. After the Socimi, nothing. I am getting too old. The valley is so beautiful at night. As beautiful as death.

Efisio owns and runs the Cantina R. in the Piazza di S. Rufina. He is about seventy years old and the locals call him The Boss. His cantina, in the coloquial jargon of the streets, is also The Boss. Not *il Boss*. He left the town in his youth, travelling to America in the flood of immigrants escaping poverty and ruin. In New York, so they say, he robbed a bank with two accomplices and started a cantina in Little Italy. The cantina became a bar and then a speakeasy. Efisio flourished. He joined a Family. They flourished. Then, as an old man, he sold up, left his Family and returned to his roots to do what he knew best. Operate a cantina.

The Cantina R. existed before Efisio bought it. It never made much money. It was too far from the Piazza del Duomo and the market, too far from the Porta Roma where the carters, long-distance truck drivers today, congregated. Yet, gradually, its reputation grew. The bar counter is made of a solid piece of oak seven metres long and nearly a metre wide, thirty centimetres thick. The wines are the best in town. The range of beer is the most comprehensive. The tables are the cleanest and made of wood not tin plate or plastic. The floors shine like those of a mediaeval monastery. The lights are low and the windows frosted. From outside, no one may see who is drinking within. The Boss is, therefore, an ideal hangout for men ducking their wives, clerks ducking their employers, shop assistants ducking their manager. Women may enter—this is not Britain with its male preserves—but seldom do unless in groups. There is no jukebox, no cheap watch gambling machine, no one-arm bandit. There are no pool tables, dartboards, shove-ha'penny slabs or skittles. This is a serious place, for drinking and talking.

I never enter alone. I do not know the regulars. Sometimes, Galeazzo takes me there for lunch. We bring our own slices of parma ham and bread, laying them on a square of greaseproof paper upon one of the tables. Then we purchase a bottle of Barolo. It is heady stuff for the middle of the day, and we have to sleep it off afterwards, but it is good to be where there is only talk.

The clientele of the cantina come from every walk of life. Giuseppe goes in sometimes, if he finds some money in the gutter. The Boss is not cheap. Maria frequents the place, one of the few females to enter alone. She is soon absorbed into a group of conversationalists. Remember, passers-by cannot see in. Husbands are safe here.

The reason I never go in alone is because Efisio is shrewd. He is what the Americans term street-smart. He is canny in the way bar-owners the world over are receptive to the human condition. They see it all. The impending bankrupts, the committers of tiny sins, the faithless and the unfaithful, the afraid and the whisky-courageous: all pass through their doors, lean upon their counters, press lips to their glasses. A customer with a friend is not scrutinised so closely, is not conversed with, cannot be plumbed and probed like a pond being dredged by police for a body believed drowned in the mud.

Of such people as Efisio I have to be extra careful. Like any priest in any confessional—and what is a bar if it is not an informal confessional, without the lattice window, the half-curtain and the muffled voices—the barman is a confessor. Yet whereas the priest generally keeps mum about what he hears, the barman is not bonded by oaths of silence. The priest sells his information for Hail Marys. God buys. The barman sells his intelligence for cash. The police buy.

This is a shame. I should like to talk to Efisio. He is a man who has existed on the fringes of my world. I am sure he has killed; certainly he has arranged the death of others. He could not be where he is, what he is, without such a past. It would, I think, be good to chat over his experiences, compare them to mine. Professionals like us enjoy talking shop once in a while. Yet, as soon as he knew of me, even caught so much as a hint of my past, he would be on the phone to the *carabinieri*, to the *polizia*. If he was really shrewd, he would bypass the locals and go straight to Rome, to Interpol, to the American Embassy and the FBI, where I am sure he must still have contacts. And, for a while, he would be feted by the popular press, interviewed on RAI Uno, temporarily become more than an immigrant bar-owner returned from exile in New York.

He would have made his mark on history.

Yet, like a bloodstain on hot sand, this mark would soon fade and disappear, enter the realms of legend which would do him no real good but would keep the bar going. The patronage would swell with the curious who would demand to know which part of the bar I had leaned against, which glass I had drunk from, what was my favourite wine. They would ogle the glass, prop up the same metre of counter, order the same bottle. The Boss would become a shrine, a sepulchre to the anti-hero.

I should not want to bring Efisio such good fortune and in such a manner, at such a cost to myself.

It would not surprise me, were I to follow this course of action and thus bare my chest to the Baretta 84 (9 x 17 mm, *polizia* and *carabinieri* issue: odds fairly long for I am not such a fool) that two centuries hence, the legend will have it, upon the spot where I fell, blood oozes from between the stones annually on the anniversary of my death. Italians love to make shrines.

I walk here every Wednesday morning.'

Father Benedetto speaks with such assurance. Being a man of his god, he has no doubts in his mind whatsoever as regards his destiny. He will continue to stroll here, in the Parco Della Resistenza dell' 8 Settembre, every Wednesday until eternity stops. Failing that, he shall come here until his god calls him into the after-life. He is not bothered which eventuality comes first.

The pine trees and poplars are silent. It is only half an hour since dawn and the sun is not yet up, but the day is light. The air remains chilled by darkness and there is no warming of the skies to create even the merest zephyr in the valley. Already, the sparrows are hopping about in their interminable search for mates and crumbs.

I spied the priest from some way off, recognised his soutane flapping as he walked, as if he was dressed still in the folds of night. There was no need for me to step into the cover and ascertain who was this early morning promenader.

As soon as he saw me, he raised his hand in half-welcome, half-benediction, as if he was covering all possibilities. I might have been a demon of the darkness wandering about in the trees, looking for my hole down to the underworld.

'*Buon giorno!*' he called when still twenty metres away. 'So you, too, walk in the park before the sun wakes.'

I greet him and we fall into slow step with each other. He walks with his hands behind his back. I prefer to keep mine in my pockets, whether or not there is something in them. This is a habit.

'It is a quiet time,' I explain, 'and I enjoy the peace. There is virtually no traffic on the roads, the people are still in their beds, the air is untainted by car fumes and the birds are singing.'

As if at some subconscious cue, an unseen bird starts to warble softly in the branches of the poplars.

'I walk here to meditate,' Father Benedetto states. 'Once a week. Wednesday, the farthest one can travel in the week from the Sabbath. I always follow the same path. The trees, they are like the Stations of the Cross: by certain trees I thank God for certain favours he has granted me, or certain gifts he has made to me and all men.

'For example, here by this pine, I pause and thank him for the sunrise. But not this time. On the next circuit. You see,' he points to the east where there is a blush on the horizon, 'the sun is not yet up.'

'You mean,' I reply teasingly, 'you only pray when the sun has risen. This suggests a doubt in your mind. Perhaps he will not give you the sun today.'

'Give me?' The priest feigns astonishment. 'He gives it to us. And he will not fail.'

'Assuredly,' I agree and grin.

He knows I am harrying him in good humour.

For a brief moment, he halts and bows his head.

'And this circuit?' I ask as we proceed along the path, our shoes crunching the gravel.

'This circuit I thank him for the many friendships I have and ask him to look after those of my friends who are troubled.'

'I just walk here for the peace of the place,' I remark. 'I have worked long hours during the night and this is a relaxation. One has to concentrate so much on fine details.'

'Butterfly wings. They demand great concentration.' He nods as he speaks but he also gives me a sideways glance which I cannot interpret.

We walk on. At a cypress tree, he bows his head once more, but I do not enquire after his prayer and he does not offer the information.

'All men seek after peace,' Father Benedetto says as we turn a corner in the path and start up a gentle slope through flowering bushes. 'You walk here in the early day, some walk here in the cool of the evening to shed their cares, some come at night and hug each other close.' He waves his hand at the bushes where the courting couples lie. 'I wonder how many bastards have been made here?' There is a terrible sadness in his voice.

'I find my peace in the mountains,' I comment as we leave the bushes.

'Is that so?' the priest asks. 'Then perhaps you will stay here and settle yourself.'

'How do you know that I might think of going?'

'Those who seek after peace seldom find it. They are always moving on, looking elsewhere. And,' he adds perceptively, 'they are usually sinners.'

'All men are sinners.'

'It is so. But some are greater sinners than others. And those who seek peace have much sinning in their history.'

'I have found my peace,' I say.

This, of course, is a lie. I never found it. In truth, I have never really sought after it. Not until now.

There has always been an element of excitement in my life and it has been prompted not only by my chosen art, not only by those who seek me out, those who dwell in the shadows, but also by my own desire to keep travelling. Life is a long journey and I am not one to get off halfway. I have always wanted to shift forwards, to turn the next corner, to see the next view and walk into it.

Yet here, perhaps, I should like to stay. This valley, with its castles and villages, its forests alert with wild pig and its mountain pastures alive with fluttering butterflies. There is a tranquility here not to be found elsewhere.

Perhaps, too, it is time to slow the excitement down, to take it easy as my years draw on and my trespass upon earth grows shorter.

I still think of myself as young. I accept that my body ages, that the cells get shrunken and the brain dies at an accelerated rate, but I have a young man's soul and ideals. I still want to go on doing my bit to shape the world.

'I would say you have not discovered your peace,' Father Benedetto breaks into my thoughts. 'You are still looking for it, still wanting. Wanting very badly, very seriously. But you are not yet done and . . .'

He pauses as we round another landmark in his prayer path, bowing his head and muttering briefly to himself, to his god.

'And?' I ask as he steps on.

'Forgive me. This is the priest in me speaking. And the friend. But you have done much sinning, Signor Farfalla. Perhaps you still do . . .'

'I have a mistress,' I admit. 'She is young enough to be my daughter, pretty enough to be my daughter-in-law, were I to have a son. We make love twice weekly, often with another girl present. We three. A ménage à trois . . .'

Father Benedetto huffs at this: it is another French expression for something immoral.

'. . . but I do not consider this sinning,' I continue.

'In our modern world,' he responds curtly, 'there are priests who share your view. However,' and his tone softens once more to the melody of the confessional, 'I do not refer to the sins of carnality. I am thinking of the more deadly sins . . .'

'Are not all sins equal?' I ask, attempting to steer the conversation; but he will not have it.

'We are not discussing theology, my friend, but you.'

The path reaches a large expanse of grass. In the centre, a number of ravens are squabbling over some morsel. As we approach, they flap into the air, one of them carrying the remains of a dead rat in its beak.

'You like this town, this valley. You should like to remain here, find your peace at last. Yet you cannot. There is something in you you cannot ignore. Some outside force. Some enemy.'

He is far more astute than I had thought. I should have remembered the lessons learnt in school: Catholic fathers not only have their god on their side, they also have the gift of prying open the box of the soul without even touching the lid.

'What work do you do, my friend?' he asks outright. 'You paint butterflies, yes. And you are so good an artist. But this cannot give you so much money. It is true one can live like a prince in the mountains here with as little as twenty thousand American dollars per annum income, but you have more than this. You do not wave your money in the air, you have a cheap car and your rent is not high, but I sense you are a rich man. How is this?'

I am silent. I do not know what or how much to tell this priest. I know him well, but not sufficiently to share my life with him. I know no one that well.

'Are you on the run, as they say?'

I do not fear him as I would others. I cannot account for this. It is a fact. He is somehow trustworthy yet I am still extremely cautious.

There is, I sense, a need to tell him something, to satisfy if only temporarily his inquisitiveness, his delving into my life. I can string him a series of untruths: not lies, for they are too readily discovered. I need to dissemble carefully, build a plausibility into my deceit which he will accept despite his priestly insights and his experience of lying confessions.

'All men are on the run from something.'

He laughs quietly.

'You are correct. All men watch at least some of the shadows, yet you watch them all.'

Confound him, I think. He has been studying me.

'So I have sinned greatly,' I admit, my voice a little louder than I should have wanted it. I quieten it. 'And I may still be sinning greatly. There is no man on earth who does not sin daily, even on a grand scale. But my sins, if such they be, are for the good of mankind not . . .'

I must say no more. I know that if I allow my curtains to part, this priest will not merely peer through my window but will swing his leg over the sill and jump inside me, have a good poke around.

'Until you relinquish your sins, until you confess and repent, how can you stop running?'

He is right. I do not agree with repenting my sins but I do acknowledge I must relinquish my way of life in order to find that elusive peace, whatever it may be.

'Do you want to tell me?'

'For what reason?'

'For your own sake. You know your reason. Perhaps I can pray for you?'

'No,' I answer. 'I may tell you for my reason but you are not to pray for me. I should not want you to perjure yourself before your god. He may punish you by destroying the world stocks of armagnac.'

I try to make light of our talk, but he still will not let me guide our talk. He is as persistent as a hungry mosquito, hizzing in the air, zooming in, dodging the swat and circling for another attack. He is as persistent as a Roman Catholic priest who sees a true, bona fide, one hundred per cent, gold-plated sinner to save.

'So?' he prompts.

'So I have little to say, little to tell. I live in a secret world and I like it that way. You are correct, father: I am not poor. I am not a poor artist. Yet I am an artist. I make things.' I demur and wonder what to say. 'Artifacts.'

'Counterfeit money?'

'Why do you say that?'

'You work in metal. You are given some steel by Alfonso, the car doctor.'

'You seem to know much about me.'

'No. I know little. I know only what you do in the town. It is not easy to hide everyday things from people. They do not talk. Except to me. I am their priest and they trust me.'

'And I should too?' I enquire.

'Of course.'

Once more, he stops, bows his head, mutters a prayer and sets off again. The sun is up now and the air is already warming. There is a small hum of cars on the roads. The sparrows are squabbling in the grass with less energy. They know the heat is coming.

'Now to walk once round with no stops,' Father Benedetto declares. 'This one for my constitution, not for Our Lord.'

'Your last prayer, I hope, was not for me.'

'And if it was, what could you do to affect it?' He grins.

'Nothing.'

I decide to give him something to quell his curiosity, to stifle for the time being his prying and prodding. This is against my nature, against my lifelong rule of silence, my almost monastic vow of silence, but I deem it necessary to put a stop to his conjecturing, pull a curtain over his persistent interest in my affairs.

This may be a mistake and I may live, or die, to regret it, but there it is. Past errors have been survived. And just as my instincts can inform me of the presence of a shadow-dweller, so do they now tell me that Father Benedetto is a man of his word I can trust, as far as I am prepared so to do.

We do not speak again until we reach the bushes.

'I will tell you this much,' I offer. 'I am what some would regard as a criminal. Perhaps even as an international criminal. I exist in police and government files in more than thirty countries, I should say. I do not rob banks, print banknotes, break into computers or sell explosives to terrorists, or governments, so they may shoot down jet airliners. I am not a spy, not a James Bond: I have only one pretty girl in my life.' I smile at him but he is frowning. 'I do not steal art treasures or peddle heroin and cocaine. I am not . . .'

'*Basta!* Enough!'

He raises his hand and, for a moment, I think he is going to bless me, make the sign of the cross over me as if I was some demon he was going to exorcise. I fall silent.

'Say no more. I know now what your work is.'

'Some would say it is the work of god.'

He nods and says, 'Yes, some would say so. But . . .'

We reach the gates of the Parco della Resistenza dell' 8 Settembre. The traffic is now quite busy, the shadows of the vehicles halted at the junction lights long and hard.

'What do you do now?' I ask him.

He looks at his cheap steel watch.

'I go to the church. And you?'

'I go to work. Painting butterflies.'

We shake hands as priest and parishioner do when they meet or

part in a public place. He goes off up the hill towards the church of
San Silvestro and I make my way through the narrow streets towards
my home.

As I walk, I worry I may have told him too much. I somehow
doubt it, but it may indeed be the case he has divined my true
employment. If that is so, I must be very wary of him and those who
may approach him.

I have already mentioned to you the Convento di Vallingegno, a
ghostly spot where spirits roam and local sorcerers rifle the monastic graves, where is reputed to be buried a Gestapo necromancer. It is
a mysterious and malignant place yet it is also quite beautiful. It has a
placidity many a holy place has lost. No tourists wander the collapsing cloisters, no lovers couple in the courtyard.

This part of Italy, for all the television aerials and telephone lines,
the ski-lifts, autostradas and proliferation of *supermercati* on the outskirts of every town, still exists in the Middle Ages. In the Yellow
Pages is a section, admittedly small, for witches, wizards, and magi-
cians. These wise folk can remove warts, abort unwanted pregnancies
without surgery or gin or drugs, cure broken limbs without splints,
restore fertility and maidenheads, exorcise spectres and cast ingenious
spells upon perfidious husbands, wayward wives, lovers and loose
daughters.

I have no interest in mumbo-jumbo. My life is clear-cut. There
are no frayed edges where reality shrouds into myth. I am no longer a
Roman Catholic.

Yet the Convento di Vallingegno has an attraction for me. I enjoy
the quietude of its interior, the timelessness of the ruins, the proxim-
ity of the grave. The inaccessibility of the monastery is pleasing to me
also: I can be fairly sure of not being disturbed there for anyone seeing my presence would keep away, fearing I might be one of the
authorities. Or a wizard. Only those with clandestine lives go there.

In the ruined wall of the chapel, there is a delicacy I am fond of hunting when the chance offers itself: wild honey.

I first tasted it in Africa. The late sixties and seventies were a turbulent time for the dark continent: wars raged, petty politicians struggled for power in the post-colonial years. It was a time for making money, those dog years of war. I was paid my highest rate ever for a job by—well, let that be as it may: he is still alive and I wish to remain so, too. Suffice to say, I was compensated fifteen thousand dollars in cash and what proved to be over forty thousand in raw diamonds and emeralds just for removing and replacing a rifle barrel. And destroying the original.

I was not told why, but could guess when I was handed the weapon. It was a one-off, a fabulously wrought stock, all filigree silver, gold inlay and ivory. The rifle had to remain in the public eye. It had been used in an attempt, I reasoned, on the life of Idi Amin Dada, madman and baby-eater, sheep-seducer and sergeant-major-cum-major-general: never believe the rantings of journalists and headline writers bent on improving circulation figures. The rifle would be carefully checked by his cronies. The rifling of a gun barrel is as indentifiable as a fingerprint. If you cannot change the print, change the finger.

I was holed up in a banda in the grounds of the Norfolk Hotel in Nairobi. A nondescript black man delivered the gun to me. Room service delivered the food. I worked for nine hours. It had to look good, look as if the rifle had been untampered with and the new barrel was the original. It was not difficult. I even distressed the metal to match the scratches.

The same man drove me in a Jeep out into the bush beyond the Ngong Hills. I fired the rifle, checked the scoring on the bullets did not match the original and showed this to my companion. He nodded his approval. He was taciturn, silent and austere, but he knew what was required. The removed barrel we then propped on some stones, sealing the breach with a rubber cork. I poured hydrochloric acid down the muzzle and we waited for fifteen minutes. When it was poured out, the rifling was almost invisible. We repeated the process. Satisfied, he propped the barrel against a rock and ran over it with the vehicle. Then, as black men do when they want to make damn sure not even the ju-ju can do anything by way of revenge, he rammed the buckled barrel down an ant-bear hole.

I was in Kenya for just sixty-one hours. The job worked out at a fraction under a thousand dollars an hour for the whole stay. In those days, that was very good money. All my expenses, including my air fare, were also met without demur.

And I tasted wild honey.

Whilst we were waiting for the acid to burn out the barrel, my companion—I never knew his name: he called himself Kamau which is to Nairobi what Dai Evans is to Newport—tipped his head to one side.

'Listen!' he exclaimed.

I listened. I did not know for what: a snapping twig, perhaps, a diesel engine, a cocking lever?

'You hear that?' he murmured.

'What?' I hissed.

I was growing alarmed. Dying is one thing: I have faced up to the inevitability all my life. Almost all of it. Yet I did not want to wind up in the hands of some African freedom fighters. They have a penchant for cutting personal bits off their victims before finally slashing the throat or poking a Kalashnikov into the nape of the neck and letting loose a short burst—short because ammunition was always precious in those guerrilla forces. Though I would not have any future use for any of the protuberances from which I should be divorced, I should like not to be parted from them whilst still sentient.

'Honey guide. Is a bird who shows you the way to honey. He likes the baby bees but he can't break the bee nest. A man has to do it for him. Or honey badger.'

It was the longest communication my companion had uttered.

When the smashed and burned-out barrel was safely down the

ant-bear hole, we set off through the bush following a distinctive 'witpurr, witpurr, witpurr' call. The bird, when we caught up with it, was about the size of an English mistlethrush, buff brown with a flash of yellow on its wings.

'What is the bird's name?' I enquired, expecting a Swahili word.

'Victor,' replied the African. 'Listen. He call his name now we are near the bee nest.'

Sure enough, the call was now a curt 'victor, victor', interspersed with a sound like a man rattling a box of matches.

The hive was in a stunted tree, about eight feet from the ground. The African took from his pocket a Ronson gas cigarette lighter and, turning the flame up high, scorched the underside of the nest. It smouldered and smoke wafted upwards. The bees began to swarm. I kept well back. Buzzing lead is one thing, bees another.

After a few minutes, the African threw several handfuls of dust at the nest and smashed it to the ground with a stick. He grabbed at it, shook it violently, tore a section off and walked swiftly away. The bees hovered in a cloud around the tree and the remnants of the nest on the ground. By the time my companion was back at my side, the bees were dispersing.

'Stick your finger.'

He thrust his forefinger into the comb and wiggled it about. He extracted it and sucked on it like a child with a lollipop. I did likewise.

The honey was sweet, thick and smoky. It tasted of bush fires and the dust of the veldt. I dipped my finger again. It was so very good, so very original a flavour. I looked over my shoulder. The bird was ravaging the remains of the nest underneath the tree, oblivious of the bees which were now regrouping, its beak darting again and again into the hive.

As we drove over the pitted, rock-strewn road, the African and I kept dipping into the nest. Within two hours, I was on a BOAC flight bound for—well, out of Kenya, anyway.

So I go periodically to the Convento di Vallingegno. I brave the witches' covens and the ghosts of the Gestapo. I brave also the climb up the walls to a first floor window. Once there, entry is simple: the windows are without frames, have never known wood or glass. To go in is to enter the fourteenth century.

Once through the window, I am in a chamber beside which a balcony runs the length of this side of the monastery. The view is stupendous—twenty-five kilometres down the valley, down the way the Knights Templar went carrying gold and fame. And history. Much of it forgotten.

The stairs down are stone, old and firm. The stillness is broken only by the breeze. Below is a chapel. It is here the witches come. The altar is made of loose blocks of stone jointed with weak lime mortar mixed with fragments of human bone. I found a finger-bone protruding from a crack upon my first visit.

Behind the altar is a tall fresco, painted on the plaster. The weather, the succession of winter cold and summer heat over the centuries, has failed to bring it down. This might be a miracle. Who can tell?

The fresco shows Mary Magdalene standing between a row of cypress trees on her left and palms on her right. The perspective is cock-eyed. Instead of diminishing in the distance, it narrows towards the foreground. Above is God. He is an old man with a crown upon his head. His arms are raised in benediction. From the back of the chapel, in the half-light, the fresco looks like the head of a goat. This is why the witches come, why the Gestapo came, why the monastic courtyard, overgrown with thistles and briars, is a maze of excavations.

There is not an unpilfered tomb in the place. A tiny room in the cellar, into which I ventured once, squeezing through a narrow slit, is full of bones: the bones of monks dead of the plague, or old age, or piety, or sickness, or at the hands of the Inquisition. Leg-bones, arm-bones, ribs, vertebræ, hips, fingers, toes, some lower jaws and teeth—but no skulls: the room is devoid of skulls. They have been stolen by the magic ones.

I am not here to steal from the dead. Only from the living. The wild honey.

The mortar in the walls has crumbled and the stones lie upon each other like a vertical cliff of gap teeth. I watch the bees making for three or four cavities. The lowest is within reach. I push through the brush, thorns snatching at my jeans like tentacles of the dead. At the mouth of the nest is a smooth, yellow stalactite of beeswax.

The bees ignore me. They do not know what is coming. I smear the wax with gunpowder, stuff some in the holes around the entrance to the hive. I step back and set a match to it. It hisses and spits like a damp firework. Clouds of dense blue smoke are given off. The bees come winging from the hive at speed, angry, confused, bewildered. Quickly, like an enemy pressing home the advantage, I tear a stone or two from the wall. Others tumble free. There, in the cavity, is the wedge of the comb. I pull at it. It snaps off the stone, breaks in half. I thrust it into a plastic bag and beat a retreat.

In the Citroën, I transfer the comb to a large jar. Later, without giving the source thereof, I present a small section to Signora Prasca. She believes the beeswax will cure her rheumatism.

Every midday, for an hour or two, the people of the town parade in the Corso Federico II. The colonnades are crowded with window-shoppers, tourists taking coffee and cakes, old women selling news-papers, office girls walking hand-in-hand and chattering like songbirds, old men discussing politics, young men discussing sex and rock music, couples discussing nothingnesses.

In the centre of the Corso, forbidden to all traffic except buses and taxis, of which there are few at this hour, men walk, arm-in-arm, some-times holding hands. This is not a town of queers, a den of queens, a goldmine for the quack with a cure for AIDS made of compounded apricot stones and quinine. This is Italy where men hold hands as they

talk about their wives, mistresses, business successes and the failures of
the government.

I like to sit, sometimes, in one of the little coffee shops under the
colonnades, a *cappuccino* and a *pasta* on the table, a newspaper in hand,
and watch this world pass by. This is the show of the warm-up acts,
the small performers upon the stage of life, the people for whom now
is everything, for whom good wine is like a woman. I think of
Duilio. They have no part to play other than that of building the atmosphere. They are the chorus, they are the crowd scene, they are the
servants and grooms and soldiers who fill out the action by the wings.
Meanwhile, mid-stage, the leading actors unravel the story. I am, I
suppose, one of them. A minor one. I have a few lines to read, a few
actions to make. They are slight, but they alter the course of the
drama. Very soon, for instance, my visitor will return. Act Four must
be drawing to a close. Act Five will soon begin.

Clara is walking along the Corso. She is with a girl I have not seen
before. A student, from the look of her, with long legs, long hair, long
sleeves to her blouse, which pushes open as a bus slides by. They are
hand in hand. The girl carries a black calfskin document case under her
arm. Clara clutches three or four books, tied round with a leather strap.
She might be a schoolgirl on her way to class. To look at her, one
would not think she was screwing her way through college and with an
old man who spends his hours clandestinely re-shaping a Socimi 821.

She sees me, nods to her friend and they cross through the throng
of boulevardiers.

'My friend, Anna,' she says. 'This is my friend, Signor Farfalla.'

They cease to hold hands and the girl offers hers to me. I half rise,
fold my newspaper and accept her greeting.

'How do you do?'

'I am very well, thank you.'

Anna speaks English. I am to be an impromptu English lesson, a
practice session with the real thing. I do not mind. A man drinking

coffee with two girls is less conspicuous than a man drinking coffee on his own, half-reading a newspaper.

'Will you take a coffee with me?' I invite them. *'Prego.'* I indicate the empty chairs.

'That would be very good,' Clara says.

She moves her chair to sit closer to me. Under the table, her knee presses against mine. Anna also moves her chair nearer to me, but to shift it out of the sun. There is no competition going on here.

'Anna is learning English also,' Clara says.

'Have you been to England?' I enquire.

'No. I have not been to England,' she replies, 'only to France and then only to Monaco. But my father has a Rover car and I have a Burberry coat.'

She is wealthy, this Anna. There is an air of well-being about her. She wears a Hermes wristwatch, the strap made of steel with inter-linking H sections in rolled gold. Upon the little finger of her left hand she wears a gold ring set with a ruby. It matches her lipstick. She does not screw for the money, just for the fun.

The waiter comes over. My cup is empty.

'Due cappuccini e un caffè corretto,' I order. I do not want wine but the *grappa* would revive me.

He takes my empty cup and disappears into the interior of the shop.

'See!' Clara exclaims. 'The book I have. I said so to you.'

She turns her pile of books around upon the table and taps the topmost volume: it is the Penguin edition of *An Unofficial Rose* by Iris Murdoch.

'Very good,' I reply. 'You will be very well-read. That is excellent.'

I am genuinely pleased: it is good to see her using her money—my money—in positive ways, not injecting it in the alleys of the night or frittering it away on raucous music. She notices my pleasure and her smile is warm, almost loving.

'Where do you come from?' I ask of Anna.

She is perplexed.

'I am sorry . . .'

It is time for me to play the teacher.

'*Dove abita?*' I help her.

'Ah, yes!' She smiles and her teeth are straight and white: even her mouth looks like money. 'I live in the Via dell' Argilla. Nearby to Clara.'

I momentarily think of what else I might teach this girl should the chance arise. But it will not and, looking from one to the other, I believe Clara is the prettier of the two. Rich girls are a pain in the arse in the sack: Larry once told me so. He knew. A client of his was killed by one.

'I see. But where do you come from? Where is your family home?'

'My home? My home is in Milano,' she replies, as if answering a question posed by a disconnected voice on a language cassette.

The coffees arrive and Anna insists on paying for them. She takes a crocodile purse from her document case and pays with a high denomination note. We talk of inconsequentialities for fifteen minutes: the weather—I am British she assumes and therefore wish this to be a topic of intercourse—the town and what I think of it, the use of learning English. I understand her father is a millionaire leather dealer in Milan, a man in the world of fashion and women. Anna states she wishes to be a model in London: this is why she is here, in a two-bit university, studying the language.

At last, they stand to go. Clara winks at me.

'Perhaps we might have a drink together soon?' she suggests. 'I am free . . .' she considers the crowded timetable of her life '. . . on Monday.'

'Yes. I think that would be good. I shall see you then.'

I, too, rise.

'It was a delight to meet you, Anna. *Arrivederci!*'

'*Arrivederci, Signor Farfalla,*' Anna says.

There is an unmistakable twinkle in her eye. Clara must have told her.

It is warm tonight, the air balmy as a tropical island, the breeze the temperature of blood. In the morning, it rained: after noon, the clouds blew away over the mountains and the sun beat down from a sky laundered of impurities. Here, that does not imply the diesel soot of Rome, the factory grime of Turin and Milan, the concrete dust of Naples. The mountain rain has cleansed the atmosphere of the pollen of a million flowers, washed out the dust of slow moving horse carts and lazy tractors dragging shallow ploughs through the stony soil, neutralised the dull electricity of heavy heat to replace it with the sharp sparks of taintless warmth.

When the rain came it did so with a Mediterranean vengeance. Here, rain is an Italian man who does not kiss hands and fawn like a Frenchman, or bow discreetly like an Englishman, keeping sex at bay, or get brazen like an American sailor on shore leave. Here, the rain is passionate. It does not fall in sheets like the tropic downpour or drizzle miserably like an English complaint, snivelling like a man with a blocked nose. It slants down in spears, iron rods of grey water which strike the earth and pockmark the dust, spread out like damp stars upon the dry cobblestones of the streets and the flagstones of the Piazza del Duomo. The earth, far from succumbing to the assault, rejoices in it. After a brief shower, one can hear the earth click and pop as it sucks its drink.

Within minutes, leaves which were hanging drab in the haze of seething air are erect, their green hands held out, supplicating for more.

After rain, there is a joy in the world. I share it. So much is rotten, is corruption, is fated to destruction. The rain seems to be a benediction, as if some law of nature had decided it is time for a baptism into reality.

I sit in the loggia. The oil lamp remains unlit. I need no light, as you shall understand. Upon the table is a bottle of Moscato Rosa. One bottle and one tall, thin glass. In an English house, a woman

would keep a single stemmed bloom in it. Beside it is a small earthenware pot and three thick slices of bread smeared with salted butter.
For later.

A dog begins to bark, somewhere outside the town, lost in the
vineyards which approach the fragments of the fourteenth-century
defensive wall still standing. It is a plaintive sound, rich in canine
melancholy. Another dog, farther away, takes up the offer of conversation and they shout to each other like men calling across a valley. A
third, in a courtyard of one of the buildings adjacent to my own, joins
the night chorus with a hoarse, gruff woof which echoes and sounds
less like a dog and more like an abusive drunk struggling to make a
point of intellectual import in a bar-room argument.

There is something timeless about their barking as if they were
revenants of all the pooches ever to have yapped, fought and
scrounged in the valley, guarded farmsteads, taunted bears in the
forests and bayed at the constancy of the moon.

From somewhere in the night drifts the scent of orange blossom.
Someone has a tree growing in a pot upon a balcony or verandah. It
is flowering late and will produce no fruit: a harvest of oranges is not
the intention. The idea of the tree is to provide this scent after a summer rainstorm.

The storms are not passed. Far away over the mountains, lightning
flickers every few minutes but it is far away, lost in the high world of
the peaks and the valleys, the cliffs of rock where bears still live. Or so
they say. It will be several hours before the storm arrives over the
town. By then, I shall be sleeping and careless of its clamour.

The wine is unique. The grape comes from the countryside
around Trieste. The wine comes from Bolzano, where the grape was
introduced before the war. It is cherry red and smells of roses, a
dessert wine as sweet as sucked cane. I prefer this rosé above all others: Lagarina is too prickly, Cerasuolo too dry and sharp for a nightcap
after such rian, Vesuvio Rosato too common—Lacrima Christi, they
call it, the Tears of Christ. Galeazzo declares it is an apt name: Christ

drank it at the Last Supper, he suggested, and it brought tears to his eyes. Christ, it seems, was an Italian, a connoisseur of good wines who knew a poor one when it crossed his lips.

The small pot was a gift from Galeazzo. He said an artist should enjoy the contents, especially one who studied butterflies and had recently wandered in the mountains painting flowers.

The contents are a jam made of rose petals.

There are no words available to describe the taste of this heavenly conserve. It is the quiddity of an overgrown garden in the deepest of sultry summers, distilled into its primal juices, dulcified with nectar and stirred with ambrosia. Spread upon the bland bread, to bite into it is to eat of a purification of all the perfumes of nature, all the essences and moods that have invoked every line of pastoral poetry since Virgil.

So. I am here, alone, in the half-darkness of the Italian night, drinking rosy wine and dining on rose blossom. The world is good. Time has stopped. The moon is hidden by the distant storm. The streets are quiet for it is just before one o'clock, even the addicts gone, curled into their puzzle of fallacious dreams, the ground too wet in the Parco della Resistenza dell' 8 Settembre for the lovers. The stars no longer move.

Yet, around the loggia, my princely tower high above the struggles of men, my own stars are moving. They flash on and off like meteors spending themselves in the stratosphere. They are tiny lightings close to. They are will-o'-the-wisps. If I was a superstitious man, I should say they were the souls of those I has assisted into eternity and, for a lucky few, immortality amongst men, or all the bullets I have ever made, ever caused to be fired, returning to haunt me.

They are fireflies, here in the centre of the town, above the rooftops, the rows of pantiles and the chasms of the courtyards and narrow, ancient streets.

Curiously, they do not settle. The stone may be too cold for them, too devoid of life. Fire has no use for stone. I quickly leave the loggia, go below to the sitting room. There is a vase of flowers there. I snatch up a few and return to the loggia. I prop them against one of the pillars.

Still, these animate flames, these tiny phosphorescences do not land. They ignore the blossoms.

I pick up the wine and sip it. It is so sweet. I think of the honey gathered from the Convento do Vallingegno. I lean back in my chair to gaze out at the mountains. The peaks to the south-east are suddenly, briefly, silhouetted against dark clouds spun with lightning. The storm is coming nearer.

In the town, a clock chimes once. This alone reminds me that time passes unavoidably onwards.

The glass is drained. I refill it. The bottle is empty now. I press the wide cork into the mouth of the rose-petal jam. Enough of that for tonight. I must save some. It is my intention to take the remnants of the preserve to Clara and Dindina, to make them eat it before we bed each other. Augustus, Nero, Caligula: they will, I am sure, have pressed such a taste upon their women before having them. Such a jam cannot be the invention of modernity. It is too delicious.

Once more I lean back in my chair and, by chance, look up into the dome above the loggia. The painted horizon I now see is, in the fresco, also bedevilled by a thunderstorm. The azure sky is pricked by gold stars. Yet they are moving now. The meteors have left the heavens and are playing on my ceiling. They are shifting in crazy patterns.

The fireflies know the storm is coming. They have no time for flowers. They need shelter before the big drops start to pummel them to the ground, knock them from their flimsy shelters under drooping leaves, flood them out of the sanctuary beneath the stones.

They dart and flicker then, gradually, as if a general in their army has given orders, commissioned billets for his infantry amidst my stars, they settle and wink on and off. Outside the loggia, on the mountains, the scanty lights of the high village also wink in the warm night. Over the hills, the electricity of the storm competes.

I sit, the wine finished, until the first fat drops of rain strike the parapet. By now the thunder is loud, the lightning coarse and cruel. It would be foolish to remain here, the highest man in the town. I go below, undress slowly and lie beneath the sheet on my bed as the rain pelts down and the storm swings over the town and up the valley like an angry wife, abandoned by her cuckold husband and looking for her treacherous lover.

As I drift into sleep, not caring for the storm, for fate will do as it will, three thoughts linger: the first is I must have the gun ready within the next two days and the second is I hope the fireflies are safe in their umbrella of private heaven. The third is less a thought than a realisation: this is an agreeable and wonderful place and I should like to settle down in it.

He is back. The shadow-dweller, the man from the street outside the wine shop. Just an hour ago, as I approached the Citroën, he was sitting at a table outside a bar. He had before him a glass of *grappa,* nothing more. He was doing the crossword in a copy of the English *Daily Telegraph,* poring over the clues but I could tell he was using it only as a pretence, to kill time that he might wait all the longer without being pestered by the waiter.

I saw him, mercifully, before he saw me. I side-stepped into a butcher's shop. Within, there was a line of women waiting to be served. I joined the end of the queue, giving myself good time in which to study the man over the slabs of meat and tripe, of offal and joints. Two old women entered and stood behind me. I stepped aside.

'*Prego,*' I said, offering my place with a gesture. They smiled at me, one as toothless as an old dog, and shuffled in front of me.

I thanked my luck that I kept the car parked well away from the house, some ten minutes' walk from the *vialetto.*

He was dressed casually, not as a tourist but not quite as a local, either. He wore a dark pair of trousers, quite smart but not of Italian cut. His shirt was open-neck and striped with faint blue lines. He wore dark glasses—the morning sun was brilliant—but no hat. In the pockets of his brown jacket he sported a pale blue handkerchief.

This, I thought, is a man of some class, of some training if not in the best of schools. Not a thorough expert at the artifice of hiding but not a complete amateur. He was making efforts to do his job.

I wondered if he was not there to tail me but to warn me. I dismissed this reasoning. If this was the case he would be more conspicuous, more arrogant in his threat. His was not a blatant stance but a surreptitious one.

He cannot be an associate of my visitor. If he was, there would be no need for him to stake out the car. He would know of and stake out my apartment, hang around the end of the *vialetto*, make himself obvious. Maybe even play a game or two with me.

I had a tail placed upon me once, in New York, by a client. He knew I knew he was there. One morning, he tipped his cap to me. Another, outside Grand Central, he walked straight up to me and asked for a light for his cigarillo. He grinned as I replied that I did not smoke, as he well knew. He feigned a puzzled air and walked away. The next day, he stood beside me on the subway going up-town. The last time I saw him he was lounging by a pay-phone in the departures hall at one of the terminal buildings at Kennedy. I had checked my baggage on the flight and was queuing at the entrance to the lounge.

'Have a good flight,' he said as I passed him.

'And you a good day,' I answered.

We both grinned and he strolled off. I skipped the queue and followed him. He left the building, crossed a walkway to a car park and opened the door of a Lincoln Continental. The alarm sounded momentarily until he punched in the code. He started the engine and drove off. I watched him go from the shadows behind a bronze-brown Dodge estate wagon. On a bumper of his car was a discreet sticker. It read 'Mafia Car Pool.' It must have been the only car in New York to have the joke turned to a reality.

The shadow-dweller shifted as I watched him. He uncrossed his knees, crossed them again and looked up from the paper as if searching the street for inspiration. The crossword was presumably too difficult for him. He waved his pen over the paper but made no attempt to write. For a moment, his eyes settled on the butcher's shop but I was certain he had not seen me and could not. There was a sunshade over the window and the shadow would have prevented him from seeing in.

If he is not with my visitor—and I am certain he is not—then he must be a real threat. He cannot be a member of the international brigade of shadow-dwellers, the CIA band and the FBI mob and the MI5 club and the gang of former KGB. They are far more skilled and, in their own ways, far more obvious. He cannot be a foreign police officer. They go about in pairs like nuns and there is only one of him. Of that I am also quite certain. He cannot be an Italian. He does not look like one, behave like one, dress like one.

So, who the hell is he?

As on the previous occasion, I packed a picnic: two bottles of chilled Asprinio, a little like the Moscato in its bouquet but *frizzante*: a loaf of local bread, a round discus of baked dough; *pecorino* is not to everyone's taste, being so strong, so I packed two clods of *mozzarella*; 150 gms of *prosciutto*; 100 of parma ham; a large jar of green, pitted olives; as before, a Thermos of black, sweet coffee. For this I did not use a rucksack but a wicker picnic basket. We might have been part players from *A Room with a View*, my visitor and I.

The rucksack contained the disassembled Socimi wrapped in squares of cotton cloth.

We did not meet in the Piazza del Duomo, nor at my apartment. Instead, we arranged to rendezvous at a rural railway station down the line from the town, down the valley and not far from the road which climbs into the mountains and our destination.

The station was little more than a halt, one platform just two or three carriages long lying alongside a single track with a two-room station house. On either side of the line, the narrow valley rose very steeply, covered in deciduous forest. Two hundred metres up the mountainside opposite the station perched a small village of buff stone houses which looked down their noses at the concrete block buildings of the halt.

The station house was locked up. The road, which led only to the station, where it ended in a circle of tarmac through the cracks in which sprouted weeds, was slippery with loose grey grit washed down the hillside by the storms. Every so often, damp slicks ran across the road, where the mountainside was still weeping. A rapid, tumbling river coursed along beside the railway track, swollen by the rain and gathering a debris of branches and grass under a steel bridge.

The sun beat down on the Citroën. I undid the clips and slid back the canvas roof. The sun was hot on my neck and I put on the panama hat I keep on the back seat of the car. Expatriate Englishmen of my age wear panama hats. So do painters, even of butterflies.

The train was on time, a three-carriage local which rattled around the bend in the track up the valley, diesel fumes pluming from its exhaust like feathers from a knight's helmet. Indeed, the track ran along the valley which had seen the Templars march to fight for God and gold, tantamount to the same thing. The trees seemed to cower back from the intrusion of the leading carriage.

There were no more than a dozen passengers aboard. No one alighted at the halt save my visitor.

We shook hands. The train belched a honking noise and the diesels thumped. Slowly, the wheels turned, gathering momentum. The train rattled over the girders of the bridge and was quickly out of sight down the line, around a bend in the forest. The trees suddenly cut off the sound of the train.

'Mr. Butterfly. How good to see you again.'

The handshake was as firm as I remembered it. I could see myself reflected in the sunglasses, the same pair that had studied me at the cheese stall in the market, surveyed me over the top of *il Messaggero*.

'Have you had a good journey?' I asked. 'Italian trains are not my favoured mode of transport. Too enclosed.'

'Indeed. Yet the journey was quite enjoyable. From . . . Well, from farther up the line, the views are spectacular. You have chosen a very beautiful region in which to retire.'

The last word was said with such irony we both smiled.

'One never retires,' I replied. 'One merely fades away.'

She laughed and removed her sunglasses, slipping them into a pocket on the navy blue sports bag she was carrying.

Yes, my visitor is a woman. It is near the end now. I can let you know. By the time you can act, we shall be gone.

Perhaps you are surprised. Once, I should have been utterly astonished. Astonished and very wary. Yet the world has changed since I began in this profession. Women have taken their place in the world— bank managers, airline pilots, high court judges, movie moguls, multi-national corporate presidents, prime ministers . . . I see no reason to exclude them from our business. It is highly select employment, ideal for the manipulator, for the cautious and intuitive. There is not a woman under the sun who has not all those qualifications. All that will have to be done is a slight tweak to the computer of the Oxford English Dictionary, or Websters': *hit-man, see also hit-woman*. Perhaps the less feminine will demand to be known as *hit-persons*.

Possibly, it takes a hit-woman to kill another woman.

Do not think I am being chauvinistic. I am not. I have no time for the intrigues of human gender classification. It is a matter of horses for courses. Or fillies for fields.

I have brought some light refreshment,' she said. I opened the rear door of the car and she slid the sports bag onto the upholstery, pushing it against the wicker hamper. 'I see you have, too.'

'There is no reason not to mix business with pleasure. It is a beautiful day and we are going—well, you shall see.'

We got into the car, snapping open the windows and drove out of the station, the Citroën swaying as it went over the stone road bridge, the walls bounding back the stutter of the engine.

'You will be hard-pressed to make a swift getaway in this,' she commented, looking around the sparse interior. 'I would have thought you to have had at least an Audi.'

'The painters of butterflies are not rich men. Not the flash sort.'

She nodded and said, 'I suppose a 2CV is as good a disguise as any.'

'Where we are going, no Audi could pass.'

'It is far?'

'Quite. Say fifty minutes. High in the mountains.'

I waved my hand above my head. She looked up at the mountain range rising steeply over us.

'Up there?'

'Yes, but we have to take the long way round. There are no direct roads.'

She eased herself back, closing her eyes. I saw the lines form, the young lines.

'The train was tiring. One has to keep alert so much in cities, in trains, in streets.'

'I understand entirely.'

'If I doze off, forgive me.'

'I shall wake you when we are out of the valley.'

She smiled again, but her eyes did not open.

I drove on, wishing the gear change was floor mounted and not one of these ridiculous French inventions which pokes out of the fascia like a walking-stick handle. It would have been pleasant, just occasionally, to brush my fingers against her skirt.

Let me describe her to you. We are too far along the highway of my story for this to do any harm. Besides, how can you otherwise trust me to tell you the truth? Of course, we know each other, to some extent, by now. I suspect you can tell some of the truth from the untruth.

She is in her mid-twenties, I should say. Her hair is cut modishly short, like a page-boy's: it curls under at her neck. She does not have one of those masculine cuts so favoured these days by young women who would rather be men, wear dungarees and working-men's boiler-suits disguised as the latest in fashion. She is blonde now, not mousy-brown as previously. Not fair-skinned, though. She has a light tan, is not one of those lie-in-the-sun-and-burn creatures one sees prone on the beaches of the Adriatic. Her cheekbones are slightly higher than normal, her lips not thin, not full, enticing. Her eyes, when they are open, are a mix of grey and brown: the former hazel must have been tinted lenses. Her eyelashes are long, not false, and she wears only the lightest of make-up. Her wrists are delicate but wiry, her arms—she is wearing a short-sleeved blouse—strong but not muscled. Her breasts do not press against the blouse but snuggle under it. She has pulled her loose summer skirt up to her knees. It is hot in the sardine-tin of the Citroën. The ventilator system under the dashboard is useless. Her legs are shapely and, I should say, recently waxed. Her low-heeled shoes are expensive. She wears no jewellery except a Seiko wrist-watch on a metal strap and a thin gold chain at her throat.

If you were to see her in the Corso Federico II, you would think she was a secretary out shopping, a tourist taking in the sights, the middle-class daughter of middle-class parents making her way through college. She might be Clara but she is not as pretty.

For all her sexual experience, there is still an innocence about Clara. When she sits astride me, and closes her eyes, and starts to moan, there is still a naïve purity about her. No matter how frantic her movements become, no matter how loud her groaning, she is still a girl at the start of her womanhood, enjoying her romping sex and also being reimbursed for it.

Conversely, there is about my visitor an air of worldly experience, of careworn time having indelibly marked her. She looks young, half asleep in the Citroën as I start to take the first of the mountain bends, younger than Clara, even. Yet there is a definite depth to her which Clara lacks, a certain edge of hardness, a severity I cannot describe or directly point to: it is just there, and I know it. It has nothing to do with understanding this young woman's secret. It has nothing to do with being in the same profession. It is more instinctive. Just as the grasshopper fears the woodpecker which, in its brief life, it has never known.

I am aware I must exercise caution with my lady visitor. She may be a cute little blonde dozing in the car but she is as ruthless as a cat with a sparrow. If she were not, she would not be alive, would not be another of death's travelling representatives.

Once the Socimi is in her hands, I am redundant and, therefore, expendable. I know her secret, know who she is. I become a threat to her, although I do not know her name, her nationality, her address, her contacts and her ideologies.

As I turned the steering wheel this way and that, negotiating the hairpin bends, struggling with the gear-change, I thought of our first meeting. I prefer her summer dress and blouse to the austere well-cut suit.

'Are we nearly there?'

She opened her eyes and spoke like a child bored with a tedious journey by car.

'No. Another twenty minutes or so.'

I glanced at her and her head tilted to one side as she smiled.

'Good,' she said. 'I am enjoying my ride. In the country I can relax, and the sun is hot.'

She stretched back to reach for her sunglasses. I checked in the rear view mirror though I knew there was no need as yet. She would not be going for a gun. Not so soon. Her hand found her sunglasses and she faced the front again but did not put them on. Instead, she toyed with them, her thin fingers wrapping around and around the plastic frame. Then she pulled the sun visor down.

I should have liked to pause at the little bar in Terranera. An *espresso* would not have gone amiss. Yet it would have been too dangerous: two foreigners, in a grey and maroon Citroën 2CV, with local licence plates, pausing in the middle of nowhere to take coffee. People might remember, put faces to vehicles, recall snatches of conversation. As we came near to the village, it was our good fortune to come up behind a slow-moving truck laden with bales of waste paper. No-one notices one vehicle following another.

At the turn off for the track, I stopped.

'Just a precaution,' I told her as I stepped from the car and pretended to urinate into a bush. A car passed by on the road below, a red Alfa Romeo sedan. The driver did not look up. There were no workers in the fields, no sounds of human activity other than the Alfa Romeo changing gear four hundred metres or so away at a sharp corner.

We set off down the track. The rain had laid the dust and the Citroën made marks on the pristine surface. This worried me slightly. Still, the sun was high and the earth drying out fast. The tyre marks would soon seem old, the tread pattern smudged by an afternoon breeze.

Eventually, we reached the alpine meadow. It was even more glorious than on my previous visit. The rain had brought out a million more flowers. I stopped the car under the walnut, facing it uphill as before, and killed the engine.

'This is it,' I said.

She opened the door and stood in the shade of the tree. The bright sunlight was a worry. I did not want the vehicle to be seen. But she had had to come this day. I could not adjust the weather accordingly.

Stretching her arms, she asked. 'Those houses? Are they empty?'

'Derelict. I checked them last time.'

'I think we should do so again, don't you?'

'Yes,' I agreed, 'but I had better do it alone. There are a lot of adders, vipers, in these mountains. Your shoes . . .'

'I shall take care,' she replied. She did not speak curtly but I knew now she did not entirely trust me.

We set off. I walked ahead to flush out any snakes and send them slithering for cover. Arriving at the cluster of overgrown ruins, she halted and looked down into the valley, up at the severe stone crags behind, along to the little lake, swollen now to half again its previous area by the rain.

'It is very beautiful here,' she observed and sat upon a loose stone wall at the edge of what had once been a terraced field. Her dress dipped between her legs. She leaned forward, resting her forearms on her knees.

I made no comment. Taking my tiny pair of binoculars from my trouser pocket, I surveyed the valley. The tussock in the pond which had been my target was now six metres out from the bank and half submerged.

'You have tested the gun here before?'

'Yes.'

She paused and watched a lizard with a bright green and yellow head peer out from under a stone in the wall, observe her and dart back into the shade again.

'There is such peace here. If only all the world were like this.'

I sensed then this young woman with no real name was a kindred spirit. She too regards the world as a rotten place and seeks to improve it somewhat. She believes the elimination of a politician or someone of that ilk would go towards this betterment. I cannot help but concur with her.

'Tell me, Mr. Butterfly, how often have you been here?'

'Just the once, to test the gun.'

'You've never brought a woman here?'

I was momentarily taken aback.

'No.'

'Perhaps you do not have a woman in your life? It is not easy for us to keep relationships. Not in our world.'

'I have an acquaintance,' I replied. 'And, no. It is not easy.'

'Friendships are transitory.'

'They are,' I confirm. 'It is the . . .'

There was a movement across the valley. I caught it in the corner of my eye and put the binoculars to my face. I sensed she was suddenly as alert as I, scanning the tree cover.

'It is a wild boar.'

I handed her the binoculars and she refocused them.

'They are quite large. And very hairy. I had not imagined that. On the farm . . .'

She handed the binoculars back. I knew she had let her guard slip and wondered if this had been intentional, a careful moment of stage management in the little play we were going through together, as formally structured as a Greek drama. If I thought she was off-guard, then I might relax and she would seize the opportunity. The double-cross is not unknown in my world: many a gunmaker has finished his job and choked on a garrote or twitched on the end of a swift blade. Trust is not a matter of knowing how things stand but anticipating how they might alter.

Dusting the earth from her skirt, she stood up and we made our way back to the car.

'Which do you wish to do first,' I enquired, 'eat or test the weapon?'

'Test it.'

I lifted the rucksack from the boot of the car and placed it upon the front passenger seat.

'It is disassembled. I thought you might like to check it from scratch.'

She unbuckled the rucksack and began to remove the wrapped sections, opening each carefully as if the contents were made of porcelain rather than steel and alloy, placing them on their wrappings on the seat, careful to avoid staining the seat fabric with oil.

'Young's gun oil is such a heady perfume,' she remarked, as much to herself as to me.

I know what she means: that deliciously cloying, awesome, addictive scent of potency which comes with every firearm, lingers upon it like incense in a temple or sweat on a man's skin.

With an easy skill, she quickly assembled the weapon and put it to her shoulder. One would have thought she was familiar with the gun. It was strange to see such a masculine, powerful object pressing into such a delicate shoulder. Yet as soon as the butt touched her blouse I could sense the change in her, as I always do when I watch a client touch the purchase for the first time. She was no longer a blond-haired young woman with alluring legs and small, neat breasts but an extension of the gun and all it meant, its potential to shape her future, the future.

'Have you the rounds?' she asked, lowering the gun and leaning it, butt down, against the wheel of the car.

'I've made up two sorts,' I said, opening the front pocket of the rucksack. 'Thirty lead and thirty jacketed.'

'I should like a hundred of each.' It was an order, her voice emotionless. 'And fifty explosive.'

'That will be no problem.' I handed her the practice ammunition in two small cartridge boxes, the shells snug in little plastic trays. 'Will mercury do?'

She smiled then, a half-smile that did not activate the lines by her eyes. 'Mercury will do very nicely.'

She held the boxes of rounds in her hand and looked down without opening them. 'I have brought my own targets,' she said.

From her sports bag, she removed several pieces of folded cardboard strengthened with split bamboo garden cane. Without speaking, she set off through the alpine blooms. In her wake flittered a confetti of butterflies and grass crickets, and I could hear the frantic sizzle of the bees as she disturbed the flowers.

'Watch out for vipers,' I called after her, keeping my voice down in case it travelled in the mountain air: most probably it would not, for the air was hot and heady, but there was no point in taking risks.

She waved back to me with her hand holding the ammunition boxes. She was no fool. Neither was I. I had the gun. I had yet to be paid the second instalment of the fee.

At ninety metres distance, she stopped beside a pile of stones, over-grown with ground creepers displaying little purple trumpet blooms like those of convolvulus: they gave an aura of amethyst to the heap. It may have once been a field shelter, perhaps a boundary-marking cairn. She unfolded the cardboard but all I could make out at such a distance was a vague silver grey shape against the stones. Returned to the Citroën, she picked up the weapon.

'Muzzle velocity?' she enquired.

'Not less than 360. The sound suppressor takes at most 20mps off the top.'

She looked at the marks on the metal where I had scorched off the serial numbers with acid.

'Socimi,' she remarked with authority.

'821.'

'I've not had one before.'

'You'll find it easy. I've re-balanced it for the longer barrel. The cen-tre of balance is just a little forward of the grip now. It should not mat-ter as you will be firing, I would suggest, from a fixed position.' There was no reply to my supposition. 'You will find no major recoil problem,' I continued, 'and should be able to hold on the smallest of targets.'

She put just two of the jacketed rounds into the magazine and stood with her feet apart, braced. The breeze under the walnut ruffled her loose summer skirt against her tanned shins. She did not rest the gun on the car, as I had done. She was younger than I, her hands steady with youth and optimism. There was the briefest of 'put-puts'. For a moment longer, she held on the target then lowered the gun, holding it under her arm. It might have been a 12-bore and she a lady on an estate in the shires, shooting pheasant on an autumnal afternoon.

'You have done a good job, Mr. Butterfly. Thank you very much. Very much indeed.'

She made a minute adjustment to the telescopic sight with her fin-gernail. She could not have turned the vertical screw more than one notch. She fully loaded and fired again.

Putting my binoculars to my eyes, I looked at the target. It was the unmistakable silver-painted outline of a Boeing 747–400, about one and a half metres long. The top cabin was elongated. Painted against the cut-out was the upturn at the end of the wing. The front doorway of the aircraft was shaded in, the first class doorway. Standing in it was the silhouette of a man. In the centre of this were two holes. On the stone above the aircraft were the scores of the ricochets.

So was she going to bring down a passenger on an international flight, embarking on a foreign mission to alter the world, or returning from a successful alteration of the same.

With the magazine containing the remaining twenty-eight jacketed rounds, she took aim again. I watched the target through my binoculars. Put-put-put-put! Where the silhouette man's head had been was another scar on the stones. A few scraps of card floated on the warm air.

'You are a very good shot,' I complimented her.

'Yes,' she answered, almost absent-mindedly. 'I have to be.'

She filled the magazine with lead rounds, snapped it into place in the grip and handed the weapon to me.

'Go to the stones,' she instructed, 'and fire towards me. Say . . .' she looked around for a target '. . . into that bush behind the yellow fronds of flowers. Two bursts, say five seconds apart.'

I went down to the stones, turned and looked up at her. The Citroën was well hidden in the deep shade of the walnut. All I could see was her dress and blouse. This was not just a test of the weapon but also a test of trust. She faced me as I raised the weapon to my shoulder.

I aimed the Socimi at the yellow blossoms, held my breath and squeezed the trigger. The first burst was done. The yellow wands of blossom seemed untouched. I was sure I had aimed straight at them. I counted to five slowly and fired again. Through the sight, I saw two stems of golden blossoms fall sideways.

'That is very good,' she praised me as I returned to the car. 'The sound suppression is superb. I could not place the direction of fire.'

From her sports bag, she took another envelope, exactly the same as the first, plain brown manilla with no marks upon it.

'I shall require the rounds and the weapon at the end of next week. In the meantime, would you please tighten the adjusting screws on the sight. They are too loose. And lengthen the stock by three centimetres. I also want a sixty-shot magazine. I know it will be slightly cumbersome, perhaps upset the point of balance, but . . .'

I nodded my compliance and said, 'I had thought of a sixty-round mag. It will, as you deduce, shift the fulcrum of the weapon. However, if you are prepared to accept this, I shall do it. Quite easily done.'

'You have a case?'

'A briefcase,' I replied. 'Samsonite. The common pattern. Combination locks. Is there any number you should like used?'

She thought for a moment.

'821,' she said.

Very efficiently, she disassembled the weapon, wrapped it in its cloth squares and replaced it in the rucksack. I put the envelope of money in with it. She collected up the spent cases.

'What do you want to do with these?' she asked.

'I threw the last into the lake . . .'

As I laid out our picnic, she walked down the valley and I watched her toss the brass shells into the water, wondering if the fish would rise to them again.

Sitting on the blanket at the edge of the walnut's shade, she picked up the wine bottle and studied the label.

'Asprinio. I do not know Italian wines. It is fizzy.'

'*Frizzante,*' I told her. '*Vino frizzante.*'

'Do you come here to paint your butterflies?'

'No. I came here to test the Socimi. And to paint the flowers.'

'It is a good disguise, being an artist. One can be eccentric, wander off the beaten track, keep odd hours, meet strangers. No one regards this as extraordinary. Maybe I shall be an artist one day.'

'It helps,' I advised, 'to be able to draw.'

'I can draw,' she answered with a wry smile. 'I can draw a bead on a human head at three hundred metres.'

I made no response: there seemed none I could make. There was no doubt about it. I was in the company of a real professional, one of the best. I wondered what events she had masterminded of which I had read in the papers or heard mentioned on the BBC World Service.

She cut a wedge of *mozzarella*.

'And this?'

'Made of buffalo milk. Probably from somewhere in the vicinity of the little village near the start of the track.'

'Terranera? I saw buffaloes in the fields.'

'You are very observant.'

'Are we not both? It is the way we have survived.' She glanced at her Seiko. 'My train leaves the town station at a quarter to six. Had we not best be going?'

We packed up the uneaten picnic and set off up the track, the Citroën pitching and tossing over the bumps.

'That is a very beautiful valley,' she said, looking over her shoulder as the car made the first ridge. 'It is a shame you brought me there. I should like to have discovered it for myself and then, some day, retired there. But you now know . . .'

'I am much older than you,' I answered. 'By the time you retire, I shall be dead.'

As I pulled in to the kerb by the station, she said, 'I appreciate that you do not usually deliver the goods. But I cannot meet you as before. Would you meet me at the services on the autostrada thirty kilometres north on the northbound carriageway?'

'Very well,' I acquiesced.

'In a week?'

I nodded my agreement.

'Around noon?'

Once again, I nodded.

She opened the rear door and removed her sports bag.

'Thank you for a lovely day, Mr. Butterfly.'

She leaned in and kissed me lightly on the cheek, her lips dry and quick upon my stubble. 'And you must take your mistress up there.'

She closed the car door, vanishing through the station entrance. Quite confused, I drove into the town.

In the Piazza del Duomo, the market bustles. There has been such a gathering here ever since the town was founded: it was probably given its charter because there was a market here before there were buildings, a coming together of traders, of shepherds down from the mountains, of itinerant monks and healers, of charlatans and fakers, of soldiers of fortune and mercenaries, of bandits and horse-thieves, of the dice-throwers and the bone-casters, of money-lenders and sellers of dreams. The whole cosmos of humanity gathered here on the hill above the bridge where the road down the valley crossed the river and the trackways from the mountains converged. Why on the hill, you ask? To catch the breeze.

Little has changed. The horses are now Fiat vans, the stalls set on trestles not on barrow wheels, the awnings are garish plastic not hessian brushed with pitch, but the traders are the same. Squawking like aged crows, old women dressed in black squat behind the riotous hues of their vegetables, scarlet chillies, loden peppers, cherry tomatoes, berylial celeriac. Young men in tight jeans, charlatans, modern pardoners and summoners, sell not promises and releases from sin but cheap shoes, T-shirts, solar-powered digital watches and ballpoint pens which leak. Older men in vests and trousers hawk kitchen utensils, copper bowls, seconds of crockery, Taiwanese steel knives and cheap Duraflex tumblers. There are stalls purveying cheese and hams, salamis and fresh fish, brought from the ocean that morning, under the mountains by way of the autostrada tunnels.

Through this mercantile mayhem pass the travellers of life, the housewives and the browsers, the middle-men and the fixers of deals, the hungry and the well-fed, the wealthy and the poor, the old and the young, the cyclists and the Mercedes-Benz drivers, the have-nots and the owners of grandeur.

This is a crazy circus, a microcosm of the world of humans, of ants, of bees, of every gregarious species which has to exist in droves, crossing and criss-crossing their paths like those complex human dance patterns devised by the sports organisations of Socialist republics, never colliding and never touching, never in touch. Everyone knows their place, knows what to do, knows how to be safe in the ring and avoid the tigers and lions in the cage. A few venture inside the iron bars, crack their whips and come out unscathed A few go in and are mauled, caught in the jaws, tossed aside like rotten meat for the scavengers to tussle over. The remainder prefer to be safe, to clown about, balance on unicycles, juggle cups, eat fire, train seals to play guitars or chimpanzees to drink tea. Some test themselves on the high wire, swing precariously on the trapeze, but there is always the net, the brake on catastrophe. Those too fearful to clown or ride a gilt-edged pony backwards sit in stalls and applaud the inanities of the show.

Nothing has changed at all, not since the early market, the early fairs and circus. There is even a soldier of fortune mingling in the crowds of the Piazza del Duomo. He is not en route for the Holy Land, not one of an order of military monks. He buys only the few items he might need for his voyage towards tomorrow, for tomorrow is his goal. Or the next day. For him, the future is immediate, can be counted on a station clock or one of the cheap watches. He does not know where his road leads nor what it passes by on its way to his ultimate destination: he knows what that is; it is death. The hydraulic buffers at the end of every line. He simply follows the way, watching the shadows ahead for bandits, cautious of the charlatans, wary of the sin-eaters and forgivers of men, suspicious of the way the dice roll.

Watch him. He buys a thin salami, accepting a slice to taste before choosing. He smiles politely to the crone in the orange head-scarf with her sharp knife and greasy hands, bobbing under the salamis hanging from the roof of her stall like obscene fruit. He does not haggle. A man with no determined future has no need of bargaining. He saves his skills in that arena for the last great bargain of them all. To die quickly or slowly, with or without pain, humiliation, suffering or sufferance. He purchases a length of small bore lead-water piping from one of the hardware merchants. He tests the ripeness of the artichokes, the apricots and peaches, the peppers and the cucumbers. He sniffs the clean leaves of the lettuce as if they were the petals of an exotic jungle flower. Whatever he purchases, he pays for it with cash, low denomination notes, and waives his right to loose change. He has no use for coins or brass telephone tokens. They are an encumbrance, a weight to slow him down.

He crosses the Corso Federico II and disappears down the shadowed gully of a side street.

Who is this enigmatic person, this invisibility, this cryptically quiet smiler, this secretive man?

It is me. Yet it might just as readily be you.

The sun is high. Father Benedetto has placed an umbrella over the table in his garden. It is blue and white and has the logo of a national bank printed on alternate panels. A long shoot from the grapevine on the north wall of the garden has reached out to it and is trying to twist tendrils round the rim.

He has been to Rome, to the Vatican. He has attended Mass in St. Peter's with the Holy Father, returned with his soul purified and two bottles of La Vie, Grand Armagnac.

The peaches being finished now and the tree bare save for the scatter of late fruit which will not ripen now, we have before us half a kilogram of *prosciutto* sliced as thin as tissue paper. It comes from the stock of two dozen hams he has cured himself, suspended like the corpses of gross dead bats in the cellar. He smokes them, too: there is a smoke oven down there. It is against the law to cure one's own hams with smoke within the town boundaries. He does the work at night, dousing the embers and glowing wood-chips at dawn, or when there is a high wind. The law has nothing to do with pollution control: it has existed for centuries, to protect the monopoly of the burgesses and guild of *prosciutto* smokers.

'Americans are uncivilized,' he says, out of the blue.

We have not spoken for a quarter of an hour. This does not matter. We are not so unfamiliar with each other that we have to chatter all the time like popinjays.

'Why do you say so?'

'In a cantina off the Piazza Navona, I saw two Americans drinking cognac—*and ginger ale!* Such a blasphemy against Bacchus.'

'And you a Catholic Father!'

'Yes . . . Well,' he defends himself, 'one has to keep standards. Regardless of faith.'

He glances momentarily upward at the sky for forgiveness but the bank umbrella gets in the way. Not that it matters: I am sure, had I mentioned it, he would have reminded me that Our Lord can see through an umbrella.

'When I was in Rome, I dined at the *Venerabile Collegio Inglese*. Do you know it?'

I shake my head. I have always avoided the narrow Via di Monserrato off the Piazza Farnese. The brothers in my public school were forever speaking its praises, telling us boys of its beauty, of its tranquillity in the chaotic heart of Rome. Every anecdote they told seemed to begin, 'When I was at the English College . . .' Some of the boys eventually trod their way there, became seminarians and fathers to perpetuate the stories. I determined at a young age never to set foot near it. It was as much an anathema to me as the gates of Hell. I envisioned it populated with brothers in soutanes, devils in disguise who, like the music master, patted boys on their buttocks as they filed out of the choir stalls.

'I know of it,' I reply evasively.

'A curious place: you know, my friend, I think the English were never meant to be adherents of our Roman church. Wherever they go—even here, in Rome, where the college has the direct patronage of our Holy Father—they keep their own particular style of . . .' He pauses, his half open hand circling in the air as if to catch from the breeze the words he requires, '. . . being Roman Catholic.'

'What do you mean?'

Father Benedetto's hand circles for a few moments more then settles upon the table.

'In the college chapel, by the high altar, there hangs a painting. All Catholic churches have these, except the modern monstrosities.'

He stops talking. His dislike of twentieth-century architecture is so strong it silences him. If he had his way, the mediaeval would be the norm.

'The painting?' I prompt him.

'Yes. The painting. In most churches, this would be Calvary, the Crucifixion of Our Lord.'

He speaks the capital letters: like all priests, certain words act like charms upon them and when they utter them one knows they are reading block text in their minds, seeing their speech as if it was a decoration on a twelfth-century manuscript.

'This painting is of the Trinity. God is standing with the body of Christ in his hands. The Holy Blood of Our Saviour is dripping not to the ground but to a map of England. And there, on the map, kneel St. Thomas and St. Edmund. It was painted by Durante Alberti. When the Faith was proscribed in England, the seminarians would sing a *Te Deum* before the picture whenever a new martyr was elevated to the side of Our Lord.'

I make no comment.

'At the base of the picture are the words, *Veni mittere ignem in terram.*'

'*I have come to spread fire over the earth,*' I translate.

It might be my own epitaph.

I help myself to another sliver of ham. Father Benedetto's silver forks are thin, long-pronged like elongated tridents. They remind me of the frescoes in the little church by the ruined farmhouse.

'Do you know a church down the valley full of frescoes?' I ask.

'There are a number.'

'This is a tiny, squalid little place, hardly bigger than a chapel. Next to a farm. Almost a part of the barn.'

He nods and says, quietly, 'Santa Lucia ad Cryptas. I know it.'

'You are thinking of another. There is no crypt.'

'There is, Signor Farfalla. A big crypt. Bigger than the church itself. It is like an oak tree of the faith. There is more below the surface than above.'

'I saw no entrance.'

'It is blocked now.'

'But you,' I guess, 'have been in?'

'Many years ago. Before the war. When I was a boy.'

'What is there?'

'You will hear many stories. Perhaps you have already?'

I shake my head and say I stumbled upon the place whilst hunting out new butterflies.

'The crypt is huge. Maybe the size of two tennis courts. It is vaulted with thick pillars. The floor is made of smooth stones. There is an altar . . .'

He stops speaking, a faraway stare in his eyes. This is unusual. He is not a nostalgic. It disappears.

'As with the church above,' he continues, 'the whole crypt is painted. The colours are more beautiful than in the nave. There is no light down there. No sun fades the colours and the temperature is still all year. No matter what the sun or the snow.'

'How did you get in?'

'My father paid the priest to take us. We were the last to enter. It was sealed a few months later. The war . . . Now no one remembers it. They think the church is what they remember so they do not look for the cavern below.'

'What are the frescoes?'

He does not answer at first but sips his brandy.

'It was my visit there decided me to take the priesthood. It was there I saw God.'

I am immediately intrigued. Father Benedetto is not an impractical man, not a dream-monger. He is, within the bounds of his faith, a realist and it is for this I find his company congenial. He may revel in the magic of Mass and the mumbo-jumbo of the rituals of Rome, yet he still has his feet on the ground. His head is not entirely in the clouds of dogma and theology.

'You saw God? You mean there is a wonderful painting down there? A portrait? The frescoes above are pre-Giotto, I am sure. Is this even earlier?'

'About the same. But . . .' He is serious, suddenly very serious. 'I can tell you only if you swear to secrecy.'

I laugh. How Italian, I think: only in Italy can one be sworn to secrecy over the contents of a church. This is a Byzantine plot in the hatching. I have enough of that sort of thing for real in my life. It is only a day or two to the delivery of the doctored Socimi.

'How can you trust me? I am not a Catholic.'

'For that reason, I can trust you. A Catholic would want to open the place up, put a turngate at the door. Charge the tourists. Encourage pilgrims. They would hold services. The colours would fade. The whole business . . .' He still holds his glass but does not put it to his lips. 'So I can trust you? Not to tell a living soul?'

'Very well.'

'When you go in—I went with a candle, like a monk of old—there is no Christ. There is no benediction. There is no altar. It is not a holy place as we think of them now . . . What you see is the Love of Christ.'

I am slightly puzzled. Love is an abstract unless translated into action: Clara's breasts, Dindina's urgent wriggling. These are love of a sort.

'More precisely, you see what the Love of Christ can do for you.'

I am none the wiser for Christ has never shown me any love. Of that I can be sure. And I do not blame him.

'Tell me, Signor Farfalla,' Father Benedetto asks, 'do you ever think of hell?'

'Yes, all the time.'

This is only a half untruth.

'And what do you see?'

I shrug.

'I see nothing. I just sense an ill-ease. Like the first twinges of influenza coming on.'

'But in the soul.'

I have no soul. Of that, there is no question. Souls are for saints and pious fools. I do not want to argue this one through: we have already stumbled along this rocky theological track together.

'Perhaps.'

'What is hell? Eternal damnation? The pit and the flames? Like the pictures you have seen in the church above?'

'I suppose so. I have not tried to visualise it.'

Standing, he turns the nut on the umbrella, tilting it to keep the sun off the *prosciutto*. I think maybe he is also doing this to have an uninterrupted view of the sky over his head. Just in case.

'Hell,' I say, 'is like your cellar: dank, musty, dark with a fire in one corner and dead flesh suspended from the ceiling.'

He smiles ironically as he sits down.

'Hell is to be without love. To be without hope. Hell is to be alone in a place where time never ends, the clock never stops ticking but the hands never move. Do you know the writing of Antonio Machado?' He wets his lips with the armagnac. ' "Hell is the blood-souring palace of time, in whose most profound ring the Devil himself is waiting, winding a Promethean watch in his hand." '

'Bearing in mind this house of yours is off the Via dell' Orologio,' I remind him, 'and has a hellish cellar—and was once the abode of a watchmaker—I should suggest you might seek another lodging. This cannot be a healthy place for a priest.'

This supposition amuses him. I help myself to the bottle.

'I like to be alone,' I go on. 'There is nothing I prefer more. To be alone in the mountains with my paints . . .'

'That is not alone!' Father Benedetto interrupts. 'You are merely without human company. But the butterflies you paint are with you, the trees and insects, the birds. God. Whether you acknowledge Him or not. No! To be alone is to be in a void. Without even memory. Memories are a great weapon against solitude. Even the memory of love can be salvation.'

'So what do the frescoes depict,' I ask, 'that they can remind you of hell?'

He makes no answer. Instead, he forks some ham into his mouth and chews slowly upon it, savouring the flavour. This is one of the best hams he has produced in a decade of illicit stoking his private inferno.

'The frescoes—yes! They depict hell as men see it. Flames and demons, Satan in all his corruption. The three gates are open—lust, anger and greed. The dead are being punished for this. But . . .' He sighs. 'Their faces. They are blank. They show no emotion. They do not grimace at the fire, do not fight the heat. They have no memory of love, have no love to stave off the horrors, to strengthen them in their trials. To save them.'

'They had an inadequate artist paint their picture,' I reply.

'This may be so. But they are still without a past. A past of love. God has not touched them with love. His love saves us from hell. The memory of love can save us all from hell.'

I drain my brandy. It is time to go. I do not want to become embroiled again in the historical argument we always have. History simply exists. It is best to forget it, live for the future.

'You know,' I comment, 'the good thing about Muhammad is that when he invented Islam, he forged a religion with no inferno.'

'Perhaps this is why,' Father Benedetto replies with uncharacteristic wit, 'the Moslems eat no pork. They cannot smoke it without an inferno in their hell. When you eat *prosciutto* you are eating the fruits of Hell. To devour them is to destroy them.'

He forks a large slice of cured ham into his mouth and grins. He is eating the devil and all his works, he thinks, rending the evil one with his own teeth, savaging him. Later, the devil will pass the way of all filth and the concept of this is immensely pleasing to him.

'Two hundred years ago, my friend,' I advise, 'you would be accused of devilry, taking the hellish into yourself just as you take the flesh of Christ in the sacrament. It is just as well the Inquisition is over.'

'Then you should see me burn in the Piazza Campo de' Fiori. Like Giordano Bruno.'

'I should not attend. I have no wish to see you enter the flames of hell.'

'For me, there is no hell. I have the memory of the Love of Christ.'

'I shall let myself out,' I say. 'Do not get up.'

We shake hands.

'Come again, Signor Farfalla. Next week. Early.' He lifts his index finger in self-admonishment. 'No! On Monday I go to Firenze. I return on Wednesday. After that . . .'

As I leave the garden, I look back. It is a little Eden in which he is seated, pouring out another brandy under the shade of a beneficial bank. I pause momentarily. He is a good man and I like him despite his underhand attempts to drag me back into the smothering folds of his belief. I shall remember him always like this: the plate *of prosciutto,* a good armagnac and the blue and white umbrella over his head.

I park the Citroën by the end of the row of trees in Mopolino, stepping cautiously out to avoid the projecting roots and a fresh pile of dog turds covered with bluebottles. My feet grind on the gravel. The flies buzz obscenely in the air, hover about and return to their banquet. The door to the village post office has been fitted with a garish, red-and-yellow plastic strip curtain to keep insects out and the coolness in.

There is not one customer at either of the bars. I sit at the usual table, order an *espresso* and a glass of iced water and unfold the day's edition of *La Repubblica*.

For thirty minutes or so, I sip my coffee, glance through the newspaper and survey the piazza. I am particularly careful to observe the shadows. The sun is high and the doorways dark, the alleyways in deep shade—there are two leading off the piazza, one in the direction of the little church and the other leading out of the village towards a channel cut in the mountainside behind to divert either avalanches or meltwater away from the settlement.

The farmer with the cart and rotund pony arrives, the wheels squeaking. He halts by the other bar and offloads a sack of nondescript vegetables, gossiping for a few moments with the patron who has come out to pass the time of day with him. He departs and, shortly afterwards, a truck arrives and collects the sack. One of the two pretty girls walks past me and goes into the general store down the street leading from the main road. She smiles sweetly at me as she goes by.

As I drain my coffee, one of the dogs lying asleep by the trees sits up and barks. Another takes up the call with a staccato refrain of yaps. They are not barking at each other, squabbling as village dogs do the world over. This is not usual. I look up to see the shadow-dweller standing some ten metres from my car. He is wearing the same clothes as when I last saw him, only he is now also wearing a straw hat shaped a little like a trilby. It has a brown band around the crown.

He has seen me, is suddenly flummoxed, like a wild animal caught in the open by the hunter. He did not expect to find me also in the open, apparently at ease and taking a coffee.

Quickly, he turns and walks smartly back the way he came. I leave

my table and follow him, walking as quickly. I must get a closer look
at this man, perhaps have words with him.

Mopolino is not my usual terrain. I am out of my territory here,
not exactly insecure yet not entirely safe. At times like this, and when
I sense the faint smoke of threat in the air, I do not go unprotected. I
feel inside the pocket of my jacket: the Walther is there, the metal cold
despite the warmth of the sun on the material.

At the end of the street, a blue Peugeot 309 with Rome license
plates is pulling away from the curb, its engine revving hard. In the
rear window is a small sticker indicating it is a Hertz hire car. Like a
flash of *déjà vu*, I recognise the vehicle: it was in the street outside the
wine shop when I first saw the shadow-dweller. It was the car the
driver of which I saw talking to the old man on the day I went to visit
the derelict farmhouse and found the frescoes.

I return to the table and drink my glass of water. I am suddenly
thirsty, my throat dry and sore. I do not sit down.

He does not know why I come here, does not realise I use the post
office. That much is obvious. If he knew, he would not have blun-
dered into the piazza. As he is now out of the village, it is safe; so I
promptly pay for my coffee and cross the piazza to brush aside the
strips of bright plastic.

The old postmaster is behind the counter upon which he is
smoothing out a memorial notice to Mussolini. *Il Duce* is still remembered here with affection and the anniversary of his death is cele-
brated with black-bordered squares of paper pasted on street corners.

'*Buon giorno,*' I greet him in my usual manner.

In his, he grunts and juts his chin.

'*Il fermo posta?*' I enquire.

'*Sì!*'

From the pigeon-holes he takes an envelope. It is fat, was posted in
Switzerland but not registered, and separate from the bundle of general delivery correspondence. I recognise the hand which wrote the
address. I feel the weight of the article: documents for me to sign. As

usual, he does not ask for any identification. I place the fee on the counter and the old man grunts again.

There is no point in avoiding the Citroën. The shadow-dweller knows it is there, at the end of the row of trees, against the projecting root and the dog turds. I go directly to the car, get in and start the engine. I am in a hurry to leave the piazza which could trap me as readily as the ring of sand does the bull.

As I drive off, the old lace-maker from the doorstep shuffles by. She lifts her hand in a half-wave, recognising me. I wave back, almost automatically.

At the main road, I stop and look both ways. There is no traffic coming save a man on a moped, billows of smoke puttering from the exhaust. I allow him to pass. He wears a beret and is sour-faced. The blue Peugeot is nowhere to be seen. I set off towards the town, keeping a vigilant lookout for the shadow-dweller's motor. He is nowhere along the road. He does not appear in the driving mirrors. In the next village, which curves around the contours of the mountain, I pull in to the kerb by a small shop. I wait. The Peugeot does not appear. I set off again.

In the countryside, near the village of San Gregorio, where the fields are golden with a waving heat haze and shimmering wheat interspersed with patches of lentils and, occasionally, saffron, I spy the car. It is stopped, some way down a lane. The shadow-dweller has left it to walk along a path towards a small ruined Roman amphitheatre surrounded by poplars.

The shadow-dweller has not given up the chase. He is just inform-ing me he is not a threat to me at this instance and that he knows of Mopolino.

I halt behind a derelict building by the roadside. Now might be the time to confront the shadow-dweller. I need only walk down through an apricot orchard, cross the stream on a modern concrete footbridge beside an irrigation pipe and go on a hundred metres to the amphitheatre. He would see me coming and could have time to prepare for my arrival, but he could not plot an ambush. The element of surprise lies with me. I shall need to get close to him. The Walther is a useful gun at close range but not accurate over more than thirty metres even in the hand of a fictional hero. And I am no such shot, not by a long chalk.

This amphitheatre, with its round walls of thin red bricks and steps sloping like the terraces of a football stadium, its arena of short, sunburnt grass, was the place in which San Gregorio was martyred, the field of his final hours, his humiliation, castigation and pain. Perhaps it is time for the wheel of fortune to turn full circle. the ancient stones give new audience to another expedient execution.

Certainly, if I am to kill him, here is the place to do it. There is no one working in the fields and my shot, our exchange of fire, would go unheeded. Anyone hearing it would assume a man was out shooting birds. It would be an easy matter to dispose of his body. I could drive the corpse into the mountains and dump it in a gully, heap stones over it to keep the signalling crows off.

Yet I do not want to kill him unless there is no alternative. It would be untidy and someone will miss him, will come to look for him, will come to look for me. They will know he was on to something around this area, will follow up his tracks and nose about, start the whole process over.

It would be best to drive him off. I know this, yet at the same time I know such a resolution to my problem is unlikely. Shadow-dwellers do not just go away.

I want to know what he is after, what mission he is on, what is so relentlessly pushing him that he follows me but does not challenge me, does not draw near and pull his gun or flick the blade of his switch-knife.

Standing beside the car, my legs deep in wild flowers strewn about by the majestic chaos of nature, I realise my love of the mountains. I do, I know now, wish to remain here after the last commission is done, after the final farewell to the girl and her gun. This would be my haven, my final retreat after the years of wandering and working, of dodging the shadows and the shadow-dwellers.

Just as the girl is my last customer, so must this damned man in the blue Peugeot rental car be my last shadow-dweller. There must be no more of either of them. I want to be left in the peace I have found, regardless of what Father Benedetto may say on the subject. But the man in the fields below is going to prevent this, is going to ruin it all.

I am faced with the dilemma of him. There seems no way of resolving it. I kill him and I risk his confederates: I try to scare him off, he will only return, perhaps with others, in the sure knowledge that I am worth the hunt.

Right now, however, I must act in some way. Indecision is weakness. I shall move into the immediate future and see what develops. Fate will decide the outcome and I have to trust in it, like it or no.

The sun is hot on my head. The shadow-dweller is standing in the very centre of the amphitheatre, a single character in a drama all of his own making. As I watch him, he removes his hat, wipes his brow, replaces it upon his head and, although he is several hundred metres away, I can tell he sees me. I start off walking down through the apricot trees, but as I reach the concrete bridge upon which is spattered a trail of sheep droppings, I hear a car engine start up. I run to the end of the bridge and watch the blue roof of the Peugeot gliding by beyond the stone walls of the amphitheatre.

He does not want a confrontation. Either he is scared of me or he is playing with me, biding his time and enjoying my discomfiture: for it is no more than that. I am not afraid, just severely inconvenienced and angry. This I must control. Emotion is as much an enemy at times like this as the shadow-dweller. He will not face me in this uninhabited valley for it does not fit his plan. I shall have to draw him to me elsewhere, cannot risk him choosing his moment in the town. That would ruin everything.

I leave, drive quickly back to town and park the car in a piazza I have previously not used. From now on, I must leave the car in different places every day.

Back in my apartment, I open the envelope. The bank draft—typically in triplicate: the Swiss are so thorough—is there, awaiting my signature and presentation. An accompanying letter informs me of how much pleasure the bank has in dealing with my affairs, and appended to it is a statement of my account. I check the figure neatly typed upon the draft. It is, of course, correct.

My heart is racing, with anger and annoyance. I take a beer from the refrigerator and climb to the loggia. Here, I am safe from the shadow-dweller, the little red robin of a devil which squats on my shoulder. I sip the beer, it is cool and my heart slows, my anger dissolving. I try to figure out where he is from, for whom he is working, what his orders or his motives are, what it is he is planning to do. Yet there are no clues and for now I must ignore him. The delivery date draws near and there is work to be done.

There was, yesterday, a bit of a contretemps between the girls. It began after our love-making. I was lying on my back in the centre of the huge double bed. Across the Windsor chairs was spread our clothing and upon the dressing table was Dindina's handbag. Clara's shoes were next to it.

Dindina was sitting up on my left, running her fingers through her hair whilst Clara was to my right, lying on her side facing me. Her breasts were pressed against my arm and her breath, still coming in short pants from the exertion of our romp, was hot upon my shoulder. The dim street light in the Via Lampedusa was barring through the slats of the shutters to stripe the ceiling. We had switched on the lamp standing upon the dressing table, its bulb casting a rosy glow through the red silk shade to fill the room with warmth. In the tall mirror, I could see Dindina's front, her full breasts hanging slightly and swaying as she methodically combed her hair with her fingers.

Clara moved her head so that her mouth was nearer to my ear. Her breasts stuck to my biceps with sweat as she moved.

'Dear one . . .' she whispered, her sentence cut short.

I turned my head and smiled at her then kissed her brow. It, too, was damp with cooling perspiration. I could taste the salt.

'Your shoes,' Dindina remarked, out of the blue and in English. 'They are on the table.'

Clara made no response to this obvious fact. They were new shoes, made in Rome, purchased that day: she had yet to wear them and was proud of her acquisition. Quite why she had not left them under the chair with those she was wearing I did not know but I should imagine they were placed upon the glass top of the dressing table in order to catch Dindina's eye.

'On the table,' Dindina repeated.

'Yes.'

'It is bad to put shoes on a table. They have walked the streets.'

Clara did not reply. She looked at me and winked. It was a wickedly mischievous wink and I felt a warmth for her and her conniving gambit.

'Take them down.'

'They are not dirty. There is no harm and we go soon.' She looked at me for affirmation.

'Yes,' I said and I sat up. 'It is time. And I have a table booked for us in the *pizzeria*. The town is full of tourists.'

Dindina slipped off the bed. I watched her smooth, round buttocks move against each other as she walked across the room and, with a sweep of her hand, cast the shoes to the floor where they clattered on the wooden floorboards by the edge of the carpet.

'*Sporcacciona!*' Dindina spat out.

Clara leaped from my side and gathered the shoes up. One was scuffed where it had hit the floor. She showed the damage to me in mute silence, her eyes both appealing for my support and flashing with suppressed Latin anger.

'Only north peasants put shoes on the table,' Dindina remarked acidly as she reached behind her back and snapped the clasps on her bra.

'Only south peasants have no regard for riches,' Clara rejoined, deliberately replacing the shoes upon the table and tugging on her panties.

I wanted to laugh. Here was I, sitting stark naked, on a huge double bed in the top floor room of a bordello in central Italy, with two semi-naked girls arguing in English for my benefit. It was the stuff of Whitehall farce.

'Do not argue,' I said quietly. 'It will ruin a good night of love-making. I am sure,' I stood and took the scuffed shoe from Clara's hand, 'this mark will vanish with polish.'

Dindina and Clara said nothing but gave each other looks fit to kill. Whoever it was that first realised that a woman wronged is a dangerous animal, and I suspect he was a neolithic half-ape, was immeasurably correct.

We left the bordello, walking arm-in-arm along the Via Lampedusa and through the streets to the Via Roviano. It was a balmy night, the air warm and the bats audible in the sky. The stars were out so brightly one could see the strongest of them through the glare of the lights. Clara carried a plastic carrier bag with her old shoes in them. She wore the new ones to spite Dindina, who carried only her small black handbag.

Our table was by the window. I wanted this changed but the *pizzeria* was full: the patron shrugged apologetically. I was insistent and, in the end, he succumbed to shifting us to a table only half in the view of the street. I sat in the chair out of sight. To be on show in a window, like a mannequin or an Amsterdam whore, was tantamount to stupidity in my situation.

In truth, our love-making had not been so grand. Whenever the curtains of bliss began to descend upon me, to cloud over my mind and cut off the real world, a vision would dance in front of them, the shadow-dweller in the piazza at Mopolino, the shadow-dweller in the amphitheatre, the shadow-dweller leaning on a parked car as he had been when first I saw him, the shadow-dweller and the old man pointing, waving, pointing at me. I had to struggle to exorcise this Banquo's ghost from my sexual feast.

We ordered our usual: a *pizza napoletana* for Dindina, *pizza margherita* for Clara. I requested a *pizza ai funghi*. I was not in the mood for eating. Perhaps the girls' argument had soured the evening. Perhaps, somewhere close, was the shadow-dweller waiting for his chance. I should, I knew, have to be very cautious returning home. Night hides many things.

Conversation was not forthcoming from the girls. I had to make the going and it was difficult. They would talk to me, each of them in turn, but they would not address each other no matter how hard I tried to make them. In the end, I gave up, drank my wine and cut into my *pizza,* keeping an eye on those who entered through the door.

As the waiter brought my bill, Clara leaned across the table to me.

'I am sorry. I do not want to make you unhappy but her . . .' She flashed a dour look at Dindina. 'She insults me.'

Dindina, overhearing this and upset at not having taken the initiative of apology first, huffed and turned away. As she did so, she knocked over my glass of wine. It was only one-third full and that from the bottom of the bottle. I had no intention of drinking it.

'In the south,' Clara said in a forced tone of sweetness, 'it is the custom of peasants to spill wine upon the table. It is a custom . . . I do not know the English for this. We say in Italian, *pagano:* for ignorant people of no god.'

Dindina could do nothing in response. The waiter was between them, offering the bill, accepting my payment.

'Come!' I said. 'It is time to go. I must walk far into the mountains tomorrow to paint. To the only place where the butterfly I need to see lives. The only place in the whole universe.'

Normally, were I to make such a comment, Clara would want a description of the butterfly, knowledge of the location; Dindina would want to know how much the painting would be worth. Yet now, neither spoke.

We left the *pizzeria* to discover a queue of tourists waiting for a table. Looking up and down the street, I did not see him.

Dindina gave me her uncle-style kiss and I gave her her evening's earnings. I then turned to Clara with the same amount of money folded in my hand.

'No, *grazie*. I do not need so much today. For you, I love. I am no *puttana*.'

Dindina flew at her, her fists flailing. Clara dropped her plastic bag and raised her arms in front of her face for protection. I picked the bag up and moved aside. There was nothing I could do.

After a few swift but ill-placed punches, Dindina paused for breath. Clara took this opportunity and smacked her face. The blow was so hard, Dindina's head jerked to one side. She stumbled, half fell and regained her balance. Then she came for Clara, clawing and scratching and the two of them closed up, tearing at each other's clothes, pulling each other's hair, trying to kick each other's shins.

Their fury was both comical and terrifying. When men fight, there is an urgency to it. Emotion seems suppressed: the whole act of fighting takes them over with its coldness. With women, the emotions are as sharp and as obvious as the blows, the fighting merely an extension of the feelings.

The tourist queue broke up. This was a side to Italian life not promised in the brochure. They had not expected to witness such a local custom and they crowded round with all the avidity of a bull-fight audience. They shouted and chattered. They were joined by locals who enjoyed the spectacle as a form of free entertainment.

The fracas lasted scarcely three minutes. In the end, Dindina retreated. Her shoulder was bare where her blouse was torn and there were two gouge-marks on her skin beginning to weep blood. Clara was just tousled, her clothing awry but undamaged. Both of them were heaving and panting with the exertion.

'*Megera!*' Dindina ground between her teeth.

'*Donnaccia!*' Clara quipped adding, 'In English, we say *Beetch*.'

I stifled a grin. Several men in the crowd clapped and there was much masculine laughter. Dindina, not able to accept this loss of face, stalked off, bending painfully to pick up her handbag which had fallen to the gutter.

'Do not put the handbag on the table,' Clara called after her. 'It has walked the street.' She lowered her voice. 'Like her,' she said.

The crowd dispersed with a cruel joviality and the tourists re-formed their queue. I handed Clara her plastic bag and we walked slowly down the Via Roviano.

'That was not kind, Clara,' I mildly remonstrated.

'She fight first. She threw my shoes to the floor.'

'Not that, just your last remarks.'

She had been smiling with her triumph but now her mouth turned down.

'I am sorry,' she said. 'I have upset you.'

'No. You have not. You have upset Dindina. I doubt we shall see her again.'

'No . . . Will you be sad at this?'

'Perhaps . . .' I answered but this was a perverse dissimulation. I was extremely glad. It reduced the number of people to whom the shadow-dweller could make an approach, who could guide him to me.

We walked a little further and, as we passed a narrow alleyway, Clara took my hand and guided me into the darkness. For the fleetest of moments, my heart raced with instinctive panic. Such shadows, such dark niches in the walls of the town could contain my incubus, the shadow-dweller. What if, I thought, she was in league with him, that our relationship was just a ploy leading to this one moment of supposed emotion followed by the quick thrust of the Bowie knife or the jab of the hypodermic.

Yet her hand was not grasping but soft in my own. There was no urgency in her movement save that of the lover wanting love, and my panic subsided as quickly as it arose.

She halted a few steps in, dropped her plastic bag and pressed herself

against me, sobbing. I put my arms around her and held her close.
There was no need to speak.

When she was done crying, I gave her my handkerchief and she
wiped her eyes, dabbing at her cheeks.

'I love you,' she suddenly declared. 'So much. *Molto* . . .'

'I am not a young man,' I reminded her.

'This is no matter.'

'I shall not live here forever. I am not an Italian.'

As the words left me, I thought of how much I should like to
remain in the town, in the valley, in the company of this young girl.

'I do not want always to live here,' she replied.

I handed her her plastic bag again.

'It is time to go home.'

'Let me come to your home.'

'I cannot. One day . . .'

She was upset by my reply but decided not to press her demand.
We left the alley and parted in the Corso Federico II.

'Stay forever here,' she said as she kissed me. It was as much a command as a wish.

We parted and I made my way home by a very circuitous route. I
watched and listened out for every movement, even dodging into the
shadows once at the sound of a cat out mousing. The nearer I drew to
the *vialetto*, the more meticulous I became. Yet, despite all the avid
attention I was paying to my surroundings, I could not prevent a
recurring thought: Clara had fought for me, not for her shoes or her
bruised dignity. She loved me and wanted me and, I had to admit, I
loved her in my fashion.

But I had to concentrate upon the shadows, upon the doorways
deep in night, upon the alleys and the spaces behind parked cars.
Thoughts of Clara could not be allowed to interfere or she would be
the death of me.

The mercury-tipped bullet is so simple yet so utterly devastating. It is more powerful than the Chicago gangster's dum-dum, more deadly than a commando raider's soft-nose.

As I sit in my workshop, the music playing low in the background—Elgar, say: the Enigma Variations—I prepare the ammunition. Some is standard: the lead and the jacketed. The other, the explosives, I have to make.

It is a fiddly job. The cartridges have to be taken apart and a tiny hole drilled in the nose. This has to be held in a vice tightly enough to stop it revolving with the bit but not so tightly as to distort the slug. Once the hole has been drilled to a depth of precisely 3mm, these being Parabellum, it has to be half filled with mercury. This done, the hole is then plugged with a drop of liquid lead. At no time must the bullet get too hot or else it will expand and deform.

I have chosen to convert jacketed ammunition. It is harder to drill through the jacket than through a lead slug and refitting the bullet in the cartridge demands greater care and skill, but the result will be far more devastating.

Whoever it was invented this lethal adaptation was a genius, one of those men who see a simple fact and can extrapolate it into greater realities. The method of working is awesomely basic. As the bullet is fired, the mercury is compacted to the rear of the hole under the force of acceleration. It remains there until the bullet strikes its target. Then the mercury, being liquid, shoots forward in the hole and bursts the lead plug. This is released and spreads outwards like miniscule shrapnel from a tiny bomb. The mercury follows it. Bits of the jacketing peel away. The bullet makes a hole the size of an American dime on entry and a cavern the size of soup plate on exit. Or inside the target. No one survives such a hit.

My pretty young lady is going to use such a crude technology on someone.

As I replace each completed cartridge in the box, nose up, I think again of who it might be used upon. There are so many possibilities.

There are so many people alive in the capitals of the world for whom such a fate should be fitting. For many, it is too good, too noble, too quick. The light of life is on—then it is off. The heart pumps and stops. The brain sends out its micro-amps of electricity and is shut down, decommissioned as they say of wondrous power plants. The muscles relax into the last sleep. The hair, like a fool staying on after a party, continues to grow. Everything else begins to ungrow.

Yet I cannot agree with other methods. The slow debilitating decline into pain and puzzlement which is brought about by poison, or the ripping anguish as the saw-backed knife rams in and twists, or the blinding thunder as the bomb explodes, the nails and bits of wiring leaping out in a tangle of agonies.

These are not the way to do it.

I hum to the Elgar. The tang of molten lead hangs in the air and I open the shutters to dispel it. I am averse to poisoning myself.

I wonder what she will feel, the pretty lady in the summer dress, with tanned legs and a steady hand. What will course through her mind as her finger takes up the slack of the trigger and the metal parts dance in their clever choreograph? What will she see through the telescopic sight? Will it be a man or a woman, or the devil of hatred wearing a smart suit, stepping from the 747?

She will, I expect, see nothing. She will feel nothing. At the moment of firing, the hunter's mind is blank. She will not think of cause or consequence, of the chaos about to be wrought by her actions. Her mind will be utterly empty of thoughts and emotions, of fears and loves.

They say to kill a man with deliberation, with months of forethought and planning, is like dying oneself. All is silent. The assassin hears no reports, no screams or shouts. It all happens in slow motion, as in the movies. All he might see in the projection room of the mind is a single frame from his past life.

I wonder if the young lady will see the meadow of the *pagliara* as she fires.

I load the new magazines I have made, checking the three of them. Each magazine holds sixty rounds as requested. There are plenty left over. She presumes she will not escape, expects to be found and held at bay, determined to take as many of them with her as she can. She knows she will die, which takes a particular kind of courage.

Yet she will enjoy it, the sexual orgasm of killing. She will not be hiding on an airport terminal building or crouched on a roof. She will be squatting over her lover, her hands on his biceps, her thighs forcing his down and all will be in her control.

Was it not Pindar, in his Odes, written ten centuries before a Chinese sage mixed gunpowder, who wrote, 'For lawless joy a bitter ending waits?'

When I entered it, the pharmacy was not busy. It never is. I do not go to one of the larger establishments in the Corso Federico II, preferring a discreet little shop in Via Eraclea. It must be as old as the street, once the laboratory of an alchemist or a geomancer.

The shelves are old oak planks resting on stone corbels. Stone pins hold them in place. The wood is stained with centuries of spilt chemicals, potions, powders and concoctions beyond the modern medical imagination. I consider, as I stand before the counter waiting for the assistant to appear, that if one were to section microscopically a shelf there would be, open to discovery, all the strata of chemical knowledge.

On the topmost shelf are bottles which contain curious looking objects which I cannot make out in the half-light: they might be, for all I can tell, pickled stillborn babies or the antlers of chamois or twisted roots of hemlock. Below them are ranged medicines, cosmetics, bottles of patent cures, perfumes and lipsticks in display boxes. On the counter is the half-life-sized cut-out of a very pretty girl in a bikini holding in her cardboard hand a tube of factor 15 suntan lotion. She herself has faded somewhat from being previously stood in the sunlight in the shop window and now the tube of tanning lotion is a healthier colour than the girl.

The assistant came through a door at the rear of the shop. She is a young woman of about Clara's age, thin almost to the point of anorexia. Her face is wan and her hands bony. She might have been assembled by the geomancer from parts pilfered from the town's graveyards. She might be the ghost of one of the thousands of girls who must have come to this place to seek an abortion, gain a virile lover or rid herself of the pox.

'*Un barattolo di . . .*' I could not think of the expression I wanted. '. . . *antisepsi. Crema antisepsi. Per favore.*'

She smiled faintly and reached up to one of the ancient shelves. Her arm was as thin as a stick, as if she had been recently released from some hideous prison. She was, I thought, so like the cardboard sun-tan girl and felt a wave of sorrow pass over me. For the sake of a few weeks and good meals, she could be as pretty and comely as Clara.

'*Questo?*'

She held before my face a small tin of Germolene. I took it from her and twisted the lid off. The smell of the zinc oxide and the surgical pink of the cream remided me instantly of my public school, of the matron who pressed the stuff into grazes, rubbing it hard as if, by doing so, she was forcing us to repent for having disturbed her afternoon tea. I could see, as if through the mist of its metallic stink, Brother Dominic standing on the touchline and shouting incomprehensible orders to the scrum.

'*Quant'è?*' I enquired.

'Cinque *euros.*'

I purchased the tin and, while the girl sorted my change, rubbed a dab of ointment gently on a cut on the back of my hand. I had gashed the skin on the lathe, a foolish little accident. I sucked the wound as soon as it was made and took it as another sign that I am ageing, drawing near the end of my working life. Even a year ago I should not have been so clumsy.

As I slipped the tin into the pocket of my jacket, it thudded against the Walther. I am not used to having to carry a gun and momentarily forgot it was there. The tin reminded me and I shifted it to the other pocket.

I looked up and down the street before I left the pharmacy. No-one was walking on the cobbles except for two men strolling arm in arm and talking animatedly. I made my way to the Bar Conca d'Oro.

Around one of the outside tables under the trees in the centre of the piazza were gathered Visconti, Milo and Gherardo. Nearby, Gherardo's taxi was standing in the shade of a building, double parked before a row of vehicles.

Since the appearance of the shadow-dweller, it is not wise for me to sit outside. The tables under the trees can be approached from all directions and there is no way I could sit at one with my back to a wall. If the shadow-dweller was to arrive I might not see him and that risk I cannot take.

'*Ciao! Come stai? Signor Farfalla,*' Milo called.

'*Ciao!*' I replied in the usual manner. '*Bene!*'

Then Visconti shouted, 'Stay out! The sun is warm. It is good.'

He waved his hand about his head as if swatting flies, but he meant simply to stir the hot air that I might see its balm and join them.

'Too hot,' I answered and I went into the bar, sat down and ordered a *cappuccino*.

I kept a look-out on the piazza. A few vehicles drove by, cruising in vain for a parking space. Some students walked over to the fountain, removed their bicycles and pedalled away. Two men sat at one of the tables under the trees and the bar owner went out to take their order. They wanted nothing: just a place to rest. There followed a brief altercation at the end of which the men left and the patron returned indoors, muttering angrily. He grinned at me as he passed. He was pleased at his victory.

I ordered a second coffee and borrowed the patron's tabloid. The headlines, I surmised from the pictures and huge print, concerned a government scandal in which a minister without portfolio had been caught without trousers in the company of a lady best known for her tits on prime-time television. There was a photograph of her swathed in a tiger's skin. The caption, so far as I could manage to translate it, implied she had more than one tiger in her life.

A car started up in the piazza. It was Gherardo's Fiat taxi. A pall of diesel smoke was drifting over the bicycles. As I watched, Milo got into the front passenger seat. They drove away, Visconti stood up and walked across the piazza to the bar.

'So! Too hot for you, Signor Farfalla?'

'Yes. It is today. I have been working . . .'

'You take too much time for working. You should take a holiday.' He sat at my table and nodded to the patron, who brought him over a glass of orangeade. 'You been to the mountains, painting little friends?'

'No, not this week. I am finishing off some work at home.'

'Ah!' he exclaimed and sipped his juice.

I folded the newspaper and cast a quick glance outside. There was a man sitting at the tables. He was on his own, and facing the bar. I squinted. It was not the shadow-dweller. This man was old and stooped.

'My friend,' Visconti interrupted my vigil. 'I must tell you some-thing.'

'Yes?'

His face was serious and he leaned forward, pushing his glass to one side. He looked like a man about to commiserate

'A man has been here to ask a question about you.'

I tried not to look concerned but Visconti is street-wise. He is no fool. One man asking questions after another is always bad news in his books.

'Who?'

'Who knows?' He opened his hands then clasped his fingers. 'He is not Italian but he speaks it . . . so-so. Milo says he is an American because of the way he speaks some words. I am not so sure. Also Giuseppe. Gherardo took him in the taxi.'

'Where to? A hotel?'

'To the station. He waits then with the other taxis for the train. The man does not go to the train. He goes to a car.'

'What car?'

'Blue. A Peugeot. Gherardo tells me this to tell you.'

'What did he ask?'

'He ask for your house. He says he has important news for you. He will not say this news. We tell him nothing.'

I made no immediate answer. So the shadow-dweller had found the bar and the piazza as he had found Mopolino, but he seemed at a dead end in his investigations. He had not found my home.

'Thank you, Visconti, you are a good friend. And the others. Tell them for me.'

'I will tell them. But what does this mean?'

'Who can tell?'

'If you want help . . .' Visconti began but I touched his arm to silence him.

'I will be all right, my dear friend.'

'All men have enemies,' Visconti remarked philosophically.

'Yes,' I agreed. 'They do.'

I paid for my refreshment and left the bar, going back to my apartment in a very roundabout way, approaching it with all the stealth I could muster. It is only a matter of time before this damn man discovers it.

My only chance is to finish the gun before this: and that I must do for although my reputation matters no longer in that I shall accept no more commissions, there is my professionalism at stake, my integrity. Integrity cannot be compromised.

If he beats me to it, I shall be obliged to act.

Only the roof of the church of San Silvestro overlooks the loggia. Nothing else. There is no campanile, no square tower, no upper storey to which access can be gained but I assume there must be a way up to the roof: a tiny spiral staircase of worn steps perhaps, twisting upward in a cavity somewhere in the wall or a steep series of wooden ladders hidden in some far part of the building unseen by worshippers and tourists, rarely visited even by the clergy.

It is essential I discover the whereabouts of this access or ascertain for certain it does not exist. If the shadow-dweller is searching for my abode, the church will give him his best vantage-point. An afternoon spent on the roof with a pair of powerful binoculars could pay him handsome dividends.

The church is not, as it would be if it were almost anywhere else in the world, surrounded by its own grounds. There is no graveyard, no small 'garden of rest' or 'arbour of peace', not even a place for a clergy car to be parked. The north and south sides of the church are bounded by narrow streets, the walls protected only by granite posts to discourage vehicles from gouging the stone footings with their bumpers. Between the posts, deep scratches attest to their failure to deter. The western end of the church contains the main entrance outside which the puppeteer and flautist may be found. The eastern end, which is rounded, provides a steep wall to one side of a wide piazza. Against it are invariably parked a fan of expensive cars, for this piazza is noted in the town for containing the offices of three of the region's most prominent lawyers.

In effect, the church is an island of sanctity in the centre of a secular quarter. It is unapproachable without crossing a public thoroughfare: no one can clamber onto it from an adjacent building.

To be sure, I walk all round the church. It may be that there are restorations going on. The town was severly jolted by an earth tremor a year ago, and scaffolding maybe erected against walls: there is nothing, not so much as a window-cleaner's ladder.

In front of the main entrance, the puppeteer is at work, his squeaky daytime voice competing with the buzz of passing traffic. The flautist is sitting dozing in the shade of his umbrella, which hangs askew from the no parking sign. Roberto is standing by his melon stall, a blue haze of tobacco smoke hovering in the air about his head like bees about an apiarist's veil.

They have been joined by a pair of new entertainers. They appear to be a couple. The man is in his mid-twenties, handsome in an aquiline way with dark, flashing eyes. He wears a loose-fitting shirt like that of an eighteenth-century dandy or a Sixties rock star, and he has a large gold earring dangling from his left lobe. He juggles. According to his act, he tosses balls, empty bottles and eggs, with as many as seven in the air at once. Whilst juggling, he talks in a quick patter which has some of his Italian audience in stitches of laughter.

His partner is a girl in her late teens who squats or kneels on the pavement and draws paintings on the paving stones with coloured chalks. She has long, unkempt, dark hair which hangs over her face. Every so often, with a reflex action, she pushes this aside and greys her hair with chalk dust, tinting it vaguely with the colour she is using. She has a shapely waist but almost no bust and her bare feet are dirty. Around her neck, on a chain, hangs an ankh. She, too, could be a Sixties hippy not grown up.

I watch them for five minutes, at the same time looking over the crowd of spectators at their show and at that of the puppeteer. I do not see the shadow-dweller.

The steps up to the church are crowded. A party of middle-aged tourists is waiting for the arrival of a coach, sitting on the steps, standing in the narrow shade of the doorway fanning themselves. They are of various nationalities, each as easily recognised as flowers in a field. The Americans carry cameras suspended on straps around their necks; the men have the top two or three buttons of their shirts undone, the women lean upon the stonework of the church. The British sweat profusely and fan themselves with their tour brochures; the women talk to each other about the heat, the men stand disconsolately and are silent. The French sit on the steps. The Germans stand resolutely in the direct glare of the sun. The tour guide is a young man in a blue cotton jacket who flits from group to group anxiously assuring them their transport will be arriving imminently.

I push through the throng and open the heavy door of the church. As it closes behind me on a sighing hydraulic hinge, the clamour of the secular world is muffled and the delicate muted sounds of the holy world swell.

The church is cool and wide. The black-and-white chequerboard of the marble floor is loud under my feet, every footfall echoing upwards. There are no pews towards the altar, only a few rows to one side. Congregations are small. I stare up at the monstrous gold ceiling and inset paintings: the spotlights have been switched off for a shaft of sun is cutting through the air, striking off the floor and glinting on the carvings. An American, undeterred by the impending arrival of his transport, is lying on his back on the marble floor, the modern upended equivalent of a mediaeval supplicant, photographing the ceiling.

I approach the altar. Above it hangs a lurid, life-sized plaster Christ nailed to his cross, which is made of real wood. From his wounds and down the side of his bearded face drips scarlet plaster blood. The nails, it appears, are genuine metal stakes rammed through the sculpture. On either side of the crucifix are white marble angels ascending into heaven. The background is an oil painting of Calvary, with a brilliant blue sky in which hangs one black thundercloud. Beneath the cloud is a row of distant crosses, bearing insignificant figures who do not count.

I gaze at this rococo example of infinitely bad taste and then turn to survey the church, like a shepherd priest surveying his flock of sheep now that the bleating of the prayer is over.

The American has stood up and is brushing his trousers. A friend is frantically signalling to him in silence from the doorway but he has not noticed him. A woman in a shawl is making her way to the door.

She walks with faltering steps. A young couple are over to the side of the church, lighting electric candles on a display by inserting coins in a slot. They might be in an amusement arcade, playing a game. The coins fall noisily into the receptacle beneath the table.

There are no doors in the church walls. I pass behind the altar where there is a sacristy. It is a musty room filled with church garments hanging on racks, several large antique chests with modern high security padlocks, shelves of books and a desk littered with papers on the edge of which is a stinking cup of cold coffee. I look behind the rows of garments. There is no hidden door. The only place remaining which could cover an access to the roof is behind the saint's tomb.

I am about to leave the sacristy and go towards the lavish tomb when I see him. The shadow-dweller.

He is standing in the very centre of the nave as if he has just risen from the floor. He is almost looking in my direction. I duck back and look out from the comparative security of the sacristy door. He appears not to have spotted me. He turns, walks slowly across the church and stands before the tomb. The fluted pillars and gold flecked black marble tower over him and I think, in a flight of fancy, that if an earthquake were to strike now he would be crushed by the grotesque grandeur of the hideous edifice.

From behind the tomb appears Father Benedetto. He is carrying a dustpan and brush. The shadow-dweller beckons to him and they move towards each other.

I watch avidly, my ears straining to catch even a snatch of their conversation but they are keeping their voices low and any sound is lost in the immensity of the church.

Father Benedetto does not put down his dustpan and brush. The shadow-dweller does not point to the tomb, to the altar, to the ceiling. It occurs to me that they are not discussing the artistic or architectural merits of the building.

After a few minutes, the shadow-dweller shakes the priest's hand

and walks quickly out of the church. Father Benedetto goes towards the automatic candle stand and, putting his dustpan and brush down, fumbles under his soutane for the keys.

'Hello, my friend,' I say as he bends to the machine.

He is startled. Two people speaking to him in rapid succession is not common in the church. He stands up quickly. His face is pale.

'You!' he exclaims. 'You are here. Come with me.'

Ignoring his dustpan and brush, locking the money box again, he ushers me towards the altar and into the sacristy.

'A man was here asking questions about you.'

'Really?' I feign surprise. 'When?'

'Just . . .' He looks at the door as if he half expects the man to reappear. '. . . but two minutes. No more.'

'What did he ask?'

'For where you live. He informed me he was a friend from London.'

'And you told him?'

The priest looks at me with vague disdain. 'Of course, I do not tell him. How do I know him? He is maybe the police. Certainly not a friend.'

'Why do you say so?'

'A friend would know your house. Besides, friends carry no guns when calling.'

He glances shrewdly at me. I sense his eyes searching into me.

'How could you tell?'

'If you live in Italy and you are a man of the cloth, you meet many people. All kinds of men, of women. And I was once in Naples . . .'

He grimaces as if it stands to reason that anyone who has lived in Naples, if only for a short while, can tell the difference between a fat wallet and a shoulder holster.

So the shadow-dweller carries a piece. This puts a different light on the matter. He is no ordinary tail, for the man who carries a gun knows how to use it.

'What did you tell him?'

'I said I had met you several times but did not know you. I had never visited your lodging. He asked for your lodging, not your address. He asked if you came to the church. I said sometimes you came. Not too much.'

'Good.'

There is, I know, a sense of relief in my voice.

'It is all true, my butterfly-hunting associate,' Father Benedetto replies. 'I have not visited your home. I do not know of the location for I have not been there to see it for myself. I have only the word of Signora Prasca. You come sometimes to church, if only to look. And I do not know you.'

He smiles sadly and I touch him on his arm.

'Thank you,' I say. 'You are a true friend.'

'I am a priest,' he states as if this not only explains everything but is also a contradiction of the fact.

'Tell me,' I ask as I reach the sacristy door, 'is there a way on to the roof of the church?'

'No. Only God's way,' he answers enigmatically. 'You are safe.'

I leave the church with extreme caution. The tour group has departed and the entertainers are taking a break. Only the flautist works, his fluid music drifting in the hot air. No one pays him the least attention. I cross the piazza before the church, tossing a coin into his tin as I pass. For luck. I quickly descend the steps and, at the bottom, look back. I am not being followed.

Back in the apartment, I sit quietly and think. The shadow-dweller is no nearer to discovering me. No one appears to have betrayed me. Visconti has led the man nowhere and the others will know by now to keep mum as well. Father Benedetto has avoided giving the information without perjuring himself in the eyes of his god. Signora Prasca cannot have been approached for otherwise the shadow-dweller would know of my address. This leaves only Galeazzo and the two girls.

The former I shall speak with, spin him a line about a creditor or somesuch. Anything will do and he will be trustworthy. Of this I am sure. And Clara, too. Dindina is not such a safe bet though, not since she was so publicly belittled.

As the sun drops and the evening gathers outside the window, pulling its shadow skirts over the valley, I consider that it may be time to decide upon a hideout and any action I should take should someone sell me out.

The track up to the castle—the fortification which stands like a rampant, gray and ragged cockscomb above the valley—is very rough. Rain has gouged deep channels in it, and rocks as large as grapefruit litter the ground. The bushes on either side overgrow the way and necessitate driving with the windows closed. An added obstacle is the steep angle of the track which was made for slow moving chariots and horses, not the internal combustion engine. The farmers never come up here for the hillside around the castle is strewn with boulders and grass cover is poor. Furthermore, the two hundred metre cliff upon which the castle perches makes it unsafe for livestock. Only historians and archaeologists, and very occasionally rock climbers, venture up this far.

At the top of the track is a crude turning circle. I get the Citroën up to this, taking twenty minutes of grinding in first gear with several two-point turns at the hairpin bends. The hood, when I get out to lean on it, is too hot for the touch. There is a long scratch down the offside door.

I park the car under a dense tree and, taking my rucksack from the back seat, lock the doors.

From the turning circle, a pathway wends through scrubby, wind-pressed bushes to a stone bridge over the dry moat in which butterflies are thronging to a patch of yellow flowers. I ignore them. I have not come here to paint butterflies. The castle entrance, no more than a horse-cart width, is still sealed with the iron grid. The titanium steel chains and heavy duty padlocks remain in place as they were when I last came here, though one of the locks has been tampered with, unsuccessfully. The keyhole cover is wrenched awry. A few more fresh, as yet unrusted hacksaw blades litter the ground but the chains are none the worse for them. The bars have been jacked slightly wider apart.

They do not think, these modern invaders, do not credit the thirteenth-century builders with guile. The front gate is not the only entrance.

I rattle the chains as if by doing so I ring the bell. I am coming, I say to the ghosts within.

Around the end of the castle, just before the precipice, the moat comes to an end in a bank of rock through which a low, short tunnel was constructed. The moat was never intended to be water-filled and any water which might collect in it was allowed to drain off down the sheer face of the cliff. Yet from this tunnel leads off a second, at right angles, hidden behind an apparently unmovable boulder. It was a means of surreptitious escape in time of siege. It is about two metres high and a metre wide, with an arched roof and a paved, stepped floor. It rises through a series of sharp-angled bends at each of which are plainly visible the massive stone bolts upon which once stood defensive doors. Without hacksaw or hydraulic jack, one can gain access to the castle grounds armed with nothing more than a reliable flashlight.

I am certain no one alive knows of this entrance. Each time I visit, I place a twig across the passageway, a few metres in. It has never been disturbed.

Careful not to be observed, though I have yet to meet anyone at this precarious place, I enter the sluice and, switching on the pocket flashlight, start up the passageway. I step over my twig alarm. My footsteps are flat. There is no echo here. I arrive beneath a tangle of brush. It is easily pushed aside, and I am in.

The castle is built along a ridge. The area of the keep, some two hectares I should guess, is far from flat. In the centre, where the land is highest, one can look over the curtain walls which are still substantial even if crumbling around the few windows cut in them. Into the rocks and slopes of the hill within the fortress are what were once stables, workshops, storerooms. Above them were quarters for workers, for soldiers and serfs. The buildings are reduced to rubble now, with no walls higher than three metres, the hollow notches for timber trusses and stays in the stonework are crammed with the debris of birds' nests. Even these appear to be derelict and no longer used. Narrow lanes pass between the buildings, grassed over. Trees grow from within the stonework, spreading leafy canopies where once were wooden and tiled roofs. Creepers festoon some of the walls—ivy and a kind of clematis. Several fig trees grow out of the natural rock, spreading over the stone remains of men.

Higher up the castle interior are the grander buildings. Here were the lord's apartments, now destroyed completely, here a small chapel of which only the altar remains, cracked and subdued by the weather. In winter, this place is under snow. In summer, as now, the sun beats down as mercilessly as a plague fever.

At the highest point is a fortification. It, too, has all but crumbled away. Yet here the curtain wall is low, not from time's ravages, but from choice. Here there is no need for a wall at all. The cliffs suffice.

I lean carefully over, sure to have a firm handhold on the pliable but strong trunk of a woody bush. It is a sheer drop from my chin to a village below, tucked in against the base of the cliff. If I were to throw a stone outwards, it would surely arc out and hit a rooftop. I can see the pantiled roofs spread below me like a crazy patchwork, like the bleak fields of East Anglia, but painted reddish and viewed from an aircraft. The campanile of the church is not a tower but a protuberance. The village piazza is a dusty oblong upon which children no bigger than mites are riding bicycles. In the streets, in the shadows, a cube moves. I see the vehicle yet no sound rises.

I stand erect, step back from the brink a pace or two. From here, the whole of the valley is in view. I can see the town, far off to my left, squatting on its hump of hill like an Italian Jerusalem. I can just make out the dome of S. Silvestro and can judge the whereabouts of my apartment: somewhere in the haze lies my temporary home and the Socimi.

The builders of this place were like me. They controlled death. In the valley below, on the mountains behind, nothing stirred without their knowledge or consent, nothing lived save by their concurrence. Their enemies were treated with chivalry. Imprisonment was dishonourable. It was better to die. They killed and were killed, swiftly, with the vengeance of their gods bunched in their fists and forged into their steel. There was not a sword, not a spear head, not a quiver of arrows or a crossbow in this whole place which was not blessed at the altar.

I sit on a flat-topped boulder and swing my rucksack to the ground. A skink rustles through the tough grass and dead leaves. I see its tail flick under a stone.

For all intents and purposes, I am come home. Whatever I may say to Father Benedetto about the role of history—and he says to me—I have to admit this much: I am part of the process. It is just that I do not allow it to affect me. I accept I owe allegiance, owe precedent to the men who lived here once, to the ghosts who inhabit these walls and tangles of branches. They, too, were a part of the process.

For them, they were not shaping history, not letting it shape them. They thought only of today and the consequence of it upon tomorrow. What was done, was done. They existed to see things improved.

This is just what I am doing. Seeing things improve. Through change. Through the young lady in the skirt with my handiwork pressed to her shoulder and her eye to the 'scope. The future is, as youths say these days, where it's at. I cause where it's at to happen.

There is a great debt due to me, to the young lady. Without us, things would never change. Not truly. Not drastically. And drastic change is what moulds the future, not the gradual, tidy metamorphosis of government and law. Only floods cause the building of arks;

only volcanic eruptions the making of islands; only epidemics the discovery of wonder-drugs.

Only assassination alters the world.

And so I acknowledge now, in this place, high in the mountains of the Old World where the dreams began, where bees make smoky honey in the ruins and the lizards scuttle, where the birds wheel in the mountain updraughts and the thermals of the plain, the debt I in turn owe to men who blazed the trail of the spear, the trail of the sword and the gun.

I open the rucksack and spread upon the rock beside me a meagre picnic. This is no feast such as I took to the alpine meadow. Just a hunk of bread, some *pecorino*, an apple and a half-full bottle of red wine.

I break the bread as if it is the host of some long-forgotten god, some pagan deity. This is not the white fine bread of Rome or London but a local loaf, brown as the desiccated earth and just as gritty with wheatseed and the occasional husk which escaped the winnowing. I bite into it and then, in the same mouthful, snap off a fragment of the cheese. It is hard going on the jaw but satisfying. Before I swallow, I take a swig of the wine. It too is local: not the magnificent vintage of Duilio but a coarse crude liquid better only than vinegar. I masticate these flavours in my mouth and swallow hard.

This is what they ate, the men of the castle. Hard food for hard men, crude wine for fighters. I am only maintaining the custom.

Surely this is all I do, me and the girl. Maintain an accepted practice, remove those of power so power may be shared, re-assessed, re-assimilated. And, in time, when the power has corrupted, re-distribute it once more.

Without the likes of the girl and my technology, society would stagnate. There would be no change save through the gradations of politics and the ballot box. That is most unsatisfactory. The ballot box, the politician, the system can be corrupted. The bullet cannot. It is true to its belief, to its aim and it cannot be misinterpreted. The bullet speaks with firm authority, the ballot box merely whispers platitudes or compromise.

She and I are the vehicles of change, we are the lions of the veldt-lands of time.

I do not consume all my picnic. After a few mouthfuls, I stop and spread the food on the ground—the bread with the cheese beside it. Onto the parched earth beside the food, I pour the wine. The bottle empty, I toss it onto the rocks. It shatters in the sunlight like brief water. The sound of breaking glass is barely audible in the heat.

This, then, is my benediction, my offering at the temple of death.

I quarter the apple with my pocket knife. It is very tart. After the rough wine, its acids seem to skin my teeth. I throw the segments of core into the bushes. Many years hence, perhaps, there shall fall a harvest of apples in the castle.

Already, a thin stream of ants has discovered the food. Their tiny mandibles are at work on the bread. They are the ghost army. In each insect dwells the spirit of a man of this castle. They are carrying away the crumbs to stockpile just as the soldiers here stored loot within the caverns of the rocks.

I move across to a spot from which I can survey the entire valley across which the mountain summits are rising to meet the gathering afternoon clouds. The villages are becoming wraithed in a dusty haze now the sun is lowering its angle through the air. A thread is moving through the valley. It is a train. Minutes late, as it pulls out of a wayside halt, I hear the blow of the horn warning of its arrival.

The forests below the snowline are darkening. The trees are changing from their daytime lazy green to a deeper, more sombre hue as if night brings them out to discuss serious problems with each other: they are like the old men who gather at the village bars in the dusk to reminisce and regret.

The roads are busy. The sun is too low to strike off the windscreens but the main routes are a line of motion like the convoy of ants now working on my offering of bread and cheese. On the road into the village tucked under the cliffs there are cars. They are being held up by a motorised farm plough chugging along at a sedate, rural pace.

A horse and cart passes it. I see the rachis of filthy smoke pumped out by its exhaust into the still evening. The sun is catching the rocky slopes of the high mountains. They look old and grey yet they are young mountains, still growing, still flexing their muscles like adolescents arm-wrestling, reminding the men in these mountains of their frail fallibility.

There is a noise beyond the bushes behind me. It is a soft noise, like a quiet laugh. I am instantly alert. It is at these times, when the job is virtually done and the customer ready for the next and final rendezvous, the dangers occur of double-cross, cf betrayal. Those who are my clients carry no references, no credentials, no papers, no indentification. There is always the risk they might not be as they seem. So much in my world is dependent upon instinctive trust.

And then there is the shadow-dweller.

I slip nimbly to the rucksack and from the outside strapped pocket remove my Walther P5. Mine is a Netherlands police issue model. I thumb the de-cocking lever and, hunched over, move towards the ruins of a building in which is growing a sweet chestnut tree. The spiky orbs are filling on the branches. It will be a good nut harvest.

I am at the end of my trespass upon earth. If there are a hundred of them—and a whole brigade of *carabinieri* are more likely than two or three: it is the way Italians do things—then I shall take some of them with me across the Styx. But if there are just a few, and these are not Italian but British, or Americans, or Dutch, or Russians, then I stand a chance; they are trained in the schools and on the ranges of their services. I was trained in the streets. If this is the shadow-dweller, however, things might be different again.

I cannot believe he has found me here. I was not followed out of the town, across the valley, up the mountain roads. They twist and cavort like serpents and, at each twist, I looked back down the way I had come. There was nothing—not a blue Peugeot, not so much as a farmer's motorised plough.

There is no human sound. Now, I am acutely aware of every

noise. The murmuring, sawing crickets are raucous: the lizards scuttle as if as played through stereo headphones. I can pinpoint every source of sound. My pulse is the loudest.

I edge very slowly forward. There is a jag-topped wall before me. I study it for loose stones, branches which may snap underfoot, a bird which might disclose my position.

Then I hear it again, a mumbled voice. It is Italian. I do not comprehend the words, but recognise the tonal quality. There is no reply. Orders are being given.

If I can get to the tunnel, I shall be safe until they bring in dogs. I look at the sun. Unless they have them already present as a precaution, it will be dark before then and I shall be clear away.

There is a hole in the wall. Beyond it I can see a screen of chestnut branches. I decide to risk a glance and move forwards on my knees, slowly, like a hesitant penitent. I can see nothing. Not a movement. No olive green flak jacket, no dark uniform or shiny peak of cap. As my face nears the hole, more of the interior of the building and the trunk of the chestnut come into view.

The ground around the tree is covered in short grass. It might have been cropped by sheep and kept irrigated, so close and verdant is it. It is an oasis in the centre of a desolation of fallen stone.

There is the voice again. It seems to be coming from immediately under the hole in the wall. To put my head through the stones would be extremely foolish. Instead, I half stand and, checking to left and right to ensure I am not being outflanked, look downwards.

On the grass are two lovers. She lies on a green carpet of grass and leaves, her skirt around her waist, her legs apart. She is so close to me I can see the soft down on her belly and her fuzzy black V. He is standing a metre away, removing his trousers. He drops them to the ground beside her slip and knickers. He takes his underpants off and, as they reach his foot, he flips them upwards into his hands. The girl, watching this, laughs lightly. He lowers himself upon her and her arms encircle his waist, tugging his shirt up and pulling him down.

His white buttocks contrast with the tan of his legs and the small of his back. He starts to move them from side to side.

They are oblivious to everything, the tree with its prickle fruit like tiny sins, the bird calling at their presence, the rustle of the lizards and scratching of the cicadas and grasshoppers. If the whole garrison of the castle were to return from the Crusades at this very moment, they should not notice it.

I move back from the wall. I am not a voyeur. This is not how I get my kicks, thrill my senses.

Was it not Leonardo da Vinci who said, quite astutely, that the human race would become extinct if every member of it could see themselves having sex? There is something ludicrous in the sight of lovers screwing. There is no beauty in the thrusting buttocks and grinding thighs. There is an urgent animal delight, but this is not beautiful, merely absurd. All that is beautiful about sex is that, for as long as it lasts, it appears you are shaping the world. They believe, those two, that they are approaching their own Armageddon, their own glorious final sunset, their private nirvana.

This is the fallacy of sex. It seems at the time that one is so utterly indestructible, so completely omnipotent, so totally in control of the whole world. Yet one cannot control the world. One can only change it. Most people do not realise this. They are fast in the big sleep, lulled by politicians and power-brokers, by guardians of law and ranks of the judiciary, by game show hosts and soap opera stars, by lottery winners and ministers of faith: any faith, any god, the dollar or pound or yen, cocaine or the credit card. Most of those who realise their ability make no effort to exercise it.

I am not one of those, the power-dreamers, the waiters on chance. Nor is my lady client. We cannot control the world. We can change it. We are not in the conspiracy of the big sleep. And change is, I allow, a form of vicarious control.

There are other voices now, from elsewhere in the ruins. The lovers, who are finished, kiss and unhurriedly dress. Another couple appears, holding hands. They know each other and talk lightheartedly but in subdued tones.

I thumb the de-cocking lever again, pocket the pistol, go swiftly to my rucksack, grab it and head for the tunnel. A glance towards the castle gate shows the bars have been levered further apart: beside the grill, tucked under a bush, is a small hydraulic car jack.

I am out of the castle and back at the Citroën before the four romantics appear from the direction of the main gate, cautiously, watching out for a vehicle they may recognise.

'Good afternoon,' I say, politely and in English.

The men nod at me and the girls smile sweetly.

'*Buon giorno*,' one says, the other, '*Buona sera*.'

They have their car parked close to mine. It is a dark green Alfa Romeo with local plates. I have checked it over before they arrive: it is an ordinary private vehicle.

I start up my car and push the gear-shift. At that moment, an awful dread climbs my spine. I know the shadow-dweller has arrived. I look in the rear view mirror. Nothing. I look from side to side. Nothing. Only the lovers who are standing now admiring the view.

Can one of the two men be him? Surely not. I should have known, I should have been able to tell.

I start the Citroën down the track, the bodywork swaying uncomfortably. Around the first bend, tucked in below a thick bush, is the blue Peugeot with Rome registration.

Damn him! He has found me this far off the beaten-track, this unprepared. I am underestimating this son-of-a-bitch. And that is dangerous, very dangerous indeed.

I stop the Citroën alongside, take out the Walther and cock it. Now to see who this bastard is. I open the door and step out, the gun at the ready. In the distance I can hear the courting couples laughing.

The Peugeot is empty. No driver, nothing on the seats, no clues. I look quickly into the bush. He is not crouched there. I glance around the bush. He is up the hillside, talking to the lovers.

I shiver. He had chosen his moment and I was utterly oblivious of it. Save for the lovers' presence, he would have had me at his mercy: but for them, we should have had our confontation and the whole business would have been settled. One way or the other.

I take out my knife and deftly cut off the valves from two of his tyres, which will stall him here for an hour or two. He must have followed me into the hills, no doubt tracking my progress from the valley below with a pair of binoculars, but he will not tail me back to the town.

This may be somewhat surprising, yet it is a fact: a man in my line of business has a distinct, not inconsiderable pride in his work. You might assume, because my handiwork is usually temporary, used only the once and abandoned at the site of action, I do not regard it highly.

I do.

And I have a trademark.

Many years ago—I shall not say when, but it was soon after the commencement of my present career—it was my task to provide a weapon for the assassination of a major heroin dealer. In those days, a reputation having to be earned, I spent much more time on my craft than I now do. There is, I admit, a degree of eventual redundancy built into my present-day products, just as there is into every modern car and hi-fi and washing machine. It is in the interest of the manu-facturer to have a specific, designed obsolescence. However, I do not, as do the makers of cars and hi-fis and washing machines, produce shoddy work.

I was shown, at that time, a block of opium. It was fresh from the Golden Triangle, enclosed in grease-proof paper, the covering as neatly folded and sealed as if the package had been gift-wrapped by the counter-staff of Harrods. The corners were creased as if pressed by an iron. Upon this brick of visionary death was branded '999—Bewaare of imitatiouns.' It gave me an idea to which I have adhered ever since.

Upon every weapon I make, or re-make, in place of the serial numbers or maker's name, I engrave my own—how shall I term it?—cachet. There is a practicality to this apparent vanity: the engraving cuts into the acid-burns which eradicate the registration numbering. These days, forensic scientists can read an erased number with X-rays as easily as they do the newspaper but the engraving confuses this substantially. Yet I readily admit egotism plays a larger part here than protection.

When Alexander Selkirk, Defoe's supposed model for Robinson Crusoe, died at sea of fever on December 12, 1720, he left very little in his bequest: a gold-laced suit, a sea chest which had been with him in his island solitude, a coconut cup he had fashioned, later mounted on silver, and a musket.

I saw the gun once, long ago. It was a nondescript weapon, out of proof for sure. Yet he had carved upon it his name, the picture of a seal on a rock and a rhyme.

To put my name upon my handiwork would be to condemn me to the rope, the chair or the firing squad, depending upon which organisation or government found me out. Even a pseudonym was, I considered, risky: I was never one deliberately to seek a sobriquet like Jackal or Fox or Tiger. Better to be known as nothing.

Ever since, instead of a name, I have put the same rhyme on every gun I have fashioned.

Tonight, I am etching the Socimi with this little poem, burning it with acid, cutting the words first in wax. It is a simple process and takes but a few minutes, the wax being dripped over the metal and the poem impressed into it with a little steel brand I carved many years ago.

It is a simple little ditty. I have kept Selkirk's spelling:

> *With 3 drams powther*
> *3 ounce haill*
> *Ram me well & pryme me*
> *To Kill I will not faile.*

I have made mistakes and half-mistakes. I acknowledge this fact. Although I have done my best to avoid errors, they have occurred. I am only human. Every so often, I sit down and recant these blunders, recalling each one individually. In this way, I do my best to avoid repetition.

There was the gun that jammed, that winged the philanderer and nobbled the mistress. There was, on another occasion, an explosive bullet which did not explode. This did not matter, in the event: it was a head shot and the target was dead in any case. A wooden stock split on a G3 I was adapting. This was not really my fault. The G3 is not manufactured with wood but the customer required it. I found out why in due course, as a result of the international press. The customer was using the gun in a very hot location and he was afraid the plastic stock would warp. A foolish and unnecessary fear, but there it is. I make the guns, I do not dictate the orders.

My worst errors have not, however, been concerned with my craftmanship but with my own life, or the conduct of it.

Twice, I have stayed too long in a place. London was one, and that led to my having to bring about the demise of the idiot panel-beater. The other was Stockholm and the fault was mine. I grew to like the place.

I lie. I grew to like Ingrid. Let me call her that, though that was not her name, but there are tens of thousands of Ingrids in Scandinavia.

The Swedish are a humourless, sterile race. They regard life as an intensity to be experienced, not a rest from the slog of eternity. For them, there are no lazy hours in the bar, no strolling down the street with an easy gait and a Mediterranean nonchalance. They are like bulldogs, always up-and-at-'em, barking and making an efficient job of it.

For the Swedes, sex is a bodily function. Breasts are primarily for feeding infants, legs for walking or running on, thighs for bearing the next generation. Like their climate and endless coniferous forests,

they are cold, reserved, unremittingly boring and insufferably pretentious. Their men are handsome Nordics with blond hair and an arrogance borne of being a one-time master race. The women are
beautiful, blond, lithe, supple automatons who are as haughty as well-
bred race-horses and as punctilious as accountants.

Ingrid was half-Swedish. She had the looks and body of a Norse
goddess. Her mother came from Skellefteå in the province of Väster-
botten, three-quarters of the way up the Gulf of Bothnia, two hundred kilometres south of the Arctic Circle: a more god-forsaken spot
would be hard to find. Her father, however, hailed from Lissycasey,
County Clare and from him she inherited an un-Swedish softness, a
lazy voice and a loving nature.

I lingered too long with her. That was my mistake. I did not like
Sweden and I hated Stockholm, but she made up for much of the
frigidity of the atmosphere. There was something delicious about
going to the countryside with her—she owned the Swedish equivalent of a *dacha* two hours' drive from the city—and spending the
weekend snuggled in animal furs on a wooden settle before a blazing
pine-log fire, fornicating every hour or so and drinking Irish whiskey
straight from the bottle. Of course, I was younger then.

This idyll lasted for as long as I was working on a commission.
Once the work was done, I had planned to leave by ferry for Gotland,
change clothes and vessels there for Ystad, travel by road to Trelleborg
and catch the night crossing to Travemünde. From there I was to hire
a car to Hamburg, then fly out to London and beyond.

Ingrid held me. She knew I was going. I told her so. She wanted
one last weekend with me in the snowbound countryside. I let my
defences slip and agreed. We drove out in her Saab sedan and arrived
late on the Friday night. By Monday morning, she was still not ready
to relinquish me to the future. I agreed to remain until the Wednesday.

On the Tuesday evening, as we walked a few kilometres through
the forest and down to a lake frozen solid as stone, I sensed someone in
the trees. Conifers are forbidding. They hold a private night beneath

them like no other vegetation, deep and impenetrable: I have, since that night, understood why Scandinavian culture has such a pantheon of trolls, goblins and supernatural ne'er-do-wells.

I looked about. There was nothing. The thick snow blanketed the world and muffled any sound. There was not the slightest breeze.

'Why do you look about you?' Ingrid asked in that singsong accent of her parental land.

'Nothing,' I replied, but my ill ease was evident.

She laughed and said, 'There are no wolves in the woods so close to the cities.'

Two hours' drive was not, in my book, close; still, I let it pass.

We reached the shoreline of the lake. There were indistinct animal tracks going out across the ice. Ingrid announced they were a snow-hare's. Those beside them were a man's. A hunter, she decided. But the hare was heading out on to the ice and the footsteps were heading in.

I spun round. There was no one, but a low branch dipped and a thick rug of snow slid from it. I pushed Ingrid down into the snow. She grunted, winded. I lay beside her and heard the crack of a bullet. It might have been a bough snapping under the weight of winter but I knew it was not.

I pulled my Colt out of my parka and cocked it. It was a hunter for sure, but he was not after small game. I bobbed up and down once. There was a crack from the trees. I pinpointed the spot from the drift of blue smoke, almost invisible in the winter air. I rubbed snow into my woollen hat, edged up until I could just see over the snow and pumped three shots into the darkness under the tree. I heard a mut-tering groan then a sliding noise as if I had shot a toboggan. More snow fell off the tree.

We waited, Ingrid gathering her breath but losing her wits.

'You have a gun,' she murmured. 'How do you have a gun? Why should you carry such a weapon? Are you a police officer? Or . . .'

I made no reply. She was busy thinking. So was I.

I stood up, slowly, and walked towards the man. He was slouched forwards in a drift of snow, his body deep in the white softness. I kicked at the sole of his boot. He was dead. I grabbed his collar and turned him over. I did not recognise him.

'Who is he?' Ingrid blurted out.

I fumbled at his buttons and rummaged in his clothing. In his breast pocket I found a military identity pass.

'He is a shadow-dweller,' I replied, thinking of the trolls and goblins. It was the first time I used the phrase: since then, it has always seemed so appropriate.

'He is not dressed like a hunter. Why is he alone? Hunters always go in pairs, for safety.'

Hunters always go in pairs, for safety. In that she was surely right. He might not be alone. I removed the bolt from the man's rifle and tossed it far into the trees.

'Go for help,' I instructed her. 'Call the police.'

There was no telephone in the *dacha*. She would have to drive to the village six kilometres away. I needed her Saab. She set off, stumbling up the track we had made through the snow. I shot her just the once, in the nape of the neck. She twitched in the snow, her blood staining the white fur of her coat collar. She looked at a distance like a shot snow-hare.

At the *dacha* there was another man, standing by a black Mercedes-Benz sedan. He was holding an automatic pistol but he was not on the alert. The bleak winter and the snow-covered trees had prevented him from hearing our shots. I felled him easily with a bullet in the ear, removed the clip from the Colt and reloaded it. I then took my holdall and few belongings out of the house, smashed the two-way radio in the sedan and removed the distributor cap from the engine, burying it deep into the snow just in case there were others about. I then drove off.

I admit to crying on the drive to Stockholm, not only from sorrow but also from the realisation of my stupidity. It was a lesson well learned, but at a cost.

And now, I admit, I should like to stay here, in the Italian mountains, in a little town where my friends are loyal, the wine is good and
another young woman loves me and wants me to linger.

Yet my safety is at jeopardy. The shadow-dweller has come here. I
should not want Clara to follow Ingrid into the short but drastic cata-
logue of my expediencies.

In Pantano, in the village piazza, there is a *pizzeria*, the Pizzeria la
Castellina. They serve, I consider, the best pizza in the whole valley, perhaps in all Italy. One eats at tables on a patio overlooking a
garden of rose bushes and fruit trees. Upon the tables are placed simple oil lamps and a candle in a pot beneath an earthenware saucer
containing perfumed oil. This keeps the midges and moths away.

Usually I go alone, exchange a few words of greeting in broken
English with the owner, Paolo: he shows me to the same corner table
on the patio. I habitually order *calzoni alla napoletana* and a bottle of
Bardolino. This is a man's wine.

Tonight, however, I have brought Clara. Dindina has left, quit her
classes and the town. We do not know for where exactly. To the
north. She has taken up with a young man from Perugia who drives a
Ferrari 360 Modena and sports a solid gold Audemars Piguet wrist-
watch. He has given Dindina an old but servicable MGB. And so she
has departed the university, renounced the sisterhood of the whorehouse in the Via Lampedusa, gone out of our lives. Clara declares she
is glad, but I suspect her joy camouflages a bittersweet envy. I am
mightily relieved, for it places her beyond the range of possible contact with the shadow-dweller.

I park the Citroën beside the village fountain. On the wall above is
a pre-war Fascist slogan, the lettering now barely visible. It states
something about the value to the soul of working in agricultural
employment.

Clara is wearing a tight, white skirt and a loose blouse of maroon silk. Her shoes are low heeled. Her hair is tied back by a simple bow of white ribbon. Her skin radiates youth and health: I feel old by her side.

Paolo greets us at the door. I can tell from the look on his face he is surprised to see me accompanied by a girl many years my junior. He thinks she is a whore. He is, of course, half right, but I never think of Clara as such: that she works part-time in the bordello in the Via Lampedusa is irrelevant. I regard her as a young woman who likes to be with me, who likes an older man, at this stage in her life.

We are shown to my usual table and place our order. The lamp is lit and we are brought a dish of *funghi alla toscana* and a bottle of Peligno Bianco. The little dish of hot aromatic oil is placed over its tiny candle burner. Looking up, I see bats weaving in the near night, snatching insects attracted to the lights from the dark universe of the air. Taking the first mushroom from the dish I smell and then taste the fresh oregano with which the food is sprinkled.

It is the middle of the week. There is only one other table occupied. Paolo, a sensible host, has seated the other party of three men and two women at the far end of the patio. He deems it best the elderly Englishman and his Italian enchantress should be alone to talk of love and rub knees beneath the red tablecloth.

The *antipasti* eaten, Paolo's daughter brings out our main *pizza* course: we have both ordered *pizza quattro stagioni*. The pizza is divided into quadrants: *mozzarella* and tomatoes in one, fried button mushrooms in another, parma ham and black olives in the third and sliced artichoke hearts in the last. Over the tomatoes is sprinkled more oregano and over the mushrooms fresh chopped basil. I request a second bottle of wine.

'The four seasons,' Clara says.

'Which season is which?'

Clara looks at me in silence for a moment: this is not a puzzle which has occurred to her before. She thinks before answering.

'The tomatoes are summer. They are like the red setting sun. The fungus is autumn. They are like dead leaves and you find this in the autumn in the woods. The ham is winter when we cure such meat. The . . .' She does not know the word. '. . . *carciofo* is spring. It is like a baby plant opening.'

'*Brava!*' I congratulate her. 'Your imagination is as good as your English. The word you did not know is artichoke.'

I refill our glasses and we begin to eat. The pizza is hot, the oil warm on the tongue. We do not speak for some minutes.

'Tell me, Clara: if you were to become suddenly wealthy, what would you want to buy?'

She considers this.

'You mean like Dindina?' she asks.

I detect a tarnish of envy in her words.

'Not necessarily. Just come into some money.'

'I do not know. It is not to happen so I think nothing of it.'

'Do you not dream of being rich? After you have graduated from the university?'

She looks up at me over her plate. The light of the oil lamp catches in her hair, the sheen bright and sudden like tiny electricity.

'I dream,' she admits.

'Of what?'

'Of many things. Of being rich, yes. Of living in a fine apartment in Rome. Of you . . .'

I wonder if she adds myself as an ingredient for the sake of decorum or because it is the truth.

'What do you dream of me?'

Before she answers, she sips her wine. As the glass lowers, I see her lips are moist and know they are cool.

'I dream we live together in a foreign city. I do not know where this is. Maybe America . . .'

They always dream of America. The British dream of Australia as their escape, or New Zealand; the Chinese of Canada and California; the Dutch dream of South Africa. Yet the Italians and the Irish dream of America. It is built into their blood, into their national psyche. Little Italy, the West Side, Chicago . . . Ever since these mountains were drained of entire populations in the bad years of the early twentieth century, America has been the land of opportunity where the sun shines more gently than in Italy, the money holds its value and the streets are paved, if not with gold, then at least not with pavé blocks which jar a bicycle and quickly loosen every self-tapping screw in a Fiat.

'What do we do there? In this dream America?'

'We live. You paint. I swim and maybe teach children. Sometimes. Other times I write a book.'

'Would you be a writer?'

'I should like it.'

'And are we married in your dream?'

'Perhaps. I do not know. This does not matter.'

I cut into my pizza. The knife is serrated and slices easily through the tough crust at the rim.

This girl, it occurs to me, is in love with me. I am not just a client to be humped in the Via Lampedusa, a source of income, a means of paying the rent and the tuition fees.

'You are my only one,' she declares quietly.

I sip my wine and study her by the subdued flame of the lamp. In the rose bushes cicadas are grating their evensong.

'I go to the house of Maria but not for other men. You are just my one. Maria understands. She does not make me do other business. And now Dindina has gone to her man from Perugia . . .'

I am touched by this girl's naïve honesty, her innocent declaration, her keeping herself for me.

'How long has it been so?'

'Since just after I first met you.'

'But I do not pay you much,' I remark, 'not after Dindina has her share. How have you made ends meet?'

Clara does not understand the phrase and I have to put it in simple terms, avoiding idiom. She understands then.

'I do some other jobs. I look after a baby in the afternoons. Not every day. I type for a doctor. Letters in English. And an architect. In the evenings. Because I know English a little—this is because of you. You teach me so much.'

She reaches across the table and touches my hand with the tips of her fingers. There are tears in her eyes, glistening in the yellow lamplight. I take her hand in mine. Suddenly, we are lovers at a quiet table in a little *pizzeria* in the mountains. Behind her, a tree shifts softly in a night zephyr. The peaks of the mountain are darker against the night.

'Clara, do not cry. We should be happy, out like this.'

'You never bring me here before. This is a special night. Before we always go to the Pizzeria Vesuvio. In the town. Via Roviano. It is not a place like this. And I love you, mister . . .'

She lets go of my hand, sobs briefly and presses a handkerchief to her cheeks.

'I do not know your name.' There is such misery in her voice. 'I do not know where your home is.'

'My name . . Yes,' I muse, 'you do not know it.'

I have to be careful. One slip could ruin everything. Although it is, I admit to myself, a very long shot, it may be she is not just a pretty student who fucks, types and babysits: maybe she has been bribed to discover who I am to winkle me out of my shell.

I had heard that the *polizia* had raided the bordello a while back: rumour had it, according to Milo, a senior police officer caught a dose there and the bust was a revenge. They questioned all the girls present about their johns. Could Clara have been one of them and open to suggestion or blackmail, a bit of information in exchange for the tearing up of the rapsheet?

Gazing at her now in the soft lamplight, her eyes still glittering with suppressed tears, I do not believe she can be a stoolie and I pride myself on my judgment of character.

Yet I cannot bring myself to tell her the truth although I am sure, at this moment, I can trust her. Her love is as good a guarantee as there could be and I should like to tell her about myself, share the past. (The luxury of a soul companion has never been afforded me as it is to other men.) Yet, I have to consider I am old enough to be her father and, should she run off one day with a handsome young buck in a BMW, my secret would be out and my future blown to smithereens.

Beyond these excuses which I may be fabricating to defend myself, erecting a coward's enclosure, a bachelor's barricade, there is one other which overrides the rest. If I tell her even a smidgin of the truth, and the shadow-dweller finds her, discovers she knows something he might value . . . It does not bear the thinking.

'Maybe you do not give me your name or say where you live because you have a wife,' she almost whispers, a catch in her throat.

This is not so much an accusation as a fear being aired.

'I have no wife, Clara. Of that I promise you. I have never been married. As for my name . . .'

I want to tell her something, give her a name she can use. Despite myself, I am in love with Clara. To what degree I dare not attempt to assess. It is worrying enough that love exists at all.

'As for my name,' I repeat, 'you can call me Edmund. But this is just between you and me. I do not want others to know this. No one at all. I am an old man now,' I vindicate myself, 'and old men like their privacy.'

'Edmund.'

She says it so softly, testing it on her tongue.

'Perhaps,' I say, 'in a week or so, you may visit my apartment.'

She is radiant now. Her tears are evaporated and she smiles with a warmth I have not experienced for many, many years. She holds her glass out for more wine and I lift the bottle.

'Have you painted new butterflies, Edmund?' she asks with a smile, testing the name again as the empty pizza plates are taken away by Paolo. He winks surreptitiously at me as he bends to flick bread-crumbs from the tablecloth.

'Yes, I have. Just yesterday. *Vanessa antiopa*. It is very beautiful. It has chocolate brown wings with a yellow border, the colour of cream, and along the border there is a row of blue spots. I shall paint a copy for my clients in New York and you shall have the original. When we meet next time.'

Paolo comes back: he has, he announces grandly, a surprise for the joyful couple. Clara claps her hands together with delight as the two tall stemmed glasses are placed before us. Paolo also puts glasses of Marsala on the table.

'*Budino al cioccolato!*'

Clara takes a spoonful of the dessert. I follow. It is smooth and rich and both sweet and tart simultaneously. The bitter coffee and the sugary blend of egg yolks, chocolate and cream complement each other.

'This is very wicked,' she says, holding up her spoon. 'The devil makes this. For lovers.'

I smile at her. I can tell she wants to make love. This has been a happy evening for her and I am glad I was the bringer of her gaiety.

'Why have you never married a lady?' she asks suddenly, a dusting of grated chocolate on her lips. She hopes to catch me off-guard, but I am too wily for such a ploy.

'I have never been that in love,' I tell her, and it is so good to tell her a truth.

The ammunition is packed in silica gel inside the little round tins in which one purchases fruit drops. They are produced by Fassi, the confectionery manufacturers in Turin and could be custom-made for smugglers. Each is simplicity itself to reseal as they are merely closed with sellotape. Twenty rounds will fit in each container: the silica gel is not to prevent dampness, which is not a problem, but rattling. The explosive shells I put in tins with red cherries printed upon them: I like the symbolism. The rest are in lemon-flavoured. I have not eaten the sweets. I do not like such sugary concoctions. I have flushed them down the lavatory.

The case for the gun is no more difficult. I drive for the day to Rome. I have several matters to attend to there, one of them being the purchase of a Samsonite briefcase: I recall my client mentioning a vanity case but decide against this possibility. If I have to carry it to our meeting, I will look out of place. Casual observers will remember, under skilful questioning, the man with the lady's luggage. A Samsonite briefcase can be carried unobtrusively by either sex, and they are so popular the world over they draw no attention. Once the status symbol only of the high-flying businessman, they are now used by clerks, lingerie and double-glazing salesmen, even schoolboys, and they are ideal for my need. The polycarbonate shell is tough, the handle strong and the combination locks sturdy and tamperproof. The hinge runs the entire length of the case, the internal pockets fold flat and the lid fits into a groove in the base, making the prising up of the lid almost impossible and the interior reasonably waterproof. A thin smear of mustard in the groove also fools the explosives and cocaine sniffing machines or spaniels.

I do not have to be afraid of X-ray machines: my pretty client told me as much. Yet I like to make a traditional job of such a case. It is a matter of pride. From a photographic shop off the Piazza della Repubblica, I purchase half a dozen film protection bags: from a haberdashery-type store nearby, I buy several packets of hooks and eyes such as are used in the straps of brassières.

The case requires a false bottom. This is not difficult. It will only be there to fool a casual inspection. No one rifles through a briefcase. I line the bottom and sides of the case with the film bags, cut to fit. They are lead lined. Into the base I then glue pre-shaped pieces of firm grey plastic foam to form the pockets in which the constituent parts of the gun will fit. Over this is clipped with the hooks and eyes a false tough card cover on to which are pasted papers—several invoices, a few letter heads, a shorthand notebook, some envelopes. To any casual observer looking beneath the central flap of the case, the whole is stuffed with documents. A visit to an office suppliers provides the final touches: on the central divider are a steel ruler, a small stapler, a pair of scissors, a miniature dictating machine, a very small transistor radio, two metal pens and a thin plastic box of paperclips. With the lead suppressing any X-rays, these will all appear vaguely and are positioned so as to confuse the outline of the weapon. It is not foolproof, but it will do. One might as well be prepared.

It takes an hour to work out the best positioning but once this is done, I draw an outline of the plan, item by item marked so the girl does not need to experiment herself. I provide service as well as expertise.

Finally, I assemble the gun for the last time.

I am more than pleased with it. It is very well balanced, has a good feel to it. The inscription is clear but not obtrusive. I put it to my shoulder. It is a little short for me. I could not use it. I loosely point it at the basin and wonder at what, at whom, it will be aimed within the next few months, who will die by my handiwork and her practised application of it.

It is so good to hold a gun. It is like grasping destiny. Indeed, this is what it is. The gun is the ultimate destiny machine. A bomb can be ill-placed or dropped off target, a bazooka can over-shoot, poison can have an antidote. Yet the gun and the bullet. So simple, so artful, so utterly unperfidious. Once the 'scope is aligned and the trigger is pressed, there is nothing to halt the journey of the slug. No wind to blow it off course, no hand to halt it, no anti-bullet bullet to bring it down in mid-flight.

To hold a gun is to have a beautiful power flush through the veins, cleaning out the arteries of their fat and lazy cells, priming the brain for action, pushing the adrenalin up.

I should have preferred my last weapon to be a handmade one, not an adaptation of another's product. I should have preferred to have had my expertise pushed to its limits, perhaps being asked to make a silent, gas-propelled dart gun. I should have had then to make the barrel, to sleeve and rifle it, to forge and finish the mechanisms, design

the darts. It would have taken six months of work and relentless testing. It would have cost a good deal more, too.

Yet those days are gone. I must instead be grateful my final employment is to be used in the traditional manner of the assassin, a hit from
not too long a distance, with classic, time-proven explosive shells.

I dismantle the Socimi, placing it in its snug foam. The metal is
only slightly darker than the padding.

Setting the combination at 821, I snap the case shut and spin the
little brass wheels.

The job is done. I have only to deliver it, receive payment and
retire.

The autostrada is busy. There are long-distance trucks pulling slowly
up the hills, buses filled with passengers crawling past them, holding up the sedan car traffic. Drivers flash their lights like whores
blinking cheekily at sailors in a bar. In my Citroën, I am obliged to
remain behind the trucks, frequently smothered by black diesel smoke
and only passing when there is a free half a kilometre or the autostrada
goes downhill.

Despite this unpleasant inconvenience, I am in high spirits. The
contract is fulfilled, on time and to the agreed specifications. It works
well. This one will not jam.

As I drive, I gaze at the mountains through which the autostrada
wends, twisting along the contours of foothills, spanning gorges on
breathtaking viaducts, plunging through hillsides in long tunnels in
which are suspended vast, slow moving fans to shift the traffic fumes.

This is a good place to live. The sun shines cleanly down, the summer rains are warm, the snows in winter pristine, the mountains
young and sharp and beautiful. In autumn, the wooded hillsides turn
to delicate hues of chestnut and oaken mahogany and in spring the
lentil fields in the high valleys are a patchwork of green. I like it here
within my little coterie of companions.

I allow my mind to wander. If I was to marry Clara, I would be even closer to them. Father Benedetto would be pleased to see me joined so, Galeazzo would share my happiness and probably re-marry himself under the influence of my evident joy, Visconti and the others would rejoice that I had joined them in their matriarchal state of slavery.

Yet the shadow-dweller puts all this in jeopardy. I curse him as I pull out to overtake a truck. He is the only fly in my ointment, he will not go away of his own volition, not until he has achieved his goal, whatever that may be.

All through my journey, I watch the autostrada. On the long straights, I look backwards and forwards: one can be followed from the front, if the tracker is experienced. I do not see any blue Peugeots, not even in the opposite carriageway.

It takes me a little over forty-five minutes to reach the service centre and my rendezvous. My client is correct. There is a back way into the services but I have elected not to arrive that way but to exit through it. I suspect she will do the same.

The services consist of a large petrol station with several rows of Agip and Q8 pumps, a convenience shop, a repair garage and a café selling soft drinks, coffee and buns. The car park is not large. I stop the Citroën in a slot, facing the illegal exit. There is a single bar across it but I notice this is raised and wonder if the girl did this or if she has an accomplice with her who might assist in such matters, who has already arrived.

The possibility of a second person makes me vigilant. I slip the Walther into my jacket pocket, checking first the magazine is full. Stepping out of the Citroën, I look around the car park. No blue Peugeot 309. I take the case from the rear seat and walk away. I do not lock the car, although I make a play of doing so. I want to be able to make a rapid getaway if necessary.

Inside the café, I sit at a table near the window and place the case on the chair beside me: I put a paper bag on the table next to the sugar dispenser. From here, I can see the Citroën and most of the parking lot. I am a few minutes early and order an *espresso*. Nevertheless, before the coffee is served, the girl is at my table. Today, she is dressed in a tight black skirt, a simple blue blouse and a dark blue jacket. Her flat shoes are polished, her makeup immaculate and heavier than I have seen her wear before. She looks like the kind of lady who would carry a Samsonite briefcase.

'Hello. I see you have brought it in from the car with you.'

She speaks quietly, her voice low and attractive.

'All there, as agreed.'

'And the paper bag?'

The waitress comes over with my coffee and the girl orders another for herself.

'Sweets. For your journey.'

She opens the bag and takes out one of the tins. She can immediately feel it is heavier than it should be.

'That is most thoughtful of you. Someone will enjoy them.'

'Will you not taste them?' I ask.

'No. They are for another, somebody who has, I am told, a sweet tooth.'

She smiles at me and I sip at my coffee. The waitress returns with the second coffee and I pay for them both.

She stirs her coffee to cool it. She is in a hurry. Such a place is a good rendezvous. Everyone is in a hurry here.

'I do not know the hit,' she admits quietly. 'I shall not be the . . .' She pauses to search for an appropriate phrase. '. . . end user.'

This is, to me, something of a small quandary; the gun was made for her, to fit her arm, her shoulder, her strength. I had assumed all along that she was to be the one to use it.

'I did work to your personal measurements.'

I sound like a bespoke tailor addressing a customer who has just taken delivery of a new suit.

'Those were my instructions,' she explains.

'I suppose I shall read of the event in the *Times* or the *International Herald Tribune*,' I say. 'Or *Il Messaggero*'.

For a moment, she is pensive then replies, 'Yes, I expect so.'

She drinks her coffee, holds her cup in mid-air and looks out of the window. I casually follow her gaze to assure myself she is not signalling to an accomplice. She replaces her cup on the saucer. I am confident she has not communicated with another.

'They say this is your last job.'

I nod.

'They?' I enquire.

She smiles once more and says, 'You know. The world. Those who know of you . . . Are you sad?'

I make no reply. It has not occurred to me to be sad. Life will merely be different from now on.

'Not really,' I reply candidly, yet perhaps I am: sad at relinquishing my position as the world's acknowledged best in my profession. Sad at having my desire to remain in these mountains thwarted.

'Tell me,' I ask her, 'have you put a tail on me? A minder?'

She gives a brief, hard stare.

'I did not think that was necessary. Your reputation . . .'

'Quite. But someone has. I feel I should tell you.'

'I see.' She is thoughtful for a moment. 'A description?'

'Young, male, white: slim, about your height, I should say. Brown hair. I have not been closer. He drives a blue Peugeot 309 with Rome plates.'

'This must be your problem, not ours,' she answers positively. 'But thank you for the warning.'

She drinks the rest of her coffee.

'I am just going to the ladies,' she says, standing up. 'Wait here.'

She picks up the briefcase. There is nothing I can do about this. She has grasped the initiative, taken advantage of me and I have been caught napping, wrong-footed. Perhaps, I readily convince myself, the time most definitely has come for me to retire. I wait. I can do nothing else. It is now all down to trust and distrust. I have my hand on the Walther in my pocket and carefully survey the car park, the door to the lavatory at the end of the café and the other customers.

After a few minutes, she returns.

'Shall we go?'

This is not a suggestion but a command. I am obliged to stand up and we leave.

'You don't need your piece,' she comments as we walk towards the parked cars. Her use of the noun is almost comical. This might be the scene from a television detective show.

'One never knows.'

'True, but I see no blue Peugeot here.'

She stops beside a large Ford. Seated at the wheel is a man. He has short blond hair and wears Ray-Ban sunglasses of the type US highway patrolmen use. The electric window whirs open.

'Hi!' he greets me. He is possibly an American.

'Hello.'

I still have my hand on the Walther in my pocket. Both his hands are on the steering wheel. He is familiar with the conventions of our business world and abides by them.

'Okay?' he enquires of the girl.

'Everything's just fine,' she says. I wonder then if she too is an American.

His right hand slips out of sight. I twist my wrist upwards and thumb the cocking lever. At such short range, the slug will easily penetrate the door, retracted window, interior trim and his rib cage.

'Final payment.'

He hands me the envelope. It feels right.

'We've added another six grand,' she says. 'You can buy yourself a retirement clock.'

To my amazement, she leans forward and kisses me lightly and quickly on the cheek, her lips dry. It could have been a trick and I was totally unprepared for it.

'Have you taken your mistress up to the meadow yet?'

'No. I have not.'

'Do it.'

Not *Do so. Do it.* So she is an American, after all.

The Ford starts up. She gets into the front seat and swings the briefcase into the back.

'Goodbye,' she calls. 'Take care, y'hear?'

The driver raises a hand in farewell.

The car reverses, pulls away and disappears down the slip-road onto the autostrada. I relax, thumb back the lever on the Walther, go to the Citroën, get in and drive off under the raised pole and on to a country road.

The road twists through vineyards. I keep my concentration despite the desire to relax. The gun is gone. I am in retirement. Yet I am not. Like the man who has to return the day after his company party to clear his desk, I have to see to my final affairs, the shadow-dweller. Only when he has gone, or I have escaped him, will it be over.

Two hours later in the apartment, after a circuitous route back, I very carefully open the envelope. There are no wires adhering to sticky tape, no tricks and six thousand extra US dollars. Americans are such a perplexing people.

On my way to my apartment from the Banco di Roma in the Corso Federico II, I am accosted by Galeazzo. He insists I come immediately to his shop. He has brought a new consignment of books up from his secret source in the south. They have arrived by truck in four small tea chests upon the sides of which are stencilled 'Best Ceylon Tea'.

'These cases were owned by the old lady. She is getting rid of many of her books now. She is dying and wants to go without encumbrance.'

'A colonial dame,' I remark, observing the tea chests which are lined with tin foil.

'I want to show you these,' Galeazzo says and he lifts from the table by the window one of a six volume set. 'It will interest you.'

The book is bound in green cloth with a leather spine blocked in gold. I hold it to the sunlight. It is a volume of Boswell's *Life of Johnson,* edited by Hill. I open the book at the title page and see it is the Oxford University Press edition of 1887.

'You have the set?'

'All of them.'

He pats the pile on the table.

'Worth having.'

'More so! Look inside the cover.'

I open the volume again: on the dark green endpaper is a white bookplate printed from a steel engraving. On either side are printed daffodils. In the distance between them are hills and a smoky city with a river wending to the foreground where stands, behind a scroll, the Houses of Parliament and Big Ben. On the scroll is printed, *One of the books of David Lloyd George.*

The arrogance of this old womaniser, this political tightrope walker, this Liberal do-gooder and philanderer astounds me. The peasant Welshman, the miners' Dick Whittington, has inscribed his entire library with this motif of his conceit. How small men risen to the thrones of politics like to puff themselves up like peacocks. How like peacocks they are, all colours and feathers and nothing more.

'What do you think?' Galeazzo asks.

'I think,' I reply, 'this is a masterful expression of the absurdity of power.'

Galeazzo is plainly crestfallen. He was hoping for praise at his bookbuying find, his bibliophilic success. I try to reassure him.

'As a purchase, it is of course a triumph. To find such a complete set, in southern Italy, in such fine condition, is the proof of a true book-hunter at work. Still, it is the most obscene and pornographic book in your shop.'

Knowing Galeazzo to have a private collection of Italian erotic literature, most of it illustrated quite graphically, in his bedroom, to not a single volume of which I have been privy, this statement has the desired effect. He stares at me as if I am a buffoon.

'This is literature,' he exclaims. 'The best of literature.'

'Obscenity and pornography are not restricted to stories of two girls and a man sucking each other's privates,' I retort. 'There is more gross profanity in one corner of the political world than in the whole of the red-light areas of Naples, Amsterdam and Hamburg all rolled into one.'

He decides not to enter into this argument. Instead, he pours out a glass of wine. It is pale red in colour and *frizzante*. I take a mouthful of it. It is dry and has a tar-like aftertaste.

'Parasini. From Calabria. It is good, you will agree?'

'It is good.'

The sun streams in through the grimy window and I undergo what is a unique experience for me, a positive longing to repeat this afternoon many times in the future.

I have a strong presentiment that matters in my life are coming to a head. I may merely feel this way because the gun is delivered, the money in the bank, my not altogether unlucrative career at a close. It may be in the stars, although I am not an astrologically-minded individual and I do not eagerly anticipate the weekly assessment of my horoscope in one of the tabloids. I dismiss astrology as irrational drivel.

The truth, of course, lies in the fact that the shadow-dweller is about. I feel him every waking hour and meet him, on occasion, in my sleep. I have not seen him for several days but he is somewhere in the town, his presence itching my spine like a creeping cancer. For certain, he is closing in, street by street, alleyway by alleyway, bar by bar, biding his time until his moment arrives. All I can do is wait.

Father Benedetto is to be away longer than he anticipated. He has left a message for me with his housekeeper. He has gone from Florence to Verona for he knows not how long. His bedridden octogenarian aunt, he writes, is dying and has asked for him to give her absolution. She may die tomorrow, she may last the month out. To me, the visit seems to need to be only a brief one. At over eighty, and confined to her deathbed, she can hardly commit more sins before she dies.

I am sad: I want to drink good wine and eat his home-cured ham with him, share with him my misgivings, my dilemma, perhaps ask his advice. The grapevine in his little garden is surely laden with dark mauve fruit by now, and he is certain to have offered me to taste them in abundance.

I have a horrid and insidious feeling I shall not see him again. What this means, I cannot tell. He might be able to divine it. I do not feel I am going to die: it is not time for me to turn, in panic, back to the church and stutter out a lengthy confession, struggle through an act of contrition. Be assured I shall never do that.

I want to give him a present and have painted a water-colour of his garden for him. It is not a painting of which I am particularly proud, for I am not a landscape artist. It is an impressionistic daub of only twenty by fifteen centimetres, and I am not skilled at imprecisions. I prefer meticulous detail, as in a butterfly's wing or the rifling of a barrel. But then his little patch of tranquillity is hardly a landscape.

Seldom do I ever admit to emotion, having no room for it in my life. When emotion enters the soul, reason does a runner. And reason is my saviour. Yet I should be a liar if I were to say there were no tears mixed with the colours of that picture.

I have never been adept with wood unless it is the carving of it into the smooth firmness of a stock. It takes me three attempts to get the mitred corners of the frame to fit. Metal is so much more obedient, so much more forgiving. It is hard and whispers all the time one is working it. Every rasp of the file says, 'Go easy, go easy.' Eventually, though, the surround is done and I mount the painting. It looks well from a few metres away. He will be pleased with it.

To accompany this tiny gift, I write a letter. That this is unusual for me is something of an understatement: apart from keeping contacts of a business nature, I am not a correspondent. Yet I feel a need to communicate with Father Benedetto.

I use Italian notepaper, the variety which bears no watermark and can be purchased cheaply in the market. It is made in the back-streets of Naples from recycled newspaper and rags and is not white but yellowish for no bleaching chlorine has been passed through it.

To write this letter, I go up to the loggia and sit at the table with the sun cutting a bow across the floor, the overhead panorama cast in deep shadow. The valley and mountains are swimming in the liquid air of midday, the pinnacles of the row of poplars in the Parco della Resistenza dell' 8 Settembre shimmering as if being tugged by a manic wind, but there is not the least breeze in this torrid hour.

I sit facing the valley. The castle on its rock is barely perceivable. I look in its general direction and think of the man astride his girl in the ruin under the sweet chestnut, his loins coyly hidden by the folds of her fallen skirt. I begin to write. This will not be a long letter. I begin *Dear Father* and pause.

This will not be a confession. I have nothing to confess.

If one does not believe one has sinned, one cannot be remorseful. I have not sinned. I have stolen nothing since I last went to confession: that was when I set up in my profession and ceased fencing. I have not been adulterous: all my liaisons have been with single, willing ladies and, if my sex has occurred out of wedlock, I do not consider myself sinful on this account. We live in the end of the twentieth century. I have studiedly avoided taking the Christian god's name in vain. I have respect for the religions of others: after all, I have worked for the cause of several—Islam, Christianity, Communism. I have no intention of insulting or demeaning the beliefs of my fellow man. Nothing can be gained thereby save controversy and the dubious satisfaction of insult.

I admit I have lied. More accurately, I have told untruths. I have been economical with the truth in the very best traditions of those who govern us. These lies of mine have never done harm, have always protected me at no expense to others and are, therefore, not sins. If they are such, and there is a god, I shall be prepared to answer my case in person when we meet. I shall take a good book to read—say *War and Peace* or *Gone With the Wind* or *Doctor Zhivago*—for the queue for this category of sinner will be very long and, knowing the arrogance of the Christian church, will be headed by cardinals, bishops, papal nuncios and not a few Popes themselves.

But what of the murders, you are thinking. There have been no murders. There have been assassinations, to most of which I have been a party before the fact. But what of Ingrid and the Scandinavians? What of the mechanic and his lady-friend? What of them? These were not murders but acts of expediency: I no more murdered them than the terrier does the rat.

At no time have I been associated with the bombing of a jet airliner full of innocents. I have molested no children, seduced no young boys, raped no women, strangled and burned no vagabonds. I have sold not one grain of cocaine, heroin, crack, uppers nor downers. I have rigged not one share issue, have taken part in no insider dealing at the Bourse or in the Stock Exchange: the FT and the Nikkei indexes have never been affected by me—not for my own advantage, anyway: I admit two of my assassinations caused the rate to fluctuate but that was because the death of the targets had been misinterpreted by the marketeers who were loath to lose a buck before going to the state funeral. No one has lost his job because of me, save a few bodyguards and they soon found alternative employment.

Assassination is not murder. The butcher does not murder lambs: he kills them for meat. It is a part of the process of living and dying. Just so am I part of the same process. I am like the veterinarian who goes forth from his surgery armed with needle and syringe or captive bolt gun. He shoots the horse which has shattered its leg, he injects the old dog dying in pain and indignity.

A high court judge in all his finery and black cap is no different from me. There is no trial, I grant you, where assassination is concerned. Yet it is a waste of time and money, save to the establishment and the law profession, the builders of prisons and court houses, to hold a trial on a man known unequivocally to be guilty of his crimes. And no assassin has a target that is not already proven beyond all reasonable doubt to be guilty. The president with the unnumbered bank accounts in Zurich, the drug manufacturer with his luxurious hacienda in the jungles, the bishop with his palace near the slums, the prime minister with the misery and poverty of thousands in his responsibility. Or hers. A trial would be superfluous. The crimes are there for all to see. The assassin is merely doing the job of justice.

So I have nothing to confess and my letter is not a confession.

The sun has shifted onto the corner of the paper. I move the table into the shadow and begin to write.

Dear Father B.,

I am writing to drop you a few lines with this gift. I hope it reminds you of our pleasant idling away of the sunlit hours.

I fear I may be leaving the town shortly. I am not sure for how long I might be gone. This means, for the time being, we shall not be able to argue like the old men we are, with a bottle of armagnac between us and the peaches falling softly from the tree.

I pause and read my words through. Between the lines I see my desire to remain, to return.

Over the time I have lived in your town, I have felt a happiness, an inner joy perhaps, experienced nowhere else. Where I go from here I shall try to take the essence of it with me. There is a distinct serenity here in the mountains which I have grown to love and cherish. But despite our talks, and my living in the centre of this bustling, hustling little mountain town, I am by nature a lonesome man, hermetic and ascetic. This may surprise you and I would understand that.

When I am gone, do not, I beg of you, seek for me. Do not pray for me. You would be wasting precious time. I shall be all right and, I hope, beyond the need for divine intervention.

You know of me only by my nickname. But now . . . I was never really interested in entomology and give you a name to think of me by.

Your friend,
Edmund.

I seal the letter into a cheap, matching envelope and tape it to the wooden board backing of the picture frame. This I wrap in tough cardboard and brown paper, tying it round with twine. Signora Prasca can take it to the priest when he returns.

It was early in the afternoon, the sun was high and not shining into the room. Clara lay back on the sheets and stretched. Our clothes were in a tangled heap on one of the chairs. The wine glasses on the bedside table were wet with condensation and the window was wide open. This did not bother Clara: she was quite audacious when it came to sex. It bothered me. The shadow-dweller might have found this room out and inveigled his way into the building opposite: but the bed was out of sight from the window.

I leaned over to my glass and sipped the wine. It seemed drier after our love-making.

'Will you stay all afternoon, Edmund?'

It took me a second to reply: I was momentarily thrown by the name then remembered.

'Yes. I have no other work to do.'

'And tonight?'

'Tonight I have work.'

'Artists should paint by daytime. They need the sunlight. It is not good to paint when the electric light is on.'

'Generally, that is true. But miniatures are different. I use a magnifying glass for much of the work.'

'A mag-nif-y-ing glass,' she repeated, testing the word. 'What is this?'

'Like a . . .'

I could not explain. It is such an ordinary object it defies description. And I could not help thinking how wonderful it was to be talking of such nonsense in a bed with Clara in the middle of a hot, Italian day.

'It makes things bigger to look at. Through a lens.'

'Ah!' she laughed. *'Lente—d'ingrandimento.'*

We fell silent then and she closed her eyes. I gazed upon her, lying in the reflected sunlight which softened every curve of her body. Her hair was ruffled on the pillow and her brow damp from cooling perspiration.

'Will you stay?' she asked suddenly, her eyes wide.

'I have said I will.'

'For all times.'

'I should like to,' I answered and it was the truth.

'But will you . . .'

'I cannot tell. From time to time I have to go away. Sell my work. Get other commissions.'

'But will you return? All times?'

'Yes. I shall always return.'

There was nothing else I could say.

'That is good,' she said and closed her eyes again. 'I do not want you to be lost. Ever.'

Her hand reached out and rested on my thigh. It was not a sexual touch but one of the familiarities of love. She was too loving, too innocent, too naïvely artful to put pressure on me yet she knew, as I did, this was her way to try and make me stay in the mountains, in the town, in her life. Yet her pretty guile was to no effect. She is wrong for I am already lost. I have, I suppose, always been lost and nothing will change.

Tonight, I am the hunter. The lamb has turned from the slaughter and shrugged on the wolfskin. To draw out my quarry, I have taken a few steps to confuse him, maybe to ensnare him.

Firstly, I have booked my car into Alfonso's garage for a tune-up. He will do the work as soon as he arrives in the morning, but I have spun him a line by saying I shall be away so he has agreed to keep the car overnight. This should have the shadow-dweller out in the open, searching for it.

Secondly, I have sat for some time at one of the bars in the Corso Federico II, making myself prominent, reading a paper. Twice, I have felt his presence but he has not hung about.

Thirdly, I have walked through the town window-shopping. He has followed me, from time to time, keeping an eye on me. I have made him feel he has me on edge by looking round just a little too obviously, but never in his direction.

I have discovered the blue Peugeot, too. It was cleverly parked behind a bank of rubbish containers in a residential street on the outskirts of the town. It has had two new tyres fitted to it. I am sure he does not know I have found the whereabouts of his vehicle.

It would have been child's-play to plant a bomb in it, wired perhaps to the reversing light. Yet I want to see this man, get close to him, know him for what he is. So now I am hunting him.

He is at present dining in a restaurant down a narrow street off the Via Roviano. He has been in there for nearly an hour and I expect him to reappear soon. A lone diner always eats more quickly than one with a companion but I know the service in the restaurant to be on the slow side.

It is now I who am dwelling in the shadows, standing at the

entrance to an alleyway not wide enough to accommodate a bicycle. It is not a cold night, but I am wearing a dark brown suit. I might pass for a businessman out canvassing for a whore were it not for the fact that I am wearing high-laced jogging boots, not leather shoes. They are new: I bought them this afternoon in the course of my window-peering circuit. They are navy blue with white bands which I have darkened with polish.

No one has noticed me. It is not unusual to see people standing in the shadows as I am. There are heroin addicts in the town and their pushers inhabit the alleys.

He has come out of the restaurant and is looking up and down the street. Satisfied, he is setting off towards the Via Roviano. I am on his tail.

Stalking is the sport of men. It requires patience, skill, tact, physical and mental tension and a degree of risk. I enjoy it. Perhaps I should have been the commissioner of guns, not the artist of them.

He is making for the street where the Citroën was parked. He is so confident he does not look round, does not prime his senses to discover my existence. He thinks he has me where he wants me, cautious as a rabbit a long way from its warren.

He rounds the corner and abruptly stops. He has seen a Fiat Uno in the space previously occupied by my motor. He looks about, not to see if I am there but to see if the car has shifted to another place.

For a moment, he thinks. Then he sets off at a brisk pace with me on his trail.

We are doing a tour of all the streets in which I have parked the Citroën. But we draw a blank. He enters a bar and orders a coffee which I see him drinking standing at the counter. He pays and leaves, turns left and walks purposefully down the street. I follow.

Damn the man! He is going towards Alfonso's garage. He must have guessed. Sure enough, he is standing outside the garage, looking up and down the street. He does not see the Citroën. Now he is crouching to peer through the hinges of the old steel shutters that close the garage. Inside, a light has been left on to deter burglars. It bars his face briefly. He stands up. I can sense the grin of smug satisfaction on his face.

The street is empty. It is nearly eleven o'clock and the citizens of the town are drawing to their beds. From a window overhead, I can hear the soundtrack of a late night film on television. It is a romantic film, the violins muffled and thin with sorrow. From somewhere down the street comes the faint sound of jazz.

The shadow-dweller is standing under a street lamp which hangs from an ancient bracket on the wall of a building. He is pondering his next move or trying to ascertain what mine might be.

He will soon find out. The time has come.

I take the Walther out of my pocket and, holding it behind my back, cock it. It clicks. He does not hear this. I would, in his position. He is not a fully qualified expert.

I step out from the shadows and start to walk quickly towards him. My right arm hangs by my side as if the pistol weighs heavily in the hand. It does not. I hardly feel it. It is an extension of my body, like a sixth and deadly finger. My left arm swings.

He does not hear me. My jogging shoes are silent. I have about fifty metres to cover. He is looking at the garage door as if he might wish it open.

I raise my right hand. The gun is pointing at him. Thirty metres. I feel my finger take up the slack of the trigger. Twenty metres.

A car turns into the street behind me, its headlights on beam. I drop my right arm, thrusting the Walther into my pocket. The shadow-dweller looks my way, almost casually. He sees me outlined by the halogen beams. For the merest of moments, I see his eyes, wide open and shocked. Then he is gone. I do not see where. There is no alleyway opposite Alfonso's workshop, no deep doorway, no parked vehicles close by. The car headlights are illuminating the whole street as if it were a film set. He has disappeared.

An invisible man is worse than a shadow-dweller. I double back quickly and run silently for several streets. As I go, I curse him and the driver of the car and I curse myself. Each oath is muttered in time with my breathing.

Today the regulars are at the Bar Conca d'Oro, sitting at the tables inside. Those outside are on the pavement: the Fiat drivers and moped riders have beaten the bar owner to the space under the trees. I stand and watch.

One of the tables is occupied by a group of English tourists. The father is the proud owner of a brand new camcorder: the aluminium carrying case with a navy blue webbing strap lies on the ground by his foot. His shoe is resting on the strap so that, should any street urchin grab at it, he will instantly know of the attempted theft: he is abroad where the streets teem with petty criminals and forgets the burglaries in his own home town.

I idly ponder the possibility of concealing an automatic weapon within a camcorder. It should be feasible. The size is convenient. The little jutting microphone could easily disguise a barrel, the camera itself be used as the sighting device. Indeed, it would be the ultimate tool of the assassin if it could be totally silenced: the operator could not only carry out the hit but film the whole action for future replay, much as athletes play back videotape of their races to judge, criticise and improve their performance. It is a few moments before I realise such problems are no longer mine.

I regret never having taken an apprentice. What I could have taught him. Or her. With my retirement, a facet of technology's folk-craft dies.

The tourist wife is hot and flustered. Her blouse is adhering to her back, her hair verging on the untidy. She has been following her husband all morning, filming this church and that market, this street and that view. Behind her have followed their two children, a boy of about twelve and a girl a few years younger. Both are fed up. They each have an ice cream which they are devouring with avidity, yet they are still jaded with the day. It is hot. They have not been to the seaside, only to the museum to see the skeleton of the ichthyosaurus and to the Parco della Resistenza dell' 8 Settembre to view the vista of the valley. They are arguing as to how a marine dinosaur could have been found halfway up a mountain.

For a minute or two, I study this little group with a degree of caution. If the shadow-dweller has called for back-up, these could readily be his accomplices. I recall the lesson learnt from the couple with the pseudo-daughter in Washington, D.C. Yet my observations soon confirm that these are the genuine article: they are too sunburned, too bothered, too rattled to be acting the tourist.

I leave them and enter the cool sanctuary of the bar. Even the hissing of the coffee machine is cool by comparison with the day outside. The radio is not blaring cosmopolitan rock music but Italian opera. It is just as cacophonous and artless. The obscure liquors in their fly-shit mottled bottles stand in sultry ranks on the shelves as if numbed into stillness by the din of screeching voices. The reservoir of little wooden beads in the watch gambling machine is somewhat depleted but there seems to be the same number of watches in the revolving Perspex box above it.

'*Ciao! Come stai?*' the regulars welcome me: all but Milo, who sits staring fixedly at the sunlight burning through the plastic curtain on the door.

'*Bene! Va bene!*' I reply.

If I was ill and at death's door, such would be the reply. Life is good. The illness will pass and therefore all is well.

Visconti nods in the direction of the window. The tourists are almost whitened in the burning sun as though they were cinematic aliens about to be beamed aboard their spacecraft.

'*Inglesi!*' he says with a hint of contempt, tapping his temple with his forefinger. He does not think of me as English. '*Signor Farfalla?*' He beckons to me with the same finger: this does not mean draw near, just pay attention. 'One hour, you see, the camera—putt!'

He makes a popping sound with his lips: it is like the Socimi letting go a round.

'Too hot?'

Visconti grimaces and nods sagely.

'*Giapponese.* No so good. The cameras—yes! Good. But the videos . . .'

He grimaces again, raises his hand a few centimetres off the table. A grimace is worse than a spoken criticism in the mountains.

Milo is quiet. I enquire after his problem, but he does not answer me. Giuseppe does. A few nights ago, some addicts broke into his stall in the Piazza del Duomo, looking for watches they might steal and sell to tourists in order to maintain their habits. They found nothing: he takes his stock home every evening in a suitcase. Peeved by their lack of success, they smashed the stall to matchwood. He is having another made by one of Alfonso's mechanics out of sheet steel and angle-iron, but it will be a fortnight before it is completed. In the meantime, he has had to set up his pitch under an umbrella. This makes him look more like a part-time seller of watches rather than an experienced watch repairer. Sales have dropped off.

I offer my sympathies and Milo brightens at this expression of friendship. All he needs is a little respect, he says. The *polizia* will do nothing. He shrugs and quietly says what he thinks of the municipal police.

The plastic curtain parts and the tourist wife comes into the bar. She has her daughter by the hand.

'*Scusi,*' she says.

We all look up. Armando turns around in his chair. Our sudden and apparently undivided attention disconcerts her.

'*Il . . . il gabinetto, per favore? Per una signora piccolo.*'

She holds up her daughter's hand as if auctioning the child.

'Through the door at the end of the counter.' I tell the woman who stares at me as I speak. She did not think of me as English.

'Thank you,' she says, nonplussed. 'Thank you very much.'

Gherardo moves his chair so she and the girl might pass. The little girl smiles prettily and Giuseppe is warmed by it.

With the observant nature of a photographer, Visconti remarks to me. 'She thinks you Italian.'

'*Sì!* I am Italian!'

They all laugh at my admission. Signor Farfalla an Italian? Ridiculous! Yet as I watch them, I notice we are dressed alike, that I sit as they do either hunched over my *espresso* or leaning back luxuriously in my uncomfortable metal chair. When I speak, my hands move as theirs do.

This has been my way for years, my chameleon way of blending into the background. Even if I cannot speak the language well, I can fit in as far as the casual observer is concerned.

The woman returns from the toilet and smiles at me.

'Thank you. That was very kind of you. As you can guess, we don't speak Italian. We're on holiday,' she adds diffidently and unnecessarily.

'You are quite welcome,' I reply and I sense a slight accent to my voice which sets me apart from her.

'Do you live here?'

She needs to talk to someone of her own race, her own kind. She feels lost in this bar of Italian men. She is the archetypal foreigner abroad, clinging to any friendly contact like a drowning man to a piece of driftwood.

'Yes. In the town.'

Her daughter is looking at the watch gambling machine. Giuseppe leaves his chair and crosses the bar to stand beside the child.

'You?' he asks, pointing from the machine to the child and back again.

'*Sì*' the little girl says and, turning, asks politely, 'Can I have some money, please, mummy?'

Giuseppe waves his hand in the air and thumbs a euro coin into the slot. He motions for the girl to turn the nob. She does so, using both hands, for it is stiff. There is a metallic click like a bolt sliding into a breach and a wooden bead drops dully into the cup on the front of the machine.

'I've got a wooden bead!' the girl exclaims, clearly delighted and thinking this to be the prize.

'You must now push the paper slip out of the hole in the bead,' I say. 'There is a little prong by the cup.'

The child does this. Giuseppe takes the paper and unfolds it, checking the flag against the chart in the Perspex box. The little girl has won a digital stopwatch and is handed it by the bar owner.

'Look! Look! I won a watch!'

She turns very solemnly and faces Giuseppe, who has regained his seat, smiling broadly as if he himself had won the useless thing.

'*Multo grazie, signore,*' the child says to him.

'*Brava!*' Giuseppe exclaims, his arms spread wide with simple joy.

The mother, who has not spoken during all of this, says, 'That was most kind of him. Can you say so for me, please?'

'I think he knows.'

'Can I pay him back. For the machine?'

'No. Besides, he probably found the coin. He is the street-sweeper in the market-place.'

I observe her face. Once again, she is confounded. In her safe and tidy life, one does not meet street-sweepers.

'Can you tell me where the church of Saint Silvester is?' she enquires, gathering her wits about her.

I tell her and she leaves, smiling again at Giuseppe who finds this whole episode both very touching and immensely funny. He is still laughing when I leave.

'*Arrivederci! Arrivederci a presto!*'

It is a good way to say goodbye, a good memory of the Bar Conca d'Oro and these simple, happy men with their thick coffee cups and glasses of *grappa*, their tiny conversations and their love of each other.

The night is cloudy. Instead of hanging overhead, the stars are suspended over the sides of the valley, the lights of the villages and farms, the tiny settlements older than memory. The hills look like the stage curtains in a run-down provincial English theatre, dined on by moths and darned ineffectively by little old ladies with arthritic fingers.

I sit back in the loggia and listen to the clicks of the bats flying around in the night, can just discern their radar squeaks.

How often have I gone through the process of decamping from one life into another. It is always a disturbing time. On the move, I am like a hermit crab, grown too big for its shell and seeking out another: as I drag myself across the floor of the world, making for my next abode, my delicate tail and pink-white underside are naked and I am game for any passing predator.

Some shells I leave with delight. Hong Kong was one such: the polluted hideaway in Kwun Tong with its chemical air and its plastic food, the urban rail system trundling and screeking endlessly on its piers, the diesel trucks and the offal in the gutter. No typhoon, no matter how boisterous, could shift the filth. The winds merely stirred it around like the ceiling fans in Livingstone interminably blending the hot air.

Livingstone I enjoyed, in a way. It was only a short distance to the Victoria Falls and the town was an African caricature of the Wild West: a long main street with a wide thoroughfare and with flamboyants, flame of the forest trees, shedding their petals on the pavements like globs of blood spilled by duelling outlaws and trigger-happy sheriffs. I had only a small job to do there. It required no equipment other than a set of screwdrivers, a pair of pliers, a box of miniature socket spanners and an oxyacetylene torch. So far as I know, the weapon was never used. The Zimbabwe war was in progress then, the area around the Falls out of bounds, a military zone, but I was in with one of the military there and had a pass for the month I was resident in the town. There was something doubly exciting about seeing the awesome grandeur of The Clouds That Thunder, as the falls are named in the local tongue, and knowing at any minute a round might hit me from the Rhodesian side of the gorge.

As a city, I adored Marseilles despite the abomination of my quarters. The criminality of the place was a good cover. Whereas here my friends are a priest and a bookseller, a street-sweeper and a watch-repairer, there I counted amongst my temporary chums a share-certificate forger, a marijuana dealer, a pornographic-film distributor (who was also the producer, director, cameraman, sound engineer and casting agent), a passport maker, a credit-card fraudster who could reset the magnetic code on the rear strips, and—most improbably—an illegal parrot importer. They were a rum, friendly, coarse, eccentric and trustworthy bunch. They thought my job was pressing out US dollar coins. I let them think so.

Madrid was unpleasant. There was much corruption in the lower echelons of the local constabulary, as was the case in Athens, and I try to avoid places where the squeeze is on, the touch is made, the backhander is accepted practice. It is not that I begrudge these petty men their graft. Everyone must make a living. But the man who pays the graft has, *per se*, something to hide and is, therefore, the subject of attention and gossip in the locker room or the mess of the local headquarters. I stayed in both capitals only weeks and got out as fast I could.

In Madrid, this was no loss. I despise Spain for its oily women with their slick-backed hair in tight-combed buns and its men with waists like girls. I abhor the undercurrent of blood-lust in Spanish life. The Spaniards sell little velveteen bulls with miniature picadors' shafts sticking out of red-painted wounds. The Spanish are not civilised: there is too much of the fanatical, mediaeval Moor in them.

On the other hand, Athens was a sorrow. That was in the days of the Colonels: military juntas have always been a good source of income to those of my profession much as a good storm is for a jobbing builder. In my stay there, I did not visit the Parthenon, did not take the tourist bus to Cape Sounion, did not drive to Thermopylae or Delphi or Epidaurus. I saw nothing but the inside of a dreary workshop in the suburbs and the ever-opening palm of a police officer called Vassillios Tsochatzopoulos. I complained to my employer about this man's greed. He disappeared. I was told wolves ate him on Mount Parnassus: my employer thought this was a fitting and noble end for a policeman who had written a book of mediocre verse.

It is late. The traffic in the town has died down. After midnight, in this valley, time reverses itself until dawn. I am not sitting up here just tonight. I am here on every night which has ever fallen since the building was made. Five hundred years of night are compressed into just this one, brief span.

The clouds break. The stars are through. The lights on the mountains are extinguished. The patterns of the stars have hardly changed since the loggia was roofed, since the painting within it was executed by a man who wanted not only to see the vista but own it, too.

I so want to stay here. Father Benedetto was right. I have found peace: love is important.

The shadow-dweller makes it all so damned uncertain. As much as I want to stay I want him to make his move, cast the die.

I have decided to change my tactic. I am no longer hunting the hunter. For three days now, I have tried to draw the shadow-dweller. I have deliberately put myself at his mercy.

I have driven out into the countryside and, parking my car, have walked into the hills, going along paths that have wound through guillies, through copses of oak and chestnut. On every walk, I have feigned vigilance, feigned painting butterflies or sketching. Not once has he followed me. He has been offered the opportunity time and again to confront me, kill me. There have been no wayward lovers to disturb his plan.

In the evening, I have strolled through the town, frequenting alleyways and uncrowded streets. Here he has followed me, but always at a discreet distance. Once, pretending not to notice him, I doubled back on my tracks. He melted away.

I cannot fathom him out. He hovers like a vulture, waiting for the corpse to still: he is a persistent nuisance, the bluebottle one cannot quite reach with the folded sports section of the Sunday paper. He is the wasp at the picnic cloth. He is biding his time. But why?

Yesterday, thinking he might rise to a more adroitly cast bait, I acted furtively. I approached the Citroën with stealth and drove out to the derelict farmhouse by Father Benedetto's church of the frescoes. The 'for sale' sign had been removed but nothing else was changed. I parked the car as I had done on my previous visit and snooped about the house. I even entered it, a risky act for it gave him the chance to approach closely without being seen.

He did follow me in his blue Peugeot but he halted half a kilometre away. I expected him to advance from there on foot and studied him through my binoculars from deep in the shade of one of the upstairs rooms. He made no attempt even to get out of his car: instead, he backed it into the entrance to a field of vines, facing the road, and wound down the window. I watched him as he fanned himself with a newspaper and drove pestering flies away.

The ruse a failure, I left the farmhouse and drove down the road towards him. I determined to stop fifty metres from him, get out and see what he would do. It was near midday, the heat was up and there was no traffic on the road. As I drew closer to him, he suddenly swung the Peugeot out from the field entrance and accelerated away from me. I pressed my foot to the floor of the Citroën but it was no match for the larger sedan. Within two kilometres, he was out of sight.

I stopped in a village on the way to the town and entered the bar. Some old men were seated at a table near the rear, playing *scopa*. They paid me scant attention as I went to the counter.

'*Si?*' the woman behind the counter addressed me, eyeing me up and down in a cursory fashion. On a table behind her was a fresh fruit juice dispenser.

'*Una spremuta, per favore,*' I ordered. '*Di pompelmo.*'

She poured the grapefruit juice into a thick tumbler and handed it to me. She smiled pleasantly and I paid her before taking the glass outside to drink standing in the hot sun. The juice was chilled and tart, furring my teeth.

What was he up to, the shadow-dweller? I sipped the juice and wondered about him. His refusal to attack me, to confront me, was puzzling. He must know that, at some time, he must act or prompt me into making a move. And yet that is what I had been doing. I had given him the advantage: he had not taken it. I had stalked him in the night streets and he had fled. I wondered, as I drained the sludge of pulped fruit at the bottom of the tumbler, if he has been on his way to attack me in the castle or was simply following me, observing me. Perhaps the lovers had not protected me but had foiled his observations.

The manner in which he was behaving would suggest he was no threat were it not for Father Benedetto's noticing he carried a handgun. And yet, on the occasions I had succeeded in observing him carefully, he appeared not to be armed. I saw no tell-tale bulge under the armpit, no stretching of the waistband, no wider-than-average belt, no misformed jacket pocket. If he had a piece, it must be of a very small calibre, useless except at very close range. And he avoids close quarter contact.

Where was he from? I had eliminated from my mind all the obvious sources of the man, the various permutations of most likely possibility: he was not CIA, MI5, or former GRU or KGB—nothing of that sort. They would not play games. They would survey the hit, study him briefly for a day or two at the most, move in and do it. They are government men, civil servants packing heat, and they have to work within the parameters of time set by their superiors behind desks. They keep the office hours of the government servant.

What if he was a freelance operating for a government agency? No. I dismissed that option quickly. They would not employ a cat-and-mouser. Whoever came under their pay came under their rules.

He would have to get the job done as quickly and efficiently as possible: tax-payers' money and all that.

He was not from my world. I tried hard to think of who might bear me a grudge strong enough to kill me. There was no one. I have cuckolded no husbands, robbed no widows, kidnapped no children. It is true, I suppose, the mechanic's family would like to see me suffer but they all thought it was a suicide. The tabloids and the coroner told them so. Besides, they would not have the tenacity or resource to track me down so many years later.

It was over a decade since I had taken a commission for the American syndicates and then none of my weapons was used on a mob hit, not even an inter-Family rivalry. No political group for whom I had worked would kill me, not after so long. If they wanted me silenced they would have done it there and then, not waited years for me to jot down my memoirs. It was not the girl: if she wanted me dead, her driver would have blown me away in the car park of the service centre.

What else could be driving him? He was not a blackmailer: he had made no demands. He was an amateur, so was not tailing me for the joy of it, or to wear me down, or to find a chink in my armour. He could only be out for revenge—but for what?

Suddenly, I knew with utter certainty he was afraid of me, more afraid than I have ever been of him or any of his predecessors. I was just as sure why he had not acted as yet: he was plucking up his courage.

For three-quarters of an hour, I drive around the town. The shadow-dweller starts to follow me in the Peugeot and I have difficulty shaking him off. Eventually, I trick him into a short cut and it is his downfall.

Near the end of the Corso Federico II, there is a one-way street. It is only eleven metres long and local drivers are wont to ignore the restriction: by driving down it, they save having to circle a piazza, often crowded with long distance buses. The *polizia* know this and, from time to time, when the mood takes them or the traffic arrest statistics are slipping, they mount a devious roadblock at the illegal exit of the street. Today there is one. I noted it earlier, on my way to the Citroën which the damn man had staked out again.

By careful manoeuvring, I drive by the street. Ahead of me is a hold-up in the piazza and I join the end of the queue of vehicles. The shadow-dweller, seeing this and reluctant to become embroiled in the same traffic chaos, as it would give me the opportunity to approach him, swings into the one-way street. I wait a moment and reverse quickly back before another vehicle hems me in. He is halted, a policeman standing before his car with a signal bat raised in his hand. Two others, one carrying a clipboard are walking swiftly to the driver's door. Grinning, I turn and drive away as quickly as I dare.

Clara is waiting on the Via Strinella near the entrance to the Parco della Resistenza dell' 8 Settembre, sheltering in the shade of the trees lining the road there. She is holding a carrier bag: at her feet is another, made of thin blue plastic rounded out by a watermelon. I pull the Citroën in to the curb.

'*Ciao*, Edmund!'

She opens the door and sits in the passenger seat, the bags at her feet.

'I am well,' I reply and add, 'put them in the back. We have a long way to go.'

She looks over her shoulder as she pushes the bags between us, squeezing the melon between the seats. It is too heavy for her to lift clear. She settles herself down, snapping the safety belt into its clip.

'How far do we go? To Fanale?' she enquires.

Clara assumes we are going to the Adriatic coast for the day for my message instructed her to bring her bikini, suntan oil and a towel. Once, with Dindina, I drove her to the seaside and the three of us had a most enjoyable day, lazing on the beach with a rented umbrella and chairs, splashing in the water and eating *calamari* in a little restaurant close by, sandwiched between the beach and the main coast railway line. Like children, we waved at the passing trains: an English pastime, I explained, which drew no reciprocal waving hands but blank stares of dull incomprehension. Clara hinted, as we made our way back to the mountains in the gathering dusk, she would have liked for just the two of us to have gone, causing Dindina to sigh with annoyance.

'An hour. And we are not going to the sea but to the mountains.'

At my response, she is somewhat crestfallen. She had obviously been counting on my heeding her hints.

'And this . . .'

She nods in the direction of the rattan basket.

'A picnic.'

She is instantly alert, her disappointment forgotten.

'We are going for a picnic,' she repeats needlessly, continuing, 'Just us? Just two?'

'Yes. No one else.'

She puts her hand on mine as I struggle with the ridiculous gearshift, changing from third into second to descend the steep hill out of the town, down to the river and the railway station.

'I love you, Edmund. And I love to go for picnics.'

'It is a beautiful day. I am glad we have the opportunity.'

'I am cutting two classes,' she admits and winks at me. 'It does not matter. The *professore* is . . .' she is lost for the words in English, '. . . *una mente intorpidita.*'

'A dullard.'

I roll back the canvas roof and a hot wind whips in.

'Yes! A dull-ard.'

During the night, in the hour just before dawn, when time was readjusting itself to the present, the sky clouded over briefly and there was a curt but torrential rainstorm. The noise of the water on the shutters and gushing down the broken drainpipe woke me. The air was chilly and I pulled a blanket over myself. By sun-up, the sky was clear, unblemished by a single cloud. It has remained so since. The sun is therefore fiercely hot and the air unsoiled. The mountains are so sharply defined, the shadows, the trees and grass, the bleak stone, I can see every crevice and gorge, every ravine and rock-slide.

At Terranera, we halt at the bar. I do not leave the car on the road as before but reverse it up a narrow lane beside the bar. If, by some remote chance, the shadow-dweller has talked himself out of his traffic summons by waving a foreign passport and pleading ignorance in his hire car, and is following us, he will drive by and I shall see him. I pray this does not happen for I should then have to abort the picnic and have no excuse ready to counteract Clara's inevitable disappointment.

The surly girl is there and gives Clara a hard look.

'*Due aranciate, per favore. Molto freddo.*'

I smile but the girl does not respond. I am an old man with a young whore and that is all there is to it. And a foreigner, as well.

She rattles about in the icebox, puts two bottles on the counter, snaps the tops off with a twist of her wrist and pours the orangeade into two glasses. I pay and Clara and I go outside to sit at one of the tables on the pavement, in the sun.

'Is it far more?' she asks.

'Ten, twelve kilometres. That is all. Another twenty minutes.'

She pauses to work out the mathematics.

'Twelve kilometre! Twenty minute?'

'We are going off the beaten track.'

The expression is unknown to her and she looks at me with puzzlement in her eyes.

'I think you would say *lontano. Fuori mano.*'

She laughs and the sound thrills me.

'You will speak Italian. One day. I will teach you.'

No vehicles drive by and I see no sign of the Peugeot. After ten minutes, during which time I am sure the shadow-dweller would pass by if he was tailing us, we leave the glasses on the metal table and drive away. At the start of the track, I turn sharply off the road, giving no signals, the Citroën rocking over the bumps and Clara holding on to the door. I do not stop to check the road. We are safe: I sense it.

'Where are we going?'

She is startled at my taking such an insignificant track, is clearly anxious. This was not what she expected.

'You shall see.'

This heightens her apprehension.

'I think it is good we should stay close to the road.'

'There is no need to worry. I have been here before several times. On my butterfly outings.'

I swing the wheel over to avoid a particularly large rock and the Citroën pitches as if struck by an invisible wave. The suddenness of the jolt comes as a unexpected surprise to her, as the jarring of an aircraft striking turbulence might. She mutters a half-cry.

'You are not afraid of coming into the wilds with me, are you?'

'No.' She laughs, tensely. 'Of course, I am not. Not with you. But this . . .' She snaps her fingers. '. . . sentiero!' She waves her hand in the air. 'You should have a jeep. A Toyota. It is not good for a . . . una berlina.'

It is as if the danger of the track diminishes her command of English.

'A sedan car. True. But this is no sedan, no fancy Alfa Romeo or German limousine. It is a Citroën.' I strike the steering wheel with the palm of my hand. 'This was made by the French for taking potatoes to market. Besides, I have always come here in this car.'

'You sure?'

'Of course. I no more want to walk back to the town than you do.'

'I think you are crazy,' she remarks. 'This will go to nowhere.'

'I assure you it does.'

She pouts her reply. Her doubts are calmed somewhat yet she still clings to the door with her right hand, her left pressed hard into the fabric of the seat to steady herself. We do not speak again until just before the valley where the track runs out altogether into grassy shadows.

'Now there is no road!' Clara exclaims in an exasperated, told-you-so voice.

Beside the ruined shepherd's hut, I stop the car and switch the engine off. She lets go of the window. In the silence, we can hear a bird piping in the trees and the song of crickets.

'Is this where we go?'

'No. Not quite. We go another hundred metres, around those stones. But from here we just roll forward. No motor, no sound. And you will see a wonder.'

She grips the window again.

'You will not need to hold on. We shall go very slowly. Just relax and watch.'

I ease my foot off the brake and the car begins to move forward, the springs squeaking slightly. At the stones, I twist the steering wheel, applying the brakes to slow us. We roll gradually down to the edge of the meadow and under the walnut tree.

The valley is as it has been for the past few weeks, a riot of flowers. Despite the direct blaze of the sun, they are not bleached but still brilliant in their colours. At the edge of the lake stands a heron, still as a grey fence post, its neck straight and leaning forward.

'How did you know of this place?' Clara asks.

I shrug: it is sufficient an answer.

She opens the car door and steps out. The heron bends its neck and crouches into the reeds but does not fly off. I watch Clara. She moves slowly round to the front of the car and stands before it, surveying the valley, the woodlands, the high austerity of the rock crags above and the ruined buff stone buildings of the *pagliara*.

'No one comes here?'

She speaks so quietly, I can hardly discern her words.

'No. No one. I have been all over the valley. Up to the buildings. No sign of people.'

'Just you.'

'Yes,' I lie and recall my final client's advice: *you must take your mistress up there.* I can again feel her dry, quick kiss on my cheek.

Clara has unbuttoned her blouse and dropped it on the grass. She is wearing no bra. Upon her back dapples the shadows and patches of sun eking through the branches of the walnut. She kicks off her shoes, which curve through the air to disappear in the grass, and unzips her skirt. It falls to the grass. She bends and steps daintily from her knickers, her buttocks tight and rounded, whiter than the rest of her skin, her waist slim. She turns to face me her long tanned legs slightly apart. Her small breasts do not hang but stand out from her chest, proud and immaculate. Her nipples are firm and brown, the skin around lighter like an aura around tiny dark moons. I look at her stomach, at the taut muscles and the notch of hair below it and I step out of the car.

'Well?' I enquire.

She is coquettish and tosses her head. Her auburn hair swings from side to side, brushing against her face.

'Well?' I repeat.

'I am going to swim. In the lake. Are you coming?'

She does not wait for my reply but starts to run through the grass.

'There are vipers!' I call urgently. '*Vipera! Marasso!*' I add in case she does not understand me. I can feel dread creeping up my spine like age.

She looks fleetingly over her shoulder and replies, 'Maybe. But I am lucky.'

The heron takes to the wing. It rises from the reeds with an ungainly flapping, its long legs swinging forward and backwards. It crooks its neck, raises its legs and flies down the valley with slow, lazy wing-beats. It is an Italian heron and we have disturbed its siesta.

I undress. It is many years since I last took my clothes off out of doors, except at the beach, which does not count: then, at least, I had a towel of modesty behind which to cower.

My body is old. My skin is smooth and my flesh has yet to metamorphose into the flabby waste of many of my peers, but my stomach is no longer tense and my chest muscles sag a little. My arms are too

sinewy and my neck is just beginning to scrawn. I do not feel ashamed
or embarrassed. Just not young. And, with the caution of years, I do
not remove my shoes until I reach the bank of the lake.

Clara is splashing in the middle. She has not wet her hair.

'Come in here,' she says, her voice carrying softly over the surface
of the lake, her hand risen from the water and pointing to a tumble of
cut stone which might once have been a slipway for a cart or water-
ing beasts. 'There is no mud there. And there is no mud here. Just
baby rock.'

I wade out to her. The water is pellucid, is almost blood-warm and
rises deliciously up my body as I go in deeper. She is standing on the
bottom, the water up to her armpits. I stand by her and look up at the
cloudless, merciless sky.

'Stand by me.'

I obey her order and she takes my hand under the water, holding it
out in front of us.

'Watch. Be still.'

As the ripples of my arrival peter out in the reeds, small fish no
bigger than minnows appear in a shoal to gather about our hands.
They hover like slivers of glass just under the surface then move in to
nibble at the skin on our fingers, their lilliputian teeth rasping infinitesimally at our flesh. I think of the mice, discovered in the Valley of
the Kings by nineteenth-century Egyptologists, which had nibbled at
the corpses of the pharoahs.

'If we stay here for a year, they will devour us.'

'It is said if these fishes bite at two hands holding, then love is good
for the people.'

She kisses me then, pressing herself against me, her skin and body
as warm and as pure as the water.

'Do you make love in water?' she asks.

'I have not.'

She places her arms around my neck and raises her feet from the
stones, wrapping her legs around my waist and pushing herself on to

me. I put my hands beneath her but the water is taking her weight. The shoal of fish dart around us for a few moments then flee for the reeds, travelling with the rings swelling to the bank.

We leave the water and slowly walk, hand-in-hand, back to the Citroën, the sun scorching into us, drying us before we reach the car. I spread a blanket upon the ground, just inside the boundary of the shade, but she pulls it into the sun.

'We do not want to hide from the sun,' she rebukes me. 'It is good. We can lie still and when the blood is hot again we can make love again.'

She takes from her carrier bag a tube of suntan lotion and waves it at me. The air fills with the scent of coconut oil as she commences smoothing the lotion into her skin. I watch as her hands rub it round her breasts, pushing them aside, pressing them upwards. She caresses the lotion into her belly and down her thighs, bending at the waist as she works it into her shins.

'Will you put this on my back?'

I take the plastic tube and squeeze a snake of the lotion on to my palm; then I smear it across her shoulder blades. I work downwards, smoothing it into her flesh.

'Go right down,' she requests. 'Today I shall be brown every-where.'

And so I put more of the lotion on my hands and stroke her but-tocks with it, feeling the firmness of her young body and thinking of how my own is older, looser.

This done, she rubs the lotion into me. Then, the sun full upon us, we lie side-by-side on the blanket, she upon her back and I upon my front. I close my eyes. Our hands just touch.

'Tell me, Signor Farfalla,' she asks, her voice lulled by the sleepy heat, her words tinged with irony, 'why are you afraid?'

She is wiser than her years. Working in the Via Lampedusa has taught her more, I suspect, than ever the university might be able. She knows to seduce first a man's body, then his mind, before searching for the kernel of his being. She is using the same technique upon my soul as a real whore might upon the wallet of a sex-hungry sailor in Naples.

Yet I am not so easily fooled. I am more experienced in the protection of self, of privacy.

'I am not afraid.'

'You are brave, yes. But are you afraid. To be afraid is not bad. You can still be like a hero as well as afraid.'

I do not open my eyes. To do so would be to give credence to her accusation, her astute observation.

'I assure you I have nothing to be afraid of.'

She raises herself from the blanket and leans upon her elbow, her head resting in her hand. With her other hand, she traces the lines of perspiration on my back.

'You are. I know it. You are like the butterfly they call you. Always afraid. Moving from one flower to another flower.'

'I have only one flower in my garden,' I declare and immediately regret it.

'Maybe this is so, but you are afraid.'

She speaks with finality as if she knows the truth.

'Of what am I afraid?'

She does not know: she makes no answer. Instead she lies back on the blanket and closes her eyes, the sun making tiny shadows of her breasts.

'Of love,' she says.

'What do you mean?'

'You are afraid of love.'

I consider her accusation.

'Love is complicated, Clara. I am not a young, romantic buck in the Corso Federico II, eyeing the girls with a marriage and a mistress on the horizon. I am an old man getting older, drawing towards death slowly, like a caterpillar to the end of its leaf.'

'You will live long yet. And the caterpillar becomes a butterfly. Love can do this.'

'I have lived many years without love,' I tell her. 'All of my life. I have had relationships with women, but not ones of love. Love is dangerous. Without love, life is tranquil and safe.'

'And dull-ard!'

'Perhaps.'

She sits up now, hunching her knees to her chin and hugging her legs. I turn over, open my eyes and watch as the sweat on her shoulders forms into droplets. I should like to kiss them from her.

'But it has not been dull with you, Clara.'

Her shoulders shrug. The sweat starts its journey down her spine.

'If love is dangerous for you, then you are afraid. Danger makes afraid.'

I sit up next to her and put my hand on her shoulder. Her skin is hot.

'Clara. This has nothing to do with you. I promise. You are sweet and very pretty and innocent . . .'

'Innocent!' She laughs ironically. 'I am a lady of the Via Lampedusa.'

'You are but a traveller through there. You are not Elena or Marine or Rachele. You are not Dindina just waiting for a better time to come along. You are there because . . .'

'I know why. I need money for my studies.'

'Exactly!'

'Also, I need love.'

For a moment, I think she means sex but then know this is not the case. She is a young woman who wants a man to love, to love her. The cruelty of fate has given her to me, an old man with a price upon his head and a shadow-dweller pacing in his footsteps.

'You have love.'

'Yes?'

'I love you, Clara.'

I have not admitted this before: not to Ingrid, not to anyone, not even in order to get what I may have wanted. She is correct. I am afraid of love not only because it is a lowering of the defences, a risk to my security, but also because it places a certain moral obligation upon me, and I have never been one to accept any responsibility save that for myself and the efficiency of my work. I have, sitting in this paradise, to agree there is a point to Father Benedetto's diatribe on love. He, too, is right. I need it after years of telling myself it was irrelevant. The irony of finding it now, when life is so uncertain, stabs into me.

'And I love you, Edmundo.'

I am aware that I have been manoeuvred on to heavy matters, and stand up, stretching. The sun seems to have shrunk me. As I flex myself, I feel my skin tighten like a jacket grown too small.

From the back of the Citroën, I remove the rattan basket.

'We can eat.'

She tugs the blanket into the shade and I open the basket. There is not a lot of food within: some *prosciutto,* bread, olives. In the polystyrene vintner's cool box is a bottle of Moët et Chandon and two dozen strawberries in an aluminium container. Beneath it is a small package wrapped in a plastic bag.

'You have champagne!'

I think of what Father Benedetto might say if he saw me sitting, stark naked by a beautiful young nude in the woods, with a French sparkling wine.

She takes the bottle and peels the foil off, tossing it into the basket. Deftly, she untwists the wire and thumbs the cork out. It pops and soars away into the grass. The champagne runs out of the bottle and she holds it so the spillage trickles over her breasts. She sucks her breath in as the chill runs down her.

I hand her the package. It is cold from resting next to the champagne and ice.

'This is for you.'

'What is this?' she asks, intrigued and unfolding the plastic.

'Your escape. No more Via Lampedusa.'

She takes out the money and looks fixedly at it in her hand. It is the proceeds of the bank draft, a bundle of American bills tied round with rubber bands.

'Twenty-five thousand US dollars. In hundreds.'

Tears begin to form on her eyelashes. She places the money on the blanket, very carefully as if it were fragile, and turns to face me.

'How can you have so much?' she asks. 'You are a poor man, a painter . . .'

She needs an explanation but I do not feel I require to give her one.

'Do not ask.'

'Have you . . . ?'

Her question is unformed, yet I know what she thinks.

'No. It is not stolen. I have not robbed a bank. It was earned.'

'But so much . . .'

'Tell no one,' I advise her. 'If you put it in a bank, you will be taxed. People will know. Better to be silent and use it.'

She nods. She is Italian. Such advice is a reminder, not an instruction. For her, this sum of money is a yacht over twenty metres long.

The tears are slipping down her cheeks and her breath is coming in small jerks as if she has just run up from the lake. I realise she wears no make-up, is naturally quite exquisitely beautiful, and I am embarrassed by her beauty and crying.

'There is no need for this.'

I wipe away her tears with my finger, smudging them. Very slowly, she puts her hand to my face and cradles my jaw in her fingers. Her eyes are wet with more tears but her breathing is steadier. She leans forward and kisses me so lightly I hardly feel it. There is nothing she has to say to me and, besides, she has no words.

Pouring the champagne into two plastic glasses, I give one to her, adding a strawberry to it. She sips it and the tears stop coming.

'No more talk of love,' I demand, quietly. 'Just drink and enjoy the valley.'

I wave my glass in the air and cover the whole of the valley with the motion. She looks down the meadow of flowers to the lake. The heron has returned to angle for the tiny fish, and the shadows under the trees are deepening as the afternoon progresses. I follow her gaze but my attention is taken by the pile of stones covered in ground creepers. I can visualise upon it the silhouette of the target. The butterflies dancing in the air are shards of cardboard.

I open the door to the courtyard. Signora Prasca has left a dim bulb glowing at the foot of the stairs. The water in the fountain drips noisily in the night.

I hold Clara's hand and press my finger to my lips. Barefoot, we climb the stairs, the stone steps almost painfully cold under our soles where water has leaked from the broken gutter: it must have rained in the valley while we were in the mountains. I unlock the door to my apartment and lead her in, quietly closing the door behind me and switching on a table lamp.

'So! You are here. This is my home. Will you have a drink? There is wine or beer.'

She does not respond to my invitation but gazes about her. I think of my customer who was studying the room for safety's sake. Clara observes it with curiosity. She looks at the paintings on the wall.

'Did you paint these?' she inquires incredulously.

'No. I bought them.'

'That is good. You are much better than this.'

She crosses to the bookshelves and tips her head slightly to one side to read the titles.

'You may take—borrow—any you wish. I do not read a great deal.'

She moves to the table, looking at the paintings lying there, mostly those of the swallowtail. She bends to look more closely at them.

'This is best. You should not have ugly pictures on your wall. Only more beautiful.'

I step to her side, pick the paintings up and tap them into a neat pile. There are perhaps two dozen.

'These I want you to have. They are not for sale or to be sent away. They are for you. To put in your place. To remind you of the valley.'

I push the pictures carefully into a large envelope and she takes them and looks at them much as she did the wad of dollar bills.

'Grazie,' she murmurs, 'molto grazie, tesoro mio,' and puts the envelope delicately on the table. She goes to the window where she stands with her back towards me, looking out across the valley now bathed in the thin, miserly light of a new moon.

After watching her for some moments, I go out to the kitchen and return with two glasses of Frascati, one of which I give her and, once again, take hold of her hand.

'Salute! Clara.'

'Evviva!' she replies, almost solemnly and letting go of my hand, returns to the table.

'I wish to live here. With you,' she states bluntly. 'I wish to live here, and care for you.'

I do not reply. It is too painful, suddenly. Her wish is now my wish and I dearly want this to be the future, she a part of it.

Yet the damn shadow-dweller, who will not act, prevents it. If only he would say his piece, make his move, matters might be ironed out. If he wants to blackmail me, let him: I will pay. Then I shall follow him and kill him. It will look like an accident, like a suicide.

I cannot, at this moment, take Clara across the border between the present and the future, regardless of how much I want to. I have chosen the game and have set the rules by which I have lived and I cannot bend them, cannot deviate from them, have nothing with which to bribe the fates. I am caught like Faustus in a snare of my own device.

'Come with me,' I say at length.

She motions to put her glass on the table.

'Bring your glass.'

Perhaps Signora Prasca was right. I should share the loggia with someone. I guide Clara along the passageway, past the first bedroom. She glances in and stops me, taking me backwards.

'No. Not now. There will be time . . .'

It is a lie. I am trapped by circumstance and there is, I realise as I look at her face in the moonlight, no alternative to the future. It is as immutable as the past, as fixed and predictable as the sunrise.

'You live very . . . *Vita spartana.*"

I look at the roughly-made bed, the cane-seated chair and the pine chest of drawers. The room is somehow ominous in the sparse moonlight filtering through the shutter slats.

'Yes. I am not a man for frills.'

'But the bed is big for us. Just two now.'

'Come with me,' I repeat and together we go up the short flight of steps to the loggia.

She stands by the wrought-iron table and looks about her. The town is still a little noisy. It is not yet eleven o'clock and cars are moving in the chasms of the narrow streets, lights still on in some of the distant houses. Yet there is no sound of music, or human voices.

'You can view all the valley from here. When it has rained in the morning and the sun is going down, there is nothing you cannot see—the castle, the foothills and the mountains, the villages. Almost as far as,' I pause but it cannot be avoided now: the sentence is made in my head and she knows how it will go, 'our valley.'

She looks up at the painted sky inside the dome, faintly illuminated, with the gold stars glinting.

'Did you draw the sky?'

'No. It is hundreds of years old.'

'Here,' she replies, 'we are hundreds of years old.'

Then, through the night comes the liquid strains of the flautist's instrument from up the hill by the church, at the head of the marble steps. The melancholy of his music drifts not as if it comes from the piazza before the church of S. Silvestro, but from the bleak caverns of a long-forgotten past. He is not a street musician now but a minstrel playing in the courts of time, a magician whose melody can weave spells of curiosity and stop the clock.

Clara kisses me and whispers she wants to make love, but I deter her. It is late, my back is sunburned, I say. We have made love twice today, I go on, once in the water and again after the champagne, her breasts sticky with wine. I warn her tomorrow she has classes to attend. Another time. And so she sips her wine and leaves her glass upon the iron table. We go down the steps, along the passageway, through the sitting room and out of the door. She almost forgets her paintings and I have to remind her. She is reluctant. She can always see them here, she says, but I insist. I walk her as far as the Piazza del Duomo, her carrier bag swinging in her hand and holding my pictures and her future.

'When shall I see you?'

'Saturday.'

'How will you call . . . ?'

'Can you find your way to my apartment?'

Her smile is radiant. She believes she has broken down my door, entered my defences, bridged the moat of my privacy.

'Yes,' she answers emphatically.

'Good. Ten o'clock.'

She kisses me very lightly on my lips.

'Buona notte, il Signor Edmund Farfalla.'

'Good night, Clara, my dear,' I say, and I watch as she walks away, her step light and young and carefree. At the corner of the Via Roviano, she turns left, waving once as she disappears.

The sunlight was shining in the window as I was wakened by Signora Prasca tapping politely upon the door and gently calling my name. I struggled to sit upright for my back ached and my eyes were sore from tiredness. I had nodded off on one of the settles in the living room and had slept uneasily, twisting this way and that and cricking my spine. My head was clear, however: I am careful never to imbibe too much. I looked at my wrist-watch. It was just after nine o'clock. I had not slept in this late for many years and wondered if this was the pattern of retired folk.

'*Un momenta, signora!*' I called and straightened my clothes, running my fingers through my hair and using the glass on one of the paintings as a mirror to make myself look less tousled, more respectable. Signora Prasca knew I was an artist but even bohemians have to maintain standards: she told me so, once. I unlatched the door.

She was standing with her back to the door as if expecting me to appear in my pyjamas or, worse, all but naked. No doubt she had had a similar experience with the previous occupant, the Lothario.

'*Buon giorno, signora,*' I greeted her.

Half-turning with a coyness more suited to an innocent girl, she noticed I was fully dressed and faced me, holding out her hand in which she grasped an envelope.

'*La posta?*' I enquired. 'So soon?'

She shook her head.

'*No! La posta . . .*'

Her empty hand vibrated slightly in the air, dismissing my question. The post did not usually arrive until after ten in the morning. What was more, she never brought the mail to my door.

'*Un appunto.*'

'*Grazie, signora,*' I thanked her, curious she should have come all the way up the building. She bobbed her head as a maid might and scuttled off towards the stairs.

The envelope was unstamped and bore no address, just one line in cursive, neat script— '*Signor E. Farfalla.*' I did not recognise the hand: the initial E threw me. It might be from Clara. It might be from the shadow-dweller.

At the thought of him, my mind filled once more with the uneasiness of my night's slouched sleep. I tore the envelope open with disregard for the contents. The letter was written on heavy, cream laid paper of almost book weight. There was an elaborate watermark in the single sheet which had been folded crisply in two.

My Dear Friend, I read, *I am returned to the town, my relative now recovered somewhat from her ailing, and have received your beautiful painting and most moving letter. Come and see me. We should talk, as man to man. Or maybe as man to priest. But let this not 'put you off'. I am in the church until noon.* It was signed *Fr. Ben.*

Re-folding the letter, I let it drop to the settle where I had spent the night. I stretched and looked out of the windows, across the valley. The sun was well up, swifts or martins soaring in the air, the shadows beginning to shorten. Over the edge of the town I could see a raptor of indefinable species riding a thermal thrown up by the mediaeval wall which remained standing in that quarter. As the bird turned, I could just note the upturn of the tips of the wings and could imagine the individual feathers spread out like fingers, gripping the up-drafting currents.

Going to my bedroom, I stripped off my rumpled clothes and took a long, soothing shower, the warm water sluicing over me and wiping away not only the sweat of the restless hours but also the dull pain in my back. I lathered myself thoroughly with shower gel and shampooed my hair, towelling it dry. Then I dressed in fresh clothes and slipped on a comfortable linen jacket. Before I left the apartment, I checked the Walther. It was clean and shiny, looking like a toy gun rather than a deadly weapon. I smelled it, the sweet perfume of the oil lingering in my nostrils as I closed the door and tested the handle.

The streets were busy as I made my way towards the long flight of steps leading up to the church. As I walked, keeping an eye open for the shadow-dweller, I pondered upon what he was packing, what piece the movies or the television or the gun catalogues had recommended to him. It did not matter to me: I was only curious in a professional way. I had had years of practice with the Walther, knew it as well as a journalist of old knew his old battered Olympia, its every quirk, its metallic foibles, its impetuosities and its limitations.

At the bottom of the marble steps, I paused and gazed up. From the angle of the hill, it looked as if the facade of the church was leaning backwards into the sky, reclining like a tired old man resting on a bench in the Parco della Resistenza dell' 8 Settembre.

The steps were strewn with the usual litter of central Italy: Kodak and Fuji film packets, the rind of a section of melon, cigarette butts and a few soft drinks cartons. I saw no hypodermic needles, but there was a cracked and filthy plastic syringe lying jammed between two marble paving slabs.

At the top, I halted and looked along the row of cars parked at the kerb. So far as I could see, there was no blue Peugeot 309.

The morning's activity before the church was in full swing. The puppeteer was giving his show to a group of about a dozen children behind whom stood adults. All were tourists. The puppet in mid-stage as I stopped was a brigand with a tricorn hat upon his head and a cutlass sewn into his hand. He was chattering in high-pitched Italian. Another puppet popped up from below. He was the hero, come to slay the brigand and he also had a cutlass. The two puppets duelled, the puppeteer cleverly interspersing his dialogue with steely clicks and clashes from his tongue. The children stood spellbound by the action.

The flautist was nowhere to be seen but the juggler was commencing his act with three eggs one of which he pretended every so often to drop. His companion was halfway through a chalk sketch on one of the paving stones. I stood over it and gazed down: she had done the outlines of what was virtually the view from the loggia and was now colouring in the sky.

On the steps of the church was a party of tourists with a guide who was pointing out the architectural merits of the building. As I watched them, they started to file in through the door. I crossed the street and was about to follow them when a strident voice called out behind me.

The time had come. I knew it would and was, deep in my mind, annoyed it had arrived in such a public place. It did not bring any emotion to the surface of my being. Emotion ruins everything and makes the wits slow.

'Hey! Mister Butterfly!'

The voice was almost as high-pitched as the puppeteer's, somehow effeminate and, for the briefest of instances, I thought it might be Dindina's: it had the same stridency as did her voice during the fight with Clara. The accent was American, unmistakably upper-crust. It cut through the sounds of the tourists, traffic and the town.

I turned quickly and glanced up and down the street. There was still no blue Peugeot in sight and nothing seemed out of order except that, pulled in to the kerb between the puppeteer and the no-parking sign to which the flautist tied his umbrella, was a dark grey Fiat Stilo. It was illegally parked and the driver was sitting in it but this did not arouse my suspicions for such a sight is commonplace in Italy.

Then I noticed the engine was idling. I looked more closely. It had a registration plate from Pescara but these are not uncommon in the region: people from Pescara have houses in the mountains hereabouts. Yet on the windscreen, in the centre and next to the registration documents, was a little yellow disc.

My hand was in my pocket, my fingers snug around the Walther.

'Hey! Mister Butterfly!' the voice shouted again, lower in tone, more controlled now.

It was the driver of the Fiat. I could not see him clearly for he was in the car and I was in the sunlight.

I did not reply. I wanted to shade my eyes against the sun.

The car door opened and he stood up. Now I could see him at a range of about twenty metres, his slim torso and brown hair trimmed short. He was wearing the designer cut, stone-washed jeans he had had on when first I saw him, a loose brown jacket over a cream shirt. It might, I thought, have been silk.

'You. Mr. Butterfly,' he called.

It was as if he was not too sure and, for a moment, I felt like bluffing it out, turning my back on him as if I had not understood, had mistaken the first call. But this would not drive him away, it would only prolong the business.

I still did not answer him. I just nodded my head.

'You son of a bitch!' he yelled more loudly. 'You goddamn, useless son of a bitch!'

'What do you want?' I called back.

He seemed to think for a moment before answering, 'I want your fucking ass, you incompetent bastard.' The voice was in pitch again. 'You bastard!' it repeated.

He was definitely American. Now I knew, could tell from his pronunciation of *bastard,* the long first *a* like the short bleat of a sheep. His voice was strangely vaguely familiar, too. I tried to place it, give a name to it, but I could not.

His bellowing caught the attention of the tourists who ignored the puppeteer and the juggler and looked around at the disturbance. An alternative entertainment was commencing.

'You have been following me. Why?'

He made no response and a taxi drove by between us, momentarily blocking him from my view. My hand took the Walther out of my pocket.

In the two seconds it took the taxi to go by, he stepped free of the door of the hired Fiat and as he came into my view again I saw he had a submachine gun in his hands, holding it at the waist. The sun was bright and the gun pointed at me: I thought it was a Sterling except that it had a telescopic sight mounted on it.

As if my attention was focussing through a lens, I saw his finger tighten and I threw myself to one side. There was a quick burst of popping explosions and the rending sound of splintering wood. Nothing more. The noises of the day continued unaffected.

The Walther fired as if independent of any action I could make. The shadow-dweller ducked as if he could see the bullet coming, swung the submachine gun and fired another brief burst. I heard the buzz of spent rounds and the crack of the muzzle but not the retorts of the discharges.

Rolling along the steps, I spread my legs, faced him and fired again. Two shots. One smashed the Fiat windscreen, the other I saw penetrate the rear door just beside the shadow-dweller's leg. He flinched and was momentarily off-balance. I rolled back again.

Now there were screams, people shouting and shrieking, footsteps running to and fro. The puppeteer's kiosk had been pushed over and he was scrabbling inside it.

Over the cacophony of panic, I detected a sound behind me. I could not turn. It would have been most foolish in the circumstances. It was not close to me but not far off, either. It was a soft noise like leaves rubbing in the breeze.

It could not be an accomplice, for I could see the shadow-dweller's face assume a mixed feeling of fear and confusion.

He took two quick paces to his left, to alter his arc of fire, and opened up again. Slugs bounced off the steps beside me, chips of marble stinging against my calves.

Again, I fired. He dropped his weapon and fell to his knees, slouching slightly forward. I took hasty but careful aim. He was nothing more to me now than the tussock in the pool high up in the *pagliara*. For the briefest of moments, he was not surrounded by the street, the church and the parked cars but by the oak and chestnut forests of the mountains, the clear air of altitude.

I did not go for a head shot. I wanted to see who he was and a bullet in the skull would blow half his face away. I aimed at his neck and the Walther did the rest. He reeled back under the impact of the slug, his hand flashed to his throat then dropped. He fell against the Fiat and slid to the ground.

There was silence now. The traffic seemed to have stopped, the town holding its breath.

At a half-crouch, I ran across to him, looking round. Everyone was lying on the ground except the puppeteer, who was crawling out of his kiosk. I knelt by the shadow-dweller.

His hand twitched spasmodically. There was a crude scarlet mess in the left side of his chest. His shirt was torn in a jagged gash around it. The mercury-filled bullet had done its job. His neck was oozing blood which was flowing down the nape and on to the back of his jacket. His head had fallen forward. On the side of the Fiat was spattered blood, which was running down like poorly applied gloss paint.

Rapidly, I searched his jacket pockets: nothing, no wallet, passport.

I gripped his chin and lifted his head up. It weighed little in death. One of Roberto's watermelons was heavier.

I did not know him although there was something about him I could not place. Perhaps, I thought, he was merely a stereotype of all the shadow-dwellers I have ever seen or sensed and, for this reason, was familiar. I let his head drop forward. It lolled to one side. His right cheek had a tic in it. There was his blood on my fingers and I quickly wiped them clean on the shoulder of his jacket.

Then it occurred to me: he was an American and Americans keep their wallets in their trouser back pockets. I pushed him slightly to one side, fumbled under him, found the button, tore the pocket open. His wallet was there, his passport, with the United States insignia on the cover, folded into it. I opened the pages.

Now I knew him, the shadow-dweller. And I knew where I had heard the voice before.

Beside him on the road lay a Socimi 821, the barrel extended with a sound suppressor. In dropping it, he had knocked the scope awry. There were thick gobs of gellified blood on the metal yet I saw the last line if the inscription—To Kill I will not faile.

I went to pick the gun up. Perhaps that was what the shadow-dweller had wanted in his death, for me to mark his weapon with my fingerprints. Yet I did not touch it. Instead, I stared at it from the core of a silent darkness within myself. My mind filled with the one thought, that my last gun had in the final test failed to do its job.

The tourists were still not getting to their feet. Everyone lay prone. Then a child called out in a voice shrill with uncomprehending panic. I could not understand its words but it shook me alert.

I ran back to the entrance to the church. The main door, splintered by the Socimi and the ancient wood showing brighter where it was newly split, was open and, on the ground before it, was a black heap.

Father Benedetto was lying crouched on his side like a foetus, his hands to his belly. Between his fingers was a thick clot of blood and flesh. He was breathing in rapid, shallow swallows as if hurriedly testing his last glass of armagnac. From his glazed eyes, I could tell he was only semi-conscious.

As I put my hand on his shoulder, he shrugged at the touch but I took this as a sign of acceptance rather than dismissal. One does not give the worst interpretation at such a moment.

'Benedetto,' I whispered. It might have been, *'Benedicte.'* I have never been quite sure.

There was a whipping screel of a siren drawing closer and I could hear running footsteps from further down the street, in the direction of the Corso Federico II. The tourists were stirring. I fired again, into the air. There were distant shouts and the footsteps abruptly ceased. The tourists dropped to the ground again. The child squeaked briefly like a rat as the trap springs shut.

I sprinted across the street, jumping over the prone bodies of those lying on the pavements and went headlong down the marble steps towards the quarter in which was my apartment.

The grazes I had suffered on my shins and calves from the shattering stone were slight: they required nothing more than Band-aids and a smearing of Germolene. I collected my battered holdall from the wardrobe in the bedroom and had a last check round. The ashes in the fire were thoroughly crushed. No forensic scientist would ever glue them together again. I inspected myself in the mirror. The toupee looked good, my jacket was neat, my spectacles polished and the homburg hat balanced nicely upon my head.

As I went to leave, I glanced up the steps to the loggia. I could just make out the dull gold of the stars on the sky in the dome.

Getting out of town, I anticipated, would be difficult: the Italian authorities are much practised at the art of roadblocks. Vehicle checks would have been established within twenty minutes of the shooting. I walked to the Piazza Conca d'Oro, perfecting a limp as I went and took a bicycle from the fountain. It was not one of those lightweight racers or expensive mountain bikes but just a traditional, black sturdy machine. I hung my holdall from the handlebars and, swinging my leg slowly over the saddle, as an old man might, took a last look at the bar. The tables were before the door—the drivers had beaten the patron to the shade under the trees—and seated at one were Visconti and Milo. They looked cursorily in my direction but did not recognise me.

Following an escape route I had reconnoitred long before, through the passageways and alleys to the outskirts of the town, I reached the countryside and, at a leisurely pace, cycled down lanes and paths and farmtracks to a village about fifteen kilometres away where I knew long distance coach services over the mountains halted on their way to the autostrada.

The bus for Rome was barely half full. I boarded the steps, purchased my ticket and took a seat at the rear. Even here, some distance from the town, the *carabinieri* were on the alert, two officers standing by the entrance to the bus, scrutinising those boarding and asking questions of several passengers. They ignored me. The doors hissed shut and the driver engaged first gear. By four o'clock, the bus had gone through the first of the autostrada tunnels which cut through the mountains. By six o'clock, I was in Rome.

From the Piazza della Republica, I walked a short distance to the Metropolitana in the Piazza del Cinquecento, travelled to the station in the Piazza del Partigiana and caught the suburban train to Fiumicino. At Leonardo da Vinci airport, I locked myself in a cubicle in the gentleman's lavatory in the departure concourse, changing into my new form. Like a caterpillar, I became a chrysalis then broke free into the finished creature, the imago: I am, indeed, a butterfly. Now was the time to find a thermal, rise over the hill and descend into a new, uncharted valley of flowers and nectar. I collected my leather baggage from the left luggage locker. It smelled musty from being there for so long.

You want to know the identity of the shadow-dweller. He was a millionaire's son, the asset-stripper's offspring, the syphilitic philanderer's brat. And I was right: it was revenge which was his motive for his hunt. His mother had killed herself and his father remarried.

All this I had in my last letter from Larry, who did not condemn me. He was a man of the world, he understood: but he also warned me. The boy had his connections, or the father had: the letter was ambiguous and I could not tell from it which of the two of them was friendly with some of Larry's more press-worthy clients in Chicago, Miami, or Little Italy. The failure of the attempted killing, he wrote, would not be overlooked. And the public nature of it was, of course, a part of the process. It was his opinion, furthermore—and he should know—that they would consider the lesson had not been learned. As he put it, another teacher would be employed in due course. His post-script was *At least you've put the poor asshole out of his agony.* I had to agree with him.

I could not believe the irony of it. This vindictive dilettante had succeeded where the agencies of the world's governments had failed. Certainly, it had taken him years to track me down. I wondered if this had been a full-time quest or a pastime when he was not otherwise engaged: the sort of undertaking such as Americans make on their summer vacations in Europe, seeking to trace their ancestry.

Yet the fact is that he made it in the end. There is nothing so per-severing—or so perverse—as a vengeance waiting to be redressed.

That he used my own gun was another of those artful tricks laughing fate plays upon us. It is one I now savour, albeit sardonically. Once he discovered my whereabouts, he must have gone to his 'connection', asked for the best to be hired on his behalf. His wish was obeyed: I was employed. He was not to know that it was I who was the finest.

And there is a moral there, I would suggest: it is up to you to decide upon what it is.

It was he who ruined everything. The whole of my future brought to devastation by the determined, petty hatred of a deranged mother's boy.

In my retirement, I often think of what might have been. I tell myself this is a pointless exercise but I cannot avoid it. But for him and his never-ending vendetta, I should still be in those peaceful mountains, seeing out my end years secure amongst trustworthy folk. And with Clara.

Clara: she was much on my mind in the weeks immediately after the shooting, the days and nights of running and hiding, ducking and dodging, swerving and backtracking across the world.

I kept recalling her visit to my home. She had somehow fitted there, had not been out of place amongst my books and pictures, sitting on my chairs. I believed she would not have been out of place in my bed and the more I think of her the more I see what I have lost: she doing her work by my side, perhaps translating from the Italian into English with—when it was demanded of me—my help, whilst I read and painted and allowed myself for the first time to fall into a routine of bar and Galeazzo's bookshop, dinner weekly with Father Benedetto.

I would have been happy. My friend the priest might have shared this: he could have married us in his ornate church with the grotesque ceiling. The service would have meant nothing to me but I suspect Clara would have wanted it. Onlookers—the puppeteer and the flautist and Roberto—would have wondered how an old bugger like me could be attractive to a young slip of a girl like her. I should have enjoyed that moment of publicity before the quiet years enveloped me once more.

We could have travelled, Clara and I. There are still places to which I could go, where I have not worked. There are a few cities I could have returned to with her as adequate disguise, spending a month or two away each year, always returning to the town, the beautiful seclusion of the mountains.

Of course, we need not have lived in the town. I could perhaps have purchased a house in the countryside around—the derelict farmhouse, perhaps with a hectare of orchards and vineyards, make my own wine as Duilio did, named it *Vino di Casa Clara*. That, I considered, had a certain ring to it. It would have been blood red, full-bodied, like kisses. Her kisses.

All that is now an impossibility. The shadow-dweller and his backers put paid to it with, his public shoot-out, his puerile *High Noon* mentality. I often think, as I sit alone in the evening, that he chose that moment deliberately, knew that by calling my play in front of the church he was killing not only me but also my hopes. Just as I, I suppose, had killed his own.

Worse, I often consider, is what Clara must think of me. I abandoned her. I paid her off with a princely sum as if she was nothing but a high-class tart, let her down, reneged on my protestation of love which she so needed. I admit to myself to hoping she used the money, did not throw it away in a moment of Italian pique. Several times, I have thought to write to her but have never gone beyond picking up the pen. Perhaps, by now, she has discovered her young man from Perugia.

And what of the others' thoughts—Galeazzo, Visconti, Milo, Gherardo . . . I was the cause of the death of their priest. I am the Englishman who brought death close to them. They dine out on the story. I am sure I am still a topic of conversation in the bar, will be for many decades. Yet the blood which legend will ooze from the flagstones in

front of the church of S. Silvestro will be that of Father Benedetto. This
much I have given him, a place in history.

Where I have flown off to is a secret. I have to remain a private
man, reborn into my new existence and comfortably settled
into it. I have my memories, of course. I have not forgotten how to
paint insects, that the cyclic rate of a Sterling Para Pistol Mark 7A is
550 rounds per minute and the muzzle velocity 365 metres per second; nor have I forgotten that it is developed from the last shadow-
dweller's gun. I can recall quite vividly the basement in Marseilles,
Father Benedetto's little garden, the stink-hole in Hong Kong, blood-
red wine like the kisses of girls, the workshop in the arches in South
London, Visconti and Milo and the others, Galeazzo and Signora
Prasca and the exquisite beauty of the *pagliara*. I shall never forget the
view from the loggia.

You do not, naturally, expect me to divulge into whom I meta-
morphosed. Suffice to say Mr. Butterfly—*il Signor Farfalla*—still sups
at the wild honey of life and is comparatively content. Similarly, he is
quite safe.

Yet I cannot drive Clara from my mind, no matter how I try.